MW00576361

Catfish

A Novel

Madelyn Bennett Edwards

Copyright © 2017 by Madelyn Bennett Edwards

All rights reserved. Published in the United States by Madelyn Bennett Edwards

This is a work of fiction. Names, characters, businesses, places, events and incidents are either the products of the author's imagination or used in a fictional manner. Any resemblance to actual persons, living or dead, or actual events, is purely coincidental.
The point of view of Susie Burton, used in the first person throughout this book as narrator, has no reference or relation to the author and is purely a fictional character.
The town of Jean Ville, Louisiana is similar to the town where the author grew up, Marksville, Louisiana; but most of the specific places such as the Quarters, St. Matthews Church, Assumption Catholic School, and other areas, streets, and places are all fictional.

Printers CreateSpace and IngramSpark
Book design by Mark Reid and Lorna Reid at AuthorPackages.com
Edited by JT Hill and Jessica Jacobs
Photography by Brenda Oliver Vessels

Library of Congress Cataloging-in-Publication Data
Names: Edwards, Madelyn Bennett, author

ISBN: 978-0-9994027-0-2

Subjects: Coming of age, romance, race relations, Jim Crow, 1960's, KKK, LSU, Southern University, Sarah Lawrence, Louisiana, Cajun

Manufactured in the United States of America

First Edition
Copyrighted Material

Dedication

For my mother
Mary Frances Taylor Bennett

Who died just before Catfish *was published.*
I wanted you to hold it.

My friend
Sue Couvillion Laprairie

You were the best of us.
You would have been proud of me.

My nephew
William Joseph "Joe" Bennett, Jr.

You left us way too soon.
We all wanted to see what you would give to the world.

When I began graduate school in 2015 and while I wrote, *Catfish,* Mama, Joe, and Sue were very much alive. Sue died in March, 2017 as I completed final revisions. Joe died in June, while I submitted queries to publishers. Mama died in August, just as I received the cover design. Your deaths inspired me to take this to the finish line without delay, because we have no idea whether we will be here tomorrow.

Acknowledgements

Gene. My IR, Ideal Reader. My partner. My husband. My biggest cheerleader. This would never have happened without you.

Lulie, Paul, David and Gretchen, my children, and to Dane, Marie, Taylor, Jacob, Sarah, Clare, Matthew and Adeline, my grandchildren, you make me want to be all that I can be.

Christopher, Anna, Lee, Sean, Kristine, my chosen children, and to Cooper, Max, Griffin and Gray, my inherited grandsons, you bless me with your love and acceptance.

Lenoir-Rhyne University Center for Graduate Studies, the Thomas Wolfe Center for Narrative; Dean Mike Dempsey; program director, Laura-Hope Gill; professors, Jessica Jacobs and Dale Neal—you opened a door I didn't know was closed and beckoned me forward into this brave world as an author.

For my writing groups and partners: Taryn Hutchison, Susan Sojourner, Francine Hendrickson, Kacy Burke, John Hickman, Dan Waters, Tanya Davis, Marie Horton, Heather Wood-Buzzard and all the students with whom I had the privilege of being in class with from 2015-2017—you made me a better writer.

My friends who read countless drafts of *Catfish* and other pieces: Lisa Mezzetti, Paula Rosenblatt, Chalayne Sayes, Evin Willman, Becca Willman, Lisa Stasevich, Carol Kinder.

Brenda Oliver Vessels for her photographs of me for the back cover and on my web site and marketing advice.

Lori Hill for designing my website.

JT Hill and Jessica Jacobs for detailed editorial advice and Sally Dubroc and Paula Rosenblatt, Lisa Mezzetti for extraordinary line editing.

Mark Reid for the cover design and Lorna Reid for interior design, and for walking me through self-publishing like a child through a scary movie.

My siblings, Johnny, Billy and Sally who are what's left of our family of eight and who provide me with a place to go "home," to;

and to Benny and Bobby, our brothers, who are preparing our permanent home in heaven.

Angela Bauldree, whom David made my sister.

My mother, whose dream to be a writer and poet was usurped by motherhood, into which she poured her whole life, and to my dad, who taught me that discipline and hard work pay off. Maybe you rest together in eternity.

To God, who has been so good to me. Thank you for giving me what I need, not what I deserve, and never leaving me alone.

"From the first page of *Catfish,* I entered the 1960s world of Louisiana bayous, racial strife, and domestic violence. Edwards' full-bodied characters listen to Catfish weave his tales of slavery, while writing their own story: a new story of forbidden love. A relevant novel for today."

Taryn R. Hutchison
Author of *"We Wait You"*

"*Catfish* is a story that draws you in with its very first pages. I chose the novel's opening to feature in Embark because of the authenticity of Edwards' voice in depicting a young girl in 1960s Louisiana, and because of the striking scenes that Edwards created for her vivid, complex characters. Young Susie's world is filled with conflicts and threats but also with love, curiosity, and unexpected connections. I'm delighted to recommend her story to all readers."

Ursula DeYoung
Editor of *Embark: A Literary Journal for Novelists*

Contents

Part One: 1963

⌒ Chapter One ⌒

∾

Night Raid
1963

FTER MY GREAT uncle died, Daddy bought the biggest house in Jean Ville, Louisiana from his widow and moved us up South Jefferson Street from our small ranch-style house. I was eleven, going on twelve, and my bedroom, which faced the road, had floor-to-ceiling French windows that opened onto a deep front porch that spanned the entire front of our antebellum home.

We had only been in the Big House a year when I was reading in bed and smelled smoke through the opened window. It seemed to hang in the air, mixed with a distinct barnyard smell and the stench of burning rubber. A loud roar, like thunder, rose from the ground and my bed shook. I crawled out of the high four-poster, pulled my long hair into a ponytail and tiptoed to the divan between the two front windows. Kneeling on the rough tapestry, I pulled the thick blue drapes back a few inches and peered through the blinds.

Engines revved and horns blared while horses galloped over the sidewalk and through our front yard. I watched as if in a dream while three pickup trucks, their beds loaded with people in white sheets, dunce hats and white fabric over their faces with two holes for eyes, pulled into the driveway and drove across the wide, front lawn.

It was summer, almost five months since Mardis Gras. What was the occasion for this parade, or was it a celebration? Whitecostumed people in pickups and on more than a dozen galloping horses waved torches in our front yard.

Two of the men—now I knew they were men because I could see their boots and jeans under the sheets that flapped open in the front—jumped out of a truck bed and ran towards the front of our house. Their boots thumped up the thirteen steps onto the porch. They were so close I could have touched them. I cowered behind the heavy curtains, still peeking through the opening but instinctively backing a few inches away from the window, stretching the drapes out in front of me. One of the men held a can of paint while the other dipped a brush into it several times and wiped it across the white wood. He saw me peeping through the open window.

"Get away from here, girl. Go back to bed," he said. "You don't need to be involved."

I backed away and moved to the other window.

Three other ghost-clad people carried what, from the back, looked like a huge crucifix into the middle of the yard. When they stood it up, it was twice as tall as the tallest of the men. Two more men ran up behind them with shovels, dug a hole and within seconds planted the body-less cross.

Then they packed the dirt around the bottom with their boots and lit the cross on fire. The men on the porch joined the ones in the yard to form a circle around the cross and chanted something I couldn't understand. All the while horns blew, men yelled, trucks revved, and horses galloped in circles around the ring of men, tearing up our yard and making so much noise I saw the lights go on in Dr. David's Switzer's house across the street.

I was so enthralled I didn't hear Daddy come into my room.

"Get back to bed, Susie!" he said, pulling the drapes fully opened and lifting the blinds in one whisk. I backed up and stood behind him. He put one of his big hands on either side of the window and leaned forward as if to make his head go through the screen. When he saw the action he stormed out of my room, through the hall and onto the porch, just as the men jumped into the beds of the pickups, and the caravan of trucks and horses with men carrying lighted torches paraded down South Jefferson Street towards the Quarters, where Tootsie and Catfish lived.

"Hey, you renegades," Daddy yelled. "Get off my property before I call the sheriff."

But it was too late. They'd already left and no one moved to stop them.

Daddy called the sheriff and spoke to a man who said he was the only deputy on duty and couldn't leave the jail; he'd give the message to the sheriff in the morning. Someone would come by to check out the scene. Daddy mumbled something about the sheriff being "in on this," and hung up.

The cross in our yard burned brightly for hours. I was scared and the bright light of the fire kept me awake so I crawled in bed with Mama and Daddy and laid my head in the crook of Daddy's arm and cried. He stroked my hair and whispered to me until my eyelids got heavy and I stopped sobbing. He explained that those people called themselves the Ku Klux Klan and harbored hate in their hearts. He said they wanted to keep blacks and whites separated and used fear tactics to make sure that happened, but would never go so far as to hurt a little girl.

I asked him why they came to our house.

"It's a warning," he said. "They think I should stop being friends with Ray Thibault."

Daddy said that colored people were the same as whites. He grew up on a farm in Backwoods, Louisiana, population 400, about twenty miles from Jean Ville, the parish seat of Toussaint Parish, where we lived.

"I was friends with Moses's son, Rufus," Daddy said. "We played and ate supper together and hunted and fished, like brothers.

We talked a lot. He had feelings and dreams and aspirations just like I did. God doesn't see differences because someone's skin is darker than another's.

"Jesus had dark skin, you know," he told me that night. I didn't know that. The Jesus at Assumption Catholic Elementary School I attended with my brothers was white—the one hanging on the cross, the picture with the big heart, the statue in the grotto; they were all white men.

Daddy said the KKK hated Jews, too, but they didn't bother the Switzers because they provided medical care for the Klan members and their families.

Dr. David and Dr. Joseph Switzer, brothers and two of only a handful of physicians in Jean Ville, were Daddy's friends. The older brother, Dr. David, lived directly across South Jefferson Street from our house and had delivered all five of us kids. He made house calls when I was sick and reminded me of the Santa Claus I had believed in when I was little—what with his jolly, loving manner, and all.

Daddy said God was colorblind.

But while he talked, I thought about the different things Mama had taught us. Mama was what you might call, prejudiced. I mean, she thought differently.

"I'm from North Louisiana," she said, "where Negroes are Negroes. They know their place, and there aren't many of them. We ran the uppity ones off early on." She told me and my brothers to stay away from "those people," except for our help, Tootsie. But even with Tootsie, there were lines we shouldn't cross, like going to visit her in the Quarters or kissing her brown cheek.

Mama rolled her eyes behind Daddy's back when he talked about coloreds being people and God loving us all the same. We'd laugh to each other because we knew she'd tell us the opposite once Daddy was gone. When he wasn't around she told us colored people had tiny brains and were the "inferior" race. And she treated Tootsie something terrible, didn't pay her much money and made poor Tootsie do all the dirty work like scrubbing toilets and sifting through garbage if we lost something. I always wondered why Tootsie stayed. She could have worked for any white family in Jean Ville but she worked for Mama until I went off to college, years later.

The Klan visit only made Daddy more determined not to change his stance on colored people. One day I heard him tell Mama that he had coffee with Mr. Ray Thibault at Charlie's Diner downtown every morning before heading to the Toussaint Bank where he was vice president at the time.

"I love to watch the looks on the faces of the sheriff and his cronies when they come in the front door, look around, and spot me at the corner table with Ray," he said. "They'll have to do more than burn a cross in my yard and paint words on my house to make me change who I am as a man."

"I don't know why you have to be friends with that Negro," Mama said. "There are lots of white men in this town who admire you and want to be your friend. Why do you waste your time?"

"Ray and I have a lot in common," he told her. Then he proceeded to explain all the reasons why it didn't matter what color Ray Thibault's skin was. Mama listened and rolled her eyes behind his back.

I thought about the only two colored people I knew, Tootsie and Catfish. Tootsie had been with us since I was an infant and I never thought of her as any color. She was more of a mother to me than my own, and I loved her almost as much as I loved God.

Catfish was a dark man who walked in front of our house every afternoon on his way home from work. I first met him when I was little, about six or seven.

*

A deep ravine separated the front yard of our old house from South Jefferson Street and was where we caught crawfish, tadpoles, turtles and, sometimes, after a hard rain, even minnows in its muddy waters. I held a bucket in my small hands. The weight of the hard-shelled snapper in my Daddy's galvanized pail made me bend over as I carried the load down the driveway and onto the road. I was bringing it to Catfish, a tall man my brothers and I saw almost every day. I walked slowly with the bucket, afraid for so many reasons.

I was not allowed to talk to people who lived on the other side of Gravier Road in the "Quarters." It was only about a block away, but it could have been miles, it was that much of a mystery. Our mother told us, "Those people eat white children," which, of course, only made my brothers and me more curious about them.

I was seven and I knew about vampires. I read *Nancy Drew* mysteries and even some of the *Hardy Boys.* If this tall man smiled I wondered whether I would see fangs.

But the bigger mystery that day had to do with a rumor about Catfish, who often stopped to whistle a tune or play his harmonica and dance for us, right there in the street. We'd overheard our mother and her friends talk about him during their Wednesday afternoon bridge game.

"They say he eats turtles," Mrs. Rousseau said, fanning her cards in her left hand and rearranging them with her right. "I'll bid two hearts."

"You don't say!" Miss June looked across the table at Mama who was her bridge partner and said, "I'll bid two spades."

"Turtles? Well, what do you expect from those ignorant Negroes," Mrs. Ruth said. She looked at her cards and peered over them at her partner, Mrs. Rousseau. "I'll bid two no-trump."

"Catfish is nothing but a dumb clown. He dances in the streets to entertain the kids sometimes. That's about all those people are good for," our mother said and all the women laughed. "I'll say, four spades."

"Four spades? Anne must have a strong hand." Miss June began to lay her cards on the table while Mama smiled and said, "We've got this, June." And they did—win the hand, that is. Mama always won at bridge. She was something of a phenom at cards.

My brothers stood on the hill above the ditch and watched me carry the turtle down the driveway and onto the road. My little brother Will, who was six, was worried about what would happen to me. He cried and yelled, over and over.

"Don't go, Susie. Please, don't go!"

James, our older, wiser brother was ten, and he wanted the man to eat me so he screamed out.

"Go on, Susie. Go on!"

I wasn't sure what to do but I had already yelled across the ditch and told Catfish that we had the turtle and my brothers were too chicken to take it to him.

I was a nervous child, the nails on my short, plump hands bitten to the quick, almost non-existent. My palms felt damp as they gripped the bucket's handle.

I reached the bottom of the driveway and turned right, onto the blacktop road. He stood about three or four yards away. It was hot and humid and the sweat in my palms matched the perspiration that ran down my back. I knew the sweat was not totally from the heat.

Before I got to him he called to me.

"Hey little girl." His voice was smooth and sweet, almost creamy. He sounded a lot like Tootsie. "You don't need to be scared of me."

"Who, me?" I tried to act big and brave but I knew my voice trembled. "I'm not afraid."

He laughed. It was a hearty laugh, from deep in his belly. In fact, he held his belly while he laughed. It made me want to smile, but I was too terrified.

"Come on little girl," he said. "I won't bite you."

I stopped dead in my tracks. Bite? Maybe Mama was right! It felt like my feet were glued to the pavement. My arms started to tremble and the bucket began to swing.

He took a step towards me. I wanted to run, but my feet were stuck. I gripped the handle so tight my hands started to tingle, like pins pricking my palms. I craned my neck upward and stared into his eyes. I couldn't look away. It was as if a magnetic force ran between my eyes and his.

It only took him two steps to reach me.

"You gonna hand me that bucket or you gonna hold on to it?" he asked. Creamy.

"I, uh, I, um, I'm going to give it to you," I said. But when he reached down to take it, I couldn't let go. My fingers were frozen around the handle.

His hand stopped in midair, as if he was afraid to touch my hands. We stood there, both cemented in time, staring at each other.

I noticed how long his hand was, and thin, not like Daddy's, whose hands were round and thick and hairy. Catfish's nails were not bitten. They were smooth and pink, which contrasted with the color of his skin—dark, not black, not brown, but darker than any I'd ever seen, even darker than Tootsie's.

"I promise I won't hurt you, Missy," he said. Again I noticed how kind his voice sounded. Is this a trick? "I'm much obliged for the turtle."

I didn't move.

"I'm going to make me some turtle stew." He spoke slowly, his voice like syrup flowing off the sides of a stack of pancakes. "I'm gonna boil it till I know it's dead, then I'm gonna break the shell, me. It's the meat inside that's good, yeah."

I knew the boys were excited because we had solved the mystery, but here I was, stuck in the street with this man I wasn't supposed to talk to, riveted by the sound of his voice, the depths of his eyes, the color of his skin, the length of his legs.

He looked directly into my eyes when he spoke. I'd never seen eyes so dark, like a never-ending dark hole, and I thought of how Mama said if we dug a hole deep enough we would reach China. I wondered whether the depths of his eyes reached somewhere across the ocean.

"After I gets the meat out the shell, I'm gonna cut her in little squares. Then I'm gonna dip them squares in corn meal and fry them in some boiling hot lard."

I looked down and saw him slide his outstretched hand under the handle of the bucket. The pinkness glared up at me. My mouth opened in surprise. How could one side of his hand be so dark and the other so light?

I loosened my grip and the handle fell into his palm.

It was as if he had two hands on each arm, one so dark it could have been dipped in chocolate, the other pinkish white, the same color as mine. I let my arms drop to my sides and I lifted my eyes to look at him.

"Is your name really Catfish?" I asked.

"Sure is." He laughed.

"That's not a real name," I said.

"It's my nickname. You got a nickname?"

"No. My name is Susie."

"Is Susie short for Susanna?" he asked.

"How did you know that?"

"Well, if it is, then Susie's a nickname," he said.

I thought about that a moment.

"Well, then, is Catfish short for Cadillac?"

He set the bucket on the road, held his belly, and bent forward. He laughed and laughed and, finally, I started to laugh, too. I wasn't aware of anyone else in the world. It was just me and Catfish.

Finally, when we got hold of ourselves, he picked up the bucket.

"Me and my family going to have us a good supper tonight, us," he said. "We shore will!" *Smooth, creamy, dripping in syrup.*

Oh, I thought. He has a family. Does he have children, grandchildren? I wondered how his touch might feel to a child, like me. Was it tender and loving like Tootsie's or was it harsh and rough like Daddy's? For some reason, I had to know the answer. I reached my hand up in a gesture that meant I wanted to shake his. I think he was shocked. He looked from side to side, as if to see if someone might be watching. He shifted the bucket from his right hand to his left and reached forward to fold my tiny hand into his. I looked at the long, dark hand folded around the end of my arm. It felt soft and gentle and kind. I didn't want him to let go. I wondered whether, when he washed his hands, they got lighter on the tops, or whether they stayed dark no matter how hard he scrubbed.

To a seven-year-old white girl in 1958 a decade before integration, in a small town in the Deep South, Catfish was an oddity. His eyes were as deep as the ocean; his voice soothing as molasses; his touch like a gentle breeze; and his laugh as hearty as gumbo. If that wasn't enough, his hands! Chocolate on one side, cotton candy on the other.

I watched Catfish march down South Jefferson Street towards the Quarters, legs lifted high, knees bent as he sang "When the Saints Go Marching In." He swung his arms, the heavy bucket in one hand as light to his touch as if it was filled with air. I stood in the street until long after he crossed Gravier Road and disappeared into the unknown.

My brothers were speechless as they stood in our front yard on the other side of the deep ditch and I was planted to the pavement watching Catfish march off.

*

Tootsie didn't come to work on Tuesday, the day after the Klan visit. When she got to work Wednesday, I told her what happened at our house. That's when I found out the Klan went to the Quarters, too.

"We spent all day yesterday scrubbing the black paint off the front of our house," I told Tootsie. "It said, 'N____r Lovers.'" Tootsie didn't react; she seemed not to hear me, like her mind was far, far away.

Our lawn was still torn up—tire tracks and hoof prints rutted the ground and most of the St. Augustine grass was gone. The atmosphere was overcast with a smoky residue that seemed to sit in the air, unmoving. No birds or butterflies, not even a bumble bee, flitted through my mother's prized camellia bushes and rose garden in front of the high front porch.

But Tootsie said it was nothing like the mess in the Quarters where the outhouse and one of the cabins was burned to the ground and her sister's house was scorched with holes in the roof and all along one side. She said that her daughter, Marianne, was home from school with stitches across her pretty face, black eyes and a broken nose.

"And those white men, well they did things to her she most likely never forget," Tootsie whispered to me. "I wish it could have been me, instead."

Mama was stomping mad that day and cursed Daddy under her breath. Tootsie just listened, as usual.

"I told him not to be friends with that Negro who owns the Esso station," Mama said. "Bob says that colored man is a savvy business person. I can't believe we let those people own businesses. Why, do you know Bob even has a charge account with that man and told me to go there for gas and charge it?"

Mama didn't expect an answer. She spouted off like that from time-to-time, knowing Tootsie wouldn't dare repeat what she said. In fact, Tootsie knew Mama didn't want or expect a comment—she was a non-person, like a statue Mama could shout at and take out her frustrations against. All the white ladies in Jean Ville did that, talked to their help about their problems and let their anger out on them. They had to have someone. Tootsie washed dishes while Mama paced behind her, shouting and complaining.

"I won't do it. If he wants my car filled up there, he'll have to take it himself."

When Tootsie arrived at work that morning she asked Mama for an advance on her pay, only the two dollars for the two days she'd worked so far that week.

"No," Mama yelled. "I will not loan you money. As soon as I start to loan you money and you don't pay it back, we'll have problems."

"But, Miss Anne," Tootsie said. There were tears in her eyes. "It's my baby's 13th birthday. I got nothing to give her, and she been through so much."

"You should have thought of that ahead of time and saved up. I said 'No!' Now don't ask again."

When I got home from school that afternoon Tootsie was still upset. I knew she would try to pull my dad aside when he got back from work and ask him for money, but all hell would break loose because Mama was bound to overhear or find out some way.

Tootsie was doing the ironing. She took the wet sheets from the washer after the spin cycle and, one at a time, slowly lowered them into the vat of starch and warm water on the back porch. She rung them out with her strong, brown hands and hung them over the line she stretched across the opening under the low roof. She set a dirty sheet under the line to catch the drippings that seeped down, no matter how hard she squeezed and pressed her hands to get all the moisture out. The ironing board was on the porch and it was hot outside as she pushed the electric iron over the damp sheets. The warm breeze did not dry the beads of perspiration that gathered on Tootsie's forehead before they could drain into her eyes.

Tootsie liked to iron. It was the one time of day when she had relative peace. Mama would lie down for a nap with the baby and the rest of us older ones were either playing outside or still at school. She said when she ironed at her house she watched a black and white television set my daddy had given her. I wasn't supposed to know about the TV but I found out when I overheard her thanking Daddy for it.

At our house, she daydreamed when she ironed, or she just stood with her thoughts.

"I wants to make this day special for my girl," she whispered to me when I climbed the steps onto the back porch, trying to escape the heat and humidity that had chased me all day. "She been through so much. She be thirteen today."

I followed Tootsie to the linen closet where she stacked the fresh-ironed sheets and pillow cases and mumbled about how she wanted to have ice cream and a chocolate cake and lots of presents all wrapped up in shiny paper so Marianne's special day could be long—long enough to unwrap every trinket she would buy at Mack's Five & Dime after work, if only she had a few dollars. She knew Mama was right, she should have saved and shopped and baked before today, but the Klan had messed up everything.

I thought about my own birthdays. I couldn't remember ever having a birthday party with friends and cake and lots of presents to unwrap. When my grandmother came to visit she brought a cake and everyone would sing happy birthday to me at the supper table and we'd have cake for dessert. Most years, when Grandy wasn't visiting, I didn't have a celebration because Mama said my October birthday was too close to Halloween, Thanksgiving and Christmas— I could celebrate on one of those holidays. Anyway, I never liked cake or ice cream and that became Mama's excuse.

"How can I give you a party without cake and ice cream. It just doesn't work, Susanna Christine." She also said she had too many kids to remember everyone's birthday. But the boys had parties and there had been a big bash on Sissy's second birthday, the previous year. Mama's friends came with their children for cake and games and little bags of trinkets and bubble gum to take home with them.

Mama was a gracious hostess. She had lots of friends who loved her and competed for her attention. I couldn't count the number of weekend dinner parties she and Daddy gave where Tootsie was hired to serve and clean until the wee hours of the mornings. Mama loved to entertain the Jean Ville doctors, lawyers and businessmen and their wives. All the women wore mink coats in the winter, even though Louisiana didn't have much cold weather.

Morehouse Samuels, the janitor at the bank where my daddy worked, would open the door and hang and fetch coats all evening; then he'd help Tootsie in the kitchen, because she couldn't go home until everything was in order for the next day. I figured Morehouse was sweet on Tootsie and told her so, but Tootsie said she had no time for the likes of him.

When Tootsie worked a party, Daddy paid her five dollars and there were often arguments the next day with Mama yelling that he paid Tootsie too much.

"She's going to expect that kind of pay every week," Mama would scream. "I pay her a dollar a day, you can't pay her five dollars for one night."

"I earn the money. I'll decide how to spend it," Daddy would always say, which made Mama fiery mad. Then he'd leave, slamming the back door behind him. I tried to stay out of Mama's way on those days.

Daddy was a CPA with aspirations of being mayor, then a senator. He struggled to build his practice until he ran for Louisiana Insurance Commissioner and got to know Governor Earl Long in the 1950s and 60s. Although Daddy was not on Long's ticket, the governor took a liking to the smart, young, energetic investment banker and hired him as his personal accountant and investment counselor. That job, which took Daddy to Baton Rouge most weekdays, didn't increase his income by much, but the connections he established catapulted his career. He became a lobbyist and a number of large oil companies and financial institutions began to invest with him and hired him to review their books and train their accounting departments. That's when he started to accumulate wealth and was how we could afford to live in the biggest house in Jean Ville.

That was when he became interested in politics. He constantly preached to us kids about how his reputation was important and that we should all be careful what we said and did. Any mistakes we made could reflect negatively on him and cause him to lose votes.

The afternoon of Tootsie's daughter's birthday I shut myself in my room and dug my piggy bank out of the bottom drawer of my dresser, from under my seldom worn sweaters. It wasn't actually a pig; it looked like a treasure chest that didn't open on top. It had a secret slot on the bottom that had to be opened with a tiny key that I kept in a sock in my underwear drawer.

I counted five dollars in quarters, nickels and pennies but saved the silver dimes as they were good-luck. I found an old, blue fuzzy sock and put the coins in it, pulled the top up and tied it in a knot, then walked down the hall towards the back door. Without so much as a glance or a word, I dropped the sock filled with coins into the big pocket on the front of Tootsie's apron. She didn't look at me but a private understanding passed between us.

Tootsie would finger the weighty package and feel the wool sock and her plump fingers would massage what felt like dozens of coins of different sizes. I knew what she was thinking: *now Marianne can have that birthday party.*

~ Chapter Two ~

~

Catfish/Slave Auction
1963

TOOTSIE USED TO tell me I had goodness in me, but she also accused me of being stubborn and not holding my tongue, which got me in a lot of trouble. And she took up for Will and Robby, my two younger brothers, because she said I was bossy.

My parents called me *Troublemaker.* Maybe they were right. After all, I did cause a lot of trouble. What is it they say? "Small children, small problems—big children ...?" I guess that would describe me, beginning with my relationship with Catfish.

After I gave him the turtle when I was little, Catfish would stop in front of our house in the afternoons on his way home from work if I was in the front yard. He would dance and whistle and, sometimes, play his harmonica. And we would talk across the ditch.

When I was eleven, and we moved to the big house on the corner of South Jefferson and Marble Avenue we were now three long blocks from Gravier Road and the Quarters on the other side. My dream to visit Catfish someday seemed dashed by distance.

The first week after we moved, I stood at the corner, in the blazing South Louisiana heat and humidity, and waited for Catfish. I was afraid he wouldn't find me at the new house, and I had come to depend on his visits. You could say I loved him like a grandfather but

I'm not sure how it feels to love a grandfather, since I'd never had one—but I knew how it felt to love Catfish.

I waved at him as he skipped on the hot pavement under the canopy of moss-draped live oaks.

"Hey, Catfish," I called out. "Here I am. We moved."

"Oh, Chere, you're in the big house now. This the biggest house in Jean Ville."

"I know. It's too big. And this yard is a ten-acre park. I was afraid you wouldn't know where to find me."

We smiled at each other. His toothy grin caused his huge lips to spread across the entire bottom half of his face and made his whole expression light up.

Most days I waited alone in the expansive front yard that met the pavement seamlessly with no ditch to divide it from the street like the old house. Mama didn't know I talked with him. She thought he stopped to entertain the neighborhood children, which, to Mama, was what people like Catfish should do for white folks: act like clowns and make fools of themselves. Only I didn't see him that way. And in the new house, set so far from the street, Mama couldn't see his tall, dark figure deep in conversation with me.

We chatted like old friends. He taught me how to listen for birds singing and tweeting to each other and to hear the buzzing of bees and butterflies that made harmonic music with other insects like crickets and fireflies. He explained how to inhale deeply to appreciate the wondrous smells of camellias and pecans and fresh-cut grass. He made me see the world as big and beautiful, filled with goodness, something I didn't know much about inside the walls of the big house.

"How you doin', Missy?" he always asked when he saw me. Or he called me "chére," which sounded like "sha," and meant "dear one," in Cajun French.

"I'm great, Catfish. I got an A in Algebra this week."

"You a smart girl, you."

"And you? How was work today?"

"Oh, Missy, we kilt so many hogs at the slaughterhouse today I done loss count. An my ole back feel it, too."

As I got older and activities after school kept me from meeting Catfish every day, the visits became less frequent and I often wondered whether he would forget me. I tried to wait for him on Fridays, since I didn't have band practice before the seven o'clock football games in the fall or softball practice before weekend games in the spring.

The fall I turned thirteen, about four months after the Klan visit, I realized I hadn't seen Catfish in a month or more. I stood on the corner every afternoon after school for two weeks and waited, but Catfish didn't skip by. I panicked and didn't know who I could ask about him. I finally decided to ask Tootsie if she knew Catfish, and whether she could find out where he was, if he was alright. I pulled Tootsie aside one Friday afternoon.

That's when Tootsie told me that Catfish was her daddy. I was shocked.

"Why, in all the years you knew I waited for Catfish and talked to him, did you never tell me you were his daughter?" I whispered. Tootsie looked down and twisted the bottom of her apron with both hands. Small beads of perspiration gathered on her forehead.

"You know we not supposed to talk about our families on the job, Honey-Chile," Tootsie whispered, a hint of a sob in her voice. What she meant was that she had to follow what the white women in Jean Ville called *help-code*, a set of implied rules the help knew existed, but no one ever talked about. One of those rules was that the hired help didn't discuss their personal lives with the white children in their care.

I signaled for Tootsie to follow me. We walked down the long hall that divided the huge antebellum house right down the middle.

Three enormous bedrooms and bathrooms were on the left side of the hall; the living, dining, kitchen, breakfast room and parlor were on the other. A semi-circular staircase just inside the front door reached upward to a landing where a U-shaped gallery wrapped around three sides of the upstairs with doors on each side that led to more bedrooms, a study, a playroom, a nursery and several bathrooms. The boys' bedrooms were upstairs; mine was downstairs all the way at the end of the hall near the front door.

Mama was busy in the kitchen at the back of the house, on the other side of the hall. Tootsie and I went into my bedroom, shut the door and sat on the edge of my bed, side by side.

"Why didn't you tell me?" I asked, again.

"You never axed," Tootsie said. I was young, but I knew Tootsie's dilemma. White children should believe they were the only family the help cared about. I had learned this from my older cousin, Charlotte, who lived down the street, next door to our old house. The children were supposed to believe we were the surrogates of our help, loved beyond measure, in competition with no one for their affection.

"You can talk to me about your family. I won't tell," I said. Tootsie cried softly. I put my arm over her shoulder and thought how Tootsie knew everything about me, but I knew nothing about this beautiful brown woman who had been a mother to me for almost thirteen years. I felt ashamed, selfish—just like all the other white people in Jean Ville who didn't think colored people had feelings or lives that counted.

"I'm so sorry, Tootsie. I should have asked you a long time ago. Tell me about them."

"Well, Catfish, his name Peter Massey and he the best daddy. My Mama died when I's just about your age and I miss her. Her name was Alabama, can you believe? But everyone called her Shag."

Tootsie stopped abruptly and began to smooth the lap of her uniform.

"Go on, Toot. Do you have brothers and sisters?

"Yeah. I got me one sister, Jesse, and two brothers, Tom and Sam. They all married with children."

"Do you have children, Toot? Other than Marianne?"

"Yeah. I have four girls. Mari your age. The others is younger."

"Wow." I was speechless, trying to absorb all the new things I was learning about this woman I loved more than anyone. We were silent for a minute. I noticed how her eye lashes clumped together with the wetness of her tears as she stared down at her hands, working the starched white fabric of her apron. My heart twisted and my natural curiosity stirred. I had lots of questions, but the number one question was, "Where's Catfish?"

"He old now, Honey Chile," Tootsie said. "He don't work at the slaughterhouse no more. He stay home and rock in his chair on the porch and watch the children play."

"Oh," I had never known anyone who was too old to work. I thought about Catfish and how, to me, he didn't seem to age. He was always the same and, like Tootsie, someone I could depend on week after week, year after year.

"Do you see him every day?'

"Shore do," Tootsie said. "I lives in the Quarters with him. I got my own little cabin for me and my girls. We all there together, my brothers and sister and me and all our kids. We live all in the row."

"The row?"

"Yeah, Honey-chile. The row of cabins used to be slave quarters at Shadowland."

"Oh." I couldn't picture what she was talking about. "Toot, don't get me wrong, but you, well, uhm, you and Catfish look different." I found it baffling that a carmel-colored, pretty woman like Tootsie could be the child of such a dark skinned man.

"That's common for Negroes," Tootsie said. "Why, we got so many generations of different bloods in us we don't know how our children will come out. My Marianne, she can pass for white, and she real pretty, with grey-green eyes. My other girls is my color, sort of cinnamon, 'cept the baby, Milly, she got a touch of pecan."

Tootsie pulled me close to her big bosoms and stroked my long hair. I called it auburn, but Mama insisted I was a redhead. The sun streaked it with gold highlights in the summertime, which made it more auburn than red I thought, but I didn't argue with Mama. I'd get my mouth washed out with soap.

With my head on Tootsie's huge bosoms, I realized I couldn't remember a time in my life when she was not there for me.

"How old was I when you came to work for us, Toot?" I asked.

"Why, you was a baby, maybe three, four months old." Tootsie paused and thought. "Now don't you tell Miss Anne I told you none of this." She paused as if trying to decide whether to go on. "Your daddy, he know Catfish, and he come to the Quarters one day to axe could Catfish butcher him a hog. Your daddy saw me, I was maybe thirteen or fourteen, and he axed could I come help your Mama out. She had a hard time when you was born, James being almost three and all."

Tootsie went on to tell me more about her family and about how Mama kept having children so she needed Tootsie more than ever. I tried to listen, but all I could think about was Catfish, and wonder how I could see him now that I knew he would no longer come by my house in the afternoons.

I was more intrigued than ever about the Quarters, no longer afraid to go now that I knew Tootsie lived there. Surely Mama would let me go visit Tootsie.

*

"Absolutely not!" Mama said. "I'd better never catch you near those Quarters."

"Why?"

"I told you those people will eat you if you go near them."

"Mama, I'm almost thirteen, too old to believe that story anymore." She slapped me across the face, and blood spurted from my lip. I sucked it in so the blood would seep into my mouth, not on the blue carpet.

"Okay, then, Miss Smarty-Pants, it's because I said 'No,' and I'm the Mother!"

Being the troublemaker I was, I didn't take "No," for an answer.

Wednesday was "Bridge Day," when Mama played cards in the afternoon with her three best friends. The ladies took turns hosting and, on this particular Wednesday, the game would be at Mrs. June's house. When I got home from school that afternoon, Mama was gone and wouldn't be home until after five.

I changed into shorts and tennis shoes and hurried out the front door and across the front lawns of all the neighbors' houses, leaving my siblings in Tootsie's care. Perhaps no one would know I was gone. When I reached our old house, a wave of sadness washed over me. I walked down the driveway onto the blacktop road and stared at the low-slung white, ranch-style home where I had known a degree of childhood peace. I wondered why things had changed so drastically after we moved to the big house. Those thoughts slowed me down and I took a deep breath, to ward off the tears that seemed just under the surface.

Deep breathing helped, and reminded me to enjoy the smells in the air. Catfish would ask me about them. I inhaled roses and hydrangeas and hot tar as I slowed my pace on the steaming pavement. It was a beautiful afternoon, hot and humid, as usual, but tolerable for late September. I listened for the music of birds calling to each other and to the bees as they buzzed near the ground around my ankles, and I made my way across Gravier Road to the Quarters. I felt like I was doing something awful, and a sheet of guilt fell over me. I tried to shake it off by thinking about seeing Catfish, after so many months.

He was asleep in a rocking chair on the back porch of the first cabin in the row, his hat drawn over his eyes. I walked up the three small steps and sat in a straight-backed chair with a green, ripped naugahyde seat. I didn't say anything for the longest time, then decided to wake him.

"Hey, Catfish," I said, as if it was a normal everyday occurrence for me to be in the Quarters visiting. Catfish pushed his hat back on his head and didn't acknowledge me at first, didn't look at me, didn't speak. He rocked gently in his chair and stared straight ahead out of half-closed eyes. I tried to see what he was looking at—a big, circular, dirt yard, in front of a little garden with a crude fence, an old barn off to the right a hundred yards or so and cane fields as far as I could see. On one side of the cane field were rows of pecan trees, and live oaks were scattered here and there providing shade to the entire space—acres and acres of land.

It had been months since the Klan's raid and the Quarters looked no worse for the wear, although I didn't know how it looked before.

I wondered whether Catfish and Tootsie ever discovered why the Klan went to the Quarters the same night they came to our house and, I must admit, I felt a twinge of guilt that it could be my fault and that maybe my visit this particular day could cause more trouble. *Troublemaker.*

Sitting on his porch in total silence, I thought about it for the first time. Was I the reason?

Catfish finally looked at me. By then I was nervous, questioning whether I should be there, wondering whether I had made a rash decision that I didn't think through. That's what usually got me in trouble—barreling into something without thinking of all the consequences. I still do that. Impulsive is what some of my friends call me.

We sat in an uncomfortable silence for a while, both thinking quietly. Catfish was probably thinking the same thing I was—what if my visit caused the Klan to return? We inhaled the smells of the cane fields and the chickens in the yard and the patch of flowers in the little fenced-in garden on the side of his cabin. I could hear myself breathe, in and out. Every now and then I sighed, and exhaled heavily, without realizing it, like I was blowing out all the pain I held inside. Without changing my position I broke the silence.

"I waited months before coming because I wasn't sure."

Silence.

"Should I leave?"

Silence.

"I had to see you, Cat. I had to see for myself that you're okay. I've been so worried, especially since that night, the raids, you know ..."

Silence.

"If it was because of me, I'm so sorry. I'll leave and I won't come back."

Silence.

"Talk to me Catfish, I feel so guilty."

"It weren't your fault, Missy. Everyone knowed I stopped at your house. That's been going on for years and years. Nobody paid that no mind."

"Then why?"

"Not sure. Maybe we'll never know."

"They came to our house, too."

"Yeah. Tootsie tole me."

"That's what made me think it was my fault."

"Coincidence."

We didn't say any more about the Klan. Neither of us was convinced it was *not* my fault. I kept thinking about Daddy saying it was because of his relationship with Ray Thibault. But why the Quarters, too? What was the connection?

A beautiful light-skinned girl with long, wavy hair, a deep shade of reddish-brown like the mahogany dining table Mama was so proud of, stepped onto the porch next door. The houses were so close the girl could have almost stepped onto Catfish's porch from hers. She was tall, at least as tall as me, and she carried a book.

"Are you Marianne?"

"How you know my name? Who're you?"

"Your mom works for us. She told me about you." Catfish watched us, inhaling our exchange. He seemed a bit skittish, like he was afraid we might start fighting or something.

"Oh, you must be Susanna Burton," Marianne said. She almost spat the words, as if they disgusted her. She walked down her steps into the yard.

"Susie."

We sized each other up. I heard Catfish exhale, quietly. Tootsie had told me that her daughter was distrustful of white people since the Klan's visit. I knew I was probably a threat to her, that maybe there was some jealousy over Tootsie, even Catfish. I smiled at her. Her stare lightened a little and she took a breath, relaxing some.

"Hey, you girls. Remember me?" Catfish said. He laughed his belly laugh and tugged on his right ear lobe. "Mari, Sweet Baby, this the girl I talks to when I walks home from work. Remember I tole you about her? She the one gave me that turtle that time, remember? She and I been friends a long time. Ain't that right, Missy?"

"Yeah. That's right ..."

"You didn't tell me she was Mr. Burton's kid," Marianne said. Again, she spat the words. Staccato.

"I never axed her who was her daddy. Didn't seem to matter."

"Well, it does matter. To me," Marianne pouted and folded her arms across her chest, the book flattened against it, tucked under her chin, but she didn't move from her spot in the yard.

"I'm so happy to know you, Marianne," I said. I smiled my best smile and skipped down the three little steps to the back yard, a sea of dirt and dust. I tried to hug Marianne but she hugged herself and turned her head to the side. I tried a handshake, but she wouldn't let go of herself to extend her hand. In the end I patted her on the back and attempted a conversation.

"You are as pretty as your Mama said. I thought she was just being a proud Mama, you know, one of those who believes all her children are special. But she was right." Catfish watched. Marianne took a step back, as if I was in her personal space. I took a step forward and put my arm around her shoulder and squeezed it. Marianne looked at me like I fell out of a tree. I ignored the innuendo and sprang back up the steps and into the chair next to Catfish.

"I was worried about you, Catfish. When you quit coming by my house I asked Tootsie where you were. She said you retired. You never told me Toot was your daughter."

"You never axed, Missy," he said. "I thought you had that figured."

"What? Just because both of you are colored I'm supposed to know you're related? That's like saying I'm related to Billy Boudreaux because he's white and Cajun." I attempted a laugh at my own joke. Catfish hesitated, then realized I wasn't making fun of colored people and he began to chuckle. Then he broke into a hearty laugh. He laughed so hard Marianne and I both started to laugh with him. That broke the ice and Marianne finally walked onto the porch and sat at Catfish's feet, against the corner post.

"I was going to read you a book this afternoon," Marianne said. She glanced at me with a look of disdain, as if I messed up her plans. I ignored it.

"Well, Chile, I thought I might tell you girls a story." He looked thoughtful.

"Okay, Granddaddy. How about you tell us about the slave days, before the Civil War." She turned to me for the first time, like it was normal for me to be there. "His Granddaddy was a slave until Mr. Lincoln declared all people free."

"That's right. My granddaddy, named Samuel Massey. That's who I named your Uncle Sam for," Catfish said to Marianne. "Well, my granddaddy was a slave on this very plantation. Lived in this very cabin, yes he did. "

He looked at us, one, then the other. When we didn't comment, and he was assured he had a captive audience, he went on.

*

Slave Auction
1854

'Well, Granddaddy was born to a slave woman on Kent Plantation over in Alexandria, and in those days, that thirty-five miles between Kent and Shadowland was like five hundred miles is today. They didn't have no cars. They traveled by horse or mule or buggy pulled by an animal. It could take all day to get from Alexandria to Jean Ville.

'Samuel, my granddaddy, he was taken from his mama, the housekeeper at the Kent Plantation, when he was about ten or so—they didn't keep track of actual ages in those days—and thought to be big enough to work in the fields. He missed his Mama so bad and grieved for her every day after they were separated. Tears would bunch up in his eyes years later when he told Granny, that was his wife, named Anna-Lee, and later he told his boys,—that be my daddy and them—about the last time he saw his Mama. It was a story he told every year, right around the time of summer when he was taken, a story passed on through the generations by those who either could not write or had no tools to record the history.

'Granddaddy said, "She was holding me so tight I couldn't breathe. I wrapped my arms around her and grabbed both my wrists with the opposite hand. I thought they couldn't take me from her if I held on tight.'

'Then he heard the wheezing of the whip and the snap of the sharp, thin blades of leather, but he said he didn't feel nothin. His eyes was closed so tight against the tears behind 'em that when the foreman swung the long rope and popped it in the air he thought that man just put the fear of the Lord in him.

'My grandaddy said he knew what it looked like, that ole whip. He saw it often, in the hand of Mister Reynaud when he rode his horse through the fields and gripped its handle polished, like priceless silver.

"It was several thin strings of twine braided together about three or four feet long with five or six leather strips on the end of it, plaited into a braid and held together with a silver ring, Granddaddy said. "On the other end was a handle, made of whittled wood, smooth and curved to perfectly fit his hand. No one was allowed to touch that cat-o-nine-tales but Mister Reynaud. And it was always in a position to strike.

"I was still a boy, so I didn't get whipped, but I knowed it wouldn't be long fore it was my time, and I thought that day had come. You never want to hear that sound. Never. If you do, you can't never forget it."

'He said he didn't feel no pain but he noticed his Mama's grip around him loosen a bit. Still, he held on to her.'

"She was a skinny little thing, but her arms was strong and she could do the work any man could do, that's for shore," Granddaddy said.

'There was lots of hollering, men screaming at them to let go, but no one touched me or Mama or tried to pull us apart. I heard the whip again. This time Mama's arms almost released me, but I was holding her tight, around her waist, so she didn't fall. I tried not to open my eyes to look at her, but, after the third wiz of the whip, I made myself glance up and saw the agony in her face. That's when I knew she was the one Mr. Reynaud's whip was hitting, not the wind.

"Now that I'm a daddy, I know that look in her face had more to do with losing me than the whipping she was getting." Je used to tell us when he tole this story.

'At this point my granddaddy would stop and a tear would run down his cheek. He said he knew she woulda just stood there and took it as long as he held on to her. He always stopped here and wiped his eyes. Eventually he would continue.

"I had to let go," he'd say over and over. "I just had to. I didn't have no choice. They'd of killed her, just for disrespecting. I had to let her go. I had to."

"When I released my grip on her she fell to the ground in a heap."

'Here, Granddaddy would always stop and look in the distance like he was talking to the trees. It was like none of us was there anymore. He was talking to hisself, I guess.

'There was blood all over her and I bent down to help her, she wasn't more an a hundred pounds. That's when the men grabbed me. They put my arms and legs in chains and attached them to a ring around my neck. Then they sat me in the back of a wagon that moved over rocky, rutted roads all day long. No hat to cover my head, no food, no water and the heat pounding on me.

'When they got here—he didn't know till later it was Jean Ville— they put him on a block in the middle of town. He was only a boy,' Catfish said.

"I missed my Mama and my home, the only place I'd ever known. The Man at Kent House was mean, but I was safe with

Mama. I didn't know what would happen to me away from her. And what about Mama? Would she be all right? If she died it would be my fault cause I wouldn't let her go of her,'

"Granddaddy heard men calling out numbers and, after some time, he was put in another wagon, turned out to be Mr. Van's. The men who took him away from his Mama got the chains off him and he waited for new ones, but they didn't come. Mr. Van went around the back of the wagon with a scooper of water and axed Granddaddy did he want some. He was thirsty. It was dusty and hot. His mouth was so dry he couldn't answer. He just nodded and Mr. Van handed him that scoop and put a bucket full of clear, fresh water next to him. Next thing he knowed they was going somewhere in that wagon and the man driving didn't put no chains on him or take the bucket or the scoop back. That was the first clue he had he'd been bought by a good man.

'He cried hisself to sleep every night, but during the day he was too busy to think about his Mama and Kent Plantation. There was some other slaves here back then: old George and a kind woman named Bessie who took sympathy on him.

'Granddaddy didn't know where Kent Plantation was or how far. He didn't see his Mama for twenty years. By that time he was married and they had Sammy. That was my daddy. He was about three, and she was pregnant with their second . . .Whew! I tired now. You girls run along, You done wore me out.'

"Wait, Catfish, you didn't finish the story. What happened? You said he saw his Mama again?"

"Yeah, Missy, but I too tired to tell you the rest. I'll tell you more next time you come around."

That was the best invitation I was going to get, so I took it. I was happy he wanted me to come back.

"Okay, Cat,"

*

41

Catfish seemed different at his own house, rocking on his own porch. I know he was surprised to see me, but I think he was happy, once everyone settled down. He looked old and worn out, and that worried me, but I acted like he was just the same ole' Catfish who'd danced and chatted with me so often over the past six years.

I tried to take it all in. The quarters had five little wood houses with back porches that almost touched each other, in a semi-circle around a fire pit in the center of the yard. It looked like there had been six cabins at one time—there was a pile of burnt rubble at the far end of the row. I figured that was where the charred smell that hung in the air came from.

Between the porches and the fire pit was dirt, and beyond the fire pit was more dirt that led to a small garden with a path on one side. From Catfish's back porch, past the fire pit and the dirt yard, past the garden with sticks that stood vertically in rows, past the pecan grove with straight lines of trees that looked like huge umbrellas with only slithers of sunlight on the ground beneath them, I could see the cane fields that went on for miles.

I didn't go inside his cabin, but from the outside I could tell that none of the houses had more than three rooms, some only two. It looked like, when they added a room, they added to the front of the cabins, where there were no porches, only a set of steps that led to a door and faced South Jefferson Street Extension. The cabins were practically hidden behind more pecan trees and huge live oaks that formed a dense canopy for at least 100-yards to the narrow street.

I was amazed at how close the five houses were to each other. Someone could sit on each of the five back porches and have conversations with the people on the other porches, never raising their voices. Except for the two houses on either end, there wasn't enough room on the sides of the cabins to add a room, unless new rooms connected the houses together.

Catfish told me the cabins were called "shotgun houses."

MADELYN BENNETT EDWARDS

"They came up with that name during slave days because the plantation owners said you could shoot a shotgun through the front door and the buckshot could kill a varmint in the back yard. We don't waste no space on halls. One room goes into the next." But he didn't invite me to go inside to confirm his story.

I walked home that afternoon thinking about the story Catfish told. I wanted to write it down before I forgot all the details. It was hard to believe people were treated that way, bought and sold like property, taken from their families, whipped, deprived of water and food. I thought about Mr. Van, who was a kind slave owner, but he still bought and sold people like they were cattle. What did that say about him?

Looking back I realize that was the beginning of my desire to be a writer. It all started with Catfish's story. It caused something of a metamorphosis inside me, a revolution of sorts, about the way Negroes were treated. Through the years I would become outraged that nothing really changed, even as laws said they did. I made it my life's mission to make people see what a travesty this was.

I sit here today and wonder whether anything has really changed in the almost half-century since my first visit to the Quarters when I was not quite thirteen years old.

*

I tried to make friends with the girls in my class at Assumption Catholic where my brothers and I went to elementary school. No one seemed to like me. I was bullied, criticized and some of the girls from the country tried to beat me up, and they succeeded every now and then. I learned to run, fast, and became a track star in high school, which I attribute to the mean girls who chased me every day. I never understood what I did to make them dislike me, and the harder I tried to please them, the worse they treated me.

"You should just go somewhere and die," Megan Dauzat said.

43

"Yeah," Melanie Gremillion said. "You just take up space. No one likes you, anyway."

There were lots of incidents. One girl held my head in the toilet and flushed. They chased me, and if they caught me, they'd throw me on the ground and beat me up. They wouldn't invite me to parties or to their houses for what people today call play dates. If I invited them, they'd laugh, or accept and not show up.

The nuns sided with my classmates and alternately singled me out or ignored me. Sister Adrian pulled me down the hall by the ear. Sister Celeste told the class I peed on the bathroom floor. When I asked why, the only straight answer I ever got was, "We were told to put you in your place and keep you there!" Now I understand it was Mama's way of making sure I didn't become conceited—or, at least, that's what she told me years later when she said, "I did it for your own good, Susanna Christine."

I was in seventh grade when everything came to a head at Assumption Catholic.

A new family moved to Jean Ville, the first Hispanic family in town. They had seven children; five were school age. The Martinez kids came to Assumption on "scholarships" and the eldest, Randy, was in my class. He was fifteen; I was barely eleven. Randy didn't speak much English and couldn't read or write, but he set his sights on me from the first day. He was big and had whiskers and the other boys were no match for his strength or his pernicious plans. He bullied Jeffrey Marks out of his desk directly behind me and Randy began a series of malicious flirtations that kept me in constant trouble, while he was never blamed. He played with my long hair, shot spitballs at me, popped the back of my training bra and tried to raise my skirt. He wouldn't leave me alone. Each time he was caught, I was punished for "leading him on," and Randy got off Scott-free. When I told Mama about the new boy and how he badgered me and got me in trouble she told me I was "leading him on," too. I didn't know what that meant.

One day when the bell rang after recess to signal it was time to return to the classroom, I stood at the end of the line of girls and waited for Sister Clement to emerge from the building to lead us up the steps from the dirt yard. It was hot and dusty and I needed to stop at the water fountain inside, so I was fidgety. I was usually second from last in line because Katie Gagnard was the tallest girl and I was next to tallest. Katie was home sick that day so I was at the end of the line.

Randy ran up behind me without warning and scooped me up like a man would carry his bride across the threshold. In one fluid motion he ran towards the hedges that separated the schoolyard from a ditch and formed a boundary between Assumption and the Gaspard's house next door. He threw me over the hedges into the trench, then dove over the bushes to land on top of me. I rolled away just in time and I guess he landed in the ditch. I got to my feet, ran through the shrubbery, up the back steps and into the classroom, unaware that I was disheveled with leaves and grass in my hair, my skirt hiked up and dirt smeared across my face, arms and legs. Randy was right behind me, laughing. Looking back I can see how it must have seemed to Sister Clement who, before I could open my mouth to explain, pointed to the door and sent me to Sister Adrian's office.

Sister Adrian took one look at me, bruised and dirty, and called me a, "whore" and a "slut" and sent me home, after a sound whipping.

"And don't come back to Assumption," the nun screamed. "We are done with the likes of you. You are a disgrace to our school and our students."

When I got home, Mama was changing the baby and Tootsie was hanging clothes on the line outside.

"What are you doing home so early?" Mama asked without looking at me.

"What's a whore?" I asked. She turned her head and lifted an eyebrow which caused a crease to form on her forehead. She slapped me across the face.

"Don't you ever say words like that, young lady! Where did you hear such vulgarity?"

"Sister Adrian. That's what she called me when she sent me home and told me never to go back to Assumption. She also called me a slut."

"I told you not to say those words!" I just looked at her. *What words?* I wondered.

"You must have done something awful," Mama yelled.

"I'm not sure what I did. That new boy, Randy, threw me in the bushes and I got away. Then Sister Clement sent me to the office and Sister Adrian whipped me and called me those words."

"What did you do to make that boy come after you?"

"Nothing, I swear. I was just standing in line ..."

"Don't swear and don't lie to me!" She slapped me again. This time I felt my lip split and I tasted blood. "I know better. You are boy-crazy! Go to your room. Wait till your daddy gets home!"

When Daddy got home he came to my room, didn't ask questions.

My hero rode in on a big horse and galloped over me, using a lasso, leather with a belt buckle on the end, to whip me into shape. I made myself into a haystack, tight and round to hide, but the horse took bits out of me and left holes that oozed from the inside out. The light was like sunshine blazing down so hot I began to sweat and a whoosh of urine ran out from under me. The sun fell from the sky and everything went dark and flat as I slid under the protection of my bed and slept, the dust ruffle around the bottom making me feel walled in and safe. The hardwood floor smelled like wax and ammonia and moisture crept up my lumpy stack of bones by osmosis. There was a small glow from the lamp beside my bed, and when I opened my eyes I could see where the holes had sprouted red liquid that pooled on the floor and smeared my face and hands.

On my knees I crawled across the hall to the bathroom and pulled myself up by hanging onto the lavatory. The blood was coming from a cut on my butt where the buckle must have landed. I tried to clean it with a wash cloth and cold water, then someone began to bang on the bathroom door.

"What's all the noise?" Mama yelled. I opened the door and stood on one foot, hobbling on the other, holding onto the doorknob. She gasped and shoved me back into the bathroom, followed me in and closed the door.

"Sit on the toilet," she said and she lowered the lid. I sat on the open wound on my butt. She started to wash my face with soap and water and became exasperated, then filled the bathtub halfway and told me to get in.

"Wash yourself with soap, Susanna, and shampoo your hair," she said. "Then get some clean pajamas on and go to bed." I did as she said, but it wasn't easy. I couldn't sleep, I kept waiting for the horses to return and stampede through my room. I felt tiny and vulnerable.

In the morning Tootsie brought me aspirin and soup at lunch and I tried to sleep off and on. Daddy came in my room that evening. I was afraid so I cowered in the bed, my neck against the headboard, legs stretched out in front of me. He gently pushed my legs over and sat on the edge of the bed next to my butt, facing me.

"Are you okay, Pretty Girl?" he asked. He put his hand on my cheek and stroked it. Tears streamed down my face. I nodded. Daddy took his handkerchief out of his back pocket and wiped my eyes, cheeks and neck, then he handed it to me. I blew my nose.

"I need to explain what's going to happen. You will not return to Assumption. There are only a few weeks left in this school year and

Sister Adrian has agreed to give you a report card for the full year, all As, of course. Your mother will get you registered at the public school and you'll go there next year."

"But Daddy," I started to cry again. "Next year is eighth grade. I won't get to graduate."

"You'll graduate from the public school."

"What about Will and Robby? Will they come with me?"

"No. Will has two more years and Robby four, and you'll be in high school in one year, so it's no use to move them."

"But the nuns ..."

"I know. But I promised your grandmother I'd make sure you all got a Catholic education. Assumption only goes through eighth grade, so you would have to go to public school in ninth grade, anyway."

"But I don't know anyone." I couldn't stop crying. I was confused and felt betrayed but I didn't understand why, at the time. And I was sick and humiliated and Daddy acted like everything was normal, that I wasn't recovering from a brutal spanking. It was confusing to an eleven-year-old.

"Just think how much better it'll be. When you start high school, you'll already know all the kids in public school. Now, don't cry anymore. It's going to be alright."

I knew it wouldn't be alright, but at least Daddy wasn't mad at me anymore, and it didn't look like I was going to be punished for getting kicked out of school. Anyway, I didn't have to go to school the last three weeks. That was something. I didn't hear another word he said.

～Chapter Three ～

～

The Quarters/Mama
1963

I RAN AS FAST as I could while Alice and Megan chased me to the back corner of the school grounds where I was trapped by the fence. I had nowhere to go so I waited a few seconds and they jumped on me, threw me to the ground and beat the crap out of me. I was still alive when the bell rang after noon recess. The girls ran off and I got up slowly, dusted myself off and felt around for injuries. I was late entering class, but it wasn't the same as at Assumption where the nuns would call me out. Mrs. Gautreax took one look at me, reached in her purse for a handkerchief and sent me to the bathroom to clean up.

The brush burn on my cheek and cuts on my legs were minor. I'd had worse. I'd been at the public school for six weeks and these beatings were regular events, but I was tired of them. Nothing I could do or say would persuade the girls at my new school to include me, and I had come to grips with that. What I couldn't get accustomed to was the country girls attacking me.

After school that day I stayed back and asked Mrs. Gautreax if I might help her during recesses. She was kind, and her hands were full with thirty rough eighth-graders, but she agreed and I began to clean the blackboards, grade standardized tests and run errands in the building during breaks.

The high school band teacher, Mr. Goudeau, was the best man I'd ever met, other than Catfish. He agreed to let me spend lunch recess in the band room, where he helped me learn to play the clarinet. I told him I wanted to become a majorette and he explained I had to learn an instrument and march with the high school band for one year before I could try out for one of the five coveted spots on the twirl team.

Troubles at school were minor compared with home. If I came home with bruises, Mama would scream and yell at me.

"I don't understand why you can't make friends. What's wrong with you?" she'd say and when Daddy came home she'd complain about me to him and he'd come in my room angry.

"Don't you understand I'm trying to earn a living in this town, and I'm running for mayor. You can ruin me with your troublemaking ways," he'd say and, if I was lucky, he'd spank or slap me. If he'd been drinking, well, that was another story.

If that wasn't enough my older brother, James, hated me and tried to turn Robby and Will against me. Boys against girl, he told them.

"Get her," James would scream at the two younger brothers I loved more than anyone—at least that was true before I started going to the Quarters. They'd chase me and trip me. We were playing chase in the yard one day and James hid a yard rake, the kind with iron firs, under a pile of leaves. I chased Robby and he went around the pile but I went through it, a short cut, I thought. I stepped on the rake and two of the teeth went through my foot. I had a tetanus shot and antibiotics for two weeks.

My life was miserable everywhere I turned.

The day I met Marianne was the best day of my life. I liked her immediately and it seemed, she eventually took a liking to me. By the time Catfish finished his story, during my first visit, we had developed secret looks and giggles in a sweet conspiracy of sorts. After Catfish shooed us off to the barn, we began to share all sorts of secrets we'd stored deep inside and couldn't tell anyone. I guess we felt safe—in part because neither of us knew the people in the other person's life, and because we shared a loneliness that we didn't need to explain to each other. Marianne didn't have girlfriends, either.

I remember being on-guard, at first, and unsure how to begin. And Marianne seemed more afraid than I was, but we had chemistry from the start, almost an inner knowledge and shared history that couldn't be explained. We laughed when we said the same thing in tandem and were both amazed at how much we thought alike and shared the same disappointments and trials in the world.

We had differences, too, but those divergences were not about skin color.

Marianne had a loving home and supportive extended family. Catfish and Tootsie were gentle and kind, never raised their voices and didn't believe in spankings. Marianne's younger sisters adored her. If she had a bad day at school, she went home to love and understanding. She didn't have a dad, but she had Catfish, which was better.

I went to the Quarters almost every Wednesday afternoon, except on the fourth Wednesday when Mama and her friends played bridge at our house. Sometimes Marianne was there, sometimes not. Sometimes Catfish was happy to see me, sometimes he was too tired to talk. It didn't matter. I sat on his porch and stared at the cornfields and felt a peace that I didn't feel anywhere else—not at home, not at school, not at church, nowhere but in the Quarters.

Marianne and I laughed freely about Catfish and the way he delivered his stories. We usually went to the old barn, sat in the sparse grass and leaned against the outside of the once red building, its paint faded and peeling.

Marianne eventually told me about the night the KKK came and two white men attacked her.

"They touched my private parts," she said. I just listened and felt deep empathy for her. I thought about how different the Klan acted at our house versus in the Quarters.

She recounted the horror as if it was something she'd witnessed, something that happened to someone else. She said she was in the outhouse when she heard the commotion. Tootsie and her three smaller daughters were asleep in their cabin and Marianne was in the dark alone, when she heard the noise and smelled burning kerosene. The earth moved so fiercely Marianne thought it would open up and swallow all six shotgun houses.

"Hurry. Get in here!" Catfish called out of his back door above the noise.

Marianne watched, frozen in the doorway of the privy as her mom, sisters, aunt and uncles and all her cousins flooded into Catfish's little house from their own cabins. Tootsie ran barefoot with the baby in her arms. Marianne wanted to call to her for help, but couldn't get her voice to work any better than her feet.

"It's the Klan," Catfish yelled. "They got fire and they coming fast! Everyone inside." He didn't need to repeat himself.

By the time Marianne recovered her legs and voice, her granddaddy had closed and bolted the door and dozens of men draped in white sheets came rushing into the dirt yard with an urgency and force she had never witnessed in her almost thirteen years on this earth.

She said that blazes of fire in their hands lit up the night sky and revealed her tall, lithe body standing at the back edge of the yard. When they saw her they whooped and hollered, adding to the thunderous roar of engines and hooves that shook the little outhouse like a ship on a rough sea.

Marianne didn't have time to think. She had to hide. She knew she couldn't make it to her granddaddy's cabin so she darted across the dirt yard to the nearest house, her Uncle Sam's. She ran, stooped over, knees bent, head down, then fell to the ground when she reached the back porch and rolled under it. She scooted as far under the porch as she could and lay on her stomach with her arms folded over her head. She tried to block out the noises of the engines and the fiery sky that smelled like burning kerosene, but she couldn't block the shouts and curses from the dozens of white men on a rampage.

She smelled something else burning—not the torches, but something like wood on fire. She peeked from under her arms into the back yard. The outhouse was on fire. She'd been there just a minute before. And the clothes that hung on the clothesline were burning, too.

Oh, God, she thought, *please don't set Uncle Sam's house on fire. I'll burn to death under here.*

She trembled all over. She told me that her tears made mud puddles under her face.

There was only one empty house in the Quarters. It was a one-room shanty in bad shape on the edge of the row of the other cabins, and it was closest to the outhouse, two cabins away from the one where she hid. Marianne watched that shack catch fire. Her Aunt Jesse and Uncle Bo's house sat next door to it and would go up in flames, too, if someone didn't get out there and start spraying it with water.

Thank God everyone was in her granddad's cabin on the far end, hopefully out of danger.

She heard boots stomp on the porch above her and she scooted further under the house, petrified.

Suddenly she felt a hand grab her ankle and begin to pull, then another gripped the other ankle and she slid quickly out from under the house. The dark night was lit by dozens of torches.

She screamed and kicked and flayed her arms.

Within seconds she was caught from behind by two strong arms and she said she could smell the body odor and sweat of the man behind her. His breath smelled like smoke and whiskey and she felt the stubble of a beard bury itself in her neck.

She screamed and a huge hairy hand clasped over her mouth.

She tried to kick and claw at the creature behind her when another man in white grabbed her legs and, before she knew what happened, the two men had flipped her in the air and onto her back on the porch of her Uncle Sam's cabin, her head hitting the floor hard enough that she blacked out.

When she came to, she felt someone grabbing the waist of her shorts while the man behind her held her down with his knees on her shoulders, one big hand over her mouth, the other on her chest. Their horrible throaty laughs were mixed with vulgar words about her body that made her sick.

She tried to yell.

Marianne said she tried to bite the man who held her down while the man in front of her yanked on her shorts and panties until he had them binding her ankles, hog-tied and helpless.

She fought hard and they laughed nasty, wet laughs.

"I'll never forget what that man said," she told me. She stared straight ahead, her eyes blank, her mouth a straight line. I smelled fear mixed with Ivory soap come from her as we sat on the ground, our bare shoulders touching.

"We got lucky, Jack. It's a white bitch!" She said a throaty laugh came from the other man who yelled. "I'm gonna get me some of this black ass, even if it looks white."

"Save some for me, you pecker wood," the first man said. She said he spit when he talked and the thick, crusty tobacco-laced saliva sprayed over her and fell on her bare belly.

The man in front of her was on his knees and he grabbed her down there and squeezed till she screamed and cried and begged him to stop. Then she bit the man's hand that covered her mouth, hard.

The man between her legs slapped her across the face, on both sides. Her neck snapped, one way, then the other, like it wouldn't hold, and her head hung to the side. She felt blood drip from her nose and mouth and everything around her was in a fog.

When Catfish realized Marianne was not in his cabin, he looked out the window, searching for her. He saw the two men with her on Sam's porch and opened his back door to run out. Marianne could hear her mother and Aunt Jesse scream, "No, Daddy. They gonna kill you. Whatever they do to Marianne, she'll get over it, but no one get over dying."

Then the man who hit her stood up and pulled off his mask and hat. He had dark curly hair and mean dark eyes. He opened his robe, started to unbuckle his belt, then cursed as the robe got in his way. Finally he pulled the white sheet over his head.

Marianne said she screamed and twisted and turned and tried to kick, but her clothes were wrapped around her ankles and the man holding her down put his fist in her mouth, like he was nailing her to the floor with his hand. She told me that his other hand was inside her shirt grabbing at her breasts.

"I think we got us a virgin, Larry," the man behind her said.

Marianne thought she heard her grandfather's voice again, "That's my baby out there. I done spent my life, she just beginning hers. Let me go get her."

Marianne tried to scream, but it came out like a grunt. The man called Larry let his jeans fall around his boots and Marianne saw his big, white penis spring out and point straight at her before she closed her eyes as tight as she could. She felt him grab her pubic hair with both hands. He pulled her britches all the way off and she felt his knees spread her legs so wide she thought she would rip in half.

"That white man, he said something awful, something that haunts me every day," Marianne told me. She was quiet a moment. I didn't push her.

"'Oh, Larry, she likes it!' he said. I was horrified. I didn't like it. It hurt like hell. They were so rough, and when the one behind me grabbed my titties and started to pinch them, I screamed. I felt like he would push me through the boards onto the dirt under the porch. I cried and cried, but no one heard me."

As she told me her story huge, alligator tears ran freely down her cheeks and pooled under her chin. She twisted a strand of hair that sprung from her temple. I tucked some of Marianne's mahogany waves behind her ear, then put my arm around her shoulder and tried to look at her, but she turned away and shut her eyes.

Marianne played with the grass between her crossed legs, but I didn't turn away. A red bird landed on a low branch of the pecan tree in front of us and began to chirp.

"'Oh, God,' I thought, 'please don't let him put that thing inside me.' I was terrified. I tried to scream but the other man had his fist in my mouth. He was so strong. I knew if things got any worse, I'd faint. Maybe I did faint because the next thing I knew that man with the big white penis was laying on top of me. He was so heavy I couldn't breathe and something burned like fire between my legs. I can still feel it—searing and hot."

She stopped talking and looked at nothingness. It seemed the red bird stared at her, almost lovingly. I didn't say anything. I just reached over and took her hand out of her lap and held it. She squeezed my hand and glanced at me through the corner of her eye.

"You ever done it, Susie?"

"Done what?"

"It, you know. Sex."

"No, I don't know much about it. What you told me is the most I ever heard."

"I think, with the right person, if they aren't rough, it might be okay."

"Really?"

"Yes. I think so." She was quiet for a while.

"My Mama wasn't much older than me when I was born. I think she was fourteen or fifteen."

I was so naïve. I didn't know what Tootise having Marianne at fourteen had to do with sex but I didn't admit it. I knew I could find the answers in the library, which was my favorite place—that is, before I discovered the Quarters.

"Finally I heard a truck rev loudly and blow the horn and a man's voice hollered, 'Come on, Larry, Jack, we're leaving,'" Marianne whispered. "'You going to walk home?' the man yelled.

"'Shucks, Jimbo, I was jus' starting to have me some fun,' the man named Larry said. I think that was when I fainted."

She said she fought through a deep fog until she could hear horses galloping towards South Jefferson Extension and, finally, the engines sounded like they were pulling out of the Quarters. She heard another man scream out.

"Hey, Jack! You and Larry better jump in the back of one of these trucks, or you'll be spending the night with a bunch of niggers, yeah." He laughed. "And you get burned up, you."

"Shit, man. I didn't get my turn, me," the man named Jack said.

"Get in or get left, you coon-asses," the man yelled. Larry got off her and pulled his jeans up, held them with one hand while he grabbed his robe, hat and mask with the other.

The next thing Marianne knew she was in her mother's lap, on the floor of Catfish's cabin, rocking back and forth. She had a headache and couldn't open her right eye and the smell of charred wet wood filled the thin air—everything except her mother's voice:

"And if that mockingbird don't sing, Mama gonna buy you a diamond ring;

"And if that diamond ring don't shine, Mama gonna buy you a Valentine..."

Marianne didn't say any more about the Klan. She just sat there and let tears wash down her face like a waterfall recently released from its dam. I squeezed her hand again. She squeezed mine back.

We sat together and held hands for a long time in comfortable silence. My heart broke for her.

A bell rang.

"Oh, God!" I said. "How late is it? I'm going to be in so much trouble."

I ran out of the Quarters, crossed Gravier Road and cut through all the neighbors' backyards. I reached the back door of our house just as Mama yelled, "Susie, it's time to set the table."

I strolled into the kitchen, composed, but hurting inside for my friend.

"Sorry, Mama, I was in the bathroom."

"Well, get a move on. You know your daddy wants supper on the table at six-thirty."

"No problem. How was bridge?"

"I won, as usual," she said. "Ten cents. We're high rollers!" She laughed. That was a good sign—Mama had a good bridge day and had no interest in my after school whereabouts. Whew!

I cleaned the kitchen and mopped the floor after supper and thought about Marianne. She didn't look colored, except for her lips, which were larger than most white people's, but not overly large, not like Catfish's—more like Tootsie's. The two of us looked so different—me with bluish eyes, reddish hair and pale skin, so white that the sun caused my face to turn pinkish red. Marianne was beautiful, with dark hair, grey-green eyes and olive skin that glistened in the sun and had just a hint of Indian blood. We were both tall and thin, with long legs and small, firm breasts, just beginning to bud out and needing a bra. Her thin, perfect nose was not wide like Catfish's, and actually seemed a little pugged at the tip.

I pictured Marianne with her long, brown hair, not black or kinky; it fell in soft waves down her back. She wore the sides pulled up in a barrette and a few wavy tendrils sprung out around her oval-shaped face. Her eyes were different, beautiful, almost inviting. I thought they held a hidden meaning. Thick, brown eyebrows framed her eyes with long, dark lashes, like fans that seemed to protect them from the glare. It was the look in her eyes that was striking and gave her a mysterious, intriguing quality. Against her olive skin, the green-grey color turned almost violet in the sunlight and the colors danced and caught reflections that bounced into the air, like prisms. They were eyes that said Marianne was smiling, even when she wasn't.

I had always wondered what books meant when they described a person as *sensuous*. Knowing Marianne, I thought, at that time in my life, I might understand. She seemed fearless, a person who would accept a dare, someone who would try anything once. To me, someone who didn't have much to smile about, Marianne was intriguing. In fact, you might say I was taken with her.

The best thing about Marianne was that she seemed to like me and want to be with me. This was a first for me, a real girlfriend.

That sweet thought was interrupted by a cloud, a sense of danger because I knew I had to keep our friendship a secret. I shuddered when I thought about what might happen if my parents found out.

I was young for my grade. I had started first grade at five, then I skipped sixth grade, because I was so far ahead of the others—maybe because I was such an avid reader, my escape. I also liked to write—poetry and fictional stories about girls my age whose daddies loved them and mothers were attentive. My characters always had lots of friends; they were popular and happy. There wasn't much conflict.

That summer I was preparing to go to high school, even though I was not quite thirteen. Yikes! The kids in my class would be at least fifteen. On the one hand I was too young to ride around in cars, or have boyfriends or listen to music by the Beatles, the latest rage from England that all the girls talked about. Teen magazines like *Seventeen* or *Cosmopolitan* were taboo for me and the *Twist* was considered a vulgar dance by the Church—if I got caught practicing the moves,

I'd be grounded, or worse. On the other hand, Mama expected me to behave like a fifteen year old.

"You need to grow up and start acting like the girls in your grade," Mama said.

"But the girls in my class are two years older and I can't do the things they do, listen to the music they like, read teen magazines, learn the newest dances. They think I'm a baby."

"You have to act like you are their age because you are in the same grade. You can't use being 'younger' as an excuse. That's what's wrong with you, Susanna Christine, you always have an excuse."

Excuses? So I was a troublemaker who made excuses. I'd have to work on that.

One day, while Tootsie brushed my hair I asked her why girls didn't like me.

"Marianne likes you," Tootsie said.

"And I like her, but why don't white girls like me?"

"They's just jealous, honey-chile. Look at yourself in the mirror."

"I can't change the way I look. I was born this way. What can I do?"

"Well, they's jealous because you smart and talented, too."

"I feel trapped. Trapped in this body, trapped in this mind, trapped in this face. I just want to be normal. I don't want to be different."

"My Marianne feel the same way. She don't have no colored girlfriends. She have the same problems like you. They jealous of her."

"I can see why. She's so beautiful and smart and, no offense Toot, but you'd never know she was colored unless someone said so. Do you fuss at her and punish her because she can't make friends?"

Tootsie didn't answer. *Help-code,* The subject dropped, and I was left to ponder.

I think I made the decision to become a writer after Catfish told me the second story in a long list of "'yarns" he'd spin for me over the coming years. As usual, Catfish was on his back porch, sleeping in his rocker when I climbed the steps and sat in the other chair. It was much too hot to sleep inside the little cabin, I expected.

It was a perfect day; sunny with a breeze, budding azaleas and dogwoods brought smells of summer and I had skipped down South Jefferson with a spring in my step. After a few minutes sitting, watching the corn grow, as Catfish would say, I tapped him on the shoulder. He woke with a start and looked at me. I laughed at his surprised expression. After a long pause, he began to laugh, too. We both felt more at ease now that nothing had happened during all the months I'd been visiting.

"Hi, Missy," he said. I wondered if he knew my real name. I liked his pet name for me but I wondered. Then I remembered our first meeting when I was seven, "Is Susie short for Susanna? ... then you have a nickname." I laughed under my breath.

"What you been doing?" I asked him.

"Oh, Missy. I been watching the grass grow." I laughed and looked at his profile set against the backdrop of pecan trees and tall live oaks with branches that curved up, then down and reached almost to the ground. It was as if the Quarters was hidden in a forest. You couldn't see it from South Jefferson Extension and, if you didn't know where to find the one-lane dirt drive hidden in the trees, you'd never get there. I would creep into the little clearing where the cabins were, by following a foot trail Tootsie told me about that had its entrance on Gravier Road. Once I took three steps onto the trail it curved sharply and I could no longer see the road or any signs of life other than the foot path that weaved through the trees and bushes. I wondered how the Klan knew how to find the Quarters.

"Are you feeling okay?"

"Fit as a fiddle," he said. We both laughed.

"Look," he said. He motioned to his right. "Here come Marianne." I waved at my best friend. She smiled broadly and waved back.

"What you doing here?" Marianne asked. She climbed the steps and sat next to Catfish's chair, facing me.

"Do I need a reason to visit my favorite old man and best girlfriend?" Catfish chuckled, and we giggled. "I was hoping Catfish would tell us the rest of that story about when his granddaddy was taken from his mother"

"Will you, Granddaddy?"

"Let's see, girls. If I remember correctly, the last time I tole you about when my granddaddy got sold and came to Shadowland, right?"

"Yeah, that's right." He looked off into space. I followed his eyes and thought they watched a robin flit from one pecan tree branch to another. He was lost in thought and I didn't interrupt. Finally he began the story.

*

Mama
1878

"It was a normal day in 1878,'"my granddaddy would say. "Almost twenty years after I came here to Shadowland.

"A horse pulling a flat board buggy trotted up the long, tree-lined drive you could hardly see from the main road, hidden by a grove of oak and pecan trees that shadowed the entry to Mr. Gordon Van's plantation house.

'That's why they called it Shadowland, you know,' Catfish commented. 'The house and all the fields was hidden in the shadows. You had to know it was here. Anyways ...'

"A young light skinned man sat on the elevated bench with the reins in his hands as the horse trotted up the long, circular drive," Granddaddy said. "He stopped the horse in front of the steps that led to the wide, wrap-around porch. Columns the size of oak trunks braced the roof, two stories high. Everything was painted white except the black shutters and the black front door.

"The man, dressed in baggy, once-white pants and a thin, loose fitting cotton shirt, sat on the wagon bench and didn't move. His hair was lighter than most of his kind and not bristly like mine. His eyes was bluish-green. He had a long, thin nose, not wide and flat like most us coloreds on Mr. Van's plantation.

"The man didn't climb down from the wagon, didn't call out, didn't make no noise, he just sat on the wagon bench, looked straight ahead, and held the reins patiently.

"Before long, Mr. Van's house girl, Lizzie, opened the front door and axed what he needed.

"'I need to see your boy named Samuel Massey,' he told her.

"'I'll go see can Mr. Van come talk to you,' Lizzie said and disappeared through the tall, black double doors with long windows on either side.

"The man in the wagon tried to peer through the glass, but couldn't see nothing. Soon, the girl returned with Mr. Van behind her. He was a tall, white man with thick, dark hair that had shocks of grey at the temples and above his ears. He wore a white suit, white shirt and a skinny black necktie with a silver clasp. He held a black felt derby hat in one hand and a pair of black gloves in the other. He slapped the hat with the gloves as he stood on the edge of the porch and glared at the man in the wagon.

"'What you want, boy?' Mr. Van axed.

"'Sir, I gots a sick woman in the back of this wagon needs to see your boy, Samuel. I been told he stay here.'

"'Samuel, yes, yes; Samuel works for me,' Mr. Van said. 'You'll find him in the Quarters, or he might be in the fields nearby. You passed it on your way here. Go back down the drive and turn right. The next turn into my property will take you to him.'

"'Much obliged, Sir,' the young man said, and he led the horses around the circular drive and off the plantation grounds. The horse-drawn wagon pulled into the property by the cabins.

'That was right here,' Catfish said. 'Right in front of this porch where we sitting, and Granddaddy was in the field planting corn. Granny, her name was Anna Lee, saw it first, coming towards the Quarters.'

"Dust rose under the horses' hooves and stirred up under the wagon wheels. Granddaddy didn't see the wagon but he knew something was coming up to the Quarters, because he smelt the dust in the air.

"'Samuel,' Annie hollered. 'Get over here.' Annie grabbed Sammy,

'That was my daddy,' Catfish explained. 'Sammy was his name. He was about three-years-old at the time'

"Little Sammy stood on the back stoop and waited, wide-eyed and afraid," Granddaddy said. "This was a stranger and they didn't have strangers come to our place unless it was trouble.

"Granddaddy looked up and watched the wagon appear out of the cloud of dust as the powdery ashes settled," Catfish said. "Then he walked slowly towards the horse and never took his eye off the younger man on the wagon seat. He took his time so he could size him up and Granny was yelling at him to hurry. She was scared."

'The driver looked to be about ten or twelve years younger than me, and he had lighter skin. In fact, you couldn't tell was he a white man or colored. He had long legs and didn't wear no hat to cover his light brown head and straight hair, cut short, above his ears.'

'As Granddaddy got close to him he noticed the man's eyes,' Catfish said.

"They was big as moon pies and a shade I'd never seen on a colored man, but, somehow, I knew he was colored, cause he seemed familiar, almost like I'd known that young man from somewhere," Granddaddy said..

'Granddaddy would later say he knew that man wasn't here to cause no trouble, he could tell from the man's face.'

"It was kind-looking and sad," Granddaddy said. "He's the one looked scared.

"What can I do for you," Granddaddy axed him when he got up even with the wagon.

"'I got someone want to see you,' the man said and he cocked his chin towards the bed of the wagon.

"He spoke so low I could hardly hear him. The young man just stared straight ahead and then he popped his chin to the side and said, 'In the back.'

'Granddaddy walked around to the back of the wagon and Granny met him there with my daddy in tow,' Catfish said.

"Little Sammy didn't want his mama to hold him so she let him down and he followed behind her, close. We all three looked in the back of the wagon over the sides that rose about a foot or so from the floor bed.

"Lying on burlap sacks, under a thin gray blanket was a frail, grey-haired woman with her head resting on a bedroll. She must have known we was there because she opened her clouded eyes and looked at me and Anna Lee standing there and little Sammy crawling up the back of the wagon.

"Then, the old woman started to cry."

'Right away Granddaddy said he knew who it was,' Catfish said. He climbed in the back of the wagon and picked her up like a baby and laid her across his lap. She weighed so little she felt like a pillow.'

"Mama," Granddaddy cried.

'He said tears rolled down his face and the dirt and dust made ridges, like tiny streams that cut through a muddy field, and they almost ran together and collected under his chin until his entire face was wet and made the mud stick in the crease of his neck, but he didn't pay it no mind. Tiny dollops of muck fell on the blanket.'

"Oh, Mama," he said.

'He just held her and she let him cradle her as she nestled into his arms that he tightened around her as tight as he could without hurting her, and he rocked her like a baby. He stroked her thin, graying hair and kept saying, "Mama. Mama. It's really you.

"I don't know how long we stayed out there, in the back of that wagon," Granddaddy would say. "Even Anna Lee couldn't tell you."

'Granddaddy'd look over at Granny and she'd have tears and she'd just nod. Finally, Granddaddy carried his Mama into the cabin and laid her in the bed. Once she was resting peacefully, he and Granny, Sammy on her lap, sat down at the kitchen table with the young man, who said his name was, Thomas.

"The aroma of freshly brewed coffee mixed with the muddy taste in my mouth as we sat there, quiet-like, and tried to figure out how to talk it out. Turned out that Thomas was my half-brother. He didn't know who was his daddy, but he was told it was a white man that worked at the Kent House. Thomas said Mama'd been sick for the past few months and she'd been crying at night to see Granddaddy.

"'I knew if she kept up that crying she would die,' Thomas said. 'So I finally made a deal with The Man and brought her here to Jean Ville. She said she always knew where you was, because she made some kind of deal with one of the men who brought you here. She never stopped yearning for you,' Thomas said. 'She missed you every day.'"

Granddaddy tole Thomas that he missed her, too, every day and every night. He tole his half-brother he never stopped believing he would see her again.

'Granddaddy was much obliged to Thomas for bringing his Mama to see him. She died a few days later, but he got to spend time with her and introduce her to Granny and my daddy Sammy, her only grand chile.

'Thomas took Mama back to Alexandria to bury her on the Kent Plantation because he had that deal with The Man.

Granddaddy didn't try to stop him. He didn't want to make no trouble for Thomas.

'You know, if my granddaddy had stayed at Kent House in Alexandria, I guess I wouldn't be here, or Tootsie, or Marianne or none of us,' Catfish said. He stared at the cornfields beyond the pecan groove. He looked reminiscent.

"Wow, Catfish, that's quite a story," I said, and meant it. I started to think about his stories, how these incredible pieces of history would die off with him if someone didn't write them down. I thought how important it was that they be told.

I knew I had to become a writer. I would record his stories and let the world know what white men did to other human beings. I would make readers think about how it would feel if those same things happened to them, because of the color of their skin.

"You bet it's a interesting story. Just when I think we coloreds have it bad now, I remember some of the stories about my granddaddy and my daddy and I think I have no room to complain."

You do have room to complain, I thought. Things are not much better now. White men still think they can put black men down in order to make themselves feel like men, when, all along, it's the Negro, strong and resilient, who is the strong one. The joke's on Whitey, I thought. Then I remembered that I was white. Who was I to tell the story of slavery and the injustice done to colored folks? That was my dilemma—a white girl telling the story of Negroes: pretty unreliable. I knew, even back then, that I'd have to work through that. I've spent years trying figure that out.

"Now you girls run along. You done wore me out, again!"

We hugged his neck and kissed him on the cheek. Then we skipped down the steps in the direction of the barn.

Catfish watched us. I could always feel it, how he looked from one of us to the other as if trying to figure something out.

*

I knew how much Tootsie loved me, I never questioned that, but now that I knew Marianne and realized how much Tootsie loved her own daughter, I wondered whether it made Toot love me less. She told me later that when she got to the Quarters from our house early one Wednesday and saw me climb the steps onto Catfish's porch she felt afraid for me.

Tootsie knew that if Mama found out I was in the Quarters, there'd be hell to pay. Tootsie wanted to protect me, to send me home, to tell me to never come back. On the other hand, she knew I made Marianne happy. And Marianne was lonely and she needed me, almost as much as I needed her.

Marianne told me that her cousin, Rodney, visited on occasion, and Marianne liked him. She said they were related twice. Rodney's uncle, Bo Thibaut, was married to Marianne's Aunt Jesse, Tootsie's sister. Bo was Marianne's uncle by marriage, and Rodney's uncle because Bo was Ray Thibault's younger brother. Rodney was a couple years older than Marianne, and Tootsie began to worry about what the boy might teach her little girl. They'd go out to the barn to talk and Tootsie was glad Marianne had someone to be with, but as a mother, she was concerned.

In Tootsie's eyes, I was a much better friend for Marianne. I was immature and innocent, and Tootsie secretly hoped some of my naiveté would rub off on Marianne, who seemed to grow up way too fast after the KKK incident. But it usually worked the other way around—the older girl would teach the younger one, and Tootsie knew I was more than likely to lose my innocence than I was to give some of it to Marianne.

Tootsie told me she watched me with Catfish, the way he smiled when I was around and the way Marianne seemed to come to life when she was with me. Tootsie wondered why I didn't make the white girls at my school smile. Tootsie knew that some of my teachers sent notes home about me and that the nuns never liked me and finally found a reason to expel me, even though I was stupid enough to keep being nice to them.

Tootsie said she heard Mama tell her Bridge Ladies all the trouble she was having with me. One of the ladies, Miss Bertha, took issue with Mama. She said Mama shouldn't talk that way about her own daughter. Tootsie liked Miss Bertha, because she said what she thought.

"Anne, you should be ashamed of yourself talking about your little girl that way," Miss Bertha said. "You know those girls at the public school are jealous of her. They feel threatened. She needs a friend and she'll find one where you don't want her to if you keep pushing her away."

"Yeah, Anne," Miss Judith said. She was Miss Bertha's sister-in-law. They were close. "You need to be Susie's friend and stop criticizing her. Let her confide in you. You're just pushing her away. Before you know it she will have an older boyfriend, get pregnant and bring shame on you and Bob."

"Oh, she won't do anything like that," Tootsie overheard Mama say. "She's such a Goodie-Goodie that she'd never betray us or do anything to hurt Bob's political future."

"A girl her age gets lonely enough, you don't know what she'll do," Miss Bertha said.

"Yeah, Anne. It would be easier for you to be her friend so she has someone to talk to, rather than to risk her going elsewhere."

"Maybe you're right. I'll think about it."

The next day, when I got home from school, Mama sat down with me in the kitchen. She was nice to me and let me tell her about how the girls treated me at school. She pulled it out of me. She didn't fuss or criticize, she just listened and held my hand. Tootsie said she knew it was a trick, that Mama was just pretending she cared about me. Of course, I didn't know that, I was so glad to have Mama's attention.

When Daddy got home Mama took him in the bedroom and Tootsie could hear them talking about me. She said she couldn't hear everything, but she knew Mama told him what I said. Tootsie wanted to warn me, but she knew her place. *Help-code.* She felt stuck. She had to watch what happened and couldn't do anything about it.

"That poor girl, she don't have no one," she said she thought. "She trapped. Don't none of the white girls like her and she's ain't allowed to have a boyfriend, a colored friend, a grown friend. When she try to turn to her Mama or Daddy, she get it worse."

Tootsie knew something I didn't know until much later: that Mama was jealous of me, her own daughter, and did everything she could to turn Daddy against me. That was why Tootsie stayed with us all those years. She said she felt I needed someone in my house who would love me and look out for me.

I could tell that Tootsie liked Daddy—and he was nice to her, which made Mama mad. Tootsie tried to explain to me, much later, that Daddy was caught between his beloved daughter and his demanding wife. Tootsie couldn't explain to a 12 year old that if Daddy didn't do what Mama wanted, she won't give him sex. That was something Tootsie understood. Of course I, on the other hand ... sex?

Tootsie could tell that, lately, Mama worked harder to turn Daddy on me. Tootsie knew the breaking point was near. It was a story that repeated itself time and time again. She couldn't count the number of times she got to work and found me in my room with an injury or illness that no one tended to. It was her job, as the help, to put me back together, like Humpty Dumpty. She said she was always afraid that she would arrive at our house one morning and there wouldn't be enough pieces left to make me whole again.

Tootsie said when I started going to the Quarters, she could feel it in her bones—the day was not far in the future when I'd be beyond repair. She was a wise soul.

Part Two: 1964-65

~Chapter Four~

~

Rodney
1964

I MET RODNEY THIBAULT the summer before I turned thirteen. He stood next to the gas pumps at his dad's Esso station at the Y-junction of Jefferson and Main when my dad drove up in our green Mercedes with me in the front seat.

It was hot and humid, a typical summer day in South Louisiana and I didn't really notice the boy who filled the car with gas. I was reading, as usual, and he knew I was unaware of his presence. Invisible. That's how he told me he felt the first time he saw me, and he was probably right. He explained that, but for my dad, he felt unnoticed around white folks, like he was nobody, but that conversation came much later.

The tall athletic boy came to my side of the car to wash the windshield and he touched the tip of his baseball cap, a gesture of respect, I thought. I looked up and smiled at him through the glass, like I would anyone who tipped his hat at me. I mean, you acknowledge that, right? My smile must have surprised him. He gulped and I noticed his Adam's apple protrude, remain there for a second, then recede. I'm not sure why I remember that detail, but I do, like it was yesterday.

Rodney said he didn't figure I would talk to him, but that he couldn't help hoping. My window was down and he began to wash the side mirror near it.

"Oops," he said. "I almost sprayed you with windshield cleaner. I didn't know your window was down."

"No problem," I said. I didn't look up from my book. He wiped and re-wiped the side mirror. He began to hum, softly. Then he just blurted something out—something like, "That must be some good book." I didn't look up. "Hey, how you doing this afternoon?"

"Uhmm. Fine. You?" I still didn't look up; I was in the middle of a paragraph.

"Good. Doin' good. It's just too hot to work outside."

I let my eyes lift from my book, a little irritated, I'll admit, but resolved. I glanced at him then turned my head and looked out the front windshield towards the gas station office. Then I looked back at him, like a double take.

He was gorgeous—I mean the most handsome boy I'd ever seen, and with three brothers who were rather cute, I had lots to compare him to. The ironic thing is that I'd never really noticed boys before. I was too busy trying to make straight As and survive at home and school, toe the line, follow the rules that kept changing on me.

"Yeah," I finally said, almost in a whisper. He didn't speak. He just stared at me. I guess I was staring at him, too. "One thing good about it being hot is we know summer's here. No school."

"You right about that." He paused like he thought I might say something else, but I felt tongue-tied. Finally, after what seemed like infinity, he said, "I love summers." His words surprised me because I was in a trance.

"Yeah? What do you do in the summers?" I asked, not really thinking about what I said.

"Oh, lots of things." He kept wiping the mirror, like he wasn't aware he was doing it. He'd look away for a few seconds, then I could feel his gaze on me again. After a while he leaned against the car with his forearm above my window, which put his face only a couple of feet from mine.

Where'd he come from, I wondered? I'd never seen him at school, but then I might have missed him since he looked like he was a couple years older. I spoke slowly. It was the first conversation I'd ever had with an

older boy, other than James's friends, and they didn't count.

"My parents send me off to a few camps, then they make me go visit my aunt and her family in Houston." I said. I watched him watch my mouth as I spoke and I felt like my lips were moving in slow motion. He leaned his forehead against his forearm, his eyes now only inches from the top of my head. I had to look up to see him and when I did, his eyes, green with amber specks, were focused directly on mine. He didn't blink. He was so close I could smell his breath when he spoke and it rattled me. I think I was fixated on his lips, full and moist. The nipples on my developing breasts throbbed and something like pin-pricks tingled in my crotch.

"I wish I could go away in the summers," he said. "I have to work here." There was dead silence for a minute, then I blurted something.

"Do you get paid?"

"Sure. It's not much but it makes sweating all day worth it."

His arm dropped it to his side. He moved the sprayer to his right hand with the towel and put his left hand on the roof of the car. He stiffened his arm so he was further away from me, but still attached. He took a deep breath and glanced past the gas pumps at the office over the top of the car, nervous-like.

"That's good." I started to look back at my book, I needed to break the spell, but he stopped me.

"Yeah. A little spending money is good. I'm saving for college."

"Oh, really? Where're you going to college?"

"I'm not sure, yet. I'm just going into the tenth grade this fall, but I'm thinking Southern. I might want to be a lawyer. They have a good law school there."

"Where's Southern? I haven't heard of it." A cloud moved overhead and cast a shadow over the car, me and the boy.

"It's a colored college in Baton Rouge. It has a good reputation. Or I could go to Grambling, in North Louisiana, but I'm more comfortable in the South." I looked at him again, this time thoroughly, searching his eyes, trying to see under his cap, watching his lips, his nose. None of his features looked anything like most of the colored people I knew, except for Marianne, but she was unusual.

"Southern College is for coloreds?" The cloud moved on and sunlight filtered through the windshield again.

"It's Southern University," he said. "Yes, it's for Negroes." I couldn't quite put two-and-two together.

"You're colored?"

"Of course I am. I thought you knew. Your dad and my dad are friends," he said. Then he whispered, "And there are people in this town who don't like it."

I turned to look at our dads through the glass door and sidewalls that hemmed in the air-conditioned, soundless gas station office. It felt intimate, personal, that our dads were talking, were friends. The boy automatically looked in the same direction. My daddy's back was to us, his dad was facing the gas pumps and I thought I noticed Mr. Thibault's cheekbones lift. He squinted accusingly.

"I'm sorry, it's just that ..." I turned back towards him. He looked into the car window and saw me staring at him. He grinned.

"I know. I get it all the time," he spoke softly, almost in a whisper. "I could pass for white, especially when I wear a cap, like this one." He tipped the bill of his Navy blue cap, "Cowboys," in white letters stamped across the front. I could only see the part of his hair just above his forehead and it was cut so short the texture was undetectable.

"But I'm not," he said. I was totally confused. He changed the subject, diverting the topic from his race to college. Smart.

"Southern and Grambling are big rivals in football!" He laughed. "Grambling is a good college, too. They beat Southern in the Bayou Classic almost every year."

"I want to go to LSU," I said. "It's in Baton Rouge, too. My daddy went to college and grad school there, and my older brother says that's where he's going when he graduates next year." I whispered, as if it was a big secret, just between the two of us. It felt like we shared something hidden. There was suspended silence for a minute.

"I play football," he blurted.

"You do?"

"Yeah," he said. His voice mesmerized me. It was soft, yet firm with a hint of a Cajun accent, just enough drawl to make it interesting, even sexy, but what did I know about "sexy" at thirteen? I still played with paper dolls—when I wasn't studying or dodging bullets. "I'm the quarterback of Adams High's football team. Well, second string last year, but our first string quarterback graduated in May, so I'll be first string this fall."

"If you are such a good football player, why don't you go to Grambling?"

"Uh. What?" He looked at me, looked at the office, then back at me and a shadow crossed his face. "What'd you say?"

"Why not Grambling? You know, the better football team and all." He probably thought I was making fun of him, but really, I was too young and stupid about boys to do that. He started to laugh but it sounded more like a weak chuckle.

"I don't know whether I'll play football in college. It's very competitive."

I liked football. My dad took us to LSU games and we listened on the radio when they were out-of-town. And my brothers played, so the topic didn't bore me, and this boy certainly didn't either.

He stood still. My natural instinct was to go back to my book, but something kept me from looking away from him. His skin was as light as my dad's, whose Cajun bloodline was strong and gave him an olive complexion. I got my coloring from my mother who was what she called "American-Scotch-Irish." My youngest brother, Robby, and I looked like her and had blue eyes and reddish hair and sunburned easily. James and Will looked more like Daddy, darker skin, brown hair and brown eyes. This boy's eyes were almost green, with golden flickers that picked up the sun. Even Marianne's eyes were not as light.

"Uh ... uh ... hey ... uh. My daddy thinks very highly of your dad," he said. I didn't look at him. I'm not sure why, but I felt terrified. Looking back, I think the way he looked at me made me feel powerless, out of control. "I'm sure you realize how unusual it is, a white man being friends with a colored man." He looked at our dads in the office and was quiet for a moment.

"It might be unusual for other white men, but not for my daddy."

"How about you? Do you have any colored friends?" That surprised me. I turned towards him and looked him square in the eye. It was impulsive and I was immediately sorry I had reacted. The sun bounced off his eyes and sent rainbows of color onto his smudged white T-shirt. I wanted to touch the reflection and was tongue-tied. I swallowed hard, then tried to speak but it came out a whisper.

"My best friend is Marianne Massey." Slowly his bottom lip bent into a half smile, as if what I said made all the sense in the world. He spoke softly and slowly.

"You don't say? I mean ... really? Uh, Marianne, well, she's my cousin, twice. Her aunt Jesse is married to my uncle Bo. We're really close. Me and Uncle Bo, dad's brother. I go to the Quarters a lot." I felt like I had a mouthful of wet bread, stuck to the roof. I couldn't swallow.

"Marianne and I used to be close," he said. He massaged his right earlobe with his thumb and forefinger. "Until, uh, well, uh, something happened to her ... but she's a good girl." He said the last four words rapidly, like he spit them out as an afterthought.

"I've never seen you there." I said, barely above a whisper.

"You go over to the quarters? he asked.

"Oh! I spoke out of turn." I looked down at my book. "I shouldn't have said that. My parents don't know."

"Not even your dad? He has colored friends."

"I know, but I'm not allowed to go to the quarters. Mama thinks it's dangerous and Daddy, well he said he better never catch me there."

"I won't tell a soul, I promise," he said. Somehow I believed him and felt better. "What made you go there in the first place?"

"To the quarters?"

"Yeah. Why'd you go?" I didn't answer right away. I gathered my thoughts while he stared at me as if anticipating some big revelation.

"One day I went to see about Catfish, after he quit coming by our house in the afternoons. That's when I met Marianne." He looked confused. "What's your name?" I asked. His head made tiny side-to-side movements as if shaking off a feeling of déjà vu.

"Huh? Uh, uhm, Rodney. Rodney Thibault," he whispered, his voice almost non-existent. I could taste the minty, orange flavor that came from his mouth each time he exhaled. It rested gently on the tip of my tongue.

"Marianne's mentioned you." I whispered, too.

"Really?" He didn't seem too surprised.

"Yes, I remember your name from a conversation we had."

"How often do you go to the Quarters?"

"Usually on Wednesday afternoons when my mama plays bridge, except every fourth Wednesday when she plays at home. It's harder to sneak away on those days."

"What's your name?"

"Susanna. Everyone calls me, Susie. Susie Burton."

"How old are you, Susie Burton?"

"I'm almost thirteen, but I'm going to ninth grade."

"Thirteen's young to be in high school."

"I know. I'm a couple years ahead. Mama says I'm going to finish high school in three years, too." I giggled. His smile was wide and broad and showed his straight, white teeth. He was downright beautiful. I couldn't take my eyes off him. I felt like I was making him uncomfortable, but darn, I liked looking at him. Thinking back I realize I was probably head over heels already, but I was too young to understand and too innocent to think it then.

Daddy returned to the car with Ray Thibault behind him. Rodney backed away from the window when he saw them coming.

The two men talked and laughed, then shook hands. Rodney glanced at me, but I had my head in my book. I had seen them coming, too.

Daddy reached for his door handle and looked at Rodney over the top of the car.

"How are you, son?"

"I'm doing fine, Mr. Burton. How're you?"

"Great, Rodney. I was just telling your dad how lucky he is to have such a hard-working son like you."

"Why, thank you Mr. Burton. I appreciate the good word." Daddy laughed. He got in the car and we drove off. I felt like I left something important at the Esso station that day.

*

"Ray Thibault sure has raised a fine, young son, there," Daddy said as he drove away from the Esso station. "He's real smart. Makes straight A's. I told his dad I'd hire him after he's finished high school, but Ray says the boy is set on going to college. He'd be the first in his family to get a higher education, in all the generations since they came here." I knew Daddy referred to the Negro race and meant since slavery. "I saw you talking to him. What'd you think?"

"Nice boy, I guess." I knew better than to let on I liked a boy, any boy, much less a colored boy. That would really cause trouble for Daddy and his political plans. *Troublemaker.*

"He's colored, you know. He might look white, but a Negro is a Negro."

"Okay," I said, careful to acknowledge I heard him, but not saying anything.

"You'd better not be thinking about boys, yet. I'll decide when you can have a boyfriend and I'll pick him out for you when the time comes." I didn't answer. The less said the better.

"Let me tell you something," Daddy said. His voice rose as if he thought about something that made him angry. I cringed. "We have to draw a line with coloreds. You realize we can't have mixed relations, don't you?"

"Dad!"

"Well, you'll be in high school in September and, thank God there are no coloreds at Jean Ville High." His voice was getting louder and higher in pitch. "You'll be younger than the other kids but there are some things you need to know." I knew when to keep my mouth shut.

"Whites and blacks don't date each other, don't marry," he said. I could see his face start to flush, blood rising from his neck upward. I began to shake. "Some can be friends, but that's as far as it can go. Do you understand?"

"Yes, sir."

"But do you understand?" He was louder. I cowered against my car door.

"Yes, sir."

"Interracial marriage is against the law."

"Hummmm?" I'm non-confrontational by nature. I'll do anything to avoid a fight or an argument, anything disagreeable. I went into defensive mode.

"Just last month in the next parish over, the Klan shot a fourteen-year-old boy because he whistled at a white girl. Last year, in Bogalusa, two colored men were murdered as they drove their car down the highway," He was talking faster, louder. "They say it's because one of them offered to carry a white lady's groceries to her car. You need to understand these things. You might be all right, but if you talk to a colored boy, he could be hurt, even killed. Understand?"

"Yes, sir, I think so." He continued like he didn't hear me.

"I have colored friends, but I don't support breaking the law. And I don't want anything to happen to Ray Thibault's son." He drove a few blocks without talking. I had a burning question on my mind but needed to word it in such a way that it didn't trigger Daddy's anger any further.

"Daddy?"

"Yes, Sweetie." Whew, he'd calmed down.

"About how old should a person be before he or she can have a colored friend?"

"Do you mean a man with a colored man friend or a woman with a colored woman friend?" His change in attitude always baffled me. He could go from a maniac to the most gentle daddy in milliseconds. I never knew which daddy I'd get.

"Either. I was just wondering."

"Well, a man should be grown and have a family of his own before he is mature enough to know which colored men are good enough to befriend. A woman, well that's another story. Women can't be friends with coloreds." I was curious as to why, but I figured I'd better not push it. I had the answer to my burning question—can I be friends with Marianne? The answer was, "No."

"See," he said. I was surprised when he continued. "Colored women work for white women, so they can't be friends. You can't be friends with someone who works for you. They'll take advantage."

"I understand." But I didn't understand, I just wanted to drop it before it went any further.

"I'm not sure you do," he said. Oh, shoots! Here we go, I thought. His voice was rising again. He pulled into the driveway and switched off the ignition, then turned towards me. His face was red. I didn't know whether he was mad at me, mad at himself or mad at the laws—but he was mad. I started to shake.

Just then my eight-year-old brother, Robby, came running to the car yelling, "Daddy's home. Daddy's home!" I could have kissed him. He climbed into the car through Daddy's window and sat on his lap. Daddy cradled Robby. Conversation forgotten, I hoped.

I opened the car door and slipped out with my book, *To Kill a Mockingbird*. I'd waited a year for my name to get to the top of the library's list so I could borrow the only copy in Toussaint Parish. I tucked it under my arm and went straight to my room, lay on my bed and tried to read. It was hot, even though the windows were open. The attic fan blew in the hall and made a roaring sound that could disturb the deaf, but it didn't cool my room when the door was closed. I perspired. It was the trade-off for privacy.

I thought about what Daddy said about it being against the law to date or marry a colored person. That didn't make sense. Who would make a law like that?

I thought about Rodney Thibault. He was a nice boy and he was so handsome, almost beautiful. I didn't feel like we were that different—or that Marianne and I were different. They were people, and I liked them. And they were nice to me. None of the white girls or boys at my school were nice. My brothers weren't nice to me, even my parents ran hot and cold. In fact, other than Tootsie, Catfish, Marianne and, now, Rodney Thibault, the only other person who was kind to me was Dr. David Switzer.

Dr. David and his wife, Erma, lived in the two-story, red brick house directly across South Jefferson Street from our house. They were older than my parents by about ten years and I looked at Dr. David as a grandfather of sorts, seeing as how I'd never had one.

When we sat on our front porch we had a clear view of the circular concrete driveway and double front doors on the Georgian style home. Our two houses had the only private swimming pools in town, unless you counted the plastic pool the owner of the Pelican Bar was said to have.

When I was sick, which was pretty often, Dr. David was extra kind to me and I felt like he looked at me a little longer than he needed to, as if he was searching for some secret I might be hiding. I knew I could trust him, but I was afraid to tell anyone, even Dr. David, what went on in our house—mostly because, if I said it aloud, I'd be admitting it to myself.

Daddy was good friends with Dr. David and his brother, Dr. Joseph. The three men played cards, drank pots of coffee laced with whiskey and talked politics. I heard my daddy tell Dr. David that he and Joseph were the only people in town, besides Ray Thibault, who shared the same views of equality, integration, and abolishment of Jim Crow.

I thought about how a Jew and four Negroes were the only people I could really trust, the only ones who made me feel normal, accepted, even loved.

After supper that night I went back to my room to read. I thought about Marianne and wondered what she was doing in that hot cabin. I needed to talk to her about Rodney, get the scoop. Meanwhile I wanted to find out what a mulatto was.

Lots of things had come up over the past few weeks that I knew nothing about—like puberty and masturbation that Marianne talked about, and laws that governed relationships among the races that my dad mentioned. I considered myself above average, intelligence-wise, but there were many things I didn't know, and I thought that might be what made me different, unaccepted, bullied—my naiveté.

My best source for information was the public library. It was next door to the Fox Theater, only about five or six blocks from our house, just past Assumption Catholic. I didn't have to ask twice to go to there, that was one thing Mama encouraged. The walk took about twenty minutes and it was miserably hot, but I walked briskly, with a lilt in my step. I felt free, even if for a couple hours.

Inside the air-conditioned building with glass windows across the front, I found a table tucked in the back corner and looked through the card catalogues for books and magazines. I was a whiz with the Dewey Decimal System, I'd spent so much time in the school library and this one. That afternoon I pretended to be there to do research for a paper, in advance of high school. Before long I had all sorts of materials spread on the table, opened so no one could read the titles if they walked by. I made notes in the composition book I'd brought along, writing key words with my blue ball point pen, but not making detailed entries in case Mama or Daddy found it.

I returned home with another new book, *Ship of Fools,* by Katherine Anne Porter. The librarian recommended it when I turned in *To Kill a Mockingbird* and told her I was too mature for *Nancy Drew* mysteries. More importantly, I'd learned about interracial relations, called miscegenation, and about mulattoes and how they had one or more white parents or grandparents. I was shocked that the laws said if a person had only a few drops of Negro blood, they were Negro. What if there was a Negro great-great grandfather somewhere in the past, but all the grandparents and parents were white? Where did that put the child? It not only seemed unjust, it seemed stupid.

～Chapter Five～

～

The Hayloft
1964

I WENT TO THE Quarters the following Wednesday after school and told Marianne about my visit to the library.

"What'd you get?" She twisted a strand of hair in front of her ear that fell out of the barrette holding up the mahogany locks.

"I didn't get anything, but I read everything I could find about sex. I even saw pictures. I actually know what a girl's private parts looks like, inside and out. I can't see my own, but I saw one in a book."

"What else did you see?"

"A picture of a man's penis, and diagrams of the inside of a woman's body and what happens when that stuff comes out of the man and goes inside her. It's called sperm, and there are tons of them and they swim. If a woman has an egg somewhere in her, the sperms will find it, fertilize it and make a baby. It's fascinating!"

"Really? I thought I knew all about sex but I didn't know that." Marianne paused. "I'll bet I know something you didn't read about in those books."

"What?" I asked.

"I know what it feels like." Marianne said.

"You know what, what it feels like?"

"I know what it feels like to have what they call an orgasm. That's sex, but it's not about having babies." I didn't say anything—I was trying to figure out what she meant. I'd missed that in the books.

"I can show you how to do it, if you want me to," Marianne said.

"Show me what?"

"How to have an orgasm."

"I don't think so. I'll figure it out myself if I want to," I said. I thought for a minute. Maybe she's talking about masturbation. I'd read about that, but I didn't mention it.

"Okay." We were both quiet. Marianne reached over and took my hand. I gave hers a slight squeeze and smiled at the sky. There was a warm breeze from the cane fields that blew a sweet, green fragrance around us. We watched robins pecking the ground near the garden. When I finally spoke, what I said seemed like the last thing Marianne expected.

"I met your cousin, Rodney." Marianne gasped, dropped my hand, hesitated, then took a deep breath. She curled her hand towards her face and began to work the cuticles of her fingers with her thumb. I could tell it surprised her but she didn't want me to know anything shocked her. She was good at making people believe she was tough and didn't have feelings, but I knew better. After all, she was my best friend.

"Where'd you meet him?" She emphasized, *him,* as if it was a bad word.

"At his dad's gas station. I was there with my dad."

"Oh, then you weren't alone with him?"

"Sort of. I mean he came to my window while Daddy was in the office with Mr. Thibault and we talked."

"You and Rodney talked?"

"Yes."

"What? What are you thinking? What is he thinking?"

"What do you mean? We just talked."

"You can't talk to Rodney. You'll get him killed!" I was so surprised by the passion and anger in her voice that I was speechless.

"You need to listen to me, Susie Burton," she turned to me, her eyes on fire, mouth twitching.

"You're jealous," I said, and I started to laugh. She jumped up and stood in front of me, her legs spread, feet planted, like she was ready to fight.

"Jealous? You're crazy. You just don't understand, do you?"

"Understand what? What's the matter?"

"You'll get him killed. That's what's the matter."

"Don't be so melodramatic, Mari." She walked away towards the cane field. I jumped up and followed. "Wait. Don't be mad," I called after her, but she just kept walking. When I caught up with her I touched her shoulder and she turned towards me abruptly.

"Listen. White Girl! You can't talk to a colored boy. Never! Get it?" I froze. She'd never talked to me that way. Her expression had hatred written all over it, like the first time we met and she looked like she wanted to kill me. I took a deep breath. I could feel tears begin to pool and tried to stop them. My best, my only friend, I thought. This can't be happening.

Marianne looked at the ground where she was making circles with the toe of her tennis shoe. It stirred up a small cloud of dust around her foot. I watched the ground where her shoe began to dig a small hole, then the hole got bigger. I don't know how long we stood like that. Eventually she stopped digging and pushed the dirt back into the hole with the side of her shoe, then stamped it down. Finally she looked at me. I was crying.

"Look. I didn't mean to yell at you. It's just that I don't think you understand the kind of danger you could cause Rodney, his family, us."

"I'm sorry, Mari. I didn't mean anything by it. I just think he's a nice guy. And it doesn't hurt that he's so handsome."

"That's what I mean. You can't talk like that. You can't even think like that."

"Well, if I can't talk to you about him, who can I talk to?" That seemed to get her attention. She took a deep breath.

She begged me not to mention Rodney to anyone and I promised I wouldn't. But I needed to talk about him. She kept telling me how dangerous it was and that I should put him out of my mind.

What is it about being a teenager and having someone tell you not to do something that makes you want to do it more? When I think back on that day I feel like Marianne's reaction made Rodney seem even more intriguing. She kept saying, "He's colored."

"I don't think of him as colored, Marianne. I don't think of you as colored or me as white."

"What color do you think we are then?"

"No color. I don't know. Maybe the color of *glass*? "

"Glass?"

"Or *air*? I'm not sure. I just think of us as two thirteen-year-old girls, that's all."

"And Rodney?"

"He's gorgeous."

"Oh, no, Susie!" Marianne screamed. "You can't say that about a colored boy! It's hopeless."

"I'm not saying anything about wanting to be with him. I'm just saying I think he's very handsome. What do colored girls think of him?"

"Well, the girls at school think he's amazing, good-looking, sexy. They go gah-gah over him. Funny thing, Rodney is pretty shy, but around girls, he has the big head. He'll go out with any girl who'll put out for him, and there are lots of them who will."

"Put out?"

"Yeah. Have sex with him."

"He has sex with girls?"

"Grow up, Susie." She looked at me like I was a little girl and she was the wise one. "You need to leave this alone. You understand, don't you? You don't need to think about how handsome he is. He's colored."

I told her what my daddy said about being friends with colored people and she got really mad.

"That's the stupidest, most two-faced thing I ever heard. He can have colored friends but you can't? How do you feel about that?"

"You know how I feel about it. I'm here, aren't I?"

"Yeah." The bell rang once. I jumped up and ran.

That evening Rodney went to the Quarters. Marianne told me about it the following week. She said she told him I'd been there but he'd missed me. When he asked her when I was coming back, she snapped at him.

"Why do you care, Rodney? She's my friend." She said she acted like I'd never told her that we'd met, but he kept asking her things about me.

"Are you sweet on her?" Marianne asked.

"No, of course not. She's white."

"Good thing. Keep it that way." She knew what could happen to Rodney and her experience with the KKK made her even more afraid for him. She also knew my daddy would kill me if he found out I was friends with any colored people, especially a boy.

"Her dad and my dad are friends. They have coffee together almost every morning."

"He's a hypocrite, her father. Watch out for him." Marianne told Rodney what I told her about my dad saying a white person should not make the decision to have a Negro friend until he was grown and that, really, women couldn't be friends with coloreds. Poor Rodney was surprised because, at that time, he had misguided notions about my dad.

"Even when I was seven, eight, Mr. Burton shook my hand and treated me like an equal," he told Marianne. "And he was the first white man who told me I should look him in the eye when he spoke to me."

"He's two-faced, I told you. If he makes you feel like that—it's not true. He doesn't see you as an equal or special. He sees you as a common N____r, believe me. I know!"

Rodney knew better than to push his luck with Marianne. If there was something she wanted to share with him, she would; otherwise no amount of probing would make her.

"She's really beautiful," he said. "That red hair and scattered freckles. And the bluest eyes I've ever seen, like the Caribbean."

"What do you know about the Caribbean?"

"I've seen pictures." He laughed and drew an oval in the air, indicating the sea.

"You ARE sweet on her! You're as crazy as she is!" She said she wanted to scratch him, to knock some sense into him but when she looked at him she knew it was too late. "He was already hooked on you," she told me later.

"What do you mean, 'you're as crazy as she is?'"

"She said, 'He's gorgeous!'"

"She said that about me?" Rodney wanted to know more about what I said, but Marianne told him to forget it. He said he couldn't forget it and he wouldn't let it go. So she screamed at him.

"Forget it. She's white, Rodney. WHITE!"

"I know, Mari. I'm well aware. I just want to know what she's like, I mean, what kind of person is she?"

Marianne said she told him I was just about the best person she'd ever known. That made me blush and feel a mixture of pride and embarrassment. She said she told him she didn't know how I got to be that way, being raised the way I was. She said he wanted to know more but she wouldn't say anything further. She said it made Rodney angry, and that he turned and walked toward the cane field, away from her, like he needed space, like he needed to think without being badgered, but she followed him.

"What did ya'll do in the barn?" Rodney asked. Marianne said he avoided looking at her. He walked past her through the rows of cane, taller than himself. Marianne said she followed him, chewing on her cane and stopping to look at each stalk he pulled down as if she was helping him to find the ideal one.

"Nothing much," Marianne told him. She said he walked slowly through the first row of cane, pulling stalks down a foot or two as if looking for the perfect piece to cut. He probably didn't even look at the cane, she said. More than likely, he looked through it, through the stalks, through the rows, through the fields.

"I wanted to show her what you showed me last year about sex," Marianne said. "She chickened out, but I won't give up." Marianne told me she said that to make him look at her, to stop ignoring her. She said it worked, that Rodney turned around abruptly and faced her and that it surprised her, even frightened her a bit, even though she wanted it to happen, but that she shrugged her shoulders to make him think she didn't care, wasn't afraid. That's how she was, tough as nails on the outside, a mess inside.

"You're a girl, Mari. You should want to have sex with boys, not girls!" Rodney told her. I'm sure he was incredulous, furious as he tasted the sweetness of the cane and the orange soda he had on his way to the Quarters. Marianne probably stared at him with a steady gaze, expressionless, like her soul was dead. He would look into her grey, green eyes and see darkness, despair, uncertainty and want to hug her like a big brother, to tell her everything would be alright, but he didn't know if it would be alright, whatever IT was.

"I hate boys, men, all males, since those white men, well, you know," Marianne told him, barely above a whisper. I can see her trying to hold back tears, being brave, putting on a front, embarrassed

93

that he, a boy, witnessed her vulnerability. I'd seen her do that before when she was trying to hide hurt feelings.

Rodney probably spoke softly, like a dad would speak to his hurting child. He was kind that way. Marianne didn't have a dad, she was the strength of her family, the oldest, the first. Her sisters had a dad, but she was her own dad.

"You'll get over it." Rodney looked down at her, but I'm sure she looked away so he didn't see her thick eyelashes clump together from her tears. "Not all men are pigs like those cowards who wear masks while they do their dirty work."

"I don't know if I'll ever get over it, Rod," she told him. "Anyway, do you think about having sex with Susie Burton?"

She said he didn't answer. I know now what he thought, but then?

*

A few weeks after Rodney went to the Quarters, my dad and I went to the Esso station with Will and Robby in the back seat. I was in the front. I watched Rodney walk towards the car and I was afraid he would try to talk to me. He shook hands with Daddy and I heard Mr. Thibault tell Rodney to fill the car and check the tires.

He washed the front windshield and, when he looked at me through the glass, I guess I was staring at him. I smiled. He smiled back and winked at me. I was surprised and without thinking, I winked back, then I was embarrassed. I looked down at the book in my lap.

He walked to my side of the car. The window was opened and he started to wash the side mirror. He must have noticed my little brothers in the back seat. They were playing a game.

"Hey, it's good to see you," he whispered. I put my index finger to my lips to indicate we needed to be quiet, and I smiled. I couldn't help myself. There was something about him that made me tingle all over.

"It's good to see you, too," I mouthed and I looked at him. It was sort of intriguing, as if we were having a clandestine meeting.

"I went to Marianne's a few weeks ago, hoping to see you."

"Shhhhh," I whispered, and giggled. He looked at the finger I held to my lips and grinned. I felt my gut melt into a pool of hot liquid that ran through my veins. My insides burned.

I could hear his heart thump against his chest and almost laughed, but I didn't want to embarrass him. The smell of gasoline, oil and dirt evaporated and I could detect a strange scent, one I'd never smelled before—like sea air. I wondered whether the saltiness came from my pores or his.

"Sorry," He just moved his lips, no sound.

"I know, Marianne told me," I whispered. He looked in the backseat. The boys didn't pay attention, in fact they were fighting.

"You look nice ... beautiful, in fact," he pantomimed. I think when he realized what he said, he was surprised at himself. I was flustered, too. No one ever complimented me and I loved it, but I didn't know how to react.

"Sorry," he murmured. At the same time I said, "Thank you." We both laughed.

"You probably think I'm crazy," he whispered. I was the one who felt crazy, so I didn't know what to say to that.

He placed his arm on the top of my window and leaned his forehead against it. His face was so close to mine I felt like we touched. I turned to stare out the front windshield, glancing to my left to make sure Daddy wasn't watching. Rodney could see our dads in the office over the roof of the car.

"I need to talk to you," he whispered as quietly as he could, shifting his eyes to look at my brothers every few seconds. They were still busy, ignoring us.

What he said scared me at first, so I hesitated. Then I turned and looked at him.

"Okay." That's all I said. I guess he wondered what it meant. Heck, *I* wondered what I meant. I didn't stop to think about the where, when, or how. I just thought that if he wanted to talk to me, well, I'd like that. Then I felt a blanket of fear come over me and I looked at our dads through the glass. They were still deep in conversation so I turned to Rodney and smiled, then I felt afraid again and looked at my book. I hoped he would take the cue to walk away from the car window. He did.

Marianne and I were in the hayloft the next Wednesday afternoon involved in a disagreement about sexual experimentation. I guess all 13 year old girls are curious and want to explore, but I was uncomfortable about doing it with Marianne. I think subconsciously I knew she was attracted to me in a way I wasn't attracted to her. She had made a number of comments about how she preferred girls, an attitude since the Klan visit that I thought would pass in time. It never did.

"I do love you," I told her. "You're my best friend. But I don't want to have sex with a girl."

"We won't have SEX, Silly. I'm just going to show you."

"I don't know."

"Take off your shorts," Marianne begged.

"I don't want to, not yet. Give me time."

"What are you worried about?"

"I'm not sure. I'm just confused. It doesn't seem right. You're a girl and my best friend. Something tells me this is supposed to be between a boy and a girl who really love each other, not like best friends, but another way."

"Hey! Anybody here?" A male voice called from below the loft.

We didn't answer. I'm sure he could hear shuffling, and dust probably rained down on him from the hay that stirred up and fell between the slats in the floor.

"Marianne, are you up there?" Marianne and I looked at each other. She mouthed, RODNEY, and I nodded. I could hear the ladder squeak and knew he was climbing it. He was about midway up when his head emerged. Marianne was on her knees, frozen, facing him. She was stunned, like a raccoon when you shine a flashlight in its eyes at night. Rodney stopped as if to give her time to adjust to his presence, then he took a couple more steps up the ladder. I knew he was there but couldn't see him until I crawled around and knelt next to Marianne.

Rodney swung his knee to the side of the ladder and onto the floor of the loft. His other knee followed. He looked directly at me and smiled. I was afraid, at first, but happy that my uncomfortable disagreement with Marianne had been interrupted.

Rodney scooted towards me on his knees and reached his arms out. I didn't know what to do at first, but when I looked at him and he smiled with the most genuine look I'd ever seen, I moved towards him. He touched one of my hands and I shivered. He let his fingers walk up my arm while he slowly scooted closer to me, until he could grip my shoulder. His other hand found mine and he took it into his as if he had just asked me to dance and I gracefully placed my hand in his. All the time he stared at me and I looked over his shoulder at Marianne who mouthed, "What are you doing?" I shrugged my shoulder and looked back at Rodney. Oh, God, I thought, he is so gorgeous and the look on his face, well, I can't describe it but I can still envision it today, all these years later.

Looking back it seems so impulsive, crazy, but that day it just seemed natural, almost like we'd planned it or had done it dozens of times. Of course, we hadn't.

He held my hand, sat with his back to the side wall, legs out in front of him, and pulled me next to him. We sat with our thighs and shoulders touching. Rodney picked up a long piece of straw and put it in his mouth. He was still holding my hand. Marianne faced us, sitting on her heels, knees in front of her as if she were praying, but got tired and leaned back.

"What are you two doing?" she asked.

"We aren't doing anything. Just sitting here," Rodney said. I loved the sound of his voice. It was deep and a bit raspy with just a hint of Cajun-ness in the twang. He wore the same "Cowboys" baseball cap he'd worn the first time I met him and he looked masculine and handsome and gentle all at the same time. His shoulders were broad and he seemed so big next to me—and I wasn't little, at five feet seven inches and growing. He turned towards me as if to block Marianne out of our conversation.

"You look beautiful, as always." He whispered it but I knew Marianne heard. It sounded a little, well, garrulous, and I didn't like it. Then, it was like he checked himself. "I mean, I'm sorry. I get tongue-tied when I'm around you. This is the first time I've touched you and I'm nervous." He lifted our entwined fingers and looked at them. I felt prickly pins run down my spine. His admission seemed so sensitive and honest—it balanced the strong athleticism and strength he carried.

"It's hot up here. Let's go for a walk," he said. He scooted to the top of the ladder and once he'd taken a couple steps down and his torso was still above the edge of the loft, he reached for me with one hand. I didn't take his hand. I just scooted towards him and turned around so I could back down the ladder. I caught Marianne's glare as my feet began to descend.

"What the heck?" she said.

"Come on," I said. "It IS hot up here." She followed me. The three of us walked in a line towards the cane field, Rodney in front. He reached for my hand and led me, our laced fingers behind him, like he was pulling me along. Marianne followed. When we got to the rows, Rodney dropped my hand, took out his pocket knife and pulled on one of the tall green stalks and cut a long rod of cane off the foliage. He sliced the two foot shaft in three pieces and handed one to me and the other to Marianne. I didn't know what to do with mine so I watched as he sucked his cane like a man might draw on a cigar. Marianne, well, she bit into hers, chewed for a while, then spit out the stringy pieces once the sweetness was gone. Then she took another bite. I just held mine and watched the other two.

When Rodney realized I was no longer following, he turned around and hurried back through the row towards me where I stood at the edge of the field. He took my hand and we walked swiftly back towards the barn.

"Let's go," he said.

"Where?"

"Here. I want to talk to you." We went to the back side of the barn and sat on the ground. It was shady since the sun hid on the other side of the old structure and there were dozens of pecan trees, their green foliage creating a canopy above us. I fully expected to see Marianne round the corner and join us, but she never did.

"What's your favorite thing to do?" he asked. He was still sucking on his piece of sugar cane and looking straight ahead. Our legs were stretched out in front and our thighs touched. He wore jeans and I had on shorts.

"Oh, I guess I like to read more than anything." I played with my piece of cane, stripping pieces down the sides like thin spaghetti.

"Really? Me, too. My parents give me books for my birthday and Christmas every year. Have you read Chaucer?"

"Oh, God! That's pretty heavy stuff, but yes, I have. I got it from the library—I love the library. I go there a lot—it's an escape."

"Really? I love the library, too. Of course I have to use the colored section and I'm not allowed to check out books, but I discover all sorts of things when I'm there. We don't have a library at Adams High." That sounded crazy to me—I mean, what school doesn't have a library?

I could feel an electric current run from his leg into mine, up my spine and into my panties. He reached over and took my hand and held it in front of his face, as if he was trying to determine the size, shape, color. His intensity was as impressive as his intelligence and we talked like scholars about Shakespeare, Newton and Jane Austin. We discovered we loved Mark Twain and Ernest Hemingway. I realized I'd never had anyone with whom I could have a conversation on that level. It was heady and exciting. Even so, I couldn't detach my brain from the way it felt to touch him.

"We have a few textbooks, but not enough to go around so we share them in class," he said. "But we can't take them home."

"That stinks," I said. "I mean, how do you do your homework?" He shrugged.

"You get used to it, I guess."

"I volunteer in our school library," I said without thinking. "When the covers come off the books at school, or if some of the pages tear or the binding begins to crumble, they throw them in boxes in the storage closet." The librarian asked me to help out during the summer and one of my jobs was sorting the old, thrown out books, boxing them and stacking the boxes in an attic closet.

"Your school throws out books?" He was incredulous and I realized how wasteful it must sound to someone like him.

"I might be able to get some of those old books for your school," I said without thinking about how I'd sneak them out and get them to the colored school.

"Wow. Could you really do that? I mean, how?" We talked about what books he needed and we went off to find Marianne, to ask her for a tablet and pencil so he could make a list for me of the subjects he'd be taking in the fall. Marianne got excited, too, and made a list of the books eight graders used at Adams. I promised to look through the boxes of discarded books.

The three of us returned to our spot in the shade on the backside of the barn and we talked excitedly about the prospect of getting books for Adams High. Marianne wrote neat lists in columns on the tablet and Rodney kept remembering certain volumes, like *The Atlas of the Universe* and *New Biology*.

At one point he put his arm around me, over my shoulder as if it was the most natural thing in the world. With Marianne sitting in front of us, busy writing, he gripped the top of my arm while he held my other hand in my lap, his shoulders twisted towards me so I could see his face when he spoke. I wore a sleeveless white shirt that buttoned up the front and the heat from his hand created a current of warmth that radiated from inside him onto my skin. It felt right and I had such peace, like a weight lifted from my soul and I was connected to him in a way I'd never been connected to anyone before. I wondered how he felt.

As our talk about books branched into finding texts for younger kids, too, tears pooled in his eyes and made them glassy, but nothing spilled out. He seemed happy, almost relieved, although I couldn't for the life of me figure out why. He kissed one of my dimples, laughed and said, "I've been wanting to do that, to see what it felt like to kiss a hole." We all laughed, even Marianne who, initially, seemed angry.

When we were all quiet, thinking of how we could pull off the great textbook heist, he began to hum. His face was close to my ear and it sounded like, "Don't Worry Baby," by the Beach Boys—one of my favorites. His voice was deep and beautifully calming and the fear I always carried with me, that "walking on eggshells" kind of feeling, lifted and I was lighter during the time I was with him than I'd been in as long as I could remember. I leaned my head on his shoulder and we stayed that way a long time.

"Did you hear the bell?" Marianne asked.

"Oh, no. Did it ring?"

"It's just been a few minutes, but the two of you seemed lost in another world and I hated to disturb you."

"Thanks!" I said and jumped up and ran out the Quarters and down South Jefferson.

I still remember every detail of that afternoon but what I remember most about those precious moments is the lifting of fear and dread inside me—a feeling of peace and freedom, even if for a few minutes, that I had never felt before. I didn't even know what it felt like to be unafraid, not to expect the anvil to drop at any moment, until that afternoon as I held Rodney Thibault's hand and he put his arm around me.

That summer I started to sneak old textbooks out of the library in my book bag. I'd hide them under my bed until Wednesday, then I would load them in my back pack and bring them to the Quarters. I didn't keep count of how many I squirreled away with Marianne during those months, but Rodney told her he was able to share them with classmates and that it was exciting to have books to take home at night. I thought how we white kids just took things for granted and how lots of kids actually complained about having to take books home to study.

Each time I went to the Esso station with Daddy, Rodney would come to the car and he would thank me for the textbooks. We had this secret—a mysterious mission to save the world together. At thirteen and fifteen, we felt we were making an impact, and we did it together—me, Rodney and Marianne. Soon even Marianne didn't think about us as being colored and white. We were teenagers on a mission.

∾ Chapter Six ∾

∾

Troublemaking/Boy Troubles
1965

IT WAS AGAINST the rules to go to the quarters and I wondered when, not if, my parents would find out I went there. I tried to convince myself it didn't matter because I was right and they were wrong. What was the harm in visiting an old man and listening to his stories?

Sometimes when I got there, Catfish was sound asleep in his rocker. I'd just sit still and watch the kids play in the yard until he woke up. If Marianne was home we'd go the barn to talk or we'd swing the jump rope for her sisters and cousins.

One day I was sitting in the chair next to Catfish, humming softly and thinking. I often thought about Rodney, especially when I was alone and quiet—otherwise I tried to put him out of my mind. I knew Rodney was aware that I went to the quarters on Wednesdays, but two months went by and he didn't come when I was there. I wondered whether he forgot about me, or maybe I was just an acquaintance who could help him get books for his school. When I had those thoughts I remembered the way he looked at me and how his heart beat so hard against my ear, how tears pooled in his eyes when he kissed my dimple—and I told myself that wasn't something you could fake. Surely he felt something for me, too.

Catfish woke up and looked at me sideways, and I could feel his stare out the corner of my eye, like he didn't want me to know he was awake. We played that game while Marianne walked across the yard. I could tell she was happy to see me.

"There's my girl," Catfish said as Marianne climbed the steps to back porch.

"Hey, Marianne," I said. "Are you just getting home from school?"

"Yes, I had to stay late to help my teacher. She is so excited about the books and keeps asking where I got them." She sat on the floor near Catfish's feet and laughed. "I said, 'If I told you, we'd both have to die,' and she laughed so hard her eyes filled with tears."

"I hope she doesn't force you to tell her," I said, suddenly afraid of the repercussions if our secret was uncovered.

"Don't worry. She's cool." And she dropped the subject. "What are ya'll talking about?"

"We weren't talking. I was sitting here waiting for Catfish to wake up, hoping he would tell me another story about his daddy."

"Yeah," Catfish said as he spread his arms out and stretched. "I got a story for you. Funny, I was just dreaming about Daddy and what he told me happened after the war, about 1880." He fingered his chin as if trying to remember something. His brow wrinkled and his eyebrows came together in thought.

"You mean the Civil War, Cat?" I asked.

"Yeah. We call it the war between the states. You know my granddaddy didn't go fight in the war, and Mr. Van stay home, him too. They was afraid all the time the Yankees would come kill them and burn down the plantation. Fact is, the Yanks never found Shadowland, it being tucked in all these trees where you can't see it from none of the roads, and all.

"You know, my granddaddy named my daddy for hisself, Samuel the second. But they called my daddy, Sammy. He had two younger brothers, my daddy did, Simon and Jacob. I guess they were

104

my uncles, but I never met them. My daddy, he talked about them a lot. Simon, he was born in 1877 and Jacob, he came the next year. My daddy told me a story about the night those boys almost got kilt.

"Seems this particular story, the one I'm fixin' to tell you, happened when the boys was young. Daddy was, hmmm, maybe five, and Simon, he was about three. That would make Jacob, two."

"You never told me about them, Granddaddy."

"Well, chile, you just in time."

*

Boy Troubles
1880

'Anna Lee, that was my grandmother. I called her Granny. Well, Granny gave birth to two more boys after my daddy, like I said. Then in 1880 when she birthed Benjamin, she bout bled to death. The baby and Granny was both in trouble. My granddaddy paced back and forth in the kitchen while the women cared for my Granny and the new baby in the front room. Sammy, that's what they called my daddy—did I already tell you that—well, anyways, my daddy and his two little brothers, played in the dirt in the back yard, right here, on this very ground.

'I'm hungry' Jacob said.

'Yeah,' said Simon.

'We don't got nothing to eat out here,' Sammy told them.

'Can you get us something?' Simon asked his big bother.

'Pop told us not to go inside,' Sammy said. 'I don't want to get whipped.'

'But we's hungry,' Jacob started to cry.

Sammy got hisself up, dusted his pants with his hands, and climbed the three steps onto this very back porch. He could see his daddy through the window, pacing back and forth in that room behind me. That was before we added the front room, so this here room served as kitchen and family room," Catfish said. "The family slept together in what is now my sitting room.

My daddy, Sammy, remember he was only bout five, opened the screen door slowly so it wouldn't creak and slipped into the overly-warm kitchen. A kerosene lantern sat in the center of the wooden table and lit the room. It smelled like urine and dried blood in the house, and there was water in pans laid out on every surface. Sammy noticed a pile of red-stained sheets in the corner.

He stood just inside the door, his hands holding each other behind his back while he waited to be noticed.

'They's both in trouble,' Bessie said to Granddaddy when she rushed into the room to ask him to put some more water on the fire in the hearth. 'The boy's not breathing good and Anna Lee, well, she just keeps bleeding. We need more sheets and towels and you needs to boil those soiled ones in the corner ...'

She noticed my daddy standing next to the screen door. Granddaddy's eyes followed hers and he saw the boy, too.

'What you doing in here, boy,' Granddaddy barked. 'I told you boys not to come inside.'

'I'm sorry, Pappy,' my daddy whispered. 'The boys is hungry. What you want I do?'

'Go look in the field for some potatoes and corn, boy,' Granddaddy said. 'You big enough to figure out how to feed the young ones. Now git!'

My daddy backed out of the room and onto the back porch. He had heard Bessie say that his mama and baby were 'in trouble.' He wondered what that meant.

He grabbed a burlap sack from under the porch and headed to the fields. The little boys followed and tried to keep up, but the five-year-old's strides were too much for their little legs and soon they got left behind. Daddy said he could hear Jacob whimpering and Simon consoling him.

Daddy dug a few potatoes with his bare hands and found some stalks of corn that looked like they were grown enough to eat. Instead of retracing his steps back to the cabin, he headed to the barn. As often as he sat and watched his dad milk Daisy, the cow, he had never tried it hisself and wasn't sure whether his hands had the strength to pull on the teats hard enough to bleed the milk out, but he found a small bucket and sat on the stool his dad used.

He had no luck at first, but he said the cow stood still, as if it wanted someone to drain the liquid that built up inside her belly. He closed his eyes and tried to remember what his pappy's hands looked like when they were pulling on the pink udders that sent milk squirting into the bucket.

He put both of his little hands at the top of the cow's teat, the backs of his hands touching her stomach. With his thumbs and the crook that they formed with his index fingers, he began to squeeze and pull downward at the same time. Success! The milk dripped into the bucket. The more he squeezed and pulled, the stronger the stream of milk became and, finally, he picked up a rhythm that sent squirts of the creamy fluid into the container parked under Daisy.

Daddy said his fingers grew tired and began to cramp so he picked up the half-filled bucket and the sack of corn and potatoes and headed home. By now it was dark, but he knew his way blindfolded. When he got home his brothers weren't in the back yard. He eased inside the house to look for the boys but his dad sent him scampering out the door. Outside he started to call for them while he walked towards the cornfield. He heard the crickets singing to the birds that tweeted back, but nothing from his brothers. He felt responsible for those boys. After all, he was the big brother.

He retraced his steps back to the field, through the potato patch and into the rows of corn stalks, then he started to walk towards the barn on Mr. Van's property. He kept whistling and calling the boys.

He heard a dog bark. He stopped to listen. The barking continued and became more intense. More barks joined in and it sounded like a pack of angry dogs that found their prey. Against his better judgment, he walked toward the noise. He hid behind an oak tree and spied the herd of dogs and five or six men on horses behind them. They carried guns aimed at a pecan tree in Mr. Van's orchard.

Daddy said he thought hard. Then he silently ran towards the plantation house. His bare feet pounded the hard earth and his slim body slipped through the cornrows as if they were invisible. When he got to the back door of the big house, he banged with both hands until Lizzie stomped through the kitchen and swung the door open. The other women were attending his Mama so Lizzie was the only worker in the house, and she was busy.

'Who's there,' she shouted into the wind.

'It's me, Miss Lizzie,' he said. She looked down to see the child standing on the stoop, eyes wide, panting.

'You been running, boy?' she asked.

'Yes, Ma'am,' he said. 'I needs to see Mr. Van. It be a mergency.'

Something in my daddy's voice made her take him seriously and she turned and walked quickly out of the kitchen into the main house. She said none of Samuel's children had ever come to ask for Mr. Van. Samuel, himself, had never done that. Lizzie knew Anna Lee was in labor, something must be wrong.

Mr. Van followed Lizzie from his study, down the long hall, into the dining room and through the swinging door to the kitchen. She opened the back door but not the screen door. Sammy was standing on the back porch, his hands deep in his pockets, his eyes staring at bare feet oozing blood in places from the brambles and stickers he ran through to get to the plantation house.

'What you need, boy?' Mr. Van barked. 'You're disturbing my family.'

'I'm sorry, sir,' Sammy stuttered, then he got hold of himself. He stood up straight, shoulders back, proud like his daddy taught him and reached out to shake hands with the big man who peered at him from behind the screen door, as if for protection. Mr. Van was taken aback, thought for a moment, swung the screen door opened and stepped onto the porch. He shook hands with the boy and remembered the first time he met this child at two or three. The little boy had performed the same brave, mature gesture in the middle of the barn by standing straight, making eye contact, and extending his right hand.

'Mr. Van, sir,' Sammy said. He looked Mr. Van in the eye and spoke clearly. He tried not to let his voice to quiver with the fear he felt. 'They's some men on horses with fire on poles. They got dogs and guns aimed at a tree on your property. My brothers is missing and they might be in that tree. Something or someone in that tree, for sure, sir.'

'Follow me,' Van said and bolted towards the barn. 'George, where are you?'

George peeked his head out of the barn,

'Here, sir.'

'Get my horse saddled, NOW!' he said. He picked up the boy who trailed behind, unable to keep up with the man's long strides.

Mr. Van carried Daddy into the barn where several buckets of water were lined up for the horses once they ate the oats George had just given them. The big man lowered Daddy's feet into one of the buckets, knelt on one knee, the other bent—a bench for the boy's rump. Mr. Van used his big hands to massage the bloody, swollen feet and toes while George saddled the sorrel.

He pulled my five-year-old daddy up and swung him round his back.

'Hold on to my neck, boy,' he said. Daddy wrapped his legs around the man's waist and held on tight while Mr. Van put one foot in the stirrup and swung his other leg around the back of the saddle.

'Okay, boy,' Mr. Van said. 'Put your legs on either side of the horse and your arms around my waist.' Sammy was barely situated when Mr. Van snapped the reins, tapped the heels of his boots against the horse's flanks and the sorrel exited the barn in a gallop.

Daddy said he couldn't see much from behind the big man but he noticed the sky lit up ahead. Something's on fire, he thought and the horse flew through the field.

'Hey,' Mr. Van hollered as they got closer to the fire. 'Hey, what you guys up to? Hey! Who's there? This is my property. What you doing here?' Daddy could feel the heat from the fire and hear a crackling sound when, suddenly, Mr. Van stopped the horse and jumped onto the ground.

'Stay there, boy!' he commanded without looking back. He moved quickly towards the men who held flaming sticks, like huge matches that stayed lit. The dogs barked so loud the men couldn't hear Mr. Van, who screamed at them as he approached on foot, long strides that moved as fast as if he ran.

'Hey, you men!' Mr. Van yelled when he was close enough to grab the leg of one of the horsemen. 'What the hell you doing?'

'Hey, Van,' the man said. He looked at the grip on his ankle and said, 'What the hell you doing. Turn me loose!'

'Not until someone here explains what the hell you men are doing on my property with torches and dogs and guns!' Mr. Van screamed, loud enough for the other four to hear. They all turned their heads towards him. One of the men barked a command and the dogs stopped barking.

'Who's in charge of this atrocity?' Van asked.

The man next to the one in Van's grip said, 'We just having a little fun, Van. Leave us be.'

'This is my property!' Van yelled. 'You have no right to be here without permission. I don't care how much fun you fools are looking for.'

'Come on, man,' the guy whose ankle Van still held. 'We just chased a couple little niggers up that tree and we having some fun watching them mess their pants cause they's so scared.'

Mr. Van yanked the man's ankle so hard he pulled him out of his saddle and onto the ground.

'You sons-a-bitches!' Van screamed. He grabbed the man's gun as he fell to the ground. In one quick motion he placed his boot on the man's neck as he lay on the ground, cocked the rifle and aimed it at the others.

The man's torch rolled towards Daddy who still sat on the back of the sorrel. He slid quietly off the horse and picked up the torch before it set anything afire, and stood beside the horse, silent, the torch in front of him so the men could not make out his little figure.

'You,' Mr. Van said. He pointed the gun at the man who had spoken. The other three sat still, the fifth one was on the ground under Mr. Van's boot. 'You and the others. Get those children out of the tree. NOW!'

'Wait a minute, Van,' the man on the third horse said. 'You don't expect us to climb that tree and handle some niggers with messy pants.'

'Not only do I expect you to do it, but if you don't get off those horses and start climbing that tree, I'm going to start shooting me some dogs. When I get through with the dogs, I'm going to shoot me some horses. When I'm done with the horses, I'm going to shoot me some men. Now! Get moving!'

The man on the ground squirmed. Mr. Van shoved his boot in the man's neck and pressed so hard the man choked.

'If you want your friend to breathe again, you better get going,' Van said. He waited a few seconds. The men didn't move. Van shot the gun in the air, cocked it and aimed it at the biggest dog.

'He's next!' The men slid off their horses.

'Buddy,' the man who was riding the third horse said. 'You hold these torches. Me and Slim will go up the tree to get those niggers.' They handed their torches to the tall, skinny man who wore a cowboy hat and had a light brown mustache.

Slim made a stirrup out of his hands and boosted the other man into the tree. The man grabbed the highest branch he could reach and pulled himself up. Sammy could see his boots climb from one limb to the next until they were out of sight. He could hear the man trying to coax the boys down.

'Come on, you dumb-ass niggers,' he barked. 'We going to get you down. I said come here! I'm not going to hurt you, just climb down so's we can get you out this tree.' The boys moved higher up the tree.

'Hey, Van, ' the man in the tree shouted. 'They won't budge. Fact is, they climbing higher to get away from me.'

'Come here, Sammy,' Mr. Van said. He motioned to my daddy without releasing the tension of his foot on the man's neck. Sammy obediently walked towards Mr. Van.

'Yes, sir,' the boy said. He looked directly at Van and stood erect.

'You go under that tree and tell your brothers to let that man bring them down.'

'With all due respect, sir,' my daddy said. 'They not coming down with that white man. If you just get them men to leave, Mr. Van, I can get them boys out of the tree myself. That is, if you could hold a torch for me to see.'

'You sure, boy?' Van asked.

'Yes sir,' he answered. 'I's sure, sir.'

'Get out that tree, Dave,' Mr. Van bellowed. "Now!'

Dave scrambled out the tree. The two men stood under the tree in front of Van, who aimed the rifle slightly above their heads. The two others sat in their saddles holding torches. The fifth was on the ground under Van's boot.

'Get up, Corky,' Van said and removed his foot from the man's neck. Corky bounced up and almost ran past Van to stand with the others, both his hands massaging his neck. 'Now, all of you, get your asses off my property and don't you ever let me see you here again,' Van howled. 'Nobody fools with my niggers, you hear?'

The men nodded.

'I'm going to keep this gun aimed at your backs till you're gone,' Van said. 'If you want your gun back, Corky, you can come up to the house with an apology. Otherwise, I just got me a rifle. Now, GET!'

The men climbed on their horses and took off before their legs cleared the saddles. The dogs followed, barking. When they was out of sight and almost out of earshot Mr. Van took the torch from Daddy and followed him to the tree. He scrambled up the big oak without help and was with his brothers in seconds.

"You okay?' my daddy asked Jacob and Simon. They shook like leaves in a brisk breeze, and they smelled something terrible. 'Come on. Simon, you go first. Jacob, hold me around the neck and I'll take you down, okay?'

It didn't take long for the boys to climb down from the tree. When each reached the lowest branch, they jumped to the ground and landed on their feet, even though the branch was at least two times higher off the ground than Mr. Van.

Mr. Van hoisted the two younger boys onto the saddle of the sorrel. Sammy walked beside the tall white man and moved his feet and legs as fast as he could to keep up with Mr Van's long strides as they made their way to the Quarters.

While they walked side-by-side Sammy explained to Van that his mama was fighting for her life and the life of her newborn.

'I's not supposed to know,' Sammy said. 'But my brothers was hungry, so I went inside to get them something to eat. I overheard Miss Bessie tell my daddy about Mama and the baby. I think it's another boy.'

'Daddy told me to go dig some potatoes and break some corn in the field to feed the boys, but I didn't come right home, so it's my fault what happened. I went to your barn to get some milk from Daisy. I guess the boys followed me and got lost when the dark came.'

My daddy said he stopped walking. When Mr. Van noticed he was no longer beside him, the big man turned around and paced about six strides back to where the boy stood, erect, stationary.

'I knew I couldn't get Pappy to come help when I saw them white men and dogs. I wasn't sure it was the boys in the tree, but I feared it might be.' My daddy looked up at the intimidating figure of that white man, while fat tears made their way down his five-year-old dusty cheeks and became drops of mud when they fell to the ground.

'You did the right thing, boy,' Mr. Van said. He patted Daddy's head. 'Next time you and your brothers are hungry, go to my house and ask Bessie or Lizzie to fix you something. Let's not lose your brothers in the field again.'

'Thank you, sir,' Daddy said. 'I'm much beholden to you for your help. Those men might of shot my daddy.'

'I know that, son,' Mr. Van said. 'Sometimes I don't understand how people around here think.'

"Me, neither, sir,' Daddy said. They walked quietly for a while. 'Can I ask you something, sir?'

'Sure, go ahead.'

'Why is you different from the other white folks in Jean Ville?'

'I'm not so different, son,' Mr. Van said. 'Remember I once owned your daddy and George and all the others. That's not something I'm proud of. I don't think God means for some people to own others, but I did.'

'Oh,' my daddy answered. They walked in silence the rest of the way home, the small boy and the big, tall man, both deep in thought.

*

"And that's the story my daddy tole me," Catfish said. His eyes were at half-mast. He was tired and began to rock and let his chin drop to his chest.

"Wow, Catfish," I said. "That was quite a story. For a while I thought you were Sammy."

"Granddaddy knows how to spin a yarn," Marianne said. She laughed and winked at her granddaddy. He winked back under heavy eyelids. "You girls done wore me out again," he said. "Now run along and give an old man a rest."

We skipped down the rickety wooded steps. I turned back towards Catfish.

"I'm going to be a writer one day," I said. "And I'm going to write all these stories you tell us. I can't wait for the next one." Catfish grinned but didn't say a word. I turned and ran off after Marianne, towards the barn.

After supper that night I sat at my desk, took out a clean sheet of paper and tried to recreate the story Catfish told me about his daddy and uncles. I wanted to record the quotes and the colloquial speech as closely as possible. Over the next few weeks I wrote down everything I could remember about the story of Catfish's granddaddy being separated from his mother and sold on an auction block in downtown Jean Ville and the one where the half-brother brought Catfish's great grandmother to Jean Ville. I hid my pages between the mattress and box springs of my huge four-poster bed, towards the middle, so even Tootsie wouldn't feel them when she changed my sheets.

~ Chapter Seven ~

The Real Enemy
1965

I WAS DREAMING ABOUT playing baseball when, suddenly, a spotlight came on and I was under interrogation in a police station. The roar of a man's voice sounded like a dragster race going around my room as this man, hidden behind the light, belted questions.

"Who do you think you are?" Before I had time to think of an answer he continued, rapid-fire.

"What makes you think you can . . ?"

"Where did you think you were going?"

The engines revved and I heard a volcano erupt on the side of my bed. I sat straight up, my arms waving in the air as if to shoo-off bats that tried to get in my hair and eyes. In a deep fog I fought to get my bearings, and I heard another loud rumble of words.

"I've had it with you!" I glanced at the clock: 2 AM!!

"God, Daddy, it's two o'clock in the morning," I yelled loud enough for Mama to hear me so she would come to my rescue. I thought I saw a shooting star just before something hard, silver, sharp, caught the side of my face and a vice grip grabbed my arm and threw me in the air. I fell in slow motion as if falling from an airplane and heard a voice filtered through the clouds I dropped through, like the sound came from a microphone below.

"It doesn't matter what time it is." Oh, my God! I smelled whiskey and sweat and knew I was headed for the side of a cliff. "You disobeyed me and you disobeyed your mother."

I couldn't make sense of the situation so I decided to jump off the cliff and sail through the air to safety. A metal object swinging on the end of a leather belt whizzed towards me and I saw a breathing monster with a look of disgust on his face and fire in his eyes get closer by the millisecond. The metal shone as it twirled around on the end, like a silver ball on the edge of a twirling lanyard. I sat up with my knees drawn to my chin, arms looped around them and wrists clasped together, hugging my legs to my chest and pretended to be in take-off position, a parachute on my back.

The face of the monster got redder as his anger grew and fire projected from its nostrils.

"What did I do?" I knew I should keep my mouth shut, but it was too late. My words were already floating in the air above the bed.

"Stand up and bend over." Fear filled me and I tried to pull the covers up and fold myself into a ball, against the headboard of my bed, which felt like a mountainside. I was virtually backed against the wall. The vice grip grabbed my arm and threw me from my perch and my head struck something hard and sharp as I went down. I saw stars and felt horses gallop over me and squash me into the dusty ground. I became flat with the earth so cars could roll over me and lions could chase tigers on my back and bees could sting my cheeks, while I was simply part of nature, one with the world. Just as I began to feel pain and noticed blue carpet, not earth, around me, an anvil fell from the sky on my head and everything went black again.

I heard a voice in the clouds scream, "I told you there would be no interracial relations and you were warned not to go to the quarters. Do you have any idea what this could do to my career and my chances for mayor if anyone finds out?"

I'm not sure how long I lay there, but light softly filtered around the edges of the blue drapes on the windows and I got a whiff of the magnolia blooms outside. I tried to pick my head off the blue carpet but it pounded so hard I left it on the floor. I couldn't open my right eye, and my left eye was buried deep in the wooly blue rug. I lifted my neck a few inches and opened my left eye, just a slit. It was still dark outside, but I heard footsteps in the hall, then smelled coffee. *Mama must be up,* I thought. She'll come to see about me soon. I tried to get my arms out from under my body, but one of them hurt so bad I couldn't move it without a jolt of excruciating pain through my entire body.

Slowly, gingerly, I rolled over on my back, and let out a blood-curdling yell. Pain came from every nerve and sinew, searing through my left arm and back. I must have blacked out again.

When I awoke sunlight streamed through the slits in the floor-to-ceiling curtains of my corner room. I tried to take stock of my condition. All I remembered was the roar of motors and the stampede of horses as I parachuted off a cliff and landed, in a heap, on my bedroom floor. My head pounded and I reached my right arm to my face and felt my swollen eye with trembling fingers. The entire right side of my head felt huge and, when I pulled my hand away, it was filled with blood. I screamed again.

Tootsie barged into my room.

"Why you yelling like that?" Tootsie demanded when she opened the door, then she screamed. "Miss Anne, Miss Anne. Please ma'am. Please come!"

Tootsie got on her knees in front of me and tried to lift my head into her lap. She slid her hands down my back and jerked them away. They were filled with blood.

"Oh, Gawd," Tootsie said. "He done gone and done it now. I'll get some wet rags and try to clean you up."

"No, Tootsie, please don't touch me. It hurts too much. Just stay here with me until I can sit up."

"You don't need to sit up on that behind, Honey-Chile. It's all blue and purple, at least the parts of it that ain't bleeding. And your pajama shorts is in shreds, your panties, too. And your shirt. Oh, Gawd, what to do, what to do?"

She jumped up and ran into the short hallway where Sissy had escaped the night before. The bathroom we shared with Mama was off that hall. Tootsie screamed for help as she gathered wet washcloths and towels. No one answered her. No one came.

She put a towel under my head and began to gently wash my face with a wet rag. After two or three swipes across my forehead, the cloth was so bloody Tootsie switched to the other one.

"Oh, Gawd, Oh Lawd, what I gonna do? Help me, Lawd. I needs help here." She just kept praying out loud while she tried to clean me up. Even Tootsie's gentle, light touches hurt and I moaned and whined. Tootsie went back and forth to the bathroom, rinsing rags and towels and returning for more cleaning. I was in too much pain and too exhausted from the long night to argue or resist.

"Can you get me an aspirin?" I whispered.

"Shore, Baby girl, I can do that. Tootsie be right back."

I didn't move. I wanted to sleep through the pain, but I couldn't get comfortable. When Tootsie came back she had an aspirin and a glass of water. It was an almost impossible task to swallow a pill and drink water, but somehow Tootsie got the aspirin down while she gently rubbed my throat. I was so thirsty I drank the entire glass of water—at least what didn't spill on me and the carpet.

I felt light-headed again, and drifted off. When I woke up, it was dark outside and I was alone in the deadly quiet room. Darkness wrapped around me like a shroud. Both doors to my room were shut and I felt like the bed was spinning.

My head pounded.

The next thing I knew, Tootsie was back and daylight streaked through the draped windows. I couldn't hear anything but a ringing in my ears. Tootsie sat on the edge of the mattress and stroked my tangled hair.

"What day is it?" I asked. I wasn't sure Tootsie heard me.

"Wednesday," Tootsie said.

"I've been here since Monday night?"

"I'm not sure. You was here yesterday morning when I come in."

"Where's Mama? Has she come into see me? I've been sleeping a lot so I don't remember."

"Yesterday she tole me she gonna make you see the light, that she not gonna come in here and baby you. She told me to tell you to, 'Straighten up and fly right.' I think those her words."

"Geez," I thought. I went into a fog. My light-headedness made me feel like I was in a dream. Rodney and I were kissing and he told me he loved me and that he would take me away from everything that hurt me and he would keep me safe. No one would ever hit me again.

When Daddy got home from Baton Rouge he took me to the emergency room at Jean Ville Hospital where Dr. David stitched up a long, deep cut on my back, above my right kidney, and gave me a shot of antibiotic. I was on the stretcher behind a curtain when I overheard a conversation between Mama and her sister, Aunt Betty, who'd come to visit from Houston.

*

"I don't know what I'm going to do about her, Betty," I heard Mama say in a faraway voice. "She's on my last nerve. It's all I can do to look at her. I told Bob that I want to send her to boarding school next month, when she starts high school, but he won't hear of it."

"Bob used to tell me how beautiful I was. Now that I've had five children, he doesn't tell me anymore, but he tells Susanna how pretty she is. In fact, he tells her all the things he used to tell me, 'You are so pretty, so talented, so smart, you make me so proud!' I could throw up. He calls her 'Pretty Girl.' He idolizes her."

"Have you told Bob how you feel?" I heard my Aunt Betty ask. She must be visiting from Houston, I thought. When I was a little girl I admired my aunt's wardrobe and beautiful shoes, but as I got older and realized Mama took money from our household allowance, earmarked for clothing for me and my siblings and sent it to her sister, I felt myself fighting resentment.

"Of course I have," Mama said. "He just doesn't hear me. He says things like, 'How can you be jealous of your own daughter?'" Mama cried and Aunt Betty consoled her. I peeked through swollen eyes to see Mama's head in her hands and her elbows on her knees. Aunt Betty leaned forward and rubbed Mama's back.

"I'm the one who made him spank her," her mother whimpered. "He didn't want to, so I kept fixing him drinks. The drunker he got, the angrier he became. I didn't mean for him to take it this far.

"I don't want to hate my daughter, I really don't. She *is* pretty and smart and talented. She can sew, draw, write poetry, dance, twirl a baton, play sports and she's only thirteen! What's she going to be like when she gets older?"

My mother hates me?

"You need to convince Bob to send her away to school," Aunt Betty said.

"I'll try again," Mama said. "The worse that can happen is for me to have her three more years."

"Only three? She's thirteen. Where is she going at sixteen?"

"To LSU, of course."

"At sixteen?"

"Yes. She'll be in the ninth grade this year and, with summer school, she can finish high school in three years."

"Anne, sixteen is way too young to go to LSU."

"She'll grow up fast," Mama said.

I lay under the white sheets in the sterile room and considered my options for the future. Survival became my primary focus in high school.

Part Three: 1966-67

⁓ Chapter Eight ⁓

⁓

Wrestling/Sharecroppers
1966

I T WAS THE summer before my junior year in high school, which was my last year—so, technically, I guess I was a senior, although I was only fifteen. I didn't have much time for Marianne or Catfish that year, but I sneaked to the Quarters every month or so. Rodney didn't come when I was there and I told myself he was over me, and that was probably a good thing, seeing as how dangerous it was. I was stupid enough to risk it, but then, what was the risk for me? I was white.

Yet, when we talked at the Esso station he said how good it was to see me and he always told me I looked beautiful. He seemed genuine and I believed him. Sometimes he passed a note or a poem to me by sticking it in the slit where the window disappeared. Most times we gave our notes to Marianne and she would begrudgingly deliver them when I came to the Quarters and when she saw Rodney at school. I wondered whether she lectured Rodney every time, like she did me.

"You two have got to stop this," she'd say and turn her head in disgust.

"There's nothing to stop, Mari," I'd say. "We haven't been together except for that one time two years ago." But she didn't believe me and she worried constantly that something would happen to Rodney. We never talked about what could happen to me. Turns out she told Rodney about the beating I got when my dad found out I went to the Quarters and the two of them, Mari and Rod, decided it was too dangerous for me, too. Here I was trying to protect him and years later I discover he was trying to protect me, which is why he never came to the Quarters on Wednesdays—although I didn't know any of that at the time or that Marianne, well, she tried her best to protect us both.

Marianne was needy and clingy when I was with her, but I didn't care. We finally came to an agreement about sex—I liked boys and she liked girls, but we loved each other.

"It's hard for me," Marianne said to me the day we finally had that difficult conversation. "I'm attracted to you."

"No you aren't, Mari," I said. "I'm just the only girl you are close enough to think that way about. Once you find other girl friends, you'll be attracted to someone else."

"That's not going to happen because none of the girls like me," she said. She pouted and her bottom lip stuck out so far it could catch flies.

"That will change when you get out of this podunk town," I said.

"You'll be leaving next year, but I might never get to leave."

"You'll go off to college, won't you?"

"I don't know, Susie. We don't have the money and, well, Mama can't do without me."

"Let's get jobs and start saving now, so you can go to Southern University. That way we'll both be in Baton Rouge." We talked a good game, but, other than babysitting jobs, my parents wouldn't let me work. It would make them look bad.

When Marianne and I talked about Rodney, all we did was argue, so I tried not to bring up the subject. She reluctantly brought his notes to me and delivered mine to him, but she'd get angry and lecture me about the Klan each time.

Sometimes, when I left the Esso station and looked in the review mirror I could see Rodney watching the back of my car. He would stand there until I turned the corner on Marble Avenue. I wanted to turn around, go back, jump out of the car and throw my arms around him and say, "Dang all of you who think the color of someone's skin can dictate who they love." But, of course I didn't.

It was August and I had just returned to Jean Ville High School the previous week for my final year. I was afraid to graduate and go off to college, but with all the tension and escalating violence at home, I needed to move on and learn to take care of myself.

It had been two years since the "accident" that landed me in the hospital and Daddy wouldn't let me out of his sight unless Tootsie was at home. If he had somewhere to go at night, I had to tag along, even if I didn't want to.

My dad had promised to take the boys to a wrestling match at the Cow Palace, a place where livestock auctions were held during the day. He insisted I go with them.

"I don't want to go to a wrestling match," I said. "It's gross. There won't be any girls or women there, only men and boys."

"You are coming with us, don't argue."

"I have homework."

"You can do your homework when we get home. Be in the car in five minutes." He started for his bedroom to tell Mama goodbye, then he turned and said, "You should thank me for this." I didn't know what he meant. Later I realized he was protecting me from Mama—but who was protecting me from him?

The smell in the arena was horrible. It greeted me outside the Cow Palace and grew in intensity as I reached the front doors. Inside, the stench was almost unbearable—horse and cow dung, pig slop, stagnant muddy water where flies and fleas hovered, and male sweat. The entire area from the parking lot to the main arena was a cesspool. Past the concession area with its concrete floor was a huge open area with a stinky mud floor and bleachers on two sides with views of where they auctioned livestock in the daytime and set up a wrestling rink at night.

"You'll get used to it," Daddy said.

Besides being unbelievably smelly, it was noisy and filthy. Men cheered and hollered, drinking beer and pulling pint bottles of hooch from their back pockets. I watched those dirty, bearded men, with wads of tobacco in their jaws, drink from the same bottle. *Gross!*

After my dad, brothers and I were settled in the stands, I excused myself to go to the ladies' room. I tramped through the muck and the mess in my new brown leather penny loafers, still stiff, and tried to avoid animal waste. I walked slowly, watching my feet and planning my steps carefully.

When I reached the entrance to the concession area, the concrete floor was a welcomed relief from the muddy surface inside the arena. I grabbed a couple of napkins from the concession counter and bent to clean my shoes. I walked slowly and continued to swipe at mud and straw attached to my pants and sweater in various places.

I wasn't looking where I was going, but I knew I was moving towards the restrooms under the staircase. I could see the feet of people as they went around me. Just before I reached the door to the ladies room I bumped into someone. It was inevitable.

"I'm sorry," I said. Or that's what I think I said, then I looked at the brown boots that were toe-to-toe with my loafers, and at the creases in the legs of the blue jeans. My eyes traveled slowly up to the light green oxford shirt tucked in behind a brown leather belt, to the full lips and amber eyes of, guess who? Rodney!

I'd run right into Rodney Thibault.

I froze. I couldn't speak or breathe. I barely felt my body stiffen and my mouth fall open. Rodney's arms rose in slow motion and rested on my shoulders. His touch sent shivers down my back and landed in my crotch where I could feel the prickly beginnings of wetness. I stared at him and tried to speak but I only stuttered and stammered.

I had relived our time in the Quarters hundreds of times over the past two years and felt his strong arm across my shoulder, his humming in my ear. Each time I saw him at the gas station I remembered, and re-enacted it in my mind, but there was always a barrier between us—the car. This time, at the Cow Palace, there was no physical barrier, and I forgot, for a minute, that there was an audience.

Something came alive inside me, something that had been dormant for two years. I stood under the staircase in a trance and stared at him. Neither of us spoke, at first. All the questioning I had done about whether he felt the same about me, whether he loved me, whether he remembered, whether his kiss meant as much to him as it did to me—all of those questions were answered by looking at him, and those fears fell away because I saw, in his face, a look I've never forgotten—complete love and submission.

I noticed for the first time how tall he was—he towered over me by at least a head. He was taller than James who was a little over six-feet.

And gorgeous. Oh, God, Rodney Thibault was gorgeous.

He said, "Hi."

"Hi," I think I said, and I swallowed, hard.

I felt a sinking feeling in my tummy and the moisture in my panties. I tingled all over.

Later I was unable to remember our exchange.

*

Rodney and Marianne said that Adams High School was a dump, but it had dedicated teachers, football and a gym where kids could shoot hoops. Marianne told me that Rodney's coach said he was a natural leader, that's why he was such a good quarterback. Rodney told Marianne he didn't play football because he loved the game, or because he needed the fraternity of other guys, he played because it kept him going, made him want to get up in the morning, helped him to forget, for a time, that he was colored and all the limitations that put on him. He said he never thought about the drawbacks of being Negro until he met me—like the fact that he couldn't go to the white school that had a library and where all the kids were given textbooks they could take home, or that he only had two choices for college. But he told Marianne that the thing that made him the maddest was that he wasn't even allowed to love who he wanted to love. How could anyone make a law about love, he asked her? She said she didn't have an answer.

Rodney said his limitations made him more determined to rise above what his race told him he could be. Marianne said he told her that he was going to be a lawyer, to become respected, show the world that just because he was a Negro didn't mean he couldn't do and be everything a white man could. She told me he was a serious student, that he studied hard and made good grades and that his teachers told him he had "potential." That he could make something of himself.

He later told me that the biggest problem he had in high school was that he couldn't stop thinking about me. And we both knew that was a dead-end street. He said he was no longer interested in other girls, so he just quit dating. I'm not sure I believed him because Marianne would tell me, every chance she got, about how all the girls loved him and chased him. She did tell me, in an off-moment, that his friends on the football team teased him and called him a faggot, because he no longer paid attention to the pretty girls who tried to get his attention.

That was the closest Marianne ever came to telling me Rodney loved me. I asked her whether Rodney's friends really believed he was gay, and she laughed and said he was too macho for that, especially on the football field, but that the guys couldn't understand why he quit taking advantage of the girls who were willing to let him have whatever he wanted.

One thing Rodney and I had in common was our love for books and the library. When I'd go to the Esso station he'd tell me about a recent trip there and some of the things he'd read. Even though he wasn't allowed to check out books at the public library because he was colored, there was a section in the back where he could read current events and articles on the microfiche reader. He said there were rarely any people in the colored section so he didn't have to hide the materials he read. He told me that he researched laws that prevented coloreds from marrying whites, especially in the South, and that he read about a case that might go to the Supreme Court— a mixed race couple from Virginia who sued for the right to be married. He was eager for the decision in that case and told me about the progress from time-to-time.

Marianne said he was obsessed with the *Loving v. Virginia* case and even wrote a term paper about it. He told her that the decision in that case would give him some idea about his future. He really believed a law to legalize mix-race marriage would change our circumstances. We were both naive back then.

Rodney told me he just wanted to be able to talk to me, like he said in one of his notes.

Susie,

I've been thinking about how unjust it is that we can't even be friends, can't talk to each other without worrying someone will see us. What kind of laws do we have in this country that can legislate how a person feels and who he loves? Have you thought about that?

I think about you all the time. I'm not sure what can or will happen between us, but I can't give up on you, on us.

I miss you,

R

Rod,

I've thought about it a lot—all the things that would have to change if you and I are ever going to be able to do simple things, like have a burger together, or take a ride, or go to a movie. It makes me sad. I feel helpless.

Yours truly,

S

Susie,

I went to mass with my family this morning and I prayed for you. Somehow I feel like you need prayers. Are you okay? Are you in trouble?

Something inside me says you are struggling with something. I want to protect you, to take care of you. I feel helpless.

I miss you,

R

Rod,

I wonder if, when you love someone, you have an inner voice that tells you things about them? It's just a thought. Are you okay? I've worried that something will happen to you since I saw you at the Cow Palace.

Yours truly,

S

*

Rodney was always more hopeful than I was that things could work out between us. I lived on the white side of the law, so I saw things differently. Rodney was ever the optimist. Even though he didn't know for sure how I felt about him, he never gave up. He said he read and re-read the short notes I wrote him until they were frayed, torn and the pencil marks were smudged. For all he knew, I could have had a white boyfriend, but he hung in, believing that one day we'd be together. I didn't, anyway—have a boyfriend, that is. How could I when I was in love with him?

The last time I went to the Esso station his dad was inside and I was the only customer. Rodney asked me if he could see me alone sometime, maybe in the Quarters. I looked around to see if someone was hiding and could hear.

"I'm afraid, Rodney. I'm sorry."

"I'm not sure I understand."

"If we get caught, I'm not sure what will happen."

"Will someone hurt you?"

"Maybe, but what's worse, someone will hurt you."

"Who?"

"I can't say. I've got to go." I drove off before he could say anything more and I cried for an hour on my bed when I got home.

I never thought we'd see each other outside of the gas station. Then we literally ran into each other at the Cow Palace. Of all places. He didn't think before he put his hands on my shoulders and spoke.

"I love you Susie. You are all I think about." I stepped back and looked at him. Time hung in the air like a thick fog that shielded the sun from the earth—and it shielded us from the rest of the world, temporarily.

I came to my senses when I heard his voice and realized where we were, who we were, and the consequences if anyone saw us together. I turned and hurried away, into the ladies' room. It just happened so fast neither of us could have predicted what might happen next.

*

Rodney later told me that he was in a stupor when his dad and brother approached him under the stairs, waiting to go up to the colored section to watch the fight. He didn't hear Jerry when he asked, "Who was that white girl I saw you talking to? You touched her. You could get arrested for that."

Rodney said he looked from his brother to his dad, who had perspiration on his forehead and a red face. That jerked Rodney back to reality.

This is what Marianne told me happened next.

"Let's go, boys," his dad said.

"We just got here," Jerry said. Rodney knew they had to leave when he looked around and saw twenty or more white men staring at him.

"I said, let's go. Now!" His dad led the way and the boys followed him out the double doors, into the parking lot and to their car. Jerry had two cokes in his hands and their dad had one. Rodney's hands were deep in the pockets of his jeans, toying with the tickets. His fingertips tingled.

They drove home in silence with Rodney in the backseat, alone.

When they pulled up to their house, his dad put the car in park but didn't turn off the ignition. He put his arm across the back of the front seat and twisted his body to look at Rodney. Jerry stared through the front windshield, trying to be invisible.

"What were you thinking, Rodney?"

"I'm not sure I was thinking."

"That's Bob Burton's girl."

"I know."

"Bob's my friend."

"I know, Dad."

"If this gets back to him ... well, I don't know what will happen."

"I'm sorry. I wasn't thinking."

"I'll say! Not thinking!" Jerry said. "Shoots, the Klan could come calling if they find out."

"I didn't do anything."

"You don't have to do anything. I've told you and your brother a hundred times—don't even look at a white person in the eye. And never, and I mean never, look at a white female. Don't look at the hem of her skirt. Don't tip your hat, don't say, 'Hi, Miss,' nothing. If you see one coming towards you, go to the other side of the street. Do you understand?"

"Yes, sir."

"I'm not sure how to handle this until I see what the fallout is. Let's just go inside. Don't mention this to your mother or sisters. Don't ever mention it again, not to anyone. Do you understand me?"

"Yes, sir," Jerry said.

"Yes, sir," Rodney said.

When they got out of the car, Rodney's dad hung back and let Jerry get ahead of them. He took Rodney aside and whispered.

"What's this all about, Rod?"

"It's nothing, Dad."

"Oh, it's something, all right; and we are going to stay outside in this heat and get eaten by mosquitoes until you tell me."

"I. I. Uh, I. Dad, I'm in love with her." He looked at his feet.

"You're what?"

"I can't help it. I just am."

"Oh, God, son. You can't be. This can't be. You get that, don't you?"

"Yes, sir. I get it." Rodney was sobbing as he glared into his dad's eyes. "But I don't have to like it." Ray Thibault put his arm around Rodney's shoulder and pulled him close. At six-feet, three-inches, Rodney was a few inches taller than his dad, so he bent his head and rested his cheek on his dad's shoulder. The tears rushed out. He couldn't stop them.

"Does she love you?"

"No. Well, I don't know. Maybe."

"What's the history?"

"We talked. I held her hand and kissed her cheek. That's all."

"Oh, God! When? Where? I don't want to know. You just have to let this go. It's an impossible situation. This is Louisiana. It's 1966. You could go to prison for talking to her. I read in the newspaper that just last week, the KKK hung a boy in Natchitoches because he carried a white girl's books for her."

"I know, Dad. It's just that I ..." He couldn't stop crying.

"It's going to be okay, son. Just cry it out, then accept it. And let's hope no one important saw you touch her."

They stayed outside a while, then went into the house and Rodney went to the bedroom he shared with Jerry, who was on his bed reading a book and drinking his coke. Rodney picked up the extra coke off the table between the two twin beds. The ice was melted and it was watered down, but he sipped it anyway. He and Jerry didn't talk. Rodney later told Marianne he didn't think a 15-year-old could understand, then he remembered that he was fifteen when he fell in love with me. Maybe Jerry would understand about loving a girl, but no one could understand about loving a white girl.

He hated his life, the South, the situation. It was so unfair.

A couple days after the night at the Cow Palace Rodney went to visit Marianne in the Quarters. She told me that he asked her if she had seen me, and she told him I hadn't been there in two or three months. Rodney told Marianne that the few times he saw me at the gas station, I was distant and acted like I hardly knew him.

"I mean, she smiles and makes small talk, but nothing personal. It's like she forgot about that day."

"Maybe she has a boyfriend," Marianne told me she said. "A WHITE boyfriend." But, she said, he wasn't buying that.

"Hummm. Maybe so . . . but what would that have to do with her not coming to see you ... or Catfish ?" Rodney asked her.

"Not sure. There are things you don't know. Things that she's afraid of, that she should be afraid of."

"What? Tell me." Marianne said he pleaded with her to tell him what she knew, but she refused.

"I can't tell you, Rodney. But her life is not what you think it is. Besides, I think she's more worried about what might happen to you. You could be lynched for looking at her. You have to stop this, now! It's insane."

Marianne said that Rodney knew she was right, but that he said he couldn't give up. He told her that he just needed a plan. He went back to the library that week and discovered that interracial marriage was legal in Washington, DC—there were a number of mixed-race couples in the north. It seemed people turned a blind eye up there, like it didn't matter. It wasn't legal or illegal. The case in Virginia was going to the Supreme Court soon. Rodney wondered whether the case would change things.

*

After I saw Rodney at the Cow Palace, I knew I had to go to the quarters to talk to Marianne. I was worried sick about Rodney. A lot of people saw us talking, saw him touch me, saw him bend to whisper in my ear. Oh, God! What would happen to him? I could think of nothing else.

Catfish looked so much older when I climbed the steps and woke him from his peaceful slumber in the rocking chair. He seemed glad to see me and returned my hug more forcefully than usual. I kissed his cheek and sat in the other chair as if I had all the time in the world, while inside, a clock was ticking. I needed to talk to Marianne and find out if Rodney was okay.

"Missy, I'm glad you're here. I been thinking about telling you what happened after my daddy came to be free."

"I'd love to hear that story, Cat. We are studying the Civil War in Social Studies this year. Anyway I want to write about you and all your stories one day. I told you that I'm going to be an author. I'm going to make sure everyone knows how badly they treated your people."

"That's good, Missy. I want people, especially my family, to remember where we come from. It's important. Keeps you grounded.

*

Sharecroppers

"When the slaves were freed after the war ended in 1865, my granddaddy, Samuel, was fifteen," Catfish said. "This is 'fore he married and had children. He didn't want to leave Shadowland, where would he go? So he became a sharecropper.

"Mr. Van let my daddy move into an empty one-room cabin, next to George's house—that's the one burned several years ago when the Klan came. You remember?"

"I remember, Cat," I said.

'Now, George stayed on to take care of the livestock and help with planting and picking when he was needed, but he was paid wages, five dollars a week plus room and board for him and Audrey. Most of the other slaves left the plantation for the north or for wages on larger plantations. Freedom meant they could go wherever they chose and work for who-so-ever they pleased.

'Simon and Jacob never healed from the scare they had the night them men and dogs ran 'em up the tree. When they was teenagers, they, along with my daddy, worked in Mr. Van's field for $20 a month each. They saved their money, so they could leave the South some day and head North," Catfish said. "My granddaddy tole the story bout that time, just like he tole us those other stories."

'Up North black men are treated like they's white,' Simon told my daddy when they were teenagers.

'Yep,' Jacob said. 'They got jobs pay $100 a month and black men wear suits of clothes like the white men and can even go to a real school.'

'You should come with us, Sammy,' Simon said.

'I'm not going up North.' Sammy said. 'And I wish you would stay here with us.'

'No, we going,' Simon said. 'You just staying here cause you sweet on that little girl works up at the house taking care of Mr. Henry.'

"Maybe,' Daddy said. Miss Maureen was the head housekeeper up at Shadowland and she had a pretty daughter named Mary, who daddy ended up marrying and she was my Mama and that was one reason he didn't go with Simon and Jacob.

'There's other reasons,' Sammy said. 'I don't want to leave Mama and Daddy. And I think there's opportunity for us here, down the road. Mr. Van's a good man.'

'You do what you want, Sammy,' Jacob said, 'But we going as soon as I turn sixteen and Simon is seventeen. They say you need to be legal age or with someone legal age to travel on the train through the south, that's seventeen.'

"My daddy told that story with tears in his eyes," Catfish said.

"About 1895, when Simon came of age, a group of young men, including Big Bugger and Wes and Lila's 18-year-old son, Norman, was going north and Simon and Jacob joined them. Lila was a lady went to church with me and Anna Lee and them. Well Miss Lila would sit on the porch with Annie in the evenings and they would weep together. Annie had taught our boys to read and write and hoped they would send letters, but Lila's children ain't been interested in lessons, so Norman wouldn't be able to write to his mama.

'Thank God, I still have Sammy,' Anna Lee would say.

'My daddy, he was always the responsible one,' Catfish said. 'He tole me he took care of his brothers and helped his mama and daddy. He worked in the field and did anything Mr. Van axed him to do. In return, Mr. Van paid him $20 a month and took special interest in him. My daddy groomed the livestock, built out-buildings, repaired the house when needed, replaced windows and kept it white-washed year-around.

'Mr. Van taught him how to ride a horse when he was ten and the mare had a foal in the spring of 1892, Mr. Van gave it to my daddy. He cared for that pony and it grew to be big, fast and reliable. He named the horse, 'Jonesie.' No reason, he just liked the name and thought the young thoroughbred looked like a 'Jonesie.'

'Daddy lived with my granddaddy and granny in their two-room cabin until his brothers left, then he axed Mr. Van could he rent the one-room shack in the Quarters where Big Bugger used to live. It was falling down, in disrepair, had no glass in the windows and the tin roof was half-missing, but daddy fixed it up good as new. He also axed Mr. Van could he have a small piece of land to share-crop. This was a new practice my daddy heard about at church. The plantation owner would let the former slave farm a certain amount of acres. The freed man of color would plant and harvest and the owner would split the sale of the crop fifty-fifty.

"I can still keep up with my work on your plantation and farm a piece of land, say about 50-acres, if you let me use your plow," Sammy tole Mr. Van. "Jonesie can pull and I can do the rest after six in the evening," Sammy said.

'We can try that for a season, Son,' Mr. Van said. 'Make sure you keep up your work on my place.'

"I'll do more than ever, Sir," Sammy said. "I appreciate the opportunity, sir."

'Daddy done pretty well with the sharecropping while Granddaddy stayed on working for Mr. Van for regular pay.

'Grandaddy would help Daddy in the fields in the evenings and, with no children at home to care for, Granny joined them when they needed her. Granddaddy did repairs when the heat was too much for him to work in the fields and Granny kept the house, cooked meals, picked cotton in the fall and took in ironing for Mrs. Van. They was doing okay, for ex-slaves—freed men of color, was what they called 'em after the war.

'It was about to be the turn of the century,' Catfish said.

*

Marianne came out of the back door of her house next door and stood on her porch. She had a bird in her hand with gauze wrapped around its leg. That was how she was, always taking care of injured animals and insects.

"What are you doing here, stranger?" she called.

"Oh, just came to see my best friends. What happened to the bird?"

"I think he got grabbed by the cat, or fell out of his nest. He'll be fine in a few days," she said. She started down the steps of her little house and I stood next to Catfish.

"You girls go on now and leave an old man to his peace," Catfish said as he slouched in his rocker, stretched his legs in front of him and tilted his straw hat forward over his eyes.

"But you didn't tell the whole story, Catfish," I said. "You were just getting started."

"Then you'll have to come back, Missy, if you want to hear the rest." He chuckled, pulled his straw hat down lower and pretended to sleep. I kissed him on the cheek, squeezed his shoulder and stared at him. In my heart I willed him to be my granddaddy.

I met Marianne at the bottom of the steps and we walked, slowly, towards the barn, both caught up in our own thoughts, not knowing how to turn them into words. She stroked the bird's wing with her thumb and cooed in its ear.

The old wooden structure that had lived through one too many storms was hidden behind a line of pecan trees, about a hundred yards from the back porches of the cabins. It had a red façade that was peeling and had faded to a pale pink. The wide doors that once slid on wheels across a long piece of iron mounted above the opening were no longer there. As we approached the building from the side I could see one of the old doors leaning against the outer wall, the other had been taken apart to make a fence around Catfish's garden to keep the rabbits and coons out. The two square openings for windows on the side of the structure never had seen glass or screens—they were there to create a cross draft through identical window openings on the opposite wall. Above where the doors once hung was another window, and one on the back side in the same position for air circulation in the hay loft.

We tried to make small talk, until we reached the barn and slid down its side to sit, thighs touching, in the thick St Augustine grass under the familiar canopy of the huge pecan tree that seemed to have grown another ten feet. I reached for Marianne's hand, but she pulled it away.

"Are you mad at me?" I asked.

"No. I'm not mad. I don't want to touch you then remember what it felt like when you're gone."

"It's September. I'm not leaving until June. Lighten up." She didn't respond. We sat in our thoughts while flies buzzed around and a bluebird landed in the live oak a few feet away. I knew she was thinking that she would be stuck in Jean Ville, in the quarters, while Rodney and I would both be off at school.

I broke the silence.

"Have you seen Rodney lately?"

"He was here Monday."

"Oh, yeah? How is he?"

"He's okay—at least, for now."

"I'm worried. Did he tell you we ran into each other at the Cow Palace Saturday night?"

"He told me."

"Is he in trouble?"

"I'm not sure. The day he came here it was still too early to know. His dad had a talk with him, but he didn't get a beating or punished, if that's what you want to know."

I didn't respond. I nursed my memories, my secrets. I watched a bumble bee buzz from one azalea bloom to the next and could hear a far-off tractor engine growl through the fields. The heat and humidity made my T-shirt stick to me and I lifted the bottom of it and bent my neck to wipe the sweat off my forehead. Then I used it as a fan, pulling it away from my chest, then in, trying to trap some of the air inside. Marianne was twirling a long, brown tendril near her forehead, lost in thought.

"I think Rodney is in love with you," Marianne finally said.

"Did he tell you that?"

"Not in so many words. But he's taking chances. I'm not sure you understand how serious this is."

"But Mari, we haven't been together except that one time, more than two years ago. I don't understand."

Marianne didn't say that Rodney was willing to take stupid chances just to see me. That he was so love-sick he wasn't thinking straight and could get himself lynched. But she insinuated as much.

"It's just that, I'm not sure Rodney sees it like you see it," Marianne said.

"What do you mean?"

"He thinks that, if you love him, he can figure out a way. He's just not sure how you feel." I grabbed Marianne's hand and turned to look at her, full-face.

"You have to tell him, Marianne. You have to tell him to give it up. Tell him I don't love him. Tell him there's someone else. I don't want to see him get hurt, or worse."

"You need to tell him yourself. That's not a message I can deliver for you."

"How can I tell him? I can't see him, EVER!"

"Are you afraid your daddy will beat you to death? Is that why you avoid him?" I had never told Marianne, or anyone, that daddy beat me. She knew things were bad at home and I wasn't sure how much Tootsie told her, but I avoided that subject with her.

The air hung stagnant between us. It was a thick silence, like a veil no one wanted to lift.

"I'm not afraid for *me*. I'm afraid for *him*," I said. Marianne didn't respond. She looked at me, deeply, as if she could see into the places I hid from the world. I felt raw and vulnerable, but Marianne acted as if I was hiding something, something deep and important.

"So, you do love him?"

"I can't love him; don't you understand?"

"But do you love him?"

"No, Marianne. I don't love him! And you need to tell him that. Tell them there's someone else."

"I'm not sure I believe you; but if you *do* love him and if he loves you, do you believe there can be a way?"

"Oh, you are a hopeless romantic. Things don't happen like that in real life, at least, not in my real life."

"How do you know? Times are changing. Who knows what the laws will be like in a few years? You shouldn't give up hope."

"The laws could change tomorrow but that wouldn't change who I am and who he is and where we live. Meanwhile I have to concentrate on getting through high school so I can go to LSU and get out of my house. I just have to." I didn't realize I said those last four words. They hung in the air like a secret let out of the bag.

Marianne squeezed my hand, but there were no words that could erase the weight I carried.

I walked back home without hiding along the tree line. I didn't care.

I thought about my conversation with Marianne for days, how she said things were changing and that if we loved each other ... I rewound it in my mind and felt it in my heart. I wanted to grab that vision and hold onto it. Somehow I thought that, if I could do that, things might work out with Rodney. I knew I needed to see him, to make sure he was all right.

Late Saturday afternoon I went to the grocery store for Mama and drove to the Esso station to fill the car with gas. When Rodney saw me he came to the car window. I turned towards him. He leaned his arm on the top of my window and put his forehead on it. He was so close to my face I could smell the cola on his breath and the sweat that soaked his stretched out T-shirt. Gasoline fumes rose from the pavement like steam after a mid-summer rain and the odor was mixed with oil and dirt that somehow had a calming effect on me. I inhaled deeply. I wanted to swallow the smell of him and keep it inside.

"Hi, Beautiful," he said. He acted like nothing was wrong.

"Rodney, we need to talk."

"That's what I've been saying to you for two years."

"No, I mean, after what happened last week at the Cow Palace."

"Oh... that."

"Look, I can't stay. Can you come to the Quarters next Wednesday about four?"

"I'll see what I can do. I have football practice and work."

"I'm sorry, that's the only time I can be there," I said.

"Susie, I want to be with you more than anything, I'm just not sure I can be there Wednesday."

"I understand."

"I'll try. No promises."

∽ Chapter Nine ∽

∽

The Unthinkable
1966

RODNEY SAID IT was dark when he heard the roar of engines and felt the earth shake under his bed. He thought he heard an eagle screech just before smoke filled his room and he realized a dozen hooded militants circled his family home above Bayou Barré on Marshall Drive.

He opened the window.

He said that flames, hot and wet and dancing in the air almost knocked him over. In that instant he noticed the moon drop behind sinking clouds, just before smoke enveloped his room with scalding heat. He reached behind him, yanked Jeffrey from his bed and jumped through the shattered window with his brother hanging around his burning neck. They rolled in the fresh cut, late-summer grass, hot from the day's heat while flames leaped after them.

He said he hollered as they rolled down the hill.

"Mama!" He felt like his breath dropped into a deep well of flames. While he grabbed at his singed, smelly hair, his other arm gripped Jeffrey and they tumbled, one eight-limbed body, down the steep ravine and fell into the chilly waters of the bayou. The shock of the cool, muddy lagoon brought Rodney back to reality, and he looked up the punishing steep bank at the horror that devoured his family's home.

He propped Jeffrey against a leafless black trunk and scrambled up the chewed-up mine field of sparks and burning debris, galloping on all fours, his pajamas shredded to ribbons, soaking wet, pushing with his feet, bare and bloody, to find the rest of his family.

Rodney said he heard angry machines that competed with chafed cries and vulgar chants, an unholy verse filtered through the smoke-filled air as if from the heavens, unseen but loud in his ear.

His throat was parched but he screamed for his dad, his sisters, his mother. He didn't have to search further than the stately live oak his dad told him had been on the property since Rodney's great grandfather escaped a Georgia plantation and settled near the Indian reservation north of Jean Ville. He saw his dad swinging like a cochon de lait, skin crackling in front of a bonfire. This time Rodney's screams found voice among the howling timber fells, truck engine roars, and the requiem chants of the white-sheeted cowards who hoisted his dad into the arms of the beloved oak.

"Stop! Let him down! You can't do that to my dad!" Although he could hear himself, the creatures tying a rope around his dad's swollen neck didn't seem to notice. He scratched and clawed and climbed on one of the ghosts, but it was as if Rodney wasn't there, at all.

He felt himself fly backwards and crack hard against the earth. Black, red and yellow film covered his brain and when he finally peeked through the darkness of subconsciousness, he was flat on his back, head throbbing, the ground an earthquake beneath him as he lay in a pool of his own fresh, warm blood. He watched four or five pickup trucks speed away and smelled gasoline and burning hair. While Jeffrey's guttural sobs echoed from the deep trench, he heard his mother scream and his sisters cry.

"Get up, get up, get up," the voices said. Rodney rolled onto his stomach and rose to his knees. He felt someone pull at what was left of his scorched hair and he raised his head to the sky filled with tongues of yellow, orange and brown flashes, that disappeared only to be replaced by more of the same.

Fourth of July fireworks in his own yard.

"Help him, Rod, help him!" They screamed. It sounded like they were in a tunnel.

Rodney said he saw his dad, hanging, like a butchered hog as if roasting for a feast. Rodney got to his swaying feet and stretched his six-foot-three frame as tall and stately as the tree, his arms like branches reaching for Spanish moss. His palms touched the bottoms of his dad's hot bare feet. On tiptoe, he pushed with all his might against his dad's pink soles and heard a small breath, a whisper that broke through the waning sounds of the eagle and the moon and the clouds and the tongues and the minefields and the dead, dying house.

"Dad," Rodney hollered. "Stand on my hands and push." His dad stiffened his legs and pressed against Rodney's flattened palms, held high above his head as if praising the heavens where smoke and flames and cries ascended in dream-like fashion.

He said someone held a hose on the fire under the tree and it smoldered, sending thick, wet smoke up Rodney's nose. He coughed and gagged, but he never turned loose of his dad's feet, pushing them higher and higher, giving his dad a platform on which to stand to relieve the tension of the rope.

"Call Bo!" Rodney screamed, but his voice was barely audible and his throat burned with the effort.

By the time his uncle Bo arrived, Rodney's arms were jelly and his toes numb and fiery. Bo backed his pickup under the hanging tree and grabbed Ray's legs while Bo's brother-in-law, Sam, climbed the tree and slashed the rope. Rodney said he watched as, in slow motion, the two strong men lay his dad in the bed of the truck, Ray's head in Bo's lap while Sam got behind the wheel and started out of the yard. Rodney jumped in the back of the pickup just before it took off and crawled next to his dad. He wanted to say something to his dad but his voice would not cooperate; instead, he lay his cauterized, bristled head, hair singed and smelly, on his dad's chest and listened for a sound, any sound—or a rise and fall, any rise and fall—or a sniffle, any ... sniffle.

It was all his fault. He knew it. His dad would know it, too, if he ever woke up to his parched lungs and blistered, raw neck. Rodney touched the imprint of hemp with gentle fingers and his hand filled with blood and pus and fear and horror and castigation.

Mea Culpa, he thought. Mea Maxima Culpa—and I can almost see him in my mind as he struck his chest over and over and over.

*

As usual, no one spoke at the dinner table but Mama and Daddy.

After Daddy led us in the Catholic blessing and began to pass the bowls of food around the table, he told Mama about the Klan burning the Thibault's home. He said the house was in bad shape—that they'd have to tear it down and rebuild.

"The worse of it is Ray. He's in the hospital," Daddy said. "They almost killed him. He has rope burns around his neck and he was beaten half to death. He looks terrible."

"You went to see him in the colored ward at the hospital?"

"Yes, and his wife told me the only reason he's still alive is because Rodney, his seventeen-year-old boy, stood on tiptoes so Ray could stand on the boy's hands. That's what kept him from hanging and choking to death."

I gasped on a mouthful of rice and grabbed my milk, greedily. I began to cough and choke.

Mama started to rant and rave about how the Klan would come back and burn another cross in our yard, and that Daddy didn't need to be associating with *those* people. Daddy ignored the chastisement and continued to explain how Ray Thibault's eyes were swollen shut and he had some broken bones and was on some sort of machine to help him get oxygen in his lungs.

"Why did they pick him?" Mama asked.

"Someone told me his boy touched a white girl at the Cow Palace one night."

My fork stopped in mid-air and shook so hard the rice fell back into my plate. I put it down with a "clink."

"I'll bet that white girl's daddy set up that lynching. You would do it, too, if it was Susie," Mama said. I held my hands in my lap so no one could see them tremble. I felt like my heart would burst open. I couldn't breathe.

"I'm sure if one of Ray's boys touched a white girl, it was innocent, or there was a reason." I stared at the food in my plate. Everything seemed to run together and become psychedelic. I felt dizzy, sick at my stomach.

"You always take up for those people." Mama sounded angry, frustrated.

My ears seemed to fill with something foamy, like dishwater that gurgled around in my head. My chest felt like I had swallowed concrete. I tried to get the rice and beans already in my mouth to slide down, but I coughed and gasped and felt the oxygen leave my body. Will reached over and slapped my back a few times and Mama yelled at me to drink some milk. In the end, Daddy sent me to my room because I caused a disturbance. It was the first time I was grateful to be sent from the table.

My heart hurt. The pain was so acute I thought my chest would crack open. I actually wished it would. Maybe if it burst, the pressure I felt inside would ease. I started to cry and couldn't stop. I cried for Rodney and for his family, and for all the colored people in the world who were oppressed, intimidated and hated because of the color of their skin. I cried for people who were not allowed to dream, to become, to achieve or to love freely. And I cried for all the people who were unloved or who could not love and be loved because of their race.

I felt like I could handle anything. I'd already survived so much I was numb to it. But Rodney! He was so protected and loved. I tried to understand what it must be like to be Marianne or Rodney. To be colored in this whitewashed world. As hard as I tried, I couldn't feel what they felt, but I wanted to be in their families anyway. When I said that to Marianne, she got angry and told me I didn't know what I was saying, that no one wanted to be colored. No One!

Maybe not—but no one wanted to be me, either—at least no one would want to be me if they knew.

⌒ Chapter Ten ⌒

⌒

Breathe
1967

THE NIGHT I almost died is like a permanent stamp on my soul. It was midnight when a brightness like searchlights suddenly blazed from the ceiling, waking me out of a deep sleep. I thought a train clamored through my room, surrounding my bed and causing Sissy to jump up yelling, as deep-throated screams bellowed in my first waking. I heard an owl hoot incessantly and the whirl of a helicopter batter against the ceiling as the burly figure of my dad appeared waving a lasso over his head, running as if chasing a herd of cattle. A shooting star whizzed by and I stood on the edge of a deep jungle with lions and bears and huge snakes creating a cacophony of jungle music with their hisses and barks and grunts.

I sat up and rubbed my eyes just as a tractor with a crane on top grabbed me and hoisted me into the sky where I dangled over the tops of trees, under which were predators waiting to eat me alive. The crane released me and I flew from my bed like a ragdoll, my face hitting a sharp object on my way to the ground where I smelled mushrooms and mud mixed with feces and blood so fresh the animals of the jungle gathered around, sniffing and prodding.

"Get up and look at me!" Through the window a silent moon sent rays of light through the camellia bush and a glow surrounded me and created an aura that seemed to temporarily protect me from the predators.

"I said, Get Up!" I heard the voice that sounded like a chorus of male screeches coming through a tube that flared out, so that the sound was loud and piercing when it reached my ears.

"I work so hard to provide for this family and this is the thanks I get?" The words were like bullets from a machine gun, shooting all around me, some landing, some whizzing by my ears. The screams were in rhythm with the hard soles of dress shoes that felt like a sledgehammer boring into my ribs.

"You've ruined me now. And with a Negro. How dare you. In public."

I rolled onto my stomach and a heavy object, like a concrete block, slammed down on my back and a dragon spewed hot breath from my mouth shooting warm red liquid across the blue expanse like a blazing flame on the ocean's surface. I swam in the salty waters and grabbed for the big fuzzy fist to save me when a huge wave knocked me over onto my back and I thought I might drown in the briny waters, turning redder by the moment.

A furry rope wrapped around my neck and lifted me up over the liquid and something sharp, like the blade of a surfboard's rudder, sliced across my cheek. Waves, salty and thick and rolling like barrels down a hill almost knocked me over again and I fought with the Loch Ness monster to keep from drowning.

I heard a deep throated croon yell fragmented words about God and fornication and disobedience and burning in hell and I waited for the flames to engulf me, but they couldn't reach below the ocean's surface as I sank to the sandy bottom and gasped for air.

Suddenly I floated above the ocean and watched my own body morph into a sea urchin, rounded and purple with pearls studding the outside in rows, that began to roll rapidly until it was scooped up by a huge shark. In the belly of the fish I heard Rodney humming the tune that replayed in my spirit over and over, "Don't worry baby, everything will turn out all right."

The spotlight went out, the helicopter flew off, the train roared on to some destination and the incessant hoot of the owl ceased. The only thing left was the smell of wisteria and camellias, the taste of honeysuckle on the tip of my tongue, as the tune hummed by Rodney sank deeper and deeper into my fading spirit. I basked in the moonshine that filtered through the flowers and opened my lips to taste its sweet, dewey drops, but they burned like fire on my tongue and my eyes smarted with millions of grains of sand.

The smell of dead birds and rotting eggs rose from Hades and filled my senses as visions of angels with tails flew above me.

*

The first time I tried to open my eyes, they felt glued shut. I knew I wasn't in my own room because I could smell the antiseptic air and I heard a far-off beeping. I tried to move, but pain shot through me like buckshot. I fell back into deep darkness.

The next time I tried to move I felt one of my hands enveloped inside two larger, hairy ones and realized Daddy was at my bedside, coddling me. I wanted to vomit.

"Oh, God!" I thought I screamed but no sound came out, only grunts. "It hurts."

"Shhh, Sweetheart," he said. His voice was gentle and concerned, as if he had nothing to do with my situation. "Just rest. Daddy's here." That's what I was afraid of. I didn't want him near me. I didn't want Mama there, either. I wanted Tootsie, Catfish. I wanted Marianne. I wanted Rodney!

I tried to sleep. It hurt too much to be awake. There was a scorching pain in my side and my right leg felt like it had nails driven into it. I couldn't move my mouth or open my eyes, and my nose was packed with something thick, so I could barely breath. It was days before I realized I had a tube in my nose to pump oxygen and nutrients into my body. And my head! It felt like there were men inside it with hammers and chisels trying to gouge their way out.

During one of my fairly lucid periods, I heard Dr. David's voice at the foot of my bed. He talked in short, staccato sentences. I could only pick up scattered words: "Broken ribs, broken leg, nose, concussion, internal injuries ...doesn't look good ... "

A nurse came in and pulled the sleeve up on my hospital gown. I felt a needle, but didn't wince. The room and voices faded and I drifted off into a drug-induced slumber.

The next time I tried to open my eyes, I felt someone hovering over me. A thumb or finger made a cross on my forehead with something oily that smelled like garlic and Latin words came from the clouds.

The first time I was able to open one of my eyes I saw Mama in a rocking chair at the end of the room, rubbing her swollen belly. Dr. David spoke in low tones. I heard him tell Mama she should call Daddy to bring my brothers and sister to see me.

"Anne, I know she didn't fall. What happened? You need to tell me. There will be an investigation if she doesn't make it. This could be serious." I couldn't hear Mama's answer, only a few words: "Girls ... school ... problems ... don't know ... found her."

The next time I was semi-conscious I heard James, Will and Robby talking softly. Daddy held Sissy, who was now five, over the bed. She tried to get in with me and was crying "Susie," but he held her back.

I retreated into the comfort and solitude of darkness and when I awoke the next time they were all still there, but they were very quiet, which was unusual for my three brothers and little sister. I could see them through a slit in my right eye. I moaned. Daddy rushed to the side of my bed and took my hand.

"Are you awake?"

"Hmmmm. Thirsty."

"I'll get you some water." He brought a straw to my lips and I sipped, little sips, at first, then I gulped. "Take it easy, Baby. No need to drown yourself. Just take small sips."

"Where's Mama?"

"She's right here." Mama came to the other side of the bed and put her hand on my shoulder.

"Feeling better?" she asked.

"No, I hurt everywhere."

"No M'am, Susanna Christine." Suddenly I hated them both. I was determined to get well, and get away. I knew that if he became angry with me again, he would kill me. I wouldn't let him win. I'd survive.

That was when I made the turnaround.

My few minutes of consciousness at a time turned to an hour a day and, then two as I fought hard to survive. One day one of my teachers arrived with books and assignments. She stayed to show me what to do to catch up. I tried to listen but my brain was foggy; however I was determined to learn, to keep up with school so I could graduate in May and leave.

I had to survive—that's what drove me to do things that, looking back, now seem superhuman.

I didn't ask how many days went by. I slept, took sips of liquids, listened to people talk or read or ask questions and tried to make words. At some point I began to read and write on my own, which took every ounce of courage I could muster.

I was afraid to go home, even though Daddy and Mama were acting like I was a precious child they wanted to protect. I knew the volcano could erupt again, anytime. I tried to fake pain and other symptoms when Dr. David came to see me each morning so he wouldn't discharge me, but, eventually he caught on.

"Susie, I know you don't want to go home, but you can't stay here forever." I started to cry. Big, fat tears that ran down the sides of my cheeks onto my pillow. Dr. David's big, hairy thumb wiped some of the drops from my face and, when he spoke, he reminded me of Catfish.

"I can arrange for you to stay with someone else, your aunt in Houston, your grandmother in Baton Rouge. You can stay with me and Erma if you like." I couldn't stop crying. "Tell me what happened, honey." He was so gentle and kind and I wanted to tell him, I wanted my parents in jail, I wanted to punish everyone for everything, but I knew, in my heart, it was all my fault.

What made me think I could love a colored boy and not poison everyone's life?

"Accident," I whispered.

"If that's the truth, I have to send you home. I'll give you another day or so to think about it." He patted me on the shoulder and left. The next morning he sat on the edge of my bed.

"You can tell me anything and it won't shock me."

"Can you keep a secret?" I whispered it, afraid to confide in him, in anyone.

"It won't leave this room. Maybe it's bad, even hopeless, but you can't keep it inside."

"It's all my fault." I couldn't hold back the tears.

"What's your fault?" I started sobbing.

"Everything. Mr. Thibault. Their home. My accident. Everything. It's all my fault."

"How can all those things be the fault of a fifteen-year-old-girl."

"It just is. I'm a troublemaker."

"Okay. Let's say it's your fault. Let's take this thing apart." He looked at me with a deep understanding, his dark eyes and overly-large nose seemed to fit his gentle spirit. He smelled like a doctor—clorox, rubbing alcohol and mercurochrome—but he sounded like a priest. "How can Ray Thibault's attack be your fault?"

"Well. Uhm. There's this boy."

"Okay, now we're getting somewhere." He removed his hands from the side of my face, sat back and took my right hand between his two thick fists. "You are a little young for a boyfriend, but I can remember thinking I was in love when I was a teenager."

"It's not about *being* in love it's about *who* I love."

"Don't tell me you're in love with a Jew?" He started to laugh at his own joke, then he saw my expression and stopped. "Oh, no, Susie, it's not a ..."

"Yes."

"Not Ray Thibault's son?"

"Yes, Sir."

"What have the two of you done?"

"Nothing. Really. I met him a couple years ago, but other than brief conversations at his dad's gas station, nothing. It's just that ..."

"Just that, what?"

"The other night I went to the Cow Palace with Daddy and my brothers and I ran into Rodney in the lobby."

"Okay, benign enough."

"He touched me. Put his hands on my shoulders."

"And someone saw?"

"Lots of people saw." He slid off my bed and began to pace back and forth in the room. His head was down and he had his left hand on his forehead, moving his thumb and fingers close together, then spreading them apart as if he tried to bring his wrinkles to the center of his forehead, then smooth them out again. He stopped at the foot of my bed and looked at me.

"Is Rodney in trouble with the Klan, too?"

"I'm not sure. I'm worried sick."

"Then I guess you need to see him, to talk to him." I just stared at Dr. David and I knew he saw the pleading in my eyes.

*

"We're wasting time, Susie," Rodney said. He walked to the side of my hospital bed and sat near me, his butt touching my side—I could feel the warmth of him through the sheet and blanket. He stroked the cast on my left arm that was bent at the elbow, the tips of my fingers sticking out of the end. He took my right hand in his. I inhaled his crisp shower scent and aftershave and realized it was the first time I'd smelled his body clean and fresh. He must have showered after work, I thought. I missed the gasoline, sweat-filled pores that seeped his masculinity into my world but I savored something consistent about him—his mansuetude, a gentleness I couldn't describe but could feel, almost as if it was velvet in my hands, my fingers rubbing the smooth softness.

With the back of his other hand, he gently stroked the length of the side of my face. He turned his hand over and cupped my face with his palm. I lifted my casted arm parallel with my shoulder and, with the tips of my fingers that stuck out of the plaster, I rubbed the back of his hand that lay on my cheek. I closed my eyes and started to cry.

He stroked my hair and tried to sooth me while tears ran down my face, unchecked, my chest heaving every now and then. I guess I felt the same way he had felt when he sobbed in his dad's arms the night of the wrestling match—frustrated, angry at injustice, confused about feelings. My tears flowed from opened eyes, and nothing could hold them back.

"You think it's all your fault, don't you?" I didn't answer. Finally I turned towards him.

"Tell me about your family," I whispered. "Is everyone okay? You dad?"

"Dad will be okay, eventually." He said it slowly, still staring at me. "It's not your fault, Susie. No one blames you." I turned away.

"I'm glad you're okay, that your dad, your family ... I've been worried ..."

He left the bed and walked to the window, a few feet away. When he did, my fingertips fell against my cheek, where his hand had been and touched the warm spot he'd left like a stamp on my face. The blinds were shut but he stared through them as if he could see the moon cast its light on the paved parking lot outside the hospital room.

"The gang who burned our house and tried to hang Daddy were not the Jean Ville Klan. They were people who follow wrestling." He didn't turn to look at me but I could hear every word.

"Oh, is that good or bad?"

"When the local Klan found out who did it, they were angry because they were blamed, and because they were not asked to participate. The way I understand it, the sheriff thinks he should be consulted about all Klan activity."

I was quiet. I just wanted to hear his voice. To be near him.

"Susie." He continued to stare out the closed blinds. He talked softly but I heard every word. "I love you. For more than two years I've told myself it's hopeless, but it doesn't change anything. I can't turn it off like a faucet." I didn't say anything. He turned around and faced me. "Look at me. Tell me you don't love me and I'll go away and try to forget you."

"I don't love you," I whispered. He came to the side of my bed, bent forward and rested his forehead on mine. Our eyelashes bruised each other's.

"I don't believe you. I know you love me. I can see it. I feel it."

"I don't love you, Rodney." I said. "This has to stop." I started to cry, hard. His lips found mine and he kissed me softly. Then he reached both arms around my back and pulled me to him. I didn't respond and let my arms hang by my side. I didn't want to touch him. Too dangerous.

He took my right arm and wrapped it around his neck, then gently placed my casted arm around his back. He pulled me close and I sobbed into his shoulder so hard my body shook.

"It doesn't matter whether you tell me you love me," he whispered. He lifted his head and I saw the tears pooled in his eyes. "I still love you. That won't change. You can love someone else, you can even marry someone else someday, but I won't stop." I wanted him to hold me and force me to tell him the truth, but I couldn't say the words. Too risky.

I tried to look at him through eyes at half-mast under wet, clumped eyelashes.

"I told my dad about us," he said. He had a half-smirk on his face and, at first, I thought he was joking.

"You, what?" My eyes flew open. It was like a knee-jerk reaction. He smiled and looked like he was holding back laughter.

"He saw us at the Cow Palace," Rodney said. "He asked. I couldn't lie."

"What did you tell him?"

"That I'm in love with you." He was still holding me and I could taste his words, almost swallow them, his lips were so close. I could see in his eyes that he knew how I felt, but I couldn't say it. I pictured a noose around his neck, gasped and looked away.

"Oh, God. What did he say," I asked.

"At first he was upset, taken aback, especially because of his relationship with your dad. But as time goes on, we talk about it more and he's learned to accept it."

"Even after what happened to him?"

"Well, we've had long conversations since then. He knows I'm here tonight, but I had to promise not to talk to you or contact you again in Jean Ville." He pulled his arms from around me and held my head in his hands, his lips so close I could taste his words. "But we, you and I, we won't be in this town forever, you know." I let those words float in the tight space between our faces.

"If my daddy finds out, it will ruin their friendship." I said.

"Right now my dad only tolerates your dad—because of what he did to you." He looked away and I knew he realized he shouldn't have admitted he knew what happened to me.

"What do you know? What does your dad know?" It frightened me that anyone might know.

"I told him."

"Marianne told you, huh? Tootsie told Marianne?" I needed the truth. "Rodney, there's something you aren't telling me." He looked unsure, like he was afraid of something. Protecting me? Shielding me? I wasn't a weakling, he should know that.

"What?" I demanded. "Tell me."

"They thought ... Um, well ... They thought you weren't going to make it." He said it slowly, as if to lessen the blow.

"Huh?"

"The priest gave you the last sacraments." I must have looked as shocked as I felt because he seemed worried.

"When? Uh. Uhm. How long have I been in here?"

"Close to a month, now."

"A month? My dad said I've been here a little over a week."

"Twenty-nine days, and counting," he said. He was sitting on the bed holding my hands. Within seconds my sadness turned to anger. I know he saw fire in my eyes. I was ready to fight my way out of the hospital and out of Jean Ville.

He took me in his arms and hugged me, gently but firmly. It felt so good to be loved that I melted into him and put my arms, even my casted one, around his waist and held him, as if by holding onto him I would survive—a life raft. He didn't pull away. Both of us were crying softly, both feeling like we were finally where we were meant to be.

Once he was sure I was okay, he kissed me. It was gentle, at first, then more urgent. I kissed him back. Our teeth hit and he pulled back and grinned at me.

"Don't open your mouth so wide," he said. "Just part your lips a bit."

"I've never kissed anyone on the lips before," I whispered.

"I know. It's okay. I'll show you." He pressed his parted lips against mine and with the tip of his tongue he licked the outside of mine. It felt good. I closed my eyes. Our mouths formed a suction and he turned his head sideways just a tad. I tried to match the gentle movement of his mouth against mine. He was a patient, gentle teacher. We shared a long kiss that felt like a perfect joining of two lost souls seeking solace and finding it in each other. His breath tasted like peppermint and chocolate and I could feel the warmth of his body against mine. I wondered if he could hear my heart pounding like I could hear his.

The kiss ended and we held each other, for a long time. Then I heard a noise outside the door and pulled away. He kissed me again, deeply, then looked at me, his face so close our noses touched. And he smiled.

"I love you Susie Burton." I could still feel his mouth on mine.

"You have to go, Rod," I whispered.

"Okay, I'll go," he said. "But know this—you don't have to tell me you love me, I know. And nothing will change how I feel about you. You'll come to your senses and I'll be here, waiting for you."

He kissed me again, on the lips, then on the forehead and he gently put my hands back over my stomach. When he reached the door to the hall he turned back towards me.

"I have a plan for us," he said. "When you realize it's not your job to protect me and my family, let me know and I'll share it with you."

He stood at the door a few seconds and waited for me to say something. I didn't. I couldn't.

I was discharged a few days later and Daddy took me with him to San Francisco on a business trip the next month. We stayed at Embarkadero Wharf where we watched the ships come into the port and could actually see Sausalito across the Bay. While Daddy was in meetings I rode the cable cars to the Ghirardelli chocolate factory, Fisherman's Wharf and Chinatown. Daddy took me to Union Square and bought me several new outfits. He insisted, and told me I looked beautiful in everything I tried on. I was almost sixteen and had developed breasts, which I was a little embarrassed about around him.

We talked about his political aspirations and he said he counted on the Negro vote to help him win when he ran for Mayor of Jean Ville the following year. I thought about how terrible it would be for him if anyone found out about my relationship with Rodney. It would probably destroy his political chances. I silently thanked God that I'd be off at college by then.

Part Four: 1968

~ Chapter Eleven ~

Graduation
1968

I TOOK A HUGE chance on graduation night at Adams High School. With Marianne's help, I disguised myself in one of Tootsie's dresses with a head scarf wrapped around my red hair. Marianne sneaked me into the gym through the girls' locker room and I stood in the little hallway just off the gym floor and watched Rodney march down the aisle with his class, two gold ropes with tassels hanging from his neck. He was so handsome. I stayed long enough to hear him give the salutatory speech and to receive the Christian athlete award, then I crept out into the dark night and made my way through the trees and shrubs to Mama's station wagon parked near the projects, about a block behind the school.

Marianne told me about the rest of the evening. She said that every time Rodney sat down, his name was called to receive another award—Math Award, Athlete of the Year Award, Literary Award. She said that he told her at the party afterwards that the only thing missing was me.

If I wasn't sure of it before, I was sure after that night what a special person Rodney Thibault was, and it made me love him more than anything. For that reason I had to get away, away from any temptation to see him. I couldn't love him, I had to forget him.

Rodney had other thoughts that I wasn't aware of until months later. He said that, in his mind, I was there at his graduation. In fact, he said he thought he saw me slip out of the gym after his speech. I didn't admit to anything.

As for my own last year of high school, it flew by. At the beginning of May Mama took me to Alexandria to buy new clothes for graduation parties and to take to college. We rode the train from Mansura and had lunch at the Bentley Hotel. She told me about her first year at LSU and how frightened she was at my age, sixteen.

"At least you have a family to come home to on weekends," she said. "I stayed on campus. It was either that or go back to the home in New Orleans." She told me about how difficult it was to live in a girls' home, and that she spent most of her time alone, reading and writing poetry.

I understood her loneliness and why she had retreated to books, and I guess I had a better grip on why she married a control freak like Daddy, who screamed at her, too. When I was eleven I heard her yell. I ran into the kitchen to find him holding her against the wall by the throat, a butcher knife in his free hand. I remember asking her later why she stayed with him and she said, "Where will I go? I have five children and no family."

I knew what it felt like to be trapped and I suffered for Mama. It was funny how, when she was away from home and it was just the two of us, she seemed so different, almost loving and motherly.

When we got home and Daddy found out how much money she spent on me, all hell broke loose. I thought we'd have to return all my new clothes, but Mama stood her ground, and after a couple days things settled down, although I don't know what type of insanity Mama suffered from Daddy's anger.

Graduation plans sort of took over. We didn't have a big celebration—just a few of my parents' friends and our family. My grandmother came from Shreveport and James came home from college with a girlfriend, who stayed in my room with me. Sissy slept with Mama and Daddy. The adults got drunk and we teenagers swam in the pool and ate grilled burgers that James had to rescue when Daddy forgot about them.

The Banner, Jean Ville's only newspaper, covered both graduations, Jean Ville and Adams High. My high school's story was on the front page, with pictures of all the graduates. I didn't receive a lot of awards or recognition since, technically, I didn't have a senior year, but my grade point average was in the top five and I garnered a number of certificates of achievement.

Rodney's name was mentioned as receiving the most awards at Adams High School graduation, but there was no mention of what they were in the one paragraph on page six, at the bottom. Whether anyone in Jean Ville knew how special he was didn't matter to me. I was so proud of him.

Rodney said that the summer following graduation passed by slowly for him. It was hot and humid as he pumped gas, cleaned windshields, made small-talk with the customers and swept the concrete in the evenings. He told me that he dreamed of Southern University, of sitting under huge live oaks with a breeze on his skin while he read Chaucer, Twain, Joyce, Fitzgerald, and Faulkner. Mrs. Jones told him that the library at Southern University held all of the classics and that students could borrow them, at no charge. It seemed like a dream, one Rodney was excited about, and that was one of the things that got him through that hot, humid summer.

It was mid-August when we finally saw each other again. I drove up to the gas pumps in the new 1967 white Camaro Daddy had bought for Will and me. Rodney hadn't seen the new Chevrolet model until now, so he was busy admiring the car, not concentrating on who was behind the wheel. When he reached my window to ask what I needed and realized it was me, he couldn't speak. He just stared at me as if I was a mirage. I laughed. It had been almost a year since that night in the hospital.

I was older, more mature, more confident. He did a double take.

"Hi, Rodney," I said. I tried to sound nonchalant but my voice came out a whisper and seemed to float in the air. I wasn't sure he heard me.

"Susie?" He stuttered. His eyes blinked several times as if to focus. He said he was afraid the image would disappear and leave him with that familiar feeling of waking from a dream.

"Remember me?" I laughed.

He stood riveted to the concrete, with his lips parted.

"Hello? Anybody there?" I laughed again. The sunlight hit the green flecks in his eyes and created prisms of color that danced in front of his face. It was like seeing a triple rainbow, so close I could almost touch it.

"Hello, yourself," he stammered. "How have you been? I haven't seen you all summer."

"I've been in Baton Rouge—went to summer school at LSU."

"Oh. No one told me." He thought for a moment. "Uh," he stammered. "How are you?" He looked at me so intently I thought he might see right through me.

"I'm fine. And you?"

"Good. Good. Glad to be done with high school."

"Yeah." I said. I smiled at him.

"How'd you do? "

"In high school?

"Yeah." I figured he'd read the newspaper and knew I received some commendations. The one I was most proud of was the volunteer award—for literacy work with underprivileged children, most of them colored. Of course the textbook program was a secret. No one knew how that happened.

"I did fine. Ancient history. I'm really glad to be done."

"I know, I read about you. Congratulations," he said.

"I read about you, too. I'm really proud of you. I'll bet you dad is, too."

"Hmmm." We just stared at each other for a minute, neither of us knowing what to say next.

"Did you like it?"

"LSU?" I asked.

"Yeah. Baton Rouge. Being away from here?"

"It's a big school, but it wasn't too intimidating this summer. I understand that when all 30,000 students show up in the fall, it will be a zoo. But anywhere is better than here."

"Yeah." He just stood there. He seemed content to look at me. Neither of us talked or moved. We just stared. Who would blink first?

"Hey, Rod!" His dad called. "You going to fill up Miss Burton's car or you going to stand there?" There was a sharpness in his voice.

"Oh, yeah." he said under his breath. He looked at me and could probably tell I wanted to laugh. He grinned. "Do you want me to fill it?"

"Sure," I said. He pumped the gas and stared at me through the side mirror. I stared back. Our connection was so strong that he forgot about the fuel until it bubbled out of the tank and onto the pavement. He jumped back and took his hand off the trigger. I laughed. He looked around to see if anyone else saw. His dad and brother were sneering at him near the car of another customer. They didn't look happy.

Rodney put the pump back and grabbed the windshield cleaner and squeegee. First he cleaned up the gas spill off the car then he came around to wash my front windshield. He asked about the car. I told him that it was Chevrolet's newest model called Camaro, and that Daddy bought it during my senior year for me and Will.

"Will gets to keep it when I'm at LSU. He still has three years of high school and Daddy says he needs it more than I do."

"That's not fair," Rodney said.

"Nothing in my life is fair," I said and laughed. He looked at me with concern and I realized he probably thought I meant that there had been more violence. He didn't ask. Maybe he didn't want to know.

"When do you go back to Baton Rouge?" he asked.

"In two weeks. I have orientation before the fall semester begins. What about you?"

"Less than three weeks."

"Excited?"

"Yes. But I hate to leave my family. Dad really needs me, and I offered to stay, but he insisted I go. I'm going to miss them." When he said that it reminded me that I didn't have a loving family. I was jealous and it was a sore spot for me. "Are you okay?"

"Sure," I said.

"I mean, really, Susie. Are you really okay?"

"I just have to survive two weeks."

"Can we talk sometime?"

"I'm not sure, Rod," I said. I looked off, through the front windshield, at the sky and beyond. I was trying to decide whether to go through with my plan.

"Okay. Whatever you want," he said. He looked sad and defeated as he stood with the wet rag and sprayer in one hand and put his other arm above my window. He leaned his forehead on his forearm. I could smell him, the familiar oozing of all the scents I loved drifting through the car window. He was only a few inches from me. I had to look up to see his face. I wondered whether he knew the effect he had on me.

"It's not what I want, Rod. It's what has to be." I whispered and I knew I wasn't very convincing.

"Please, Susie, let's not go there again. Laws are changing. Do you read current events?"

"Yes, I know about integration and anti-miscegenation, but this is still Louisiana. Things change slowly here."

"How will I know where you are, at LSU?"

"I have an address." I reached in my pocket and removed a small, folded piece of paper I had prepared in case I had the nerve to give it to him. It fit in the palm of my hand and I passed it to Rodney by extending my hand to shake his. I wanted things to look platonic, like we were just friends. I didn't want his dad to worry. Rodney took the note and after he released my hand, put it in his back pocket. I drove off.

I watched through the reariew mirror and saw Rodney stand still and stare at the license plate on the back of the new white Camaro until it disappeared in a vapor of gas and heat and moisture that radiated from the blacktop. Other cars, pedestrians and heat fumes swallowed him up the further away I got, but I watched through the review mirror as he continued to stare, his arms by his side.

That night Rodney said he sat at his desk with a tablet and pen and wrote:

August 19, 1967
Dear Susie.

I saw you today for the first time in almost nine months. You are more beautiful than ever and I'm more in love with you than ever. We can do this on your terms.

We can be friends and have coffee while we listen to beatniks recite poetry and play bongos.

I can pretend to be your servant from the plantation. I'll carry your bags and call you, "Miss Susie."

I'll be your student, you can tutor me, call me illiterate, unfortunate, pitiful.

I'll be the yardman at your dorm and you can tell me to cut certain flowers, to trim the hedges, to mow the lawn.

I'll walk your dog, feed your cat, change the water for your goldfish. I'll do or be whatever you'll let me; just let me—Be, that is. Be in your life. In any role that works for you.

This is my address at Southern University. I'll be there August 30th Please say there will be a letter waiting for me when I arrive.

I miss you.

He signed it, Yours, Forever, Rod. He told me later that he put it in an envelope and wrote my name and address at LSU on the front and his return address at Southern on the top, left corner, without his name. He walked out of the front door and headed to the post office, about two miles away, in the center of town. It was dark. He didn't notice his Dad and Mom on the front porch as he skipped down the steps.

"Where do you think you're going this time of night, Rod?"

"Oh, I'm going to the post office to mail a letter."

"Do you have a stamp on that letter?"

"No, Sir. I'll buy one at the post office."

"The post office won't be opened until eight in the morning. Are you planning on waiting outside the building until then?"

"Uh, no. I guess not."

He stood in the lane in front of their house and fingered the letter. He walked slowly up the steps, through the screened door and made his way up the stairs to his room. He slept with the letter under his pillow. It was in the mail at 8:01 the next morning.

~ Chapter Twelve ~

≈

College
1968

RODNEY SAID THAT Southern University in Baton Rouge seemed even larger than when he had visited with his parents the previous February. Nestled on Scott's Bluff overlooking the banks of the Mississippi River on the North side of Baton Rouge its buildings and fields are situated on 500 acres with pecan groves and oak-draped walking paths that ended at a wooden pier jettisoned out into the massive river, and areas of forested land a person could get lost in. The most beautiful part of the campus, to Rodney, was the John B Cade Library—154,000 square feet holding over a million volumes, nearly 2,000 journal subscriptions, 600,000 films and 1,800 recordings. On the third floor was the Camille Shade African American Heritage Collection where students could learn about their heritage and trace their ancestry back generations before slavery.

Rodney was in awe.

He said his dorm was hot, with a single fan in the window and four bunk beds, two on each wall plus one desk, one chest with four drawers and one small closet. Rodney edited the clothes and other items he'd brought and sent most of them home with his Mom and Dad. He said he and his three roommates worked out the logistics and he survived with three dress shirts, three pair of slacks, one navy

T-shirt, one pair of jeans and a sports coat. He kept sneakers and dress shoes, socks, white T-shirts and a few ties in his one drawer. There were washers and dryers in the basement. He said he'd make do.

The first evening at dorm orientation, the rector handed out mail. Rodney said he was one of the few called. I hadn't put my name on top in the return-address area, but he knew. He told me later that he fingered it as if the finest calligraphy rested in his hand. He confessed that he didn't hear much of what the rector said during the rest of the meeting. When the meeting adjourned he headed out the front door towards the library that was lit up across from the student union, looking for a place to be alone. He said he sat on a bench under a big live oak and opened the letter.

August 31, 1968
Dear Rod,
Thanks for writing. It was really great to have a letter waiting for me when I got here. As much as I needed and wanted to get away from my family I wasn't prepared for the loneliness. This summer there were fewer students and it was more of a family atmosphere. Now, not so much.

You won't believe this—I've met several girls in my dorm and they seem to like me. They actually want to be my friend. Amazing. I hope the same thing happens for Marianne if she gets to leave Jean Ville after she graduates next year. Some of us compared schedules and this girl, Becky, seemed elated to know we have the same English class. She said we can walk together. Other than Marianne, I've never had a girlfriend. This may take some getting used to.

So far I haven't noticed anyone with plantation servants, yardmen, illiterate students or pet-sitters. I'm not sure about having coffee with someone of another race, but I'm checking that out. What about on your campus? Have you seen any red-haired, blue-eyed white girls walking around?

I hope you have time to write to me.
Yours Truly,
Susie

Rodney told me that he read it again, folded it and put it in his pocket and that before morning, it was dog-eared, raveled on the edges and memorized. His reply was in the mail when the post office opened at 8:00 AM.

September 3, 1968
Dear Susie,
  Your letter! Yes, I got it. Thank you. You made my day, my week, my month, my year. I love you. More than ever. I will find a way to see you. I have to see you. We don't have to touch. Just talk to me. Tell me about your life. Help me to catch up on who you are, what you've done, where you've been.
  I know. I'm not making sense. I'll figure something out and let you know where to meet me. Give me a few days to get my bearings and talk to people.
  You know, they are attempting to integrate Jean Ville High School this year. Someone from the NAACP convinced my dad to send Jerry and my sisters to the white school. At the last minute Marianne decided to go, too. She and Jerry are both seniors and my sisters are in the seventh, ninth and tenth grades. Things are changing. I read where the US Supreme Court just passed a law that says anti-miscegenation laws are unconstitutional. Virginia cannot put the white man and Negro woman in jail or break them up. It's probably not easy for them, but they are together, legally!
  Please don't freak out. I'm not suggesting marriage, but the law says I can't go to jail for talking to you. I know what you'll say, "But this is Louisiana. We still have the Klan." Yes it's risky, but I can take care of myself, and you, too, by the way. I'll figure it out. Trust me.

I love you.
Forever, Yours,
Rod

September 5, 1968
Dear Marianne,
This campus is so big I haven't seen half of it, yet. My classes are all over the place and it takes at least thirty-minutes to walk from my dorm to the nearest classroom building. This past summer all my classes were in one building across from my dorm, so I didn't have to go far. Other than the student union and library, which were also close by, and church, I didn't see three-fourths of the Campus during the summer, so I'm trying to learn my way around now.

Tootsie said that you are at Jean Ville High School for your senior year. I hope you like it. Be aware that the white kids will be cruel and try to make you so miserable that you'll want to go back to Adams. I know you didn't have to leave friends at your old school, but it will still be lonely for you. I wish I was there to help. Only one year and you'll be in Baton Rouge, too, I hope.

You won't believe college—girls here actually like me and want to be my friend. And I don't have to pretend, or try to act like I think they want me to act. Some of them seem to fight for my attention. The same thing will happen to you when you get out of Jean Ville.

I heard from Rodney. I'm not sure whether I'll be able to see him, but at least we can write.

Please give my love to Catfish and your mom. I miss all three of you so much.

Write me.
Your best friend,
Susie

*

My first month at LSU flew by. I was overwhelmed by the size of the campus, almost ten times larger than the town of Jean Ville, in size and population. There was a lake on campus, with ducks and swans and blooming flowers that gave off a sweet fragrance, enticing students to spread quilts and blankets on the banks to picnic, study or nap under the canopy of pear, oak and pecan trees grouped in clusters around the water. Lily pads hinted of frogs and tadpoles that croaked at night and participated in a symphony with crickets and hoot owls and raccoons and foxes and other animals that guarded the entire campus. They made me think of Catfish and how much he'd love the sounds and smells.

I loved the hundreds of moss-draped live oaks that lined every sidewalk, pathway and street on the campus. In the center of all that beauty stood the Bell Tower, in a huge grassy expanse of several acres where kids threw Frisbees, played intra-mural sports and sat on benches and in the thick St. Augustine grass to breathe in the filtered heat and warm breezes, welcomed relief from the oppressive heat.

I wished I'd had a bicycle to get around, or a good pair of sneakers. I was ill-prepared for walking the 2,000-acre campus with a pair of loafers, one of Keds, knee-high white boots, and my coveted three-inch black patent leather heels that I persuaded Mama to buy me for the prom I never attended—no date. Anyway, she said I was too young and that Daddy would have to chaperone which took the glamour out of the whole concept, and I was stuck with high-heels instead of sneakers and no money. My weekly allowance barely covered vending machine meals I grabbed on the run between classes when I couldn't get to the cafeteria, and on weekends when I had no meal plan. This was the first time I experienced what it was like to choose between a meal and a pen when my Bic ran out of juice.

I tried to get a job on-campus, but my dad's income was too high. An older boy in my history class asked me if I'd like to be a model for a local department store where he worked. I was afraid it was a come-on, surely I wasn't model material, and, anyway my dad would kill me. He wanted me to concentrate on my studies, but I needed the money, so I said I'd try.

I walked the three miles to downtown Baton Rouge after my one o'clock class on Friday and found the department store called Gouchaux, named for the owners, an old Louisiana family. I took the elevator to the mezzanine and asked for Mr. Breaux, then sat and waited in one of the two chairs near the reception desk. A handsome man with a touch of grey at the temples came into the lobby and stood in front of me.

"They didn't tell me you had red hair," he said. I just looked at him, puzzled, unsure how to respond. "The blue eyes are a nice touch, but these are black and white pictures. Come to think, your hair won't show red. Come with me." I followed the unidentified man to an office. He walked around to the back of his desk, picked up a phone and punched one number.

"Margaret. Come in here." I was standing just inside the office door. "Sit down Miss .... Uh ...?"

"Burton," I said. "Susanna Burton." I took a few steps further into the office, but didn't sit.

"We'll have to take some preliminary photos to see how the camera likes you," he said. He shuffled papers and didn't look at me. I was standing behind a chair, afraid to sit and have my skirt ride up too far. It was short and I wore my white boots and a jacket that matched my plaid skirt with a green knit shirt underneath. I felt conspicuous, even though the man didn't look at me. There was a knock on the door and a lady with mousey brown hair and cat-eye glasses entered.

"Yes, Mr. Breaux." He looked up and seemed to stare right through the lady.

"Margaret, this is Miss ... Uh ... What did you say your name was?

"Susie. Susanna Burton."

"Right. Take Miss Burton to the media room and call Doug to come take some prototypes." He looked at me and did a double take, as if it was the first time he'd seen me.

"We'll, uh, uhm, I'll call you after we develop the film and take a look, okay?" he said.

"Sure," I said. I turned towards Margaret who held the door open. Mr. Breaux was still staring at me.

"Miss Burton?"

"Yes, sir."

"Why don't you come back in here after Doug takes the pictures?" I smiled but didn't answer. I'd read *Seventeen Magazine.* I knew what he meant and I wasn't falling for it. I followed his secretary to a dark room with lots of silver umbrellas clamped to tripods in various angles. She told me to stand on an X made with orange plastic tape on the concrete floor. She started to turn lights on behind the umbrellas. The room brightened and I stood on the X, clutching my book bag to my chest. Without saying a word, Margaret reached over and took my bag and placed it on a chair near the wall. A young guy entered. Margaret gave him curt instructions and left. He introduced himself as Doug, the photographer.

Doug had a kind face and was about twenty years old, give or take. He had sandy brown hair, green eyes and a quick smile. He was only a few inches taller than me but had wide shoulders and a small waist. He wore Levis, black and white Converse tennis shoes and a brown, short sleeve collarless shirt. He asked my name.

"Susanna Burton. But everyone calls me Susie."

"Nice to know you, Susie," he said. His warm smile helped me relax and soon we were chatting like old friends. He asked about LSU and my classes. He wanted me to tell him about my interests, whether I had a boyfriend, what about a sorority. I was so involved in our conversation I was surprised when he said, "All done."

"Did you take any pictures?"

"I took a whole roll," he said.

"I didn't know you were shooting."

"That's the trick," he said and smiled. "How 'bout having a beer with me. I get off at five."

"Sorry, I have homework and, really, I don't drink."

"You'll never make it at LSU," he said and laughed. "Can I have you phone number?"

"I don't think so. Maybe after I know you better." He tried to make a case for how I couldn't get to know him if I wouldn't go out with him, but I wiggled out of that conversation as we walked toward the elevators. He stood in front of the doors and stared at me when they closed. I let out a sigh of relief. When Mr. Breaux called to tell me my pictures were wonderful and they wanted to hire me, I told him I'd have to call him back. Chalk it up to immaturity, but I was too afraid to deal with the likes of him or Doug. I never returned his call, never modeled for Gouchaux's. It was a learning experience, but it didn't solve my money problems.

I had a few dates, but when they discovered I was only sixteen and couldn't go to bars, they quit calling. The older boys were crude and forward, their fraternities turned into orgies with vulgar, demeaning language. It was difficult to fight them off, especially when they drank too much, which was always. Disgusting.

It should have been easy to forget about Rodney when there was so much to do, but I couldn't. I knew there was no hope, no future, only sorrow and pain if I saw him and that the Klan was still alive and vibrant in Jean Ville and, I heard they were in Baton Rouge, too. But I was lonely and vulnerable.

October 13, 1968

Dear Beautiful,

Here's the deal. There are several girls on campus who see white guys. I haven't met a guy here who is seeing a white girl, but, that's beside the point. One of the girls with a white boyfriend is named Lucy.

She's a junior and has been dating a senior at LSU for almost two years. They meet at this place off Plank Road called, Sammy's. They say the owner is a Negro who is sympathetic to this kind of thing.

Here's the address. I know it's kind of far, so I'm enclosing cab fare. Just get there and I'll get you back to the dorm. See you Friday night, after dark, about eight.

I love you,
Yours forever,
Rod

Oh God! Help me. I can't do this. They'll kill him.

Two dollar bills fell out of the folded white paper onto the floor. It was Tuesday when I received his letter. I looked up Sammy's in the phone book and calculated it was about twenty-minutes away, near Southern University on the north side of town. I tried to figure out how to do it, how to pull it off. I'd never hailed a cab. The only times I'd ever been in one was with Daddy when he took me on business trips to Chicago, Dallas, Houston, and my favorite, New York City. How do you get a cab? How do you tell the driver where to go? What would I do when I get to some strange bar in a colored neighborhood? Did Rodney really expect me to walk into a Negro bar alone? The weight of the whole situation seemed too heavy. I couldn't do it.

I sat down to write to Rodney, not sure whether he would receive it before Friday night. I didn't want him to wait for me and feel rejected when I didn't show up.

October 17, 1968
Dear Rod,
I can't meet you. I'm sorry. I don't know how to get a cab, how to tell the driver where Sammy's is located, what to pay him or how to walk

into a colored bar alone. You probably think I'm a big baby. Maybe you're right. I'm only 16.

By the way, I'm sure they'll notice I'm white! Maybe some other time, some other way.

Sorry,
Susie

*

Saturday morning the dorm rector, Renée, came to my dorm room to tell me I had a phone call. The pay phone in the lobby was the only place where we could make or receive calls, and it was usually occupied. I hadn't used the phone in the two months I'd been in Connor Dorm. I almost ran to the lobby. So many thoughts went through my head—one of my brothers or sister was sick, Daddy had an accident or a heart attack, my grandmother fell. Oh, God! Please don't make me go home.

The receiver was dangling from the coiled silver wire. I picked it up and answered before I plopped onto the shallow bench and pulled the door shut. It was stuffy and hot inside the phone booth and smelled like sweat and ink, but it was private.

"Go to the library tonight," Rodney said. I tried to listen but I was frightened. "Just stand outside the Highland entrance at the bottom of the steps. Be there about eight, okay?" I didn't answer him. I didn't know what to say. I felt perspiration drip down my back to the top of my panties.

"Are you there?" he asked. "Susie, did you hear me?" I hadn't heard his voice since August. I'd forgotten how it felt in my ear and how it gave me goose bumps all the way down my body into my crotch. I shuddered.

"Uh... I'm here. I need a second."

"Okay, Beautiful. I'll give you all the time you need, but tell me you'll be there tonight."

"I don't know. What do you want me to do outside the library?"

"Wait for me. I'll be in a yellow cab. We'll pull up right in front of you. All you have to do is open the back door and slide in. Can you do that?"

"I guess so."

"Okay. I'll see you at eight, only ten hours."

"Rod?"

"What, Baby?" He'd never called me "Baby" before. I loved the sound of it, the way those two syllables popped softly through the telephone and made me feel like Rodney was in the booth with me. He sounded excited, but gentle and kind.

"Rod." I didn't know how to say it. "I'm afraid."

"Don't be afraid, Sweetheart. I'll take care of you. You're safe with me. I have everything worked out." Sweetheart?

"I'm not afraid for me, Rod." I let the words turn in my brain before I said them. "I'm afraid for you."

"I'll be fine, so will you. I love you. See you tonight."

I heard the click before I could protest again. Then a dial tone. Maybe I was so accustomed to being afraid that I carried fear inside. I stepped out of the phone booth and walked to one of the over-stuffed sofas against the wall, plopped down hard and put my head in my hands. I had to think.

We weren't in Jean Ville anymore. Did I need to worry about the Klan, that they would lynch Rodney or his dad, burn their house, hurt one of the other kids in the family? Did I need to worry my dad would find out and kill me, or Rodney? Was I so accustomed to worry, that I didn't know how not to worry any more?

I had to face it. I knew why I was afraid, terrified, in fact, and it was not about the Klan or my dad. I was afraid to be alone with him. I had learned to live without him, to move on with my life. I didn't want to find out that I still loved him. If I did, I wasn't sure I could pretend I didn't. Not anymore.

187

*

Rodney told me later that he was afraid I wouldn't show up, that his cab would pull up to the LSU library and I wouldn't be there. But just as he began to consider what he would do if that happened, he saw me standing there, "your light blue dress flapping softly in the breeze." He said he noticed everything—white socks and white Keds, the dusty blue sweater draped over my shoulders.

I stood there nervously fingering a small clutch purse in one hand while I adjusted my sunglasses with the other. The sun was sinking behind the classroom buildings in the distance so that light filtered through the trees in fingers of gold and yellow. I tapped my foot on the concrete and hugged myself.

The cab pulled up to the curb. It took a moment for me to realize he was there. Then I snapped out of the trance I'd been in and grabbed the door handle, pulled it open only a foot or so and slid onto the back seat. As soon as I slammed the door, the cab took off down Highland Road.

Rodney sat on the other side, near the window with his body turned fully towards me, his left leg bent across the middle of the seat and his arm across the back. His long arm almost reached me and I waited for outstretched fingers to touch my shoulder, but they didn't

I sat on the edge of the seat behind the cab driver, my knees almost touching the back. I turned my head to look at Rodney. He didn't speak. He just stared at me. I was aware of every fiber of him, his amber-green eyes, the smell of Irish Spring and English Leather, his knee so close to my thigh it emitted energy that felt like a magnetic pull, his breathing, soft and rapid. It had been three years since we'd talked in the Quarters, a year since we'd kissed in the hospital—but it was as if time erased itself and we'd never been apart.

There was no barrier between us, no car door, no Daddy, no KKK—nothing but air, and he filled it so that the space was not space but a capsule with only the two of us in it. I didn't notice the cab move or see the traffic or watch the cityscape and I don't think he did, either. He just looked at me and I felt as if something magical had happened to put Rodney and me in the back seat of that cab, away from everyone and everything that had stood between us for three years.

We were miserable at that game of playing it cool, so we just sat and stared. I knew he wanted to pull me to him and I wanted that, too, to feel his body press against me. I remembered everything about being in his arms in the hospital—his touch, his scent, the feel of his breath on my face, his voice in my ear—safety and peace.

I wondered whether he noticed that I was older, taller, had more curves. When I thought those thoughts, I blushed.

He told me later that he was afraid to say anything or to touch me and scare me away. He said he'd waited and planned for that moment, but when it happened, he froze.

"Hi," I said, finally. It was a whisper and I wasn't sure he heard me.

"Hi, yourself."

"You look good, Rod." I wasn't sure why we were both whispering, but it seemed right.

"You are beautiful, stunning, gorgeous."

"Thank you." I was embarrassed.

"Are you okay?" he asked. A slight grin spread across his face and the corners of his eyes lifted, just a tad.

"I'm fine. How about you?" I wanted to grab him, to hug him.

"I'm great. How's school?"

"It's hard and LSU is so big, but I'm figuring it out."

"I'm not worried about you figuring things out." Rodney always thought more of me than I thought of myself—that I was smart, competent and strong. But he didn't say any of those things, he just stared at me with a satisfied grin that drew me into him.

"You are too kind."

"Never. No one could ever be too kind to you. Not ever." I looked at him and felt wonder and hope.

Without thinking my hand touched his knee, which was inches away, and I patted it, as if to acknowledge I heard him but didn't have words to respond. Before I could pull it away, he covered my hand with his. Electricity shot through me. I turned my body towards him, slightly, but enough that I could see his face fully. I squeezed his knee and he, in turn, squeezed the top of my hand. I felt senseless.

That familiar feeling of pins and needles from my neck down my spine through my stomach and into my panties took me by surprise and I felt moisture gather between my legs. It embarrassed me that I could have such a visceral reaction to his hand on mine. It was as if I'd lost control of my own reflexes and my body leaned towards him without my permission. He picked up my hand and placed it on his lips where he kissed each fingertip. Then he wrapped it around the back of his neck, his hand still covering mine for a second, as if to guide it and make sure it stayed where he put it. Then his other arm fell softly from the seat back to my shoulders and gently folded around me. The feel of the back of his neck had me reeling. My sweater fell off my shoulders and his hand gripped the top of my left arm, skin to skin. His palm burned my shoulder, in a good way.

Suddenly we both realized we weren't alone and we pulled our hands away from each other as if they were on fire. But our eyes continued the embrace. There was no hunger or fierceness in his stare, although I felt like he wanted me and I could see in his eyes that he still loved me. I wondered whether I was able to hide how I felt.

"It feels better than I remembered," he whispered.

"What?"

"Just being with you," he whispered and I felt his breath touch my cheek.

"Rod?"

"Yes, Baby."

"Is there some place we can go to be alone to talk? I don't want to go to a smoke-filled bar and socialize with people I don't know. I've waited a long time." The words just spilled out on their own, as if someone inside of me had taken control of my voice.

"You've waited? You've waited?" Rodney started to laugh. His joy was contagious and I giggled. "Yeah, Baby. We can go somewhere to be alone. Make sure that's what you want because, if I get you alone, I can't promise I'll let you go."

"Oh, held captive, huh?" I laughed softly.

"Wait right here."

"I'm not going anywhere," I whispered. He sat up and leaned over the front seat to talk to the Cabbie.

"Would you drop us at 116 State Street, please?"

"Sure. Let me turn around." Rodney sat back and put his left arm over my shoulder and pulled me closer to him. I felt him gasp, softly, then he chuckled. It was endearing, everything he did was endearing and wonderful and sexy and ... I knew I was in trouble, but I couldn't help myself.

I leaned into him, lay my ear on his shoulder and sighed. I could feel his heart beating hard and fast and I giggled. I put my hand on his chest and pressed it flat against the place where his heart tried to jump out of his body, as if I could hold it in. He wrapped his arm around me like he couldn't get me close enough. I snuggled into him.

We got out of the cab and walked up a sidewalk into the courtyard of a square apartment complex. It was two stories with iron stairs on the outside and doors that faced the large grassy opening like motel rooms at the Howard Johnson where my parents would take us for long weekends in the summer forour family vacation. We didn't climb the stairs. Instead we walked under the second-story walkway to the far right corner of the complex. Rodney pulled a key out of his pocket and unlocked a brown door, number 21 on the center. He pushed the door open and guided me into the apartment with his hand in the small of my back. I heard the door shut and the light switch flip. It was a small but clean space with a sofa and matching chair, a small round table with four wooded chairs in front of a counter with cabinets hanging from the ceiling, an opening between the bottom of the cabinets and the counter about two feet high that gave a glimpse into a kitchen.

Rodney turned on a lamp near the sofa and flipped off the overhead switch. He told me it was his friend's place. I didn't ask whether he had brought other girls here, I didn't care. I just followed him inside. We stood a few feet apart, looking at each other.

He later told me that he was petrified, afraid to touch me, afraid, well, he said he was ... afraid of me. Me? Sixteen-year-old Susie Burton? When he told me that, I almost laughed. He said he was afraid that if his hand touched my skin, he wouldn't be able to stop there, that he'd want more. More? More what, I wondered. He said he'd thought about this moment so often, the moment when we'd finally be alone, that now that that moment had arrived, he didn't know what to do.

I looked at his hands, big, brown, strong. He rubbed his thumb along the tips of his fingers, back and forth, as if counting them, from the pinky to the index. All the time I watched him and breathed that musky scent I'd never forgotten. His thick eyelashes were at half-mast, his hands folded in front of him as he was waiting; waiting for what? I wondered. When I looked up from his hands he shrugged his shoulders ever so slightly as if to say, "What now?"

What now, indeed, I thought as he reached up and scratched his forehead near his hairline. It was a gesture I'd noticed him make often when he stood next to my car window at the Esso station, a thinking gesture.

He reached out with both hands, across the gulf of air that separated us. I unfolded my hands in a way that told him it was okay to take them, but I was afraid. Afraid I'd want him to hold me forever.

Somehow our hands met in that abyss that seemed to separate us by a mile. When they touched, the space between us disappeared and we were one.

All of our fears were realized. Touching was so powerful that we both knew we wouldn't be able to stop with our hands, we had to touch each other elsewhere. As innocent as I was, I knew he felt it too, because, without thinking, when my thumb began to rub the side of his hand and I lifted my eyelashes to finally let him see the tears gathering, he pulled me to him, put his hand on the back of my head and let me wipe my eyes on his chest.

*

Daddy's trips to Baton Rouge became less regular after Governor Earl Long was out of office but he'd recently been hired to lobby for the insurance industry, and he had a number of clients whose corporate offices were in and around the state Capitol building. He came to Baton Rouge several times a month.

He called James and me to see if we could meet him for lunch one Thursday about mid-way through the fall semester. James was a junior in pre-law and I never saw him since the campus was massive and we had no classes that were even in the same buildings.

I had a class at noon that Thursday so I had to bow out of the lunch date. Daddy and James went alone. After lunch Daddy came to my dorm to wait for me to get back from class. I was unaware of this, but one of my friends told me later what happened.

The telephone in the booth in the lobby of Connor Hall rang and one of the girls ran to answer it. Daddy was on the sofa in the lobby and listened to the conversation as the girl called out.

"It's for Susie," she screamed. "Go get Susie Burton."

"Susie's still in class," someone called. "She should be back in a few."

Daddy told me I couldn't date, that I was still too young. He grabbed the phone and stepped into the booth.

"Hello. Who's this?" He yelled into the mouthpiece.

"Uh, uh. I'm calling for Susie Burton," a male voice said.

"This is her father. What do you want with her?" Click. "You chicken-shit coward," he yelled into the phone. Just then I walked through the front door and turned right towards the hallway to my room. He called out.

"Susie! Susanna!"

I turned and saw Daddy standing in the lobby one foot in the phone booth, the receiver in his hand. I was surprised, then afraid, but I tried to act if I was happy to see him.

"Daddy," I said and walked quickly towards him. "What a great surprise." I held my books against my chest, as if for protection, stood on tiptoes and pecked him on the cheek.

"I'm the one who's surprised," he said.

"Why are you surprised?"

"I just hung up the phone with your boyfriend." He still held the receiver and pointed it at me.

"I don't have a boyfriend, Daddy." He hit me across the face with the phone receiver. Blood spurt from my cheekbone and my books flew in the air and scattered throughout the room. I grabbed my face as a shriek shot out my mouth. Before I understood what happened, he backhanded my other cheek and I stumbled against a sofa and slid down to the floor, my back against the base of the couch. He kicked me and screamed.

"Get up! Get off that floor." I sat there and stared at him in disbelief and horror, clutching my bleeding cheek and folding into a ball to protect myself from his pointed boots that stabbed the side of my chest. There was blood everywhere. "I said, GET UP!" He grabbed me under my arm and lifted me to me feet. But I was still bent forward, my face in my hands. Again he slapped me across my head and I lifted it in reaction, which exposed my face. He backhanded me across my other cheek and, this time blood spurted from my lip. I cupped my mouth with my hand and fought to get away from him, but his grip on my arm was strong and tight. I could hear screams and someone yelled, "Get Miss Druid. Get help."

He reared back and punched me in the face with his fist. I turned my head just in time and he connected with my already bleeding cheekbone rather than my nose. I went limp and he let me fall to the floor in a ball. Blood shot out onto the tile floor from places I didn't know existed.

He yelled. "Get up you impudent slut. I told you, 'no boys.'"

Mrs. Druid, our house mother, came running into the lobby dressed in a navy suit and black heels. She walked right up to Daddy from the side and caught him unaware. Mrs. Druid was about forty-years-old, plain-looking, with kind, intelligent eyes. We all loved her. She positioned herself between me and Daddy as his leg was in motion. Before he realized she was there, his foot connected with her ankle. She stumbled and yelled.

"Get out of here. Now."

"Butt out, bitch." he said. "This is my daughter and we are having a father-daughter conversation. This is not about you." She didn't move.

"I don't care what you say your relationship is with this young lady. You need to leave."

"You can't kick me out. I pay her tuition. She's my daughter." He was screaming. A crowd of girls began to gather in the vestibule, between the lobby and the hall to the bedrooms. They were quiet now, wide-eyed.

"While she's on this campus, she's under the direction of the Dean, and while she's in this building, she's under my direction. I'm in charge of her and in charge of this dormitory. We do not allow violence on this campus and, certainly not in this building. Get out now." Mrs. Druid stood straight, unwavering inches from Daddy, daring him to hit her.

"Get out of my way!" he yelled. He tried to move around her and reached to pull me to my feet. Two security guards entered the front door and moved towards Daddy.

"Sir," one of them said. "You need to leave. Now."

"I'll leave, but not without my daughter. She's coming with me."

"No, sir. She stays here. You leave." Daddy took a swing at one of the guards, who caught Daddy's wrist and twisted it around his back. The other guy pulled on Daddy's other arm and, before he knew it, he was handcuffed, his wrists behind his back. I sat on the floor watching the ordeal as if it was a movie.

"You can't do this," he yelled. "I know the governor. I'll have your badges before I'm done with you." Mrs. Druid got on her knees on the floor next to me, removed her jacket and used it to apply pressure to my bleeding face. I was dizzy and confused. She put her arm around me and before I knew it several of the girls were there with towels and someone appeared with a bag of ice.

"Mrs. Druid," one of the guards said. "Take pictures. Call the City Police and get this girl an ambulance."

Mrs. Druid got up, left me in the care of the rector, Amelia Thibodeaux, and moved quickly towards a door on the side of the sofa. She came back with a camera and her assistant, Angela Alford, who carried a notepad and a pencil.

"Name's Susie Burton, Angela. This is her dad," Mrs. Druid said as she clicked pictures of Daddy in handcuffs, held on either side by uniformed men. He was screaming obscenities and the guards struggled to hold on to him. Mrs. Druid snapped pictures of everything—me, the books strewn across the room, Daddy yelling.

A few days later I stood in front of her desk, the pictures spread out like a display, and I saw things I hadn't seen that day: Daddy's face, a look of hatred and anger; me balled up like a coward, blood all over my clothes, the sofa, the floor; books spread out, some of them bloody, torn, stomped on; a gang of girls standing in the foyer, looks of surprise and amazement plastered across their faces; Lauren and Amelia coddling me and a couple of girls I didn't know with towels and an ice bag.

I stood there and cried like a baby, stitches across one cheekbone and my lower lip, two black eyes, a wide ace bandage around my ribs. Mrs. Druid came from behind her desk and put her arms around me, pulled me close to her and let me cry in her arms. The last time I'd felt this kind of love was when Tootsie held me. I missed Toot. I missed Catfish and Marianne. I missed Rodney. No, I needed Rodney.

Mrs. Druid told me she had filed charges against Daddy. I didn't know what to make of that. She asked me to file charges, too, which, of course I would never consider. He'd kill me. She said that Daddy told the judge he was sending me to school in New York in January and that if I wanted to stay at LSU, she could get legal custody and keep him away from me. I told her I'd go to New York, that I'd probably be safer there. She tried to talk me into staying, but she just didn't understand and I didn't try to explain.

Part Five: 1969

ᕫ Chapter Thirteen ᕫ

ᕫ

Sarah Lawrence
1969

I REMEMBERED NEW YORK City from a trip I'd taken with Daddy when I was thirteen, a few months after he'd beat me for going to the Quarters. He always took me on a business trip after one of my "accidents," a way of saying he was sorry, I guessed. New York City with Daddy had been much different from the massive metropolis where I arrived alone that January, 1969.

As the cab traveled north out of Manhattan, and the jungle of skyscrapers fell away, I became more relaxed. The town of Yonkers was about the size of Baton Rouge, so doable. It was built around Getty Square, a charming area of shops, restaurants and government offices. I began to feel better when the cabbie drove onto the small, 49-acre campus above the banks of the Bronx River. The Tudor style buildings were tucked among dramatic outcroppings of exposed bedrock and large oak and elm trees. With about 1,200 students, the all-girls school seemed a welcomed change from LSU's 30,000-student campus.

But I was 1,400 miles from Rodney—a world away.

My first semester at Sarah Lawrence was the hardest. I was homesick. New York was so different from South Louisiana and the girls were a lot more snobbish and cliquish than the ones at LSU. It was the spring semester when I entered and the other freshman had been there since August, some since June and they'd already made friends and had their cliques. I felt like the odd-man-out.

January 18, 1969
Dear Rod,

I'm miserable up here. It's so lonely and all the girls know each other and have formed their groups. The only thing that keeps me sane is the memory of the few times we were together in Baton Rouge. I remember how you kissed me and how it felt to have your arms around me.

You make me feel safe. I'm really looking forward to your visit this summer.

Yours,
Susie

January 25, 1969
Dear Susie,

There's nothing that makes me happier than opening my post box and seeing your handwriting on an envelope inside. I live to hear from you. I can't believe he sent you so far away from me. I miss you terribly. I think about our long talks and how you put your head on my chest when we sat together on Jason's sofa. I can still smell your shampoo and that lilac, or is it lavender, scent that seems to come from your body. I love everything about you and I really miss you. I'm counting the days until I can hold you again.

I love you.
Yours, forever,
Rod

*

It wasn't enough. I thought about him all the time, no matter how hard I tried to put him out of my mind. My loneliness made me long for him more. He wrote that he missed me in every letter and told me in the conversations we had on the phone every few weeks.

I stayed in New York for summer school because Daddy said he could afford only one airline ticket a year and I should save it for Christmas.

June 3, 1969
Dear Rod,
It's June. Only six weeks before you come to visit me. I can think of nothing else. I miss you so much. I still remember how it felt to kiss you. Sometimes I wish we weren't so dedicated to wait until I'm eighteen. But it's just one more thing I love about you. You are so wise. Girls here are very open about their relationships. Half of them sleep with other girls, the other half with guys. I witness broken hearts every day and I can't count how often I've heard, "I gave it to him, and he dumped me." My daddy always said, "Why buy the cow if you can get the milk free?" His way of saying I'd be sorry if I ever did it before marriage. I'm not sure why I'm rambling on about this. I'm really glad we are waiting. It will be worth it.
Yours,
Susie

*

The campus was almost deserted in summer, only one dorm, half-filled. I counted the days until Rodney came to see me in August.

August 1, 1969
Dear Susie,
You are going to be angry, but know that I'm angrier than you are. I can't go to New York this summer. I worked two jobs but still didn't save enough money for the trip and for my dorm and meal ticket for the fall and spring semesters. I'm so sorry. I miss you more than you could ever miss me, and I think about kissing you and holding you every minute of every day.

This has nothing to do with how much I love you. Please forgive me. I feel like such a failure. I know I've let you down. I've let myself down. I never want you to think you can't trust me to do what I say I'm going to do.

I have a broken heart. I love you. More now.

Yours forever,

Rod

*

I cried for days, until I ran out of tears, but not sorrow. It was a week before I could finally answer his letter.

August 14, 1969

Dear Rod,

I'm not angry. After I cried myself half to death, I came to the conclusion that we should not hope for things that will probably never be. We should realize that none of our plans will ever be realized because of who we are and where we come from. I am learning to appreciate the memories, especially those in Baton Rouge, knowing that those idyllic times were probably once-in-a-lifetime moments. I want to be grateful for what we've had, not ungrateful for what we can't have.

Please don't be so hard on yourself. I trust you to always do what you say you will do. Remember, I know what it's like to be controlled by outside forces, unseen rules and doctrines greater and older than ourselves.

I think about kissing you, too. Maybe, one day.

Yours,

Susie

*

I met a girl from Maine who invited me to go home with her at the end of the summer term. Kennebunkport was fabulous, with its lower village and Dock Square located right on the Atlantic Ocean and the Kennebunk River. I watched schooners and ships make their way down river to the sea and was amazed at the beautiful old mansions built in the 1600's by wealthy sea captains. They reminded me of the plantation homes in Louisiana. Although the town reeked of wealth and privilege, everyone was friendly and down to earth. I understood why this beautiful port, which smelled of salt air, rich chocolate and boiling lobsters, was a vacation destination for New Yorkers. Millie's family was wealthy, but her attorney-dad, whose clients included the Kennedys, the Billings, the Sedgwicks and the Vanderbilts, was welcoming and kind.

Millie turned out to be needy and spoiled and began making sexual advances towards me. I fought her off for three weeks and slept with my eyes opened at night. I'd stare at the tall ceilings with rich crown moldings over shiplap walls and inhale the salty breeze that blew through the sheer curtains into the huge bedroom. I thought about Rodney constantly, but couldn't tell anyone about him. I felt like they'd know that he was well, I just couldn't discuss him.

I liked Millie, and I had nothing against lesbians, half the girls at Sarah Lawrence were gay—but I couldn't imagine myself with a girl. After all, I was in love with a boy. I finally had to tell Millie that it wasn't about her, it was about me being in love with someone else. She pretended to understand and then she tried to pump me for information. It was a game of cat and mouse, for sure.

Finally, the first week of September, we headed back to New York. I never thought I'd be so happy to be in Yonkers.

The girls at school were older and different in lots of ways. I began to understand how Southern girls were unlike Northerners. No one seemed to understand me, they thought I was a prude, that my manners were "stiff," that my use of "Yes, sir" and "No, ma'am," was stupid.

I was really lonely on my 18th birthday that October. It wasn't like I missed birthday parties and celebrations; I didn't have many of those growing up, anyway. It's just that it seemed eighteen was a right-of-passage that should be spent with someone who recognized that I was now an adult. I didn't tell anyone at school it was my birthday but I went into the City after my last class that afternoon, found a payphone in a coffee shop and called Rodney with the twenty dollars my dad had sent me. It was the best birthday present I could give myself.

"I was hoping I'd get to talk to you on your birthday," he said. I started crying and couldn't stop. "You're going to waste your money crying. Talk to me." Soon we were laughing and planning. We tried not to talk about seeing each other because it seemed so pointless, but we pretended we might be able to get together when I was home for Christmas in a couple months, even though he'd promised his dad never to see me in Jean Ville.

Other than that phone call, I found my sanity in the letters from Rodney and Marianne. He wrote diligently twice a week and told me how much he loved and missed me. Marianne filled me in on Catfish and Tootsie and her progress at Toussaint Vocational-Technical Institute, or Too-Vo-Tech, which was located about five miles outside of Jean Ville and had a bus that took her there every day. She was going to be a Licensed Practical Nurse in two years and she was excited about her classes. She told me about learning to give shots and bathe patients. She said she had a girlfriend and that even though they had to pretend they were just friends, they'd found a community of lesbians and a few places where they could "be themselves." I was still confused by Marianne's sexual orientation but I loved her like a sister.

Rodney was working at a gas station in Baton Rouge on weekends and during school breaks. He told me he was saving money for an airline ticket to New York. I didn't get my hopes up after what had happened in August.

When I walked around the city, scaling the skyscrapers and dodging the fast-paced pedestrians on the wide sidewalks, I would see mixed-race couples walking hand-in-hand in plain sight. I wondered at the difference in laws and rules between the North and the South. The aromas from delicatessens and street vendors made my stomach growl, but I had no appetite. My loneliness and isolation were heavy cargo and my soul felt weighted down.

Thanksgiving loomed and my depression became so acute I began to make poor grades. I lost weight, couldn't sleep and began to run a fever. Daddy called when he received my mid-term report and told me if I didn't bring my grades up by the end of the fall semester, I'd be returning to Jean Ville—for good. He wasn't going to waste his money.

The only thing worse than being in New York alone, would be living in Jean Ville. I had to get a grip! I decided to spend the Thanksgiving holidays studying and catching up.

Most of the girls left campus Friday afternoon, the week before Thanksgiving. Several girls invited me to go home with them, but I declined, afraid to be faced with another vacation like the one with Millie, plus I needed the time to get my school work done. There were a few students on campus from other countries who, like me, didn't have a place to go for the holidays, but I ignored them and concentrated on academics.

I started across Andrews Lawn the Saturday morning before Thanksgiving and headed to the Esther Raushenbush Library to begin my week of catch-up. It was a beautiful fall day. The gold, red, and amber leaves fell like rain from the ash, maple, pear and honey locust trees that lined the lawn and the breeze had a fresh sea-scent, even though we were landlocked. I inhaled deeply and considered getting my act together. I had to forget Rodney and get on with life.

Halfway across campus I heard someone call my name.

"Susie. Hey, Susie Burton. Wait up!"

I turned and thought I saw Rodney running towards me, but I knew it was a mirage. I'd been having them during sleeping and waking hours. I turned back towards the library.

"Susie. Wait!" The voice was closer, but I thought I was hearing things and I refused to give into my psychosis. I continued to plod across Andrews Lawn.

"Susie, Baby, please wait!" I stopped in my tracks when I heard, "Baby." Only one person called me that. I didn't turn around. I was afraid I was wrong, hearing things, schizophrenic.

I heard him panting as he got closer and, finally, I felt his warm breath on my neck and his arms wrap around me. His familiar scent fell into the air around me and I inhaled deeply, afraid to wake up from such a vivid dream. I thought maybe I was swooning from the stress of it all—no food, no sleep, no Rodney.

Finally, after what seemed like a lifetime, his breathing slowed and he murmured, "I've missed you," into my neck and I twisted inside the circle of his arms to face him. Tears ran down his face and I saw my reflection in the glassiness. I was crying, too. I couldn't believe he was real, that I was in his arms.

Neither of us thought about being seen in public together. We were the only two people on the planet. Eventually we walked, holding hands, to a bench under a huge live oak, its green foliage a promise to remain through the upcoming winter, the hope not lost on us. We whispered about what it felt like to be together, what the loneliness had been like, why we were meant to be together—all the while, neither of us had faith we would see each other again after this visit.

"You're so thin, Susie," he said, pulling me to him, feeling my hip bones push against his.

"I'll be better now," I said and rested my head on his chest. He stroked my hair that now reached my waist.

"Your hair is much longer," he whispered.

"I haven't thought about it," I said. "I guess I haven't taken very good care of myself."

"I like it," he said. Later he told me that, in that moment, he visualized me naked, "your golden-streaked hair draping your shoulders, barely hiding your breasts." He shuddered. I giggled, and he said he thought I read his mind. He blushed.

He'd booked a hotel room in the New York, near Harlem, for the week.

It was marvelous—riding the buses and trains together, walking on the sidewalk holding hands, having dinner at cafés, dropping into delicatessens and being served without question, having tea and talking for hours in small coffee. We visited the Metropolitan Museum of Art where we were enthralled with Nelson Rockefeller's recently-donated collection that included African art and pieces from South America.

We went to the New York Public Library three times where we found volumes on slavery and read newspaper accountings about the Supreme Court decision in *Loving v. Virginia* in the massive reading room. Rodney was especially interested in the case and found interviews with Mrs. Loving in magazine articles. She was colored, married to a white man, and they had several children.

The ceiling height in the library had to be 50-feet or more and chandeliers hung over the long reading tables between huge curve-topped windows down both sidewalls. It smelled of ink and paper and bodies—wonderful.

During our first trip to the library we just wandered from room to room, holding hands, the only sounds our gasps and breaths of amazement. Later we found a table in some out-of-the-way cafe in SoHo and talked for hours about the books we'd found, the art we loved and the architecture we admired. When we returned to the library the second day I tried to piece together, in my head, how I would write Catfish's stories, while incorporating the history of slavery in our country. Rodney was interested in how he could help Negroes achieve a higher standard of living, what the liberals in Greenwich Village referred to as Civil Rights and Equality. The Toussaint Parish Library didn't have books about Martin Luther

King and Malcolm X and other subjects that could help the colored people. All Rodney knew about the civil rights movement was what he had read on microfiche, because all libraries carried newspaper and magazine articles pertaining to current events.

We found so many books that interested us. Time ran out before we could ever run out of reading material.

The first evening we went to a free concert in Central Park and heard Bob Dylan sing "Blowin' in the Wind," and Joan Baez belt out her rendition of "House of the Risin' Sun." We were smitten with folk music and ballads, rather than Elvis and rock 'n roll. We fell in love with Simon and Garfunkel's "Sound of Silence," gravitated towards Sam Cooke's "A Change Is Gonna Come," and Marvin Gaye's "Ain't No Mountain High Enough." We loved the Temptations and the Four Tops, who mesmerized us with their performances of semi-dance and smooth harmony in "My Girl," and "Baby I Need Your Loving."

We found a little blues club in Harlem where we danced to, "Sittin' On The Dock of the Bay," "When a Man Loves a Woman," and "Stand By Me." We clung to that music for years and, even today, when I hear Otis Redding or B.B. King, I go back to the 18 year old girl in the arms of her twenty-year-old dream-boy, and my heart sinks and rises simultaneously.

During that magical week we even went to mass at St. Patrick's Cathedral together. No one bothered us. No one seemed to notice. We were wrapped in a cloud of bliss and I guess you could say our physical attraction morphed into a real, deep love that week when we found so many common interests and never ran out of things to talk about.

I finally agreed to stay overnight with him the evening before his last day in New York. I went to his hotel with a small backpack that held a few toiletries, a nightgown and a change of clothes. I told myself it made sense, because I was going to the airport with him in the morning. But I was nervous.

I tapped lightly on #1174, and he opened it immediately, before

I got my hand down and my fist uncurled. He looked serious, unsmiling.

"Is something wrong?" I asked as soon as he pulled me into the room and closed the door. We were standing just inside, facing each other, his back against the door, his hand still on the knob behind his back. I stood still, my backpack hanging on one shoulder. We looked at each other. He didn't answer.

"Rod? Are you okay?" I whispered. He just stared at me. It was unnerving. A silent fear began to grow in my chest. I swallowed hard; it tasted like bile. He just looked at me. We stood like that for what seemed forever. Finally he spoke.

"I'm afraid."

"You? Afraid? What are you afraid of?"

"You."

"Rod. You aren't making sense." Aside from a far-off siren and the soft whirl of heat coming from a vent in the floor, there was no sound but the hallow echo of his voice that hung in the space between us. I breathed deeply. The smell of old carpeting and paint masked Rodney's fresh showered smell, his shaving soap and deodorant and the starch in his green, cotton shirt with the alligator on the left breast and buttons at the points of his collar. It was opened at the neck and I could see his chest hair trying to stick out.

His hand fell from the door knob and circled in front of his body, bent at the elbow, reaching straight out from his belt. He turned his hand palm side up and opened it, his unblinking gaze fixed on my startled stare. I looked at his hand. It was cupped ever so slightly as if waiting for something to be put into it. I slowly raised my left hand, the one not holding the strap of my backpack on my right shoulder, and placed my hand lightly into his inviting palm. He gently folded his fingers around mine and tugged lightly, as you would on a fishing line to see if there's something on the end. I moved a step towards him. He inhaled and held his breath for a few seconds, then exhaled slowly, as if releasing pent-up emotions for which there were no words.

I took another step towards him and he gently pulled my hand around his waist, folding his arm around his back with mine. We stood still, our chests and the tops of our thighs touching, his breath in my hair. With his other hand he pushed the backpack off my shoulder.. He took my hand that had held the strap as the bag fell to the floor with a "clunk." He pulled that hand around his waist until both my arms encircled him, his hands still holding mine behind his back. My head fit under his chin where his collar parted and I breathed in what came from his pores, all the Rodney scents I knew and a new, indescribable one I couldn't name then, but now I know it was *desire*.

I knew he smelled it on me, too, as he rested his chin on top of my head and sighed. The only other time he had held me this close was when I was in the hospital, three years before. How could you love someone this much and not touch intimately? How could you not touch intimately and know you love someone this much?

When I lifted my face to look at him, a fat tear fell slowly from his eye and travelled down the length of his cheek. Just before it fell under his jawbone, I unconsciously licked the salty drop, then kissed the spot where it had been. Rodney shuddered. He put two fingers under my chin and lifted it to meet his lowered face. His kiss was wide and gentle. There was no urgency, no pressure. It was as if everything that had gone before us to this moment was dress rehearsal. Never before had we both known our kiss would lead us to a place we'd never dreamed we could go. We dared not ... dream.

He kissed me more deeply, released my hands and folded his arms around me. First he rubbed my back, then his hands reached lower and cupped the cheeks of my butt. His tongue found the back of my teeth and I gasped. He lifted me off the floor a few inches and pulled me against his hardness. I took a deep breath, and when I did, my breasts lifted and I felt my nipples rub against him. The wetness between my legs was like a river.

In one motion he slipped one of his arms under my knees, the other around my back, my head tucked under his chin and took me to the bed. I could feel and smell the whole of him. Wonderment seeped from his skin and I trembled.

It seemed hours before our naked bodies came together in that hotel room. His gentle, unhurried wanderings told me he wanted every moment to count, every touch to mean something, every feeling to be emblazoned in his memory—and mine. And when he started to enter me, he took his time, coaxing me, asking me if he could go further and, when we finally came together completely, he cried, his tears falling on my face and neck. He didn't try to hide them. He cried openly, without any sound, but with a passion and feeling I'll never forget as long as I live.

I've relived that moment thousands of times, and each time I am more amazed by the completeness of it. Of him. Of us.

In the morning we lay naked. wrapped in each other's arms, spent, but gloriously happy.

"Rod?" I whispered so softly I was barely audible, but I knew he felt my breath against his chest.

"Yes, Baby." I paused and took a deep breath.

"Do you still love me?" He was silent for a few seconds.

"Do you have to ask?" I didn't answer. I knew, but I needed to hear it.

"Yes. I love you. Never doubt that." I was quiet for a long time. Finally I said what was on my heart.

"I'm afraid, Rod. I'm always afraid." He pulled away from me just far enough so he could see my face.

"I know, Baby. But you don't have to be afraid anymore. I'll take care of you. I'll keep you safe." I opened my eyes fully and looked at him.

"But who will protect you? Who will keep you safe?"

He didn't answer.

~ Chapter Fourteen ~

~

Louisiana Christmas/Landowners
1969

CHRISTMAS VACATION ARRIVED and I flew home on the heels of the most magical week of my life. I tried to leave the memories in New York, to compartmentalize, but it was impossible, and Daddy seemed to hover around me and wouldn't let me out of his sight until the Monday after Christmas, when he had to go to Baton Rouge on business. He tried to convince me to go with him. I considered it, thinking that maybe Rodney could meet me somewhere, but I was afraid. In the end Daddy and I argued and I won when I explained I wanted to get a jump-start on my studies for next semester so I didn't get behind again.

Mama had a bad case of "baby blues" and ignored me, which was fine by me. I did worry about her, though, because she sat in a rocker in her bedroom and cried most of the day while Tootsie cared for little Albert.

After Daddy had been gone about an hour, and I felt sure he wouldn't return any time soon, I sneaked off to the Quarters. It had been more than a year since I had seen Marianne or Catfish. He wasn't on his porch and there were no kids in the yard. It was eerily quiet. I knocked on Catfish's back door. I heard shuffling inside, then footsteps on the porch next door.

"I didn't think you would come," Marianne said. She walked up behind me. We hugged.

"Hi. I missed you, too. You look beautiful, older, more—I don't know. You look wonderful, Mari."

"You look good yourself. A little on the scrawny side, but beautiful. You look older, too."

"I finally turned eighteen. I'm still two years younger than the girls in my classes, but it feels different."

"Yeah, eighteen is good. Sit down. Tell me about school, about Christmas." We sat on the steps of Catfish's porch.

"Where's Cat?" I asked.

"He hasn't been feeling well. He's probably in his bed. Want me to check?"

"Sure, if you don't mind," I said, tapping my toe on the wooden step, aware that I didn't have much time. "I want to see him."

Marianne went into Catfish's cabin and closed the screen door behind her. She didn't invite me inside. I realized I'd never been inside any of the houses in the Quarters, not Catfish's, not Marianne's. Suddenly I felt like an intruder. What kind of friends were these that they never invited me into their houses, offered me a cool drink? Then I remembered how many times Marianne begged me to stay for supper and Catfish asked me if I was thirsty. Tootsie would call from her kitchen window and ask if we wanted sweet tea. I'd always refused, trying to be polite, but they probably thought I didn't want to drink out of their glasses or eat at their tables. I felt so insecure. Maybe time and distance did that to people.

"I knew you wouldn't come to Jean Ville and skip coming to see me," Catfish said as he hobbled out of his back door onto the porch leaning on a wooden walking cane. He patted me on the shoulder and sank into his rocker. He looked so old. He was thin and his eyes were bloodshot. He wore his standard straw hat but I could see, on the sides, that his hair was white and thin.

"You too curious about my stories." He laughed at himself. "You going to get rich one day selling books about me." He leaned over in his rocker and laughed so hard he began to cough. He pulled out a white handkerchief and coughed into it. He quickly folded it over when he was done, but I saw the red stain on it.

"Are you okay, Cat?" I asked.

"Fine as wine, Missy." He coughed again and Marianne appeared behind him with a glass of water. He drank greedily. "Now sit down and let me tell you about how we got to be property owners. Imagine, Negroes owning land before the first war."

"Oh, I love your stories, for sure," I said. "But it's the two of you I want to see."

"Well, I been thinking about the next story to tell you cause I knowed you'd come back to see me and I want to be sure you have enough stories to write in that book one day.

"Sit down, Mari. You might want to know about your ancestry." Marianne and I shared a look of concern for Catfish, but we tried to hide our worries from him.

*

Landowners

"Let's see. Now my daddy, your granddaddy," he pointed to Marianne with his cane as he rocked, his feet rising an inch off the floor and returning, flatfooted with each back and forth movement. "Like I tole you before, my granddaddy was freed after the Civil War, then Simon and Jacob left for the North. My daddy stayed with his parents, my granddaddy and granny, here at Shadowland and spent ten years as a sharecropper for Mr. Van.

"I need to back up a little and tell you about my daddy and my Mama.

"Ten years went by for two Samuels, that's my granddaddy, Samuel the First, and my daddy, Samuel the Second, who they called Sammy."

"Why weren't you named Samuel the Third, Catfish?" I asked.

"Well, you see, I had an older brother, and he got that name. But he gone and got kilt in the first war.

'Anyways, my granddaddy and daddy talked about owning their own piece of land some day and not having to pay the half-share of crops to Mr. Van no more. They talked about it regular. One day my granddaddy saw Mr. Van by the barn—by that time Van was getting up in years, near about 80. He was old and sickly and walked with a cane, bent over. Granddaddy axed the old man would it be possible to purchase one of the slave cabins, the one he lived in, and the sliver of land it sat on, with the opportunity to eventually buy the fifty-acres he and my daddy sharecropped. Mr. Van told him to come see him up at the house the next day.

'That night Anna Lee scrubbed both Samuels' shirts and ironed them stiff.

'The two Samuels walked up to Mr. Van's front porch the next morning and Lizzie showed them into the library, first door on the left off the main hall. It was the first time they ever went through the front door of the house, much less being invited into the study. Daddy said he tried to take it all in, the hanging lights they called chandeliers, the velvet sofa and tapestry covered wing-back chairs in front of the huge mahogany desk behind where Mr. Van stood, hiding a leather swivel chair, and the ceiling-to-floor windows covered with silk draperies, tied back with gold-tasseled ropes with sheer, white curtains that floated in front of the glass. The old white man had a paper in front of him that he read.'

'This paper says you own a house and one-half-acre of land on Jefferson Street Extension and 50-acres of farm land on Shadowland Plantation,' Mr. Van explained. 'It will be filed in the courthouse after you sign it. Your payments will be 10% of your annual crop for the house and 50% for the farm land. In fifteen years, the property will be yours and you won't have to pay anymore. This means I hold the mortgage, and you owe me for the land, until it's paid for in fifteen years. But it will be in your names.'

'Granddaddy was almost 50 and was slowing down, so the work would fall on Daddy. This was just before the turn of the century and they was the first Negroes to have a paper say they owned land in Toussaint Parish.

'Mr. Van died two years later. His oldest son, Mr. Henry, came to tell my daddy and granddaddy and they all wept, specially Daddy. He loved that man. Mr. Van was good to Daddy, taught him things, gave him a horse, opportunity. No one knew how Mr. Henry would handle their futures at Shadowland.

'A few days later they found out, when Mr. Henry sent for my daddy and granddaddy. They met him in Mr. Van's study. Henry Van, handsome and stately, a few years younger than Granddaddy, was seated behind the huge, mahogany desk. He cleared off the stacks of papers and folders that had been there two years before when Mr. Van sold the 50-acres and the cabin to my daddy. Mr. Henry asked them to sit. They'd never sat in a chair in the plantation house before, they just stood in front of the desk when Mr. Van signed the papers on the property, so they didn't know what to do. Their clothes wasn't clean and they was afraid to dirty the beautiful tapestry.

'Please,' Mr. Henry said. 'Please sit down. There's something important I need to tell you.'

They sat on the edges of those fancy chairs and Henry Van came around and stood in front of them, leaning his rear on the front of the desk. He crossed his ankles in front of him.

'Our attorney read Dad's will yesterday,' Mr. Henry said. 'It included the deed to your property, marked, Paid in Full.'

They was afraid to look at each other. They just stared at Mr. Henry Van, speechless. They didn't rightly know what he meant.

'Well, Samuel, aren't you going to say something?'

"What does it mean, Mr. Henry?" Granddaddy asked.

'My father left you a gift, Samuel,' he said and he looked directly at my daddy. 'The land is yours, debt-free. You don't have to pay the 60% share. It's paid off.'

'Oh, Sweet Jesus. Thank you, thank you, thank you, Mr. Henry. I don't know what to say,' Granddaddy said. My daddy said he just sat there and stared at the white man with the kind face.

'There's more,' Mr. Henry said. 'The cabins you live in, both of them. And the piece of land they sit on. They are yours, too. In fact, all six cabins are yours because they are on one tract of land.' The Samuels didn't know what was a tract of land, but they understood they owned six cabins, the land they sat on and the 50-acres of field in front of the houses.

'The houses?' Both of them said together.

'Yes. But there's a small catch. If you ever decide to sell the land or the cabins, you need to let me have the chance to buy them back at fair market value. If I don't want them or can't buy them, you can sell to whomever you want. It's your property.'

'They was dumb-struck, speechless and motionless. They couldn't even look at each other. They just stared at Henry Van with their mouths opened.

'Samuel and Sammy, my father was a good man,' Mr. Henry said. 'I hope I can live up to his reputation and example. If there's anything I can do for you in the future, come see me.'

'Thank you, sir,' Sammy said. 'Thank you very much, sir. We'll never forget your generosity and the goodness of your father.'

'I hope that means you'll still work for me at the going rate of $15 a week."

'A week?'

'Yeah. I checked with some of the other land owners and I want to pay what they pay. I don't want you to leave and go find work somewhere else.'

'No, Sir. We not leaving you. No, Sir,' Daddy said.

"I'm happy for you both," Mr. Henry said.

'We so grateful," Granddaddy said. "We shore are.' He rose and Mr. Henry stuck out his hand and wrapped it around the skinny black hand, then enclosed it with his other hand.

'You are a good man, Samuel. You stayed with my dad when most of the Negroes ran off. He never forgot that. And you, Sammy. He always had a special place in his heart for you, like a grandson.'

'Thank you, sir,' Daddy said. They walked slowly out the study door, holding their hats in their hands, eyes down, afraid to look at each other. When they reached the front door of the plantation house, Henry Van reached around and opened it for them.

'Thank you for coming, Gentlemen,' he said. 'I'm very happy for you.'

Speechless, they walked home slowly, each in his own thoughts.

*

"That's how my blessings got started. And I been blessed ever since," Catfish said. "My parents never let me forget how hard it was to get what they got and to never take it for granted. I know I'm a blessed man."

"My daddy married Mary Williams a few months after they got the title to the property and I came into the world a couple years later, in 1901. It was a new time for us, for the Massey family."

Catfish finished his story and lay his head back. Within seconds he was snoring.

Marianne and I giggled and tiptoed off the porch.

"Your family's history is amazing," I said as we walked towards the old barn. "You should be so proud to come from such proud, successful people." She didn't answer and it gave me time to reflect on how, for the Masseys, becoming property owners set them free, in a real way.

I thought about my own bondage, held captive by parents who controlled me with money. I wanted to be my own person, proud of who I was, like Samuel and Sammy were when they got their land deed. It was like a meteor fell on my head that day and I realized the only way for me to achieve the freedom and security the Masseys had found, was to do what they did. They put in an honest day's work, told Mr. Van what they wanted and were willing to do what it took to get it. I could do that—work hard in school, get my degree and a job in New York—so I could be free of my parents' control. Maybe then, I could figure out how to be with Rodney.

I wanted to see him, tell him of my revelation, explain how I felt, and that I believed him when he said that we would be together. I'd been running from that promise. I was ready to tell him I loved him and that I trusted him to make things happen, that I'd quit trying to protect him. So I asked Marianne if I could call him to come over.

"Why Rodney?" Marianne asked. "That's not fair. You came to see me. I don't want to share you."

She had grown taller, and more beautiful. Her hair was long, dark and wavy and her eyes were as big as iris petals, and almost as purple. Nursing school agreed with her because she seemed calmer, more worldly, almost like the chip on her shoulder had grown smaller. I grabbed her hand and squeezed it. I felt proud of my friend.

"I know, and I want to spend time with you, too, but I'd also like to see Rodney."

"What's going on between the two of you?"

"Nothing much."

"I know better, Susie Burton. I can tell there is something you aren't telling me."

"Well, he came to New York to see me at Thanksgiving. But you can't tell a soul."

"I knew it. I could tell by your face that something glowed inside. Are you in love?"

"Mari, you know I can't tell you anything so private."

"Why not? Am I still your best friend?"

"Yes, but you're Rodney's cousin. Let's call it divided loyalties and leave it at that."

"Come on, Susie."

I refused to tell her any of the details and frankly, even though I knew I was in love, I couldn't tell anyone until I told Rodney—and I was finally ready to do just that.

Marianne finally relented and called him from Catfish's phone, the only one in the Quarters.

Rodney said he drove to the quarters the back way, without passing in front of my house. Marianne and I were sitting on the ground with our backs against the old barn when he walked up. He and I looked at each other and wondered how to handle Marianne, but she noticed our exchange and said she had some chores to do, she'd be back later. I thought again how much Marianne had grown.

Rodney looked at me and sighed.

We climbed into the hayloft and were in each other's arms immediately. We kissed, then Rodney pulled away and sat against the wall, next to the opened window. I thought he would undress me and make love to me like he did the last time we were together, but he seemed afraid to touch me. I sat next to him and we held hands in the hay.

After we talked about Christmas, presents, and family, there was not much else to discuss. What we hadn't shared during our week in New York a month before, we'd talked about on the phone and in letters. I didn't want to talk, I wanted his arms around me and his body on top of mine, but Rodney seemed distant and unaffectionate.

Something was wrong. A cloud hovered over us.

"What are your travel plans?" Rodney asked.

"My flight leaves Baton Rouge on January fifth," I said.

"Have you told your parents when you're leaving?"

"Not specifically."

"Do you think you could go to Baton Rouge on the fourth?"

"Let me see what I can do, if I can take the bus on Sunday. My flight leaves at noon Monday."

"That'll work," he said. He kissed me passionately, told me he loved me and left. I sat in the hayloft thinking about how I hadn't been able to share my revelation with Rodney or to tell him that I loved him. He was too preoccupied and I wondered what had happened in the past five weeks to disconnect us from the closeness and intimacy we'd experienced in New York.

Tootsie was sitting on her porch when I went looking for Marianne. I'd seen her every day at my house, but it was always refreshing to see her in her own environment, sitting in the straight-backed chair, shelling peas into a silver bowl and humming one of her old Baptist hymns.

"Was that Rodney just leaving?" she asked. She didn't look up from her bowl of peas but I knew she saw me. She smelled of rose water and rubbing alcohol, which she'd told me she used as underarm deodorant. I remember how I laughed at her concoction but how it explained the unusual scent she carried.

"Yes. How was your day, Toot? I guess things are busier with Albert?"

"Oh, it's okay. You and James is gone now so it's not much different than before. I just getting older."

"You aren't old, Toot. What are you? About thirty?"

"Going on thirty-five." She still looked seventeen to me. I noticed her bulging belly but didn't ask about it. I hugged her and kissed both cheeks. Marianne walked onto the porch and we headed back out to the cane fields where we wandered in and out of the

224

rows, talking, joking, and catching up. There was nothing like being with Marianne—it was easy and true and honest and I loved her.

*

Daddy insisted on taking me to Baton Rouge after mass on Sunday. We had a late lunch and he dropped me at the airport because I told him I had an afternoon flight. I knew Rodney was in Baton Rouge and I went to a pay phone in the airport and called the number he gave me.

"Wait an hour," I told him. "I can't trust Daddy. It would be just like him to come into the terminal to make sure I'm on the plane."

"I don't think I can wait an hour. I miss you."

"After Wednesday I wasn't sure you still loved me," I said. He laughed a forced laugh. "Okay, let's say forty-five minutes."

I thought maybe something was wrong, but I shook it off. We were always nervous about meeting in Louisiana and I remembered he'd promised his dad he wouldn't see me in Jean Ville, ever again. That was probably why he was skittish on Wednesday.

He picked me up in a cab, afraid someone would recognize his car. The cab dropped us at Rodney's dorm next to his parked car on the Southern University campus. It was cold, about forty-five degrees and rainy. The dampness in the air and the low clouds above made it feel more like thirty-five. I drew my overcoat around me and tied the sash at the waist. Rod saw me shiver and opened the car door so I could slide in out of the raw weather. He started the car and adjusted the heat then turned towards me. He took my hand and kissed my fingertips, one at a time. Then he turned abruptly and drove off.

"Where are we going?" I asked.

"I got a hotel room. I hope you don't mind. Am I being presumptuous?"

"I said I wanted to be alone with you, Rod. Am I being presumptuous?" I giggled. He stared ahead. For some reason Rodney

225

seemed nervous, which made me nervous. I tried to make small talk, but we didn't seem comfortable together. I concluded that a cloud of fear hovered over us when we were together in Louisiana, at least I hoped that was the problem and that nothing had changed between us. I turned the radio on and "I Wish It Would Rain" was playing. He turned the volume down.

"Rod? Is something wrong? Do you need to tell me something?"

"Nothing's wrong, Baby."

"Rod, I'll understand if there's someone else. You were here without me for over a year. You're a hot-blooded guy." He jammed on the brakes and pulled into the parking area at a gas station. He turned the engine off and turned to me, angry.

"How can you say that? How can you question how I feel about you?"

"What's the matter? I've never seen you angry. I know something is wrong. There's something you aren't telling me."

"It has nothing to do with us, Susie. There's no one else. I haven't looked at another girl since I met you five years ago. You are all I think about, dream about, care about. How can you question that?"

"Rod, please calm down and look at me. What's wrong?" He looked away and didn't say anything. I thought if I waited, he would talk but he started the car and backed out onto the road. He stared through the front windshield. His jaw was set, his lips clamped in a straight line, his eyes squinted. I could only see his profile but I could visualize the frown wrinkles on his forehead. I felt like he had just run away from me.

When we stopped, he got out of the car and left it running while he went into the lobby to check in and get the room key. When he came back he pulled the car around to the parking lot, got out and opened the trunk. He took my bag out and swung a backpack over his shoulder, then came to my side of the car and motioned for me to roll down the window.

"Here's your key. Room 360. Please give me five minutes, then go straight to the elevators and come up."

"Isn't this the place that looks the other way?"

"Susie, would you please do what I ask?" I nodded and rolled the window up.

I watched him walk off and had a sinking feeling in the pit of my stomach. I waited for about fifteen minutes, until my tears subsided, then I walked into the lobby of the hotel, past the front desk and got on one of the two elevators. When I opened the door to room 360, Rod met me, pulled me into the room and closed the door, quickly. He took both my hands in his. I could see gentleness in his eyes, but there was something else. Something dark and sinister. I was afraid.

"We had a visit from the Klan last night."

"Oh, God. What happened?"

"They burned a cross in front of our house and wrote nasty things all over it."

"What were the accusations?"

"Leave the white girl alone! Or else. And other stuff you don't need to know. My dad gave me an ultimatum—go to New York or end it."

"What did you tell him?"

"Susie, I love you, but I can't go to New York. I don't have the money. I'd have to drop out of college, give up on my dreams of law school." Tears ran down his face.

"Of course you can't, Rod." I walked to the window. I didn't want him to see my face, the tears that welled in my eyes, the thoughts that I tried to deny: *if he loved me he'd come with me.*

"I understand." But I didn't. Maybe my head got it, but my heart, well, it didn't. "I would never ask you to give up school, your dreams."

He walked up behind me and wrapped his arms around my waist. I didn't want to touch him. It would just make it harder to leave him. I felt his breath on the top of my head and lost all resistance. I turned inside the loop of his arms, faced him and put my hands on either side of his face—his gorgeous, handsome, wonderful face.

"I don't want to live the rest of our lives with you fighting for your next janitorial job." I tried so hard to be brave, level-headed, convincing, but tears began to roll down my face as if a dam broke somewhere inside. And that's how I felt—like my gut had split open.

Rodney didn't say anything. He looked at me and pulled me close. My head rested on his chest, and he stroked my hair.

"How did they find out?" I whispered into his chest.

"It's probably a coincidence, but it happened Thursday night, the day after we met in the Quarters."

"Who would know?"

"I'm not sure, but we can never meet in Jean Ville again. It seems like every time we've ever seen each other in that town, we've been found out. It's as if there's a spy watching us. Someone close to us, someone who knows us. We have to be more careful."

I pulled away from him, shocked by his last words.

"Be more careful? Are you crazy? We can't continue this. We have to give it up. It's way too risky. We're being selfish. And you can't decide that you don't care what they do to you. What about your family? Remember what they did a few years ago?"

"Don't you think that's been weighing on me?" He dropped my hands and walked to the window, enclosed by heavy drapes. He pulled them open a few inches, stood rigid and stared at the grey sky. I stared at his back and smelled fear swirl in the room. It came from his pores—mine, too.

Our lovemaking was intense, but sad. We didn't say it, but we both knew this was the last time. We had to let go of this impossible dream. What were we thinking, anyway? No matter where we lived, our families would always be in Jean Ville, and his family could be in danger, real danger.

Rodney's life was more important than any relationship. I knew I'd rather let him go and know he was alive walking on the same earth, than to hold onto him and have him killed.

When he took me to the airport the next day we didn't say the words, the look in our eyes said it all.

Good-bye.

He told me later that he watched my plane until it disappeared behind the clouds, then he sat on a bench in the corner of the Baton Rouge airport and sobbed.

Rodney became obsessed with finding out how the Klan got their information. How could anyone know we met in the Quarters that afternoon? We'd only been together for an hour, in the hayloft of an old barn behind Catfish's house. Who would tell? Surely not anyone who lived there. If he could solve that mystery, perhaps he could figure out how we could be together without risking danger for his family.

We talked about it when he called but we never mentioned it in letters. I began to question Marianne's loyalty, and Tootsie's. The one person I never questioned was Catfish. He'd never squeal on me. Who then?

I began to wonder how Daddy always seemed to find out when I went to the Quarters. Who would tell him? Maybe it was the same person, someone connected to Daddy and the Klan—or, was Daddy connected to the Klan? It was a mystery that, unless solved, would mean Rodney and I had no chance of ever being together.

After I returned to New York, Rodney went back to Southern University and said that he dove into his studies, determined to finish college on time and with honors. He said he *had* to be accepted into law school, which was dependent on his grades and the results of his LSAT exam. He decided to concentrate on those goals and to put me and the Klan out of his mind for the time being. He told me later that, in his mind, if he could get a law degree, he could move to New York, but that was almost five years away. What were the odds that we'd still remember each other by then?

We talked on the phone every month or so and wrote long letters at first. Then the letters got shorter and the time between them longer. I wondered what his life was like, but I didn't really want to know. We'd decided to move on but I would hear his voice on the other end of the phone and I'd be a mess all over again. I knew we had to stop calling and writing. We needed a clean break.

It took me six months to get on with my life. I learned later that Rodney eventually moved on too. Looking back, it was probably the best thing for everyone.

Part Six: 1970-71

～ Chapter Fifteen ～

～

Rodney Moving On
1970

ANNETTE DUNNING GRAVITATED into Rodney's life by accident. She worked in the law library as a part-time student on Work-Study. The summer before his senior year he began to go to the library to study for the LSAT and to do research for his final project in political science, his major. Annette was helpful. She found the books he needed, allowed him to check out more than allowed and, when he was late returning books, she stamped the correct return date on the ticket.

She was a beautiful girl with skin the color of cashews, deep brown eyes and long hair she had straightened every week. Annette was a year behind him at Southern and majored in Secondary Education with a concentration in English. She was a huge help when Rodney needed someone to edit his final papers and projects.

In his last semester of undergrad, Rodney needed to attend a number of university-related functions and was expected to bring a date to most of them. He asked Annette and she readily accepted. He bought her a corsage for graduation night and they danced until the band quit at one o'clock in the morning. Rodney's family came to graduation and met Annette. His mother fell in love with the pretty, intelligent girl from New Iberia, Louisiana. She was charming, well-read and had a bubbly personality. And she was colored, available and perfect for the Thibault family.

Rodney was a bit overwhelmed by his mother's reaction but let her talk him into accepting an invitation by Annette to visit New Iberia and meet her family before he returned to attend summer school in anticipation of law school.

When he arrived at the Dunnings' home, they greeted him as if they knew him.

"Annette's told us so much about you, Rodney," Mrs. Dunning said. "It's nice to finally put a face with a name. And not a bad looking face," she said, looking at her daughter. They both giggled. Rodney blushed.

Mr. Dunning shook Rodney's hand forcefully, and said, "So glad to know you," so many times Rodney lost count. They offered him a drink and he finally settled on a beer, although he wasn't much of a drinker. Mr. Dunning made a pitcher of Martinis, brought it out on the veranda and served Annette and her mother.

"Sit down, son," Mr. Dunning said and patted the pillow next to Annette on the small settee that required the two to sit so close their hips pressed against each other's. Rodney was uncomfortable with the arrangement but tried not to show it because the Dunnings were falling all over themselves trying to make him feel welcomed.

"Would you like something to eat? I just took some brownies out of the oven."

"He doesn't want anything sweet with beer, honey," Mr. Dunning said to his wife. "How about some nuts, Rodney, or some chips." Annette seemed nervous. He could feel her body shake a bit, so he put his hand on top of hers for reassurance. She looked at him, smiled and calmed down. Rodney was suddenly aware that he was touching another girl and drew his hand back, as if he'd been bitten. He told Marianne later that he kept trying to remind himself that it was over between us, that we'd both said we needed to move on, but he was struggling with actually doing it. Marianne told him I was probably dating some rich, white guy and had forgotten all about him.

He put his hand back on Annette's. He had to make himself learn to live without me, he said when he explained Annette to Marianne weeks later.

The Dunnings lived in a modest home on Bayou Teche and both parents were schoolteachers at the local high school, now integrated. Mr. and Mrs. Dunning were not happy with integration; they said it took kids away from their neighborhoods and placed them with prejudiced white students and teachers who made their lives more difficult than they already were.

"We thought our kids needed to go to better schools where they had access to books and other learning materials, where they would be in air-conditioned classrooms and have decent lunches. We thought it would give them a better chance to learn and grow and have more opportunities to go to college or get decent jobs," Mr. Dunning said.

"We were wrong," said Mrs. Dunning. The couple wanted to start a private colored high school after Annette returned to New Iberia with a teaching degree the following year.

Rodney liked the Dunnings, even if they were a bit overwhelming. It was nice to be accepted by a girl's family and to have her accepted by his. He also liked it that the Dunnings seemed loving and kind, like his folks, not violent and hypocritical, like the Burtons. Yes, there were benefits to dating one of his own. But the thought of marrying anyone but me, he told me much later, the thought of making love with anyone else, the thought of sharing his innermost self, well, that was out of the question.

Or that's what he said he thought at the time.

Ray Thibault called Rodney at the Dunnings' to tell him he had been accepted to Southern University Law School. Annette and her parents insisted on a celebration, a cochon de lait dinner that was an all-day affair in South Louisiana. All of the Dunnings' friends and Annette's high school classmates came to the boucherie the next day, where they butchered a hog and made boudin, cracklins and sausage out of all the innards, then spread the gutted pig like a star, between two sheets of chicken wire, fastened with twisted pieces of metal. The spread-eagle animal hung from an old swing set frame in front of a huge bonfire. Men sat on straight-backed chairs, drinking beer and poking the side of the pig with a long cane pole to turn it slowly in front of the heat. The smell of grease-splattering on burning wood spread throughout the huge backyard that sloped down to the Bayou Teche.

Everyone congratulated Rodney, slapped him on the back and insisted he toast with them to acknowledge new friendships and future success. They automatically accepted him into their fold.

By the time the pig was cooked and everyone ate, it was after nine o'clock at night and Rodney had lost count of the number of Budweisers he'd had. He'd never been a drinker. Occasionally, to fit in with his college buddies, he would buy himself one beer and nurse it all night, usually leaving a half-full bottle of warm liquid on a table or bar at the end of the evening.

After the celebration dinner in New Iberia, he was drunk. Annette asked him to take a walk with her and he decided it might help to clear his head. They disappeared into the darkness and walked until they reached a clearing on the bayou behind the Dunnings' home. There was a crude-looking boathouse with a deck on top and two boat slips that jutted out into the bayou. Holding his hand, Annette led him inside where a sofa and several outdoor chairs surrounded a fireplace. There was a bar across the back of the cabin with cabinets behind it and a bed sat in the far left corner. It smelled musty, and mildewy.

Other than a courtesy kiss on the cheek after the few dates he had with Annette, Rodney had never touched her. He didn't think about kissing her, but as soon as they entered the boathouse, she wrapped her arms around his neck and started to kiss him, passionately, probing his mouth with her tongue. He stood dumbfounded, his arms hanging limp, eyes opened wide, unresponsive. She didn't seem to notice his lack of interest.

Annette led him to the bed and began to unbutton his shirt. She stared into his eyes, but all he saw was a blur. He tried to tell her he was drunk but she kept saying "Shhhhh," and put her index finger on his lips.

She pushed his shirt off his shoulders and began to stroke his chest. She made guttural sounds like "Ohhhhh," and "Ahhhhh." Rodney tried to focus, but, mostly, he just stood there unable to respond or to walk away. When Annette began to unzip his jeans, he took her hands in his and removed them from his crotch.

"No, Annette," he said. "I'm not even coherent. I've had too much to drink."

"That's not a problem, Rodney," she said. "This might be the only way I ever get you to have sex with me." He felt dizzy and sat on the edge of the bed, his face in his hands, elbows on his knees. He must have blacked out.

The next morning he woke up with a headache and Annette, naked, next to him. His clothes were in a heap on the floor. He slipped out of bed, stepped into his jeans and went outside to pee. He walked, shirtless, into the bayou to clear his head. The water was warm and it felt good as he went under, blew bubbles to the surface, came up and shook his head to get the water off his hair and out of his ears. He climbed onto the bank and sat in the grass in his wet jeans. Unconsciously he pulled a long blade of St. Augustine grass and put it in his mouth, chewing on it with his molars.

When he looked up he saw Annette standing in the doorway of the boathouse with a grin on her face. She wore a robe, tied at the waist but opened down the middle to reveal her breasts and the hair between her legs. His eyes took it all in and he immediately looked away. She laughed aloud. *She saw me nude,* he thought, remembering that his clothes were piled on the floor when he woke up. He must have seen her naked, too, but he couldn't remember.

"How you feelin' this mornin', mon chere?" she asked. He liked the sound of her voice, her Cajun accent, her smile. He felt comfortable with her, but he wasn't in love with her. He had to end this before she fell for him and got hurt. His heart wasn't available just yet.

Rodney avoided Annette the next six weeks until he was forced to go to the library one evening, hoping she'd gotten off earlier in the day, but she was sitting at the desk when he entered.

"Hi, handsome," she said as if nothing had changed. Then he remembered nothing had, except in his own mind.

"Hi," he said. "What time do you get off. I was hoping we could grab a burger and talk."

"I'll be off in an hour. Sound good?"

"Sure," he said and he walked into the reading room and spread his books on the table. He'd take her to Joe's, sit in a booth in the back and tell her it was over. He just couldn't keep dating her now that he knew how she felt and how she had tried to trick him into *maybe* having sex.

He parked in the parking lot across the street from the restaurant. As soon as he cut the engine off, she grabbed his arm.

"I need to tell you somethin', Hon," she said.

"Yeah. I want to talk to you about something, too."

"Me first," she said. She looked excited, elated about something. Maybe she had good news. Maybe she'd be going off to graduate school.

"I'm pregnant," she said. A sound like a heavy wind blew through his ears and filled them with a roar. He couldn't breathe—he felt like he'd been hit in the gut with a pile driver. He put his arms over the top of the steering wheel and lay his forehead on them.

"Oh, God," he whispered. He heard her sniffle and knew she was crying. He didn't care.

"I thought you'd be happy." She whimpered

"Happy?" He raised his voice louder than he'd intended. "Happy?" he repeated, quieter. "Why would I want a baby just when I'm about to start law school? That would mean no law school." He didn't lift his head. It was as if he was thinking out loud.

"I didn't do this by myself," she said.

"I don't remember having sex with you, Annette," he said and he looked up and glared at her. "How do I know I ever did?"

"You think I'm lyin' to you?"

"Are you?" He started the car and drove out of the parking lot. He thought about how his dad warned him and Jerry so many times, "Get a girl pregnant, you marry her and raise the child." Rodney didn't take chances. He didn't want a child, not right now. Not with Annette. They didn't talk until he pulled up in front of her apartment.

"Annette," he said. "I need some time to think about this." He got out of the car and walked around to her side and opened her door. He grabbed her hand to help her get out. She looked up at him before she stood next to him beside the car.

"What's there to think about, Rodney? I'm pregnant with your child."

He drove off in a stew. He'd have to drop out of law school before he got started. How else could he support a wife and baby? What about Susie?

He had to talk to someone, but he couldn't talk to the person he shared all of his innermost feelings with. He told Marianne he knew I'd tell him to do the right thing and would drop out of his life, for sure. He couldn't tell his parents, or his brother. He knew what they would say. The thing that nagged at him the most was that he didn't remember having sex with Annette. *You'd think I'd remember something like that, no matter how drunk I was.*

Rodney drove to Jean Ville and went to the Quarters to see Marianne that weekend. She was studying for summer finals in nursing school. Rodney sat on the edge of her bed and watched her write in her notebook.

"What are you studying?" he asked.

"Biology."

"Hmmm. You learning anything you want to tell me about?" He laughed under his breath, but she heard him.

"What you doing here?" She looked up from her desk.

"I need to talk to you about something." She put down her pen and closed her book.

"You want something," she said. She looked at him lounging across her bed. Rodney stared at her beneath his thick eyelashes. She was a beautiful girl. She had fewer Negro features than he did. He searched her to see if there were still angsts over the Klan's abuse she had suffered seven years back. He didn't see any.

"Well, I need some womanly advice," he said. Suddenly he felt embarrassed. Marianne was no longer a little girl. Did he still know her?

"Well? You gonna ask or lay there and stew? You in trouble?" She got up from her desk chair, sat on the floor in front of the bed, and crossed her legs like a pretzel.

"Sort of." He wanted to get up and pace, but the room was small and full of piles of girlie things.

"Susie?"

"No, Annette." Marianne made a funny face, like *I told you so.*

"Hmmm. That's what you get for having too many girlfriends." She laughed, got up from the floor and sat next to him on the bed. "What'd she do?"

"She says she's pregnant."

"Oh, God, Rod. Is that possible? I mean, did you ... you know, did y'all?"

"That's the problem. I don't know."

"Well listen, older cousin. I might not be as experienced as you, but I know this—if you have sex with someone, you remember it. It's not something that slips your mind." She rolled her eyes and tilted her chin towards the ceiling so her hair hung behind her in heavy waves.

"That's what I was thinking." Rodney told her about the night in the boathouse and how he didn't remember having sex with Annette. Marianne got up and walked to the window. She looked out at her Uncle Sam's house next door. The memory of her lying on that porch when she was barely thirteen crossed her mind, but it no longer caused pain.

"She's trying to trick you." She spoke to the window, but he heard her.

"You think so? What do you mean?"

"She in love with you?"

"Yeah, I think so."

"She want to marry you?"

"Probably."

"You want to marry her?"

"No. At least not now. Maybe in a few years, if at all."

"You tell her that?"

"Yeah. I've told her I'm not ready. That I want to go to law school first."

"That's your answer."

"What?"

"Boys are so dumb." She faced him, her hands behind her back. "Want some cousinly advise?"

"Yeah. That's why I'm here."

"Give it three or four months. Don't have sex with her. See if it's true."

"You really think she would ... ?"

"90 percent."

"What do I tell her? She thinks I'm shirking my responsibility."

"Tell her you'll marry her before the baby comes. It takes nine months, you know."

"Yeah." He thought about that. Maybe. Hmmm. Maybe that would work.

He thought about it all the way back to Baton Rouge. Something about Marianne's advice bothered him. He wasn't sure what it was. He was in a pensive mood when he walked into the dorm room he now shared with Jerry, who was pulling on a pair of basketball shorts.

"Going to shoot hoops?" Rodney asked.

"Yeah. Wanna come?"

"No. I, uh, well, uh ..." Rodney sat on the edge of his twin bed and put his elbows on his knees and folded his hands almost as if in prayer.

"What is it, bro?" Jerry stood still and stared at his older brother.

"Oh, nothing. Forget it." Rodney rested his chin in his hands.

"Come on, Rod, I'm your brother. What's bothering you? If you can't tell me, who can you tell?" Rodney stared at his little brother, now two inches taller at almost 6-feet, 8-inches, a basketball standout at Southern. He admired Jerry. They had shared a room since Jerry's birth, exactly two years after Rodney's, until Rod went off the college. Rodney went home every month, holidays, and semester breaks for the first two years, then Jerry came to Southern and they resumed their roommate status. It felt right.

Now that they were both in college, their brotherhood grew into a close friendship. They were inseparable. They studied together, even took a few classes together. They bowled, went to football games, played intramural basketball and met for most of their meals. Lots of students on campus thought they were twins

Jerry would be a junior when the fall semester started in a week. He had been recruited to play basketball for dozens of colleges in the South but easily chose Southern and received the Freshman Athlete Award after his first year. His sophomore year he was the lead scorer. All the professional teams were after him, but Jerry said he would finish college before he agreed to play pro ball. No one did that. If you were called up, you went and left your education behind. But Jerry was solid, responsible. He said he'd rather be a lawyer than a professional basketball player.

Jerry volunteered at the newly-organized Big Brothers clubhouse in Baton Rouge and had "adopted" two pre-teens. He brought them to campus, took them to games, the library, the Student Union. He spent hours with them throwing Frisbees, footballs, baseballs and kicking soccer balls. And they played basketball on the outside courts on campus and at the clubhouse every free moment.

Jerry never missed mass on Sunday and often attended daily mass during the week. He kept a small bible in the back pocket of his jeans. Rodney didn't know how often he read it, but it was dog-eared and ratty.

Rodney was proud of his brother.

They talked about opening a firm together after Jerry finished law school, one that would serve colored people who couldn't afford an attorney. They spent hours discussing that dream.

Jerry had a girlfriend, a beautiful girl named Sarah, from Denham Springs who was a junior and also wanted to go to law school. Jerry said she made all As and wouldn't have a problem with the LSAT. He and Sarah were already talking about marriage. Jerry said, "When you know, you just know," which, Rodney told Marianne, made him think about me. I was the one secret he kept from his brother. What was there to tell, anyway?

Jerry thought Rodney should ask Annette to marry him. When Jerry questioned why Rodney was dragging his feet, the older brother just said he wasn't ready and he wasn't sure if she was the right one. Jerry didn't pressure Rod, but he really liked Annette, who had become close friends with Sarah.

"Do you think you'd want to marry her if she went to law school?" Jerry asked one evening as they sat at Sammy's Grille listening to the Platters and the Four Tops on the jukebox. Rodney laughed.

"That has nothing to do with it. If she's happy teaching, that's fine with me."

"What then?" Jerry asked. Man of few words.

"I'm not sure she's the one, Jer."

"What do you need to be sure?"

"How do you know Sarah is the one?"

"I just know."

"Well, I'm waiting until I know."

"I'm your brother. Explain."

"She's a great girl, don't get me wrong. But there's something missing. Maybe it'll develop."

"Oh." That's all Jerry said. Rodney felt Sarah had put his brother up to the interrogation.

Rodney told Marianne that it didn't bother him that Jerry would try to get information for Sarah. Rodney said he would have done the same thing for me. Marianne told me later.

"Ah! I thought about Susie, not Annette, when I wondered what I'd do in that case" He said his life with Jerry had always been like that—*ah ha* moments of wisdom, knowing that Jerry was born a wise, old soul. Rodney depended on him. He knew Jerry depended on him, too.

"Other than Susie," Rodney told Marianne, "I don't think there's anyone I love more than Jerry.

"Hey, you there?" Jerry asked, interrupting Rodney's thoughts. Jerry sat next to Rodney on the edge of the bed. "What's bugging you?"

"It's Annette."

"Well?"

"She says she's pregnant." Jerry stood up and faced Rodney.

"You didn't tell me y'all were ... uh, you know."

"We aren't, weren't, don't. Oh, I don't know what I'm saying."

"Then who's she pregnant for?"

"She says it's mine."

"Well? Is it or not?"

"Look, I don't remember having sex with her but she says I did."

"I can tell you this, if I ever had sex with Sarah, I'd remember it."

"That's what I thought, too. She says I was drunk and we did it."

"Did you?"

"Well, I got drunk, yes. At that boucherie her parents threw for me. And she took me to see the boat house. We kissed a couple times then I told her I was dizzy. Or that's what I thought happened. I woke up the next morning in bed with her. We were both naked."

"But you don't remember the sex part?"

"No, the last thing I remember was her kissing me and sticking her tongue down my throat and saying it was the only way she could get me to do it with her."

"That sounds fishy. You remember those details, but you don't remember having sex."

"Yup. It doesn't feel right, but I was drunk, so I don't know what happened and she was there and says it did."

"What did you say when she told you she was pregnant?"

"Crap. What do you think I said? That I'd have to think about it. It was a shock, still is."

"What did she say?"

"She cried and said I was calling her a liar and that it was my baby." Jerry moved to his own bed so he could face Rodney, their knees were almost touching. Rodney told Jerry about his conversation with Marianne. "Mari said to tell her I'd marry her before the baby comes and to wait it out. Marianne thinks Annette is trying to coerce me into marrying her, that she's not really pregnant. And Mari said the same thing you just said, 'You'd remember if you had sex with her.'"

"Have you ever had sex, Rod?" Jerry looked directly into Rodney's bloodshot eyes that seemed about to fill with tears.

"Yes."

"With whom?"

"I can't tell you that."

"You think I don't know about Susanna Burton?"

"What? What are you talking about?"

"Look, Rod, if you don't want to talk to me about it, okay. But don't think I'm stupid." Rodney stared to cry. Jerry had never seen him cry and Rod was embarrassed but he couldn't stop himself. He felt so frustrated—Susie, Annette, a baby. He was screwed.

"Listen bro. I'll have Sarah get to the bottom of this. She and Annette are best friends and girls talk. Let me see what I can find out, okay?" Rodney shrugged his shoulders. His face was buried in his hands. He didn't look up.

⌒ Chapter Sixteen ⌒

⌒

Susie Moving On
1970

I'D BEEN BACK in New York a couple of weeks when I got sick, really sick. It was a stomach virus and I couldn't stop throwing up. One day my roommate found me on the floor, out cold. She called the rector who called the housemother who called an ambulance. I learned all of this later, of course. When I woke up I was in a hospital with an IV in my arm, feeling somewhat better.

My doctor was a handsome resident named Josh Ryan. He couldn't have been more than five or six years older than me and had sandy hair, wavy and a little daring, long enough in the back that it flipped up on his collar. I guess you could say Josh, I mean Dr. Ryan, was sexy. I liked him right off. He sat on the side of my bed, his leg pulled up and bent at the knee so that his thigh touched my side through the bed sheet.

"Well, well, Miss Burton," he said. He had a sideways grin and eyes that laughed when he talked. I felt like he was laughing at me, but I wasn't uncomfortable. "You've been a busy little girl, now haven't you?" I didn't know what he meant. I guess he read the confusion in my expression.

"So you don't know?"

"Know what?" His smile faded and a seriousness wiped over him.

"Oh." He took my hand in both of his. "You are pregnant, Susie. May I call you Susie?" I couldn't talk. I couldn't breathe. I wanted to shut my eyes, to shut out the news, but I couldn't do that, either. I lay there with my mouth half opened, my eyes wide as if I'd seen a ghost. My hands trembled. I knew he felt them quiver inside his surgeon's hands.

"Pregnant?"

"Yep. Who's the lucky guy?"

"Uh. You wouldn't know him." My voice trailed off. "We broke up." I whispered, but he heard me.

"Oh. That's not good. I'll give you some time to think about this, to decide what you want to do."

"Do?"

"Yes, you have choices, of course."

"Choices?" He was right. I needed some time to think. How far along, I wondered to myself. Thanksgiving to now, seven or eight weeks. Still early.

"I can refer you to an obstetrician."

"How much time do I have?"

"You sound like you're dying. You're not. You're just having a baby."

"I can't have a baby." That was one thing I knew for sure. I couldn't have Rodney's baby. Not now. Maybe not ever. My daddy would kill me. Literally. And the Klan would kill Rodney. And what would happen to this baby?

"Well, I can't tell you what to do, but I can remind you that abortion is against the law. You could put the baby up for adoption."

"I can't have this baby. I can't put this baby up for adoption. That won't work." He looked confused and I couldn't explain to him that no one would want a mixed-race baby. When Dr. Ryan left my room I cried and cried and couldn't calm myself down. I wanted to call Rodney and tell him, ask him to come to New York and marry me. Make a respectable woman out of me. But, of course, that would ruin his life.

I couldn't have an abortion. I was Catholic. I'd go to hell, for sure, if I wasn't already destined for Hades because I'd had sex—and not just sex, but sex with a colored boy. I didn't know what to do. The next day when Dr. Ryan came to see me we talked. He asked me if I'd decided what I was going to do. I hadn't.

The following day he came in and told me I would be discharged later that day. He gave me a prescription for anti-nausea medicine and some warnings about self-care—drink lots of fluids, eat regularly, try to keep my meals down, and relax. Being pent up was bad for the baby and me. When the nurse rolled me towards the front door of the hospital in a wheelchair, Dr. Ryan caught up with us and took over the nurse's duties. He asked me how I was getting back to campus. When I told him I was taking a cab, he insisted on taking me back to my dorm in his two-seater convertible. We stopped for a drink. He had a beer, I had iced tea. He warned me about alcohol, caffeine, cigarettes and stress. A few days later he called to check up on me and asked me if I'd like to get some dinner. He said he wanted to make sure I was eating. I met him at a burger joint near campus.

"Look," he said after he ate his burger and I picked at mine. It smelled like onions and I wanted to puke, but I held it together. "I know you're in a jam. Do you have anyone you can tell about this? Your mother or father, a sibling, a close friend—the daddy." I shook my head, No.

I'm not sure how things happened between me and Josh Ryan. I was in quite a state, had no one, and he was there for me. I think I'd have died without him. After a few weeks I knew he was falling in love with me, but I had no control over his feelings. I had enough trouble managing my own. With Rodney's baby growing inside me,

I didn't have space in my heart for another being. I sort of rolled with the flow. When I look back on that time I realize I'd sort of spaced out, operated in the clouds, put one foot in front of the other and tried not to think or feel.

The spring semester flew by and I didn't really start to show until the end of May when no one seemed to care during summer classes. I worked in the English Department. I graded papers and read essays and rocked along with only adjunct professors on staff. They didn't know whether I was married and didn't ask.

One Monday I called the English Department and told them I was sick. Other than the two days in the hospital it was the first time I'd done that and no one seemed to notice. I had an appointment in Manhattan with an agency that handled "unorthodox" adoptions. It was hard for me, being from the Deep South, to realize couples who wanted mixed-race babies existed; but they did, and I was able to interview several before I selected the perfect parents for the baby I carried: a white professor at Columbia and his attorney wife. The concept of open adoption was new and unusual, but it seemed the right thing for me and this brilliant child I'd be bringing into the world.

The thing I wrestled with most was that this baby was a product of my love for Rodney and his for me. To give her-him-it away felt like I was giving up on our relationship, our love for each other. In essence, I guess I was. It was a decision I had to make.

I went into labor the last day of summer classes, as if I'd timed it—August 15, the Feast of the Assumption, I thought, ironically. I was so scared when my water broke, I called Josh and he told me to take a cab to the emergency department and he'd meet me there. He was waiting when I arrived and ushered me directly to a delivery room. I squeezed his hand and tried to breathe with the contractions. He was encouraging and assuaged my fears so that, at times, I was laughing at some of the silly things he said.

The pain was intense, but as soon as I heard the baby cry, nothing else mattered. I started to cry, too, as Josh lay the tiny naked infant across my stomach, its cord still attached to my body. Joseph and Emalene came into the room to cut the cord and hold the baby and I detached myself as best I could. I tried to find joy in watching the couple ooh and ahh over the miracle they held, their dreams to have a family finally realized after fifteen years. A girl!

Josh had not met the adoptive couple—in fact I'd just told him about them a few days before the birth, but I hadn't mentioned the race thing. I watched him look at the beautiful colored woman who held this baby Josh and I had nurtured together for more than seven months and his facial expressions changed from surprise to anger to something I couldn't detect. He walked out of the room without a word to me or anyone else.

My emotions were flooded with thoughts of Rodney, separation from our baby, happiness for Joe and Emalene, wonder at Josh's reaction. I turned on my side and sobbed until I fell asleep. When I awoke I was alone in my hospital room. Two days later I was discharged.

I had to move on. Sentimentality would get in my way of me achieving freedom. I had to finish college so I could be on my own; yet, I didn't forget our baby girl. I thought about her constantly.

On August 15, 1971 I received a picture of an amber-eyed toddler with light brown curls corkscrewed to her head and fastened away from her round face with a huge pink bow. Her smile was a big, toothless, "O," as she held onto a coffee table, totally proud of herself for standing. I cried all day; then I called Emalene, who told me I was welcome to visit if I felt I could handle it. I thought about that for a long time.

*

By my third year at Sarah Lawrence I'd decided to major in International Relations and Creative Writing. I wanted to write books and see the world, maybe write books about the world and about Catfish's world.

I didn't go home for Christmas that year. I knew it would be too painful to be there and not see Rodney, and I still had residual postpartum depression. I was afraid he would know, just by looking at me.

Rodney continued to write and call, but the letters and phone conversations became fewer and farther between, until gradually he faded into a sweet memory of first love, first kiss, first sex, first everything. Or at least I tried to push him back to that memory section of my brain.

I read all the current magazine articles about relationships. I learned that girls needed to get through their first love to understand how it worked. We could use the lessons from that experience to make the next ones better. I had learned a lot by loving and being loved by Rodney Thibault.

I figured Rodney was dating other girls since I hadn't heard from him in months. I hoped he was dating colored girls, girls he could take home to meet his parents and in whose homes he would be welcomed. He would never have that with me.

I started to date too, after I recovered and realized Josh Ryan was out of my life. My friends and roommates set me up with a few guys from some of the universities in and around New York. I'd meet them for coffee, go to football games and to an occasional fraternity party. By spring, I noticed that a Connecticut boy, Gavin McClendon, had been asking me out regularly and the other boys had backed off. I liked Gavin. He was intelligent, funny and very handsome. By my senior year Gavin and I were an item. He took me to his fraternity parties and formals at Yale University and he escorted me to the few functions at Sarah Lawrence I cared about attending. The schools were about an hour apart by train.

Gavin asked me to be his date for his senior fraternity formal at the Plaza Hotel in NYC. The Yale KA formal was a big deal to the girls at Sarah Lawrence. They ogled over me because I would be attending, and they obsessed about what I would wear. Only one other SL girl had been invited, a girl engaged to a KA.

Gavin took the train to Yonkers that Saturday morning and picked me up in a cab. The Plaza was a magical place. We arrived and were escorted into an elevator by a bellman who looked like he was dressed to march in the Nutcracker parade. Later I learned that Gavin had stopped at the Plaza and checked in before he came to Sarah Lawrence. He said he didn't want me to feel uncomfortable standing in the lobby while he registered. I was impressed with his thoughtfulness, especially since I had misgivings about staying in a hotel room with him, or any guy for that matter. Any guy except Rodney, but it had been almost two years since I'd been in one with him.

I was nervous at first. Then, when Gavin opened the door and I entered the living room of the huge apartment with Persian rugs and French Provincial furniture, I relaxed. I walked to the floor-to-ceiling windows that overlooked Fifth Avenue and Central Park. Next door was Bergdorf Goodman, Louis Vuitton and Chanel. From the outside, the Plaza looked like a castle and I felt like a princess.

I thought the moment the door closed and we were alone, I'd freak out, but Gavin had arranged for me to have a massage and mineral bath in the spa, so I was whisked away and left him in the suite. Later he met me for tea in the famed Palm Court. The magic increased as the day moved on.

My skin was clear and shiny after the facial and, with no make-up, I felt conspicuous in the famous Plaza Tea Room, but Gavin told me he thought I was the most beautiful girl he'd ever seen. I blushed and we sipped champagne and talked about school, graduation and plans for graduate school. It was like a dream and I was being swept away by a handsome, considerate guy who was easy to be with and about as thoughtful as any man I'd known. I guess it was easy to be thoughtful when you had as much money as Gavin, but who was counting?

Back upstairs in the suite, Gavin ushered me into the elegant French-styled bedroom to use the bathroom with gold-plated fixtures. He told me to take my time, then left me alone to dress for the dance. I soaked in the huge garden tub, piled high with bubbles, shaved my legs and underarms, shampooed my hair and dried off with an Italian cotton towel the size of a bed sheet. When I stepped into the living room in my silver form-fitted formal, a slit revealing my left leg, Gavin gasped. I smiled.

His right hand went to his chest, as if to indicate he was trying to keep his heart from coming out of his body and he smiled at me. I laughed at his gesture. Then he looked at my feet in the three-inch silver-glittered stilettos and let his eyes follow the slit in my dress up my leg to mid-thigh, where he paused for a second, and then his eyes continued their journey to my neck. I watched him look me over. His gawking didn't put me off. He didn't try to hide it and he had an endearing smile the entire time.

While Gavin looked at me, I looked at him. He was attractive, no doubt, with his wide rugby shoulders and slim rower's waist. His blonde hair fell across his forehead and sort of shifted sideways while the sides were cut short, over his ears. He had the bluest eyes I'd ever seen, not sky blue but almost navy blue, as deep as bottomless inkwells. He was wearing a black tuxedo with a white shirt, white bowtie and white vest. The combination was unique and, on him, stunning. And he wore a smile that lit his entire face—eyes, mouth, nose, even his forehead lifted to make him seem approachable.

I'd known Gavin for almost a year and I liked him, liked being with him. He took me to museums and on ferry rides. We rode in his convertible roadster to upstate New York for picnics and saw movies as soon as they were released. He escorted me to five-star restaurants and hole-in-the-wall pizza joints. We'd been to formal dances, sloppy football games and sock hops. But on this night things seemed different. Not so casual and fun in a friendship way. I think it was the way he looked at me that made me realize something had shifted.

When his gaze rested on the low-cut neckline of my dress that was held up by slim straps I told myself I'd asked for it by wearing a dress that showed my cleavage in such an alluring way—or at least that's what Debbie, my roommate, said. "You know he's going to fall into your cleavage. You'd better be ready." I'd laughed at her comment, but if I was honest with myself, I'd probably wanted that exact reaction I got from him.

I kept waiting for him to look at ME, but his eyes paused at my mouth where I'd taken extra care to apply lip-gloss to make them look wet. Finally, his eyes stopped on mine.

"You are fabulous," he said. I blushed and felt a hint of innocence.

Gavin didn't try to hide the fact that he was smitten with me, which was charming on him. He dropped all pretence of machismo and discarded the play-hard-to-get games. It was obvious by the way he looked at me and treated me that he was putty in my hands. I guess that's what sucked me in. His complete candor and honesty reminded me of Rodney. No pretence. No playing it cool.

Of course, for a guy who'd always had girls fawn all over him, my indifference towards Gavin over the past nine months was probably a challenge, but I didn't do it purposely. I really didn't think about him unless he called and asked me out. I guess if I'd never heard from him again, I wouldn't have noticed.

Gavin was either a complete gentleman or he was afraid of me, I didn't know which, nor did I dwell on it. I was simply happy he didn't pressure me. He kissed me after dates, held my hand in movies and pulled me close when we danced, but he didn't attempt anything further. That was the reason I felt comfortable agreeing to share a hotel room with him. I trusted him. He'd proven himself.

Looking at him in the living room of the hotel suite that night, gorgeous and unabashedly drooling over me, I guess I let my defences down.

"You smell as fabulous as you look," he said. "You found the gift I left for you on the bed?"

"Yes. Thank you so much, Gavin. That was very thoughtful." It was a beautifully wrapped gift with a bottle of Channel #5 in a navy velvet box. I, of course, dabbed it all over myself.

"It smells good on you. In fact, you give it a unique scent. Perhaps we should name it 'Susanna Number Five.'" We both laughed. The spell was broken but Gavin couldn't take his eyes off me and I kept looking at him, too. He was strikingly handsome. I felt happy, something I couldn't remember feeling since, well, when I thought about it, that week with Rodney in another part of this same city, in a far-off time.

On that magical night at the Plaza I was a princess. All my cares fell away, the past, the pain, the struggles—all of it—and I was happy.

"You look handsome, Gavin," I said. He smiled and his long eyelashes raised from half-mast to fully opened and touched his light eyebrows, almost white from the sun when he rowed and played sports. His square jaw gave him a masculine appearance and he had a deep, sexy voice.

I had a small box in my hand that I knew he hadn't noticed. I bent to set it on the coffee table, opened it and pulled out a single, white rosebud. When I pinned it on his lapel, his lips brushed the top of my head and I noticed his scent for the first time. English Leather, a familiar smell, but Gavin's was flavoured with his own porous outpourings. It was intoxicating. I didn't notice his eyes were closed until I raised my head to look at him, my hands still resting on the lapels of his tuxedo.

"You can open your eyes now, handsome."

"Oh," he stuttered a second. "Thank you. I didn't expect the boutonnière."

"My pleasure." I smiled.

I was glad he'd bought a wrist corsage for me since there was no place to pin one on my shoulder. It was ironic that the one he slipped over my hand was made of white roses—nine of them; one for each month we'd dated, he told me.

I didn't need a wrap since the dance was downstairs in the Plaza Ballroom. I held a small, silver clutch bag and he put his hand gently on the small of my back as he led me out of the suite and into the elevator. I could feel my own body warmth in the palm of his hand that became sweaty before we exited the elevator; still, he didn't remove it. He seemed to want to touch me constantly, knee to knee under the table, hand over mine when he led me to the dance floor, arms around me when we danced. It was like we were attached, always in contact with each other.

Other than the occasional glass of wine or champagne, I wasn't much of a drinker, but that night I felt so relaxed and happy that I drank past my limit. Gavin, on the other hand, who usually drank as much as his fraternity brothers, stayed sober and took care of me. He was ever the gentleman, attentive, kind and loving, a side of him I hadn't seen before, or maybe I'd never bothered to notice.

He asked the band to play "Suzanne," by Leonard Cohen and "I Can't Help Myself" by the Four Tops." When we finally danced the last dance, a slow, sensual pairing to "Unchained Melody," by the Righteous Brothers, I was in a trance. I thought I could feel Gavin's hardness against my leg, but I was tipsy and oblivious. I imagined Rodney's arms around me and pressed into Gavin. He seemed surprised by my forwardness, and pulled me closer. I let him.

After Gavin opened the door to the hotel suite, he lifted me and carried me into the room like a bride. I wrapped my arms around his neck and nuzzled under his chin, pressing my lips against his neck. It seemed natural, like I'd been here before, I thought. He didn't smell like Rodney, but I was too drunk to think about that.

Gavin took his time and was patient with me. He lay me on the bed and began to kiss my forehead, cheeks, chin, neck and shoulders. He gently slipped the straps of my dress off my shoulders and breathed on my cleavage. He sat next to me and removed his jacket.

Looking back I realize he was giving me every opportunity to stop him. It was like he only wanted me if I really wanted him, too.

All the lights were on. The only sound was our breathing and the horns and sirens in the distance. We didn't talk. I kept my eyes closed, He waited for me to stop him, but I didn't. He held me all night. He was staring at me when I opened my eyes in the morning, the sunlight streaming in through the sides of the heavy, velvet drapes. I squinted, closed my eyes and, after a pause, opened them wide.

His arm was under my head and, when I lifted it to look at him, he didn't take it away. He kissed me on the forehead. I pulled the soft, ivory sheet over my breasts, folding my arms across my chest as I sat up in the middle of the bed. He put both his hands behind his head, elbows spread over his pillow.

I looked at the grin on Gavin's face and felt humiliated. I was naked. What had we done? Then I remembered. I thought I was making love to Rodney. Oh, God! I couldn't look at Gavin. I gathered the sheet around me and slipped out of the bed, closing the bathroom door behind me. I leaned against the door and took a deep breath. I thought I heard Gavin chuckle and I felt my cheeks burn.

I took a shower, drank lots of water out of the faucet, brushed my teeth twice and emerged an hour later in the white Egyptian cotton bathrobe I found in the closet.

Gavin wasn't in the bed. I walked into the living room just as the bellman left with a fist full of cash and closed the door behind him. I smelled the bacon and sausage before I saw the breakfast feast laid out on the dining table, a vase with at least a dozen white roses in the center. Gavin, dressed in jeans and a navy Polo shirt, walked up to me, kissed me on the cheek, put the palm of his hand in the small of my back and led me to the table.

He sure was handsome and his shirt matched his eyes. He didn't speak. I was glad.

He pulled out a chair and I sat. He sat at the head, catty-corner from me, and took my hand. He held it on the beige linen table cloth. The sweet smell of roses filled the room while breakfast aromas rose from below silver-domed platters and the rich flavor of fresh brewed coffee seeped from the silver pot. I heard his breathing, or was it mine?

"Susie," he whispered. I didn't look up. He put his fingers under my chin and lifted it up. I kept my eyes downcast. "Please, look at me." I lifted my lashes and looked at him out of the tops of my eyes. I looked down again.

"Please," he repeated.

I looked at him. Tears pooled in my eyes. I couldn't help it. And I couldn't explain it. It was too complicated.

"Please don't cry. You are incredible. Last night ... well, thank you for last night."

I couldn't answer. Tears ran down my cheeks. I was so embarrassed. I'd never felt like this with Rodney, embarrassed, guilty as if I committed adultery, cheated on the man I loved. Gavin squeezed my hand.

"What can I do to make you feel better?" he asked.

"Tell me we didn't have sex."

"Okay, I'll tell you that if it will help. But, Susie, I want to remember last night."

"Well, I want to forget it," I said. I got up and stormed out of the room and slammed the bedroom door. I could feel his eyes bore through the closed door as if he could drill a hole in it, reach inside and make me come back.

I didn't want to see Gavin again but, somehow, it got to be routine. It was easier than starting over with someone new. At least, with Gavin, everything was in the open.

When I went home with him for Christmas his parents fell all over me. When we returned to New York I saw a doctor and got a prescription for the birth control pill.

*

I graduated with honors, but no one from my family was there. I'd only seen them once in the three and one-half years I had been at Sarah Lawrence, so I didn't miss them. But I still missed Rodney, who I hadn't seen in almost two years and I missed Marianne. And Catfish. And Tootsie. Rodney and Marianne wrote to me, once a month or so and, every now and then, Rodney called. I never told Gavin about Rodney and, when Rodney and I talked, we didn't mention our personal lives.

Gavin came to my graduation ceremony on campus that beautiful May afternoon, and looked handsome as ever in his preppy navy blazer complete with a Yale emblem on the left pocket, red bow tie and grey slacks. I knew we made a striking couple—Gavin, the tall blond athlete with wide shoulders and a pedigree a mile long, and me, the mysterious redheaded Southern girl with a degree from a prestigious college.

When we entered the ballroom at the Plaza that night for the graduation ball, heads turned and flashbulbs lit up the room. I smiled as if I was the happiest girl in the world. Why shouldn't I be? A gorgeous, wealthy, Yale graduate on my arm, a college degree from Sarah Lawrence, and a promising future in writing and publishing.

I knew Gavin's parents had encouraged him to ask me to marry him. He hinted at it, but I let him know I was not ready to be asked. When I wrote home and told my parents about Gavin, I built him up so they would be proud of me. From the time I was a little girl, my mother told me I would go to college, not for a BA but for an

MRS degree. Mama was proud that I had the promise of such an *exploit accomplir*. Better yet, I would live fifteen-hundred miles away from her.

Graduation night was a repeat performance of the KA formal at Christmas. Gavin and I spent it in one of the Plaza's lavish hotel suites, but this time, he brought me breakfast in bed in the morning. There was a small gift, wrapped in white paper with a white satin bow and a Tiffany's label on the bottom right corner sitting on the breakfast tray.

"Gavin, if this is what I think it is, I can't open it, not yet. I'm not ready."

"Open it, Beautiful. Don't be afraid." He sat next to me in the bed with his arm possessively over my shoulder. I looked at him and repeated my statement.

"I don't want to open something I can't accept and make you feel rejected. I'm just not ready."

"Open it. Trust me." I thought of how many times Rodney encouraged me to trust him and how he'd never let me down. It wasn't fair to compare Gavin with Rodney, but who else could I use as an example of the kind of man I could trust with my future? I opened the gift slowly, looking up at Gavin periodically and asked, "Are you sure? Can I trust that this is not something that comes with a commitment?"

"Trust me, Susie," he said. I wanted to believe he understood that, if it was an engagement ring, I would say "No."

When I flipped the lid of the black velvet case, I immediately snapped it shut.

No, Gavin couldn't be trusted. He'd tried to trick me. Rodney would never do that. I handed the untouched gift to Gavin, got out of bed and went to the bathroom. When I closed the door, I knew I'd closed him out of my life for good.

I had applied to Harvard Graduate School the previous fall and was accepted. I knew I would be able to attend only if they awarded me a full scholarship because Daddy refused to pay for further education and, anyway, I was ready for my freedom. But Harvard's offer only included tuition and books, no room and board. I spent several days in Boston looking for a job and was offered a part time position with a small publishing house. It wasn't enough to cover living expenses so I took a second job waiting tables at an all-night diner.

I moved to Boston for the summer to see if I could make it work, financially, with the two jobs. Even with a roommate in a small, one-bedroom apartment, I had to work sixty hours a week to make ends meet and I knew I couldn't continue at that pace and make decent grades in grad school at Harvard. In addition, I was terrible at waiting tables and quit that job within two weeks. By the first of June I had made the decision to leave; it just wouldn't work.

~~Chapter Seventeen~~

~

Jean Ville Summer/School Days
1971

RODNEY TOLD ME he was too busy to realize we hadn't spoken or written in months. Neither of us sent cards or letters of congratulations to each other in May. We'd both gone on with our lives and I thought that's how it should be. The craziness needed to be over and it felt like it was.

Rod said that after graduation he became obsessed with getting in touch with me. He wondered what I was doing that summer. Perhaps he could take a train to New York after summer school. He told me that he suddenly felt a burning desire to see me although, to me, the timing seemed strange. He said he went to the pay phone in the lobby of his dorm and called.

"The number you have called has been disconnected ..." He said he tried the number again, maybe he dialed wrong. "The number you have called ..." He couldn't imagine that I might have left New York after graduation without calling or writing him to say where I would be. But then, he thought, we hadn't spoken in, how long? He hadn't heard from me since, when?

He said he went to his room and pulled out the box of letters he'd saved. He flipped through them to find the most recent.

Marianne told me he called her, frantically searching for me. He knew she and I stayed in touch. He told her he wanted to shoot himself for being so neglectful of the woman he loved, even if we had decided it was over between us and he was dealing with the "Annette Issue." Marianne told me that for Rodney, it would never be over between us.

Tootsie answered the phone when Rodney called and said Marianne was at the hospital. She'd finished practical nursing school the year before and was working at Jean Ville General. She said she loved her job and was saving money to go to Our Lady of the Lake Nursing School in Baton Rouge to become a Registered Nurse.

"Have you heard from Susie?" Rodney asked Tootsie.

"Well, shore, Rod," she said. "Susie got home Monday. She was going to stay in Boston for the summer, but things didn't work out."

"Boston?"

"Oh, didn't she tell you? She was going to Harvard. They accepted her and all, but she couldn't get a job to pay for school."

"Harvard?" I knew that would be news to him. I could visualize him rubbing his forehead with his free hand.

"Yep. She's trying some other schools. I think she said graduation schools."

"Graduate schools?"

"Yeah. Maybe that's what she said. Graduation schools."

"How long will she be in Jean Ville?'

"Not sure. Until she gets in one of them schools, I suppose. She got a job at the hospital for the summer."

"Jean Ville General?"

"Yeah. Her daddy got her on with the man what runs it."

"The Administrator? Mr. Michel?"

"Yeah. That's him. I gotta go, Rodney. I'll tell Marianne you called." She hung up. Rodney said he looked at the receiver and heard the buzz of the dial tone. He left it dangling from its silver coil and stepped into the lobby of his dorm. It was Friday. He threw some clothes in a backpack, got in his old, blue Mustang and set out for Jean Ville.

*

I was nervous about being back home. This was only my second trip to Jean Ville in almost four years. My last trip home got me a black eye that, thankfully, healed before I returned to New York. On that trip I'd been home only two weeks. I was petrified about what might happen if I spent the entire summer in Jean Ville. But I was secretly glad to get away from Gavin. I'd told him we needed to move on. We'd grown apart after I refused the two-carat diamond ring and moved to Boston for those few weeks. Gavin argued, pleaded for another chance, told me how much he loved me, adored me, but I knew I couldn't trust him.

There were some good things about being home for the summer. I got to see my siblings and to know my baby brother, Albert, who was now almost four. I sneaked off to see Marianne in the Quarters and we'd have lunch together in the cafeteria at the hospital when she worked the day shift. I didn't care what people thought. I considered myself free, even if I was staying at my parents' house. Anyway, Marianne looked white, I told myself.

The best thing about being home was I got to spend time with Catfish. I went every week, sometimes twice a week, and didn't care who knew. I was emboldened by my college degree and full-time job. I felt protected from Daddy's wrath by people like Dr. David and Mr. Michel, and I didn't worry about Rodney or his family since we weren't seeing each other. Rodney wasn't even in Jean Ville that summer.

Catfish was older, slower and wore out quicker, but he told me more stories, a little at a time. He told me about how he met his wife, Alabama, and about how she died and how much he still missed her. He talked about losing his mom and dad. He said his mother, Mary Williams Massey grew up on the plantation and that she learned to read and write from Catfish's grandmother, Anna Lee who started the first school for coloreds at Legion Baptist Church.

*

School Days

'Mr. Van would give all the workers Sundays off. Now, Mrs. Van, she didn't like that none, and Bessie, the cook, would fix a big breakfast and leave dinner on the stove for the noon meal. Then she'd go on back while the rest of us'd be having a hoedown or a singing revival and fix the Vans some liver and grits or cous cous with cracklins for supper.

'My granddaddy and grandmamma, Mama and Daddy, Maureen, Bessie, heck, all the folks in the quarters, we'd walk to the Legion Baptist together on Sunday mornings. The preacher and his wife had taught my granny, Anna Lee, how to read and write do numbers and now Granny was teaching the youngsters.

'It was bout three miles to the church, and the women would bring covered dishes and have a picnic after the service while Granny taught school. That's where my daddy met my Mama. It started when Mama was about five, and when she was about eight or nine and my daddy was thirteen or fourteen, the older folks would head on back to the quarters and leave Daddy to walk Mama home, cause the lessons was taking longer and longer.

'That's when two things happened to my daddy. First, he sat in those lessons and he learned to read, write and figure numbers hisself. Second, he fell in love with Mary Williams, though he says it weren't till she was bout thirteen or fourteen. When she turned fifteen—by then he was twenty—he axed Mr. Van could he marry her.

'Mama and Daddy made sure all of us learned to read and write, too, and Mama, she taught kids with Granny and took over the colored school when Granny got too old. That was before 1920 when my mama was just sixteen, seventeen. I think. Now here we are, some fifty years later and the state's got schools for our kids. Ain't that something?'

Catfish told me about the other people who lived on Shadowland Plantation, George, Big Bugger, Lizzie and others who came in and out of Samuel and Sammy's lives. And he told me stories about the Vans, stories told by the house maids.

Each time I left Catfish, sitting in his rocker, eyes closed against the filtered sunlight, his grandchildren playing in the yard, crisp white sheets hanging on the clothesline, I'd kiss him on the cheek and hug his neck. He'd grin, but he never kissed me or even touched me, except to squeeze my hand ever so slightly when I put mine in his.

I'd go home and write everything I could remember in ruled composition books I was saving for the time when I could write Our Book.

*

Marianne told me that Rodney came to Jean Ville looking for me one weekend, but no one seemed to know where I was. He was in summer school in Baton Rouge and had to get back. All the better, I thought. We can't see each other, anyway. Too risky, and we were finally over each other, I thought. We needed to keep it that way.

After I'd been home about a month, I went to the Quarters after work on Friday at about four o'clock. I was sitting on the porch with Marianne and Catfish. He tried to tell us a story about how his daddy fell in love with his mother, who worked up at the big house, but Cat was weak and had a hard time completing sentences, so we ended up sitting together and watched a few of the children jump rope and listened to the sounds of summer.

I heard a familiar noise, a car engine that sounded like a sewing machine. I'd have known that sound anywhere. I looked at Marianne, who gave me a guilty sideways glance before she got up and helped Catfish into his house. I watched in disbelief and fear as

Daddy's familiar olive-green Mercedes drove up to Marianne's house. I saw Tootsie look out her kitchen window. That's when I realized it must be after five o'clock. Tootsie was home from work. I was scared to death. Someone must have told Daddy where I was and he came to find me in the Quarters! I climbed off the side of the porch to hide and plan my escape.

I watched in disbelief as Daddy climbed the steps of Tootsie's cabin and entered her back door without knocking. I looked at Tootsie's kitchen window and saw my daddy embrace Tootsie, then the two of them turned and walked out of my eyesight and got lost in the bowels of the little house.

Marianne came out of Catfish's back door and I whispered for her to join me in the trees on the side of the house.

"How long have you known?"

"A long time," Marianne said.

"And you didn't tell me?"

"I didn't tell nobody. Don't talk about it."

"I can't believe it. Not that I don't believe my dad would do something so dirty, but because you and Tootsie have known and didn't tell me."

"How we gonna tell you your daddy and my mama been doin' it?"

"How long has this been going on?"

"Long as I been alive, I guess. I never known it any other way."

I had to get out of the Quarters before Daddy re-emerged so I made my way home along the tree lines behind the houses on South Jefferson Street. I ran the entire way. I was out of breath when I threw myself across the bed in the huge blue room that felt like it shrank to the size of a matchbox and pressed around me. I could smell the salt and mucus run from my eyes and nose as I squeezed the feather pillow and breathed in dust mites and mildew.

I was shocked and devastated about Daddy and Tootsie.

I felt more betrayed by Tootsie than by my daddy and was hurt that Marianne had lied to me. Even Catfish must have known and didn't tell me. Anger grew inside me as I thought about how my daddy had kept me from the Quarters with his high-handed rules, yet he went there.

The worst of it was that the very people I thought I could trust and who I believed loved me, the ones I considered my family more than my own flesh and blood, those people I loved most in the world, had betrayed me. I wondered if Rodney knew, too. That would finish me off.

The more I thought about Daddy and Tootsie, the more confused and deflated I became.

Did Daddy know about Rodney? Had Tootsie told him? Was she the leak? Was Daddy the one who alerted the Klan? I tried to reconstruct the timing of the KKK incident with the Thibault family. It was a few days after Rodney had talked to me at the Cow Palace. He only spoke to me for a few seconds, and my daddy beat me within an inch of death for it.

Didn't Rod say they thought I was going to die? No one ever mentioned the incident afterwards—the last sacraments, my hospital stay, the bruises and broken bones that healed slowly, or the emotional scars the whole thing left on my soul. It was as if it never happened. And the Klan's visit to Rodney's house when I came home that first Christmas and we saw each other in the hayloft? What about that incident—the visit that ended our relationship? Who alerted the Klan then?

I wondered what else I didn't know. How long had this been going on between Daddy and Tootsie? I thought about what Marianne said, "Long as I been alive, I guess. I never known it any other way." What could that mean?

*

I joined my family at the huge round kitchen table for dinner that evening but I couldn't eat. I couldn't swallow. Something felt stuck in my throat and my chest hurt so bad I wouldn't have been surprised if I'd had a heart attack. I couldn't look at Daddy knowing he'd just been with Tootsie and was now sitting at the table as if everything was perfectly normal.

I was in trouble for not cleaning my plate, but I knew I would throw up if I swallowed even one bite of lasagna, so I excused myself and ran to the bathroom. Before I reached the door Daddy was on me like a pancake on a griddle.

"Your mother worked all afternoon to prepare lasagna because she knows it's one of your favorites and you didn't eat it. How dare you treat her that way." I hated lasagna, always had. However, that's not why I didn't eat it.

I looked at him and wanted to spit in his face. He disgusted me.

He slapped me across the face but I didn't feel it, nor did I respond. That made him angry so he slapped me again, and again, until I fell to the floor. Then he started to kick me. I rolled into a ball and thought about Rodney and the last time we were together, when we made love. I thought about the week he spent with me in New York—that glorious, wondrous time that was like a dream I could fold myself into so I didn't feel my father's kicks and slaps. I thought about how wonderful it was with Rodney, and how different it was from Gavin. I remembered when I knew I was pregnant and how it felt to carry Rodney's child inside me. I thought about Josh Ryan and his kindness, how he'd stuck with me through it all, but in the end he couldn't stomach what I'd done and who I'd done it with. And I thought about the little girl in the picture, her wide grin and amber eyes.

That's what I thought about when I was on the floor in front of the bathroom door, being kicked. My baby was almost two years old, walking, saying words, playing patty-cake. She would be beautiful, like her daddy. She would be loving and gentle and kind and she would love me, unconditionally, forever.

When I woke up from the beating, it was dark and I was in my bed. I tried to sit up, but everything hurt, so I lay back and tried to sleep. It was Friday night. The next morning I sneaked into the bathroom to look at myself. Well, I couldn't go to work like that on Monday. I had two black eyes and cuts on both sides of my face; one needed stitches. One finger was definitely broken and I had difficulty taking deep breaths. I could barely walk and everything hurt.

I got two aspirin out of the medicine cabinet and tiptoed back to my bedroom. I dressed in jeans and tennis shoes, grabbed my purse and slipped out the front door. The sun had not risen but there was a yellow glow in the distance, suggesting a new, clear day. I felt it was an omen and stopped under the huge old oak, moss draped almost to the ground and listened to a redbird sing, then a sweet tweet reply from the tall pine across the street. Love birds, I thought. Yes, a new day. I'm done with my old life.

I knew Dr. David would be awake. He went to the hospital to make rounds early, even on Saturdays. I walked across the street and rang the doorbell. He answered it, took a long look at me with sad eyes, his bushy eyebrows lowered and drawn in to the bridge of his nose. He inhaled deeply and put his arm around me then gently pulled me inside and closed the door. Without a word he led me into the den and motioned for me to sit on the large, white sectional. If it hadn't been leather, I would have been afraid to stain the beautiful sofa with the blood that seemed to come from various places.

Dr. David went into his study, adjacent to the den and came back with his medical bag. He didn't say a word, but went straight to his work, I thought, like the Santa Claus I once believed in. He gave me a shot near the cut on my cheekbone, then stitched it up with tiny, neat sutures. He set my finger and began to treat each cut, bruise and bump, systematically. He unbuttoned my blouse and pulled it open just enough to reach the abrasions, then he worked on the other side, then my back. I stood and he pulled my jeans down so he could treat my butt and the tops of my legs. Every now and then, I'd feel a little stick and he'd take a few stitches. Finally, he listened to my breathing with his stethoscope and told me I had a few cracked ribs. I pulled up my shirt and he wrapped an Ace bandage round and round my torso, below my breasts.

When Dr. David was done, he gave me a pill and led me to the first bedroom off the hall. He pulled back the covers and I got in the comfortable bed. He sat next to me on top of the feather-filled duvet and put one big, burly hand on either side of me. His face was above mine, the kindest expression I'd ever seen spread across its entirety—eyes, forehead, nose, mouth, chin, and the hint of dimples in his cheeks, not deep because his smile was only a kind grin.

"You don't have to tell me what happened. I know. I'm so sorry. I should have stopped this long ago. Each time, I guess I tried to tell myself that it would be the last time. Then you moved away and I was relieved. When I saw you at the hospital this week, I knew it was only a matter of time."

I looked at him while he talked. My eyelids began to feel heavy.

"You were very brave to come here this morning, Susie. You did the right thing."

"I want to go to work Monday, Dr. David. I don't care what I look like. I'm tired of hiding his dirty work from the town."

"You can stay here with me and Erma this weekend. I'll take you to work Monday and we'll make a plan for the rest of the summer."

I was sleepy now. I wanted to thank him, but I couldn't keep my eyes opened.

*

I enjoyed my job at Jean Ville General Hospital. I was a general flunky and assistant to the CEO, Mr. Michel, whom I liked very much. In fact, I liked all the people at the hospital and my work was fun, varied and easy. They paid me well because I had a college degree. I was determined to save every penny.

I went to work that Monday with stitches in my face, left knee, right elbow and several places on my back. I had black eyes and a broken finger, lots of bruises and hematomas. It hurt to take deep breaths, but I'd had a restful, peaceful weekend with the Switzers and felt well enough to work. When Mr. Michel asked what happened, I shrugged and said, "Ask Dr. David. He treated me." I got lots of stares and the older nurses wanted to pamper and baby me, but I shook it off and did my job. I'd been through much worse.

At noon Dr. David found me in the cafeteria and pulled me aside.

"I met with your dad. You can go home and expect to be safe the rest of the summer, unless you prefer to stay with me and Erma. We are happy to have you."

"I couldn't impose. You've done so much already."

"No, Susie. I didn't do enough. I should have put a stop to this years ago. I'm done with that, though, and I'd like to make it up to you. Stay with us."

"I'll think about it, Dr. David. But please know this—I appreciate you more than you could ever know. Somehow I knew I could trust you and you didn't let me down. Thank you.

"By the way, Dr. D, when I was in the hospital a few years ago, a certain colored boy came to visit me one night. You wouldn't have had anything to do with setting that up, would you?" Dr. David blushed and stared at me, but he didn't respond. He didn't have to. I gave him a quick hug around the neck and left the room.

I went home the next week and no one discussed my appearance or asked where I'd been. No one talked to me much at all, which was fine with me.

I went to see Marianne the following Friday, after work. I just drove there and didn't try to hide. After all, if Daddy could do it in the open, why couldn't I? Marianne told me that Rodney had come home the previous weekend looking for me, but no one seemed to know where I was, not even Tootsie.

Bile rose in my throat and tears stung the insides of my eyelids as I thought about the deception that Tootsie and Marianne had pulled off.

"I want to know why you've lied to me," I said. Marianne just looked at me, then tears began to stream down her face.

"You don't get it, do you? I never lied to you. I hate him. Telling you means saying it to myself." My anger began to melt as I watched Marianne's tortured heart break.

"He's a bastard," Marianne said.

"I agree, but he is my father. We only get one." Marianne looked at me in the most peculiar way. "What?" I asked.

"Don't you know? Don't you get it?"

"What, Mari? What are you trying to tell me?"

"You know, Susie." Marianne said. "You a smart girl. Figure it out." I just looked at her. Maybe my mind couldn't grasp it. Maybe my heart wasn't ready. I searched her face for a clue, anything.

"When?"

"Since I was born, you fool!" Marianne got up and walked toward the barn. She moved fast and her arms swung high, her knees bent as if she was marching, her chin was tilted toward the tops of the sugar cane.

I sat in Catfish's chair and rocked back and forth slowly. I needed to think. I breathed the fresh, clean air in the Quarters and tried to relax. I thought about things, like who told my daddy about my trips to the Quarters, and who told the Klan about Rodney. I wondered in my heart if Daddy was responsible for tipping off the Klan. If so, who told Daddy? I was plagued by my dad's relationship with Tootsie and thought there must be a connection.

It was easy to avoid Tootsie most of the summer. I was at work when she was at our house, and when I went to the Quarters, if she was home, she stayed in her cabin. I wasn't ready to face her. It was hard enough to look at Daddy at the supper table every night.

I didn't see Rodney all summer, a sign that he understood it was over, I thought. Of course I didn't know he was dealing with his own issues. Marianne was closed up about Rodney and, I felt sure, she didn't tell him things about me, either.

At home in the evenings when it was so quiet the only sounds were the hum of the fan and Sissy's slow, sleep breaths, I wrote letters and filled out applications for every graduate program in the Northeast and appealed for scholarships. My preference was an MFA in writing, but I'd accept anything in the liberal arts field if the college gave me a full ride.

Two weeks before the fall semester was scheduled to begin, I went to the mailbox and pulled out a large brown envelope from St. John's University in Queens. Someone withdrew their name from the fellowship program and they offered me a full scholarship in the Masters of Fine Arts program. I was elated.

With the money I'd saved working at the hospital I bought a one-way airline ticket from Baton Rouge to New York City and a bus ticket to Baton Rouge from Jean Ville, and had plenty left to help me get moved into an apartment in Queens. I didn't tell my parents about the scholarship or my travel plans. I hoped they didn't know about my last day at work. They had no say in my life anymore. That thought made me feel free.

*

I got up early and walked to the bus station on Prescott Street in the pre-dawn darkness on a Monday morning, the end of August. The world was just waking up and I watched lights begin to appear in some of the windows along Gravier Road. I had a suitcase in each hand and my purse over my shoulder. I inhaled deeply, a last whiff of the moss-draped oaks and hot asphalt, my final reminder of a childhood of love and hate, friendships and deceptions, first love and final good-byes. I would miss Catfish. I loved him like a grandfather, and he loved me. I would miss Marianne, my first and only friend, a sister in more ways than I ever expected. I would miss Tootsie, my surrogate mother, protector, and confidant ... traitor?

Catfish's family had become mine, but I was disturbed and confused by their deception. It hurt. It caught me blindsided because I'd trusted them totally, innocently. I felt a knot form in my throat that begin to tighten, like a rope used for lynching, a chokehold that renders its victim helpless.

The murmurs of waking, the soft whispers of bird calls, the hum of a bus engine, air brakes on the concrete and the beating of my dying heart were what I heard as I waited at the Greyhound station for my final escape. I wondered whether my family would be upset when they realized I was gone, but I knew they wouldn't be, only that they would be upset because I'd sneaked away and tricked them. My dad didn't like to lose and today he'd feel like he'd lost—to me. I knew his elephant's memory would come back to grab me, body, soul and heart one day.

But for now, I was free.

Marianne told me that Rodney had a job in the Clerk of Court's Office in the Baton Rouge courthouse for the summer and that he hoped they would let him work part-time after he started law school in the fall. He told her he liked the work and made decent money, plus he had time to study. He got to sit in the courtrooms and listen to interesting cases, which he thought would give him an edge in law school.

I'm not sure who answered the phone when I called. Maybe it was one of the clerks.

"You have a phone call, Rodney."

Rodney said no one ever called him at work. His parents called him at his dorm in the evenings or on weekends. He told me he was worried that something was wrong at home, another Klan visit, his mother was sick, maybe Catfish, as he hurried to the phone on one of the clerk's desks.

"Hello," he said.

"Can you tell them you have a family emergency?"

"What? Susie? Where are you?"

"At the Greyhound station."

"Where?"

"Here. Baton Rouge. A few blocks from the courthouse."

"I'll be there soon. Don't move!" I heard him take a deep breath and swallow hard. He told me later that it was like happiness wrapped in Christmas paper. He pulled up in front of the bus station in a cab thirty-minutes later. I was sitting on a bench in the 100-degree heat, fanning myself with a cardboard square glued to a popsicle stick. I tried to hide my misery and the perspiration that made my dress stick to me at ten o'clock in the morning. I certainly wouldn't miss the oppressive heat and humidity when I got back to New York, but I would miss the gorgeous man who jumped from the cab before it came to a full stop.

He grabbed my bags, threw them in the trunk, opened the back door and ushered me in. He slipped through the back door on the other side. Before his door was completely shut, he reached for me. I fell into him.

Oh, so familiar, so safe, so wonderful. The almost three years felt like three days as the familiar, gentle comfort of his arms wrapped around me and I inhaled ink, sweat, aftershave, laundry soap, and the familiar scent that came from Rodney Thibault's pores. How had I lived without this?

We didn't speak, didn't kiss, didn't grope —we just sat in the backseat with our arms wrapped around each other, my head on his chest. Every few seconds, he would stroke my back and heave.

It was hot in the cab, especially against the radiant heat from Rodney's body. The cabbie took us to a motel on Airline Highway and pulled in front of room number 12. Rodney had a key and let me into the air-conditioned room, a welcomed relief. He followed me inside with my bags, dropped them on the floor, slammed the door and pulled me to him. We had not said a word since the phone call. We kissed hungrily, then he let go and held me away from him.

"I just want to look at you," he said. I stood there, my damp dress clinging to my every curve, my ponytail askew from hugging him in the backseat, my lipstick gone from kissing, but he looked at me as if I was the most beautiful creature in the world.

"God, you're beautiful. You get more beautiful with age."

"You act like I'm an old woman." I laughed. He put an index finger in one of my dimples.

"I've always wanted to do that," he said. "Ever since the first time I saw you at my dad's Esso station. You were thirteen. I fell in love with you that day and I've been in love with you ever since."

"You look good, Rod. You are more handsome than ever. It looks like you grew another inch or two. I didn't think that was possible. How tall are you?"

"Not sure. About 6'5" or 6'6" I think."

"Wow. You make me feel so small."

"You are small, and perfect. You fit perfectly. See." He pulled my five-foot, eight-inch body to him and folded his long arms around my shoulders. The top of my head fit under his chin and tucked comfortably into the crook of his neck. He wore a white dress shirt and I inhaled starch and laundry soap plus a distinct musky scent. He looked gorgeous as ever, and older, more confident.

"You fit, perfectly. We fit," he said.

"Yes. We fit."

My head rested over his heart, a familiar position where I could hear the fierce magic of the organ that pumped blood throughout his body—and feelings, too. When I lifted my head, he bent to kiss me. I had forgotten what his lips felt like—full, wet, sweet. The urgency of our kiss was gentle, thoughtful, regretful. I wonder if he tasted my anguish because he opened his eyes as soon as tears begin to roll down the sides of my nose. He licked my closed eyes.

I was glad and sad. I'd tortured myself on the bus about whether to call him. I felt guilty, like I was messing up his life by dropping in it, knowing I'd be leaving for good the next day.

Our kisses became more intense and he sucked on my bottom lip, softly, at first, while I moved my lips and teeth around so he could get to every square millimeter. He tasted like honeysuckle. He held me gently, yet passionately. How'd he do that?

"If you continue that, you are going to cause trouble," I muttered.

"What kind of trouble?" He continued to tease me with his tongue.

"Hmmm. Not sure."

He was tolerant, pretending to enjoy my antics when I got my hands under his shirt and began to stroke his chest. He let out a deep sigh, picked me up and lay me on the bed on my back. I wanted him more than I'd ever wanted anyone or anything in my life, but I was afraid that it was because I was lonely, afraid and, mostly, because I felt so rejected by Tootsie and the people I'd come to believe loved me. Was that why I called him? Did I need something from him, something to negate the deception and disloyalty I felt from my best friend and her family? Some reassurance he wasn't in on the ploy?

Rodney knelt on the floor beside the bed and bent his head to mine.

"I forgot how blue your eyes are and that, when you look at me I can see my reflection." I saw my own reflection in his amber, gold, green eyes. There were rainbows of blues and pinks in there.

"Tell me about yourself," he whispered. "I've missed you, missed knowing what you are doing, where you are. I tried to call you and your phone was disconnected. I panicked."

"I'm sorry, Rod," I rolled onto my side so I could face him as he knelt on the floor beside the bed. "I've really tried to make a clean break of things with you. I feel guilty calling you today, but I had to see you before I go back to New York."

"When do you leave?"

"In the morning."

"Oh, so soon?" Neither of us spoke for a moment. "Do you want to talk about things?"

"No. There's nothing to talk about. Nothing's changed. I just wanted to see you one more time. I wanted to remember, to see for myself that you weren't a dream I made up."

"It sounds so final."

"This is my last trip to Louisiana, unless it's to return for a funeral."

"Oh, I see." He looked rejected, sad.

We kissed softly and he slowly unbuttoned the top of my dress. I gasped.

"Hold on, Baby. We have all night," I whispered.

"I'm holding. I'm holding."

Our lovemaking was selfless. We were all about each other. He wanted to please me and I wanted to please him. It was gentle and loving, without urgency. We pressed ourselves into each other and became one. I was happy. I had forgotten what real love was. For the moment I let myself live in a dream, unreal, a small blip of hope in a hopeless world.

After we made love I told Rodney about my daddy and Tootsie. I could tell by his face that it was a surprise. It made me feel better that he wasn't in on the cover-up. At least one of the people I trusted was who I thought he was. I told him how hurt I was that I'd been betrayed by Tootsie and Marianne.

"And Catfish," I said. "He's known all along and he never told me. I trusted him like a grandfather."

"Try not to look at it like that, Baby. Catfish has divided loyalties. Tootsie's his daughter. Marianne's his granddaughter. You can't expect him to go behind them."

"Hmmm. I never thought about it that way. I'm just so hurt. I thought they were the family I didn't have."

"They still are, Sweetheart. They are the same people they've always been. What's happened between your dad and Tootsie started long before any of them knew you and grew to love you. Trust me, they love you. This is a horrible discovery for you, but it doesn't change who they are and how they feel about you."

"Rod, have you thought about how the Klan kept getting information about you and me?"

"For a while that's all I thought about, but not living in Jean Ville... I don't know . . . out of sight, I guess."

"Yeah, me too, until I saw my Daddy and Tootsie together."

"You saw them together? With your own eyes?"

"Yes. I don't think I'd have believed it otherwise. I'm not sure if I am more shocked at my daddy's behavior or at Tootsie's." Rodney reached over and took both my hands in his.

"There are things you'll never understand about colored people and the patterns they've lived for two-hundred years."

"What?"

"Well, not all coloreds ... and not all whites ... let me see how to say this. Ever since slavery, white men have owned Negro women, like cattle, and could do whatever they wanted with them. They took them as concubines, fathered children with them, sometimes had a string of colored women waiting for them to show up, be rough and cruel, and leave. It's been a way of life, Susie. No one thinks anything about it."

"You mean you think it's normal, it's okay, for my daddy and Tootsie to have an affair for twenty years while he's married to my?"

"I'm not saying it's okay, or normal. I'm just saying old habits die slowly. Tootsie doesn't think she's betraying you. She's doing what your dad wants her to do because he's white and powerful and she's scared to tell him, No. And Marianne. Well, if it was you, would you want people to know?"

"Uhmmm. I guess not, when you put it that way."

"I don't want you to feel like this changes anything between you and Tootsie, Marianne and Catfish. They live in survival mode. You shouldn't judge people until you've lived their life." I got up and walked to the window. The sun was going down over the Mississippi River and I watched a tugboat push a big barge towards the bridge and thought about what Rodney was saying. It made me feel better, not completely abandoned by those I depended on to be there for me. Still, I couldn't rid myself of the notion that Tootsie and my daddy had something to do with the Klan's tactics and the beatings I got. Their timing seemed to coincide with each other and with times Rodney and I were together. I tried to shake it off.

"Are you hungry?" Rodney asked.

"What time is it?"

"I'm not sure, but it's dark outside."

"Oh. Are you? Hungry?"

"I could eat something."

"What's on the menu?" I asked.

"Funny you should ask. There's a Kentucky Fried and a McDonald's across the street."

"I've been in Jean Ville all summer. I forgot about civilized city food joints." We laughed at the irony of it, that McDonald's seemed civilized!

We didn't sleep all night. We were both reluctant to waste our precious time together. We talked and talked, ate Big Macs, and caught up on school and career plans. When Rodney mentioned he might go back to Jean Ville to practice after law school, I frowned.

"What are you thinking?" he asked.

"We've never talked about it, and we probably shouldn't. It's just that, I'll never live in that town again. Things are so different up north. So much more tolerant."

"Tell me about it, Baby. How do they treat couples like us? I was there for a week, but that was three years ago, almost. I don't remember it being a problem for us but of course, we were in Harlem most of the time."

"I see them sometimes, couples like us, together on the streets, in cafes, at school—black and white, white and yellow, red and brown, men and men. They walk on sidewalks holding hands and no one stops them. Some people stare and some of the old biddies whisper, but it's nothing like the South."

"It would kill my dad if I moved that far away."

"You probably shouldn't." I found my robe in my suitcase and went to the bathroom. When I came out he was in his boxers, sitting on the side of the bed with his head in his hands, elbows on his knees. He looked up when he felt me come close.

"You should go home and marry a nice colored girl and have a family."

"What about you? Will you marry a white boy?"

"I don't think I'll ever marry, Rod. I'd be afraid of what a husband might do to our daughter. The girls at Sarah Lawrence were older, so I have friends who are married now. They wed guys they thought they knew, but after the honeymoon, the husbands turned into controlling monsters. That frightens me. I don't want my child to live through what I've lived through."

That was the most I'd ever said about the abuse of my childhood. I didn't tell him about the times during and after college. I didn't tell him why I had to leave LSU after my dad talked to him on the phone in the lobby of my dorm. I didn't tell him about Gavin or Josh and I didn't ask him about girls at his school. I was sure he'd dated during the past three years. He was a normal, hot-blooded guy and I imagined every girl at Southern University wanted to go out with Rodney Thibault. I didn't blame them, he was quite a catch. But I didn't want to know.

I didn't tell him about my pregnancy. I couldn't. I never wanted him to think he owed me anything. Our baby had to remain a secret.

I didn't tell him I loved him, either, that I would always love him, that I couldn't marry anyone else because I'd never love anyone else.

I knelt on the floor in front of Rodney, who sat on the side of the bed with his head in his hands. I wrapped my arms around his waist. I just wanted to hold him and feel him and touch him and breathe in his scent of sweat and mint and manhood. I wanted to subject it all to memory—everything about him and this night, because I knew I'd never see him again. I thought he probably felt the same way because once we finally put our heads on the pillows, he held me all night and every time I opened my eyes he was awake, staring at me.

In the morning Rodney kissed me with bird kisses all over my face and ears, my nose and hair, my fingertips. His weight began to feel heavy so he rolled on his side and pulled me close. I loved the taste of him, the sweaty, sticky, sweet, sensuous flavors that seeped from his pores and rested on my palate and wrapped me in comfort and safety.

I could hear the sounds of morning outside. Car doors slammed, footsteps clicked on the concrete sidewalk, someone whistled a tune and I lay there and wished for this moment to go on forever. I didn't want to move, to disturb the magic.

It was different, making love to Rodney. There was nothing hidden in him. He gave me everything he was, all of himself, willingly. There were no tricks, no ulterior motives and no demands. He took what I could give him in that moment and gave me everything in return.

I didn't feel like he expected anything from me, and that was important because I had nothing permanent to offer him.

Part Seven: 1972-1974

~Chapter Eighteen~

Grad School and Law School
1972-73

THE CAB DROVE through the stately gates at St. John's University, onto a tree-line drive of red, gold, green and amber foliage, dwarfed by the massive stone buildings. The cabbie dropped me at the main administrative building that was topped with an iron cross set against a sky as blue as the ocean waters off the Caribbean island and named for the same saint, John the Baptist. Something about the spiritual, serene atmosphere soothed my soul and made me feel welcomed and happy.

I registered for classes and met with my department head, Dr. Merrick Harper, who helped me write the syllabus for the two freshman English courses I'd be teaching, under his direction.

I wrote my parents to give them my new address, a small apartment just off-campus set aside for professors and administrative staff who needed housing. It was adequate, convenient and cheap. Perfect.

I tried to soothe my dad's anger about my clandestine departure by boasting about the campus, my job, my apartment and the Borough of Queens in New York City.

I started graduate school and soon was in a routine of classes, studies, and my part-time job as a graduate assistant. That meant classes to teach, papers to grade, student conferences and staff meetings. When I walked to the English building I strolled around the bell tower that rose above the trees and rang out the time of day with three brilliant clangs. I crossed the two large lawns, separated by a walkway, around the old Catholic church topped by a tall, domed spire with an iron, bodyless cross encircled where the two appendages crisscrossed.

I hadn't realized how many hours college professors worked until I became one, but I was happy and felt fulfilled. I loved being in school, learning and growing, and I loved my students; many were my age and some older.

Merrick Harper was thirty-five, handsome and well-dressed. His female students went gah-gah over him, whispered about him and made excuses to meet with him. He found it amusing. He taught Literature and Poetry in the Graduate School where I was a student. He directed my Master's program so he was more than my professor, he was also my mentor and supervisor. Every graduate assistant had one.

He asked me to have dinner with him the first week. He didn't wear a wedding ring, although there were rumors that he had a family. I didn't know for sure, or care, so other than our age difference, and the fact that he was my boss, I didn't see a problem. We'd get to know each other and establish a strong working relationship.

He was charming, yet honest and forthcoming. Before long we were having dinner a couple times a week and, after the first month, he took me to his apartment, a one room, cozy study he called his writer's retreat. It had a fireplace, a mahogany desk, a bar with a sink and a small refrigerator and a Murphy bed that pulled out of the far wall between the two floor-to-ceiling windows. A pair of wonderful club chairs sat in front of the fire and I sank into one.

"You like?" he asked when he brought me a glass of white wine.

"It's wonderful Merrick. How did you find such a place?"

"Stay here long enough and things start to fall in your lap."

He sat on the arm of my chair and stroked my hair. "It's beautiful, you know."

"What?"

"Your hair. Well, everything about you is beautiful."

"Thank you." We talked about literature, his travels to Europe, my dreams to write novels, and we made love.

It was sweet, gentle and comfortable. Twice a week we went to dinner and spent the night at his retreat. When he told me he was married, I wasn't shocked, nor did it matter to me. That made it more comfortable less pressured. I knew deep in my psyche that I became involved with Merrick Harper because he had a wife, which made him unavailable. He would never pressure me to marry him.

I didn't go home for visits, feigning lack of funds, extra work during breaks, studies and other obligations. Since my parents wouldn't pay for me to fly home I wasn't under any obligation to spend my hard-earned dollars on airfare. I knew my mother, especially, wasn't disappointed when I didn't visit during the three years I spent at St. John's, even at Christmas time.

I secretly hoped Rodney would come to New York to see me and at Christmas break, I waited, but he never arrived.

Occasionally I received a letter from Sissy, or from one of my brothers, and I answered them with lots of facts about my life, school and job. I knew Daddy would read my letters so I wrote them appropriately. He called every week from his office. I didn't speak with Mama, who Daddy said, was very busy with the children.

I wrote to Rodney and Marianne, and they wrote back. Their letters were newsy and filled with their busyness. My responses were similar. Every week, without fail, I received a letter from Rodney; he called me once a month, regular as clockwork, for the first year. I wondered whether he wrote out of obligation or from habit or maybe from a feeling of compassion for me, alone and far from

home. His words didn't talk about love, the future or missing me—
they were full of humor and anecdotes but he signed them:

I'll love you always,
Yours forever,
Rod

And I thought he meant it.

The letters and calls began to dwindle during the second year,
and by the third year, our correspondence consisted of Christmas
and birthday cards and an occasional newspaper clipping that told of
people back home.

I knew in my heart there was someone else in his life; after all,
there was someone in mine. Because I loved Rodney so much, I was
happy for him. He deserved a wonderful life with a girl he could be
proud of and have children with and who would live in Jean Ville,
Louisiana. I could never be that girl. Yet, as many times as I told
myself I was happy for Rod, I was sad for myself. I missed him
desperately. I needed him.

I went to Manhattan on weekends to shop, sit in cafes and
people-watch, and to get off campus. Merrick was with his family
and it made me less antsy if I wasn't on campus thinking about being
alone while he was so busy. I looked for interracial couples, who
seemed to grow more commonplace.

Every time I saw a mixed-race couple I not only dreamed about
a future for me and Rodney, but I also thought about Emalene and
Joe and my heart yearned to see my little girl—their little girl.
Emalene sent me a picture of her at Christmas and on her birthday,
August 15th, every year, but I never called. I didn't even have the
courage to ask what they named her, much less risk a visit. I knew I
would want her, and that wouldn't be right for her or me, and
certainly not for Joe and Emalene. So I stayed away, but that didn't
mean I stopped thinking about her every day.

I also thought of Rodney everyday. Yet, although I might daydream about Rodney moving to New York; but I would never ask him to do that, never make him choose between me and his family.

I didn't want to date. I was afraid of experiences like the ones with Josh and Gavin, and I certainly wasn't interested in another proposal. My relationship with Merrick was enough. We spent hours discussing journals, literary pieces and our experiences with students. We had a great deal in common and I enjoyed his company and, I think, I became a damn good writer because of his tutelage.

Just before my graduation from St. John's in 1974 I was teaching a freshman English class when a student knocked on my classroom door and handed me a note. It said that I had a telegram.

I was alarmed as I walked briskly across the front lawn to St. Augustine Hall to pick up the message. I thought of all the catastrophes that could befall the people I loved back home—Rodney? Marianne? Tootsie? Catfish? What about Sissy or my brothers? Oh, maybe it was about my parents. My pace quickened.

I entered the student union and walked to the Western Union counter.

"Susanna Burton. There's a telegram for me?"

"Yes, Ma'am," the student said, and he took an envelope out of a slot behind him and handed it to me.

"You must be from the South," I said. "I haven't heard 'Ma'am,' since I was home last."

"Yes, Ma'am," he said. "I'm from Jackson, Mississippi."

"Well, I hope you like New York."

"So far, so good," he said and smiled his best smile.

I stepped to the corner of the room where there was a counter with pens and forms. It smelled of ink and foot odor and there was a ticking sound from the clock on the wall. The murmur of students hanging out in the student union building attached to the post office faded in the background as I unfolded the paper and read the telegram.

Granddaddy very sick. Doc says not long now. He's asking for you.
Marianne

I went to the English department and found Merrick. I explained that my surrogate grandfather was dying and I needed to go home to be with him. We were standing in the hall. A few students walked by and said hello, but it was obvious we were in a serious conversation. We knew there were rumours about us, but neither of us cared.

"You didn't tell me you had a, did you say, 'surrogate' grandfather?"

"You never asked." I tried to laugh it off. I didn't talk about my family. I told him my dad was a CPA and I had a brother who was a lawyer and other siblings, but I didn't go into detail. I certainly didn't tell him about my special family in the quarters.

"How long do you need?" he asked.

"At least a week. Of course I don't know how sick he is. And if he dies . . . funeral." I looked up at the ceiling and felt salty tears begin to gather.

"Will that give you enough time, my dear?" he asked.

"Yes, thank you, Merrick. My thesis is almost finished. I just have some final revisions to do. I should be back in a week. If not, I'll call or telegraph."

"I'm sorry, Susie. Is there anything?"

"No, Merrick. Thank you. I appreciate you understanding."

"I'll miss you."

"And I, you."

He told me he'd manage my classes through finals, not to worry. He'd finalize the students' grades for the classes I taught if I wasn't back in time. We both wanted to hug and kiss good-bye but, of course, we couldn't.

"If you can't get a flight out today, can we meet at my place to say good-bye?" he asked.

"Sure, if I can't get out, I'll call you."

I went to my apartment and packed a bag. I was able to get a flight to Baton Rouge that afternoon. At the airport I found a pay phone and called Rodney. We hadn't seen each other in three years. I hadn't heard his voice in almost two. I knew he was almost finished with law school and Marianne told me he would be moving to Jean Ville to practice at the District Attorney's office.

When he answered the phone, I hung up. I thought how selfish it would be to disrupt whatever life he had built over the past three years. Maybe he had a steady girlfriend, maybe a fiancée. Maybe he was married.

⟋ Chapter Nineteen ⟍

❧

Goodbye Cat
1974

I STEPPED OFF THE plane in Baton Rouge and it was sticky and hot, as if announcing what could be expected during the coming months. When I got to Jean Ville, the air was stifling. Even the birds hid in the shadows and refused to sing.

There was no breeze. No leaf swayed. No blade of the newly cut grass blew or skipped across the lawn in front of St. Matthew's Baptist Church on St. Matthews Road a few days later. The church had been there for one-hundred years, before houses surrounded it or a grocery store had been built on Prescott Street, within walking distance.

The Chickasaw Indian Reservation was connected to the St. Matthew's quarters by a footpath that cut through the woods. Everyone called it, "First Bridge." I stared at the trees behind the church and remembered when I was six and James led me deep into those woods and left me to wander deeper and deeper into the thickness until, petrified by the sounds and darkness, a posse of my parents' friends found me after midnight. An electric pulse ran up my back. I shook it off.

It was Friday, May 17, 1974. I had arrived from New York on Tuesday and went directly to Catfish's house. He died an hour after I told him good-bye.

I stared at the tall, handsome figure who stood next to his dad at the front door of the church, greeting people. He had a white carnation pinned to the lapel of his perfectly-fitted dark grey suit. The red and grey striped bow tie made him look sophisticated and grown-up. I couldn't take my eyes off him as I stepped out of my dad's car and stood on the sidewalk flanked by my two younger brothers and waited while Daddy parked his Mercedes.

Rodney must have felt my stare because he turned his head and looked at me. A controlled smile spread through his eyes and lifted the lines on either side of his mouth. I had kissed those full lips and had held that gaze while he gently made me his own. I would always be a part of him—my first kiss, first hug, first touch, first lover, first everything.

I swallowed hard.

In that moment, standing in front of that old Negro church between Will and Robby, I realized that Rodney Thibault was not only my first everything, he was my only everything. I stared at him and knew, in my knowing, that no matter how hard I tried, I would never be complete without him in my life. And I'd probably screwed that up by distancing myself, by not telling him how I felt.

It was a revelation that caught me off-guard. I trembled and popped my knuckles by lacing my fingers together, extending my arms in front of me and pushing my palms outward, a nervous habit Mama had tried to get me to break for years. Rodney caught my unintended gesture and laughed, then he covered his mouth as if to catch himself.

I diverted my gaze to my dad when he walked up to my brothers and me on the sidewalk and led our little group up the steps and shook hands with family members standing in the little porch on the front of the church. I could feel Rodney's eyes follow me, even while he was greeting other people.

I shook hands with Mr. Thibault then I was standing in front of Rodney.

Time seemed to stop. He took both of my hands in his and although his palms were sweaty and warm, his touch sent shivers up my arms and I could feel goosebumps form under my long-sleeved suit jacket. I breathed in the sweet fragrance of carnations, fresh cut grass in the churchyard, and gas fumes from the cars that were pulling up and parking in the lot behind Rodney. Most of all I smelled him—the sweat-filled, ivory soap-showered, Tide detergent-washed, masculine scents of Rodney—those smells that could cause chills down my spine and moisture in my panties. And I stared at the hazel, amber, azure eyes that looked directly at me and made me feel like there were no other people for miles around.

When he opened his mouth to say "Susie," I tasted peppermint and orange soda and remembered the first time he leaned against the car and said, "How you doin' this afternoon?"

"Rodney," I whispered. He smiled with his entire face, his lips parted and spread under high, lifted cheekbones and the sides of his eyes rose and his eyelashes touched his eyebrows; my eyes traveled from his bow tie to his lips to his cheeks to his eyes to his hairline, then back to his eyes and I stood there like a mannequin, composed but frozen, stymied. I wanted to say something but my voice wouldn't cooperate and neither did his, so we just stood there, my hands in his, looking at each other and smiling, broadly.

All too soon he released me and my daddy pushed me with his hips and took my place in front of Rodney. I was mildly aware of him shaking hands with my dad and exchanging niceties as I made my way through the rest of the line and into the church.

I watched Rodney throughout the long, loud service. People screamed, cried, laughed, shouted, sang, hummed, and even danced at various times. My brothers were entertained but I couldn't keep my eyes off the gorgeous being who stood with the pallbearers, focused and purposeful throughout the service.

Rodney was Catholic, like me, so I presumed he was uncomfortable in the Baptist church, too. When he looked at me, we shared a common expression of unrest.

The black station wagon led a long stream of cars up Ferdinand Street, onto Prescott, then west on Gravier Road. When the procession turned left onto South Jefferson Extension towards the Quarters, Daddy turned right towards our house.

"Please stop, Daddy," I said. "I want to go to the burial."

"Why are you are so involved in Catfish's death and burial? You don't even come home for Christmas, yet you came home for this?"

"It's complicated. Just let me out here, I'll walk to the Quarters."

"I'll just park in the Dauzat's yard and we'll all walk there together. If I park in the quarters I'll never get my car out." I could tell he was angry, but he seemed resigned. He insisted that he and the boys accompany me to protect me from "those people."

I wanted to ask Daddy what he meant when he referred to Tootsie and her family as "those people." Is that what he called Tootsie, the woman he had been screwing for more than twenty years? The who might have had his child. I wanted to ask him why he taught us, his children, to be nonjudgmental of Negroes, then he turned around and made comments like "those people." I wanted to remind him that Tootsie was Catfish's daughter and that Tootsie was family and had raised his children. I had so many questions for him, for Daddy, but I didn't ask any of them. I knew he was already angry and I also knew that even the most innocent comment could push him into violence—and what I needed to say to him was not innocent. But I had learned how to walk that tightrope, so I kept my mouth shut.

Catfish was laid to rest in the family cemetery in a pecan grove beside the cane field, near his garden. I couldn't control the tears that ran down my cheeks when they put him in the ground. I watched Rodney and the others remove their carnations and place them on top of the pine box that held Catfish's remains and I stood planted in the St. Augustine grass, tears streaming down my face. The crowd moved towards the houses in the Quarters but I held back to speak to Tootsie and Marianne. Marianne helped her mother out of the chair that sat a few feet from the coffin, and when they approached me I took Tootsie's other hand and the three of us followed the crowd in silence.

I watched Daddy's back move through the people, shaking hands and introducing my brothers. Politicking, I thought. He's running for the State Legislature and needs the Negro vote. That's when I realized why he agreed to come to Catfish's funeral: votes.

Everyone gathered around picnic tables laden with enough food to feed a small army. Chitlins, gumbo, fried chicken, jambalaya and rice-dressing filled the center of the tables. Salads and desserts were stacked on side tables. People gathered in the backyard and sat in chairs and on the steps of the five back porches that formed a line in front of a large fire. A pig stretched out like Jesus on the cross was the main event. The cochon de lait was almost done. Men and children gathered to admire the crucified hog that burned at the stake.

Daddy waited for me to catch up with him and the boys, but I was with Marianne and Tootsie. We watched the men turn the pig, drink beer and tell stories. I thought about how many times Catfish sat in one of those iron chairs with torn, green naugahyde seats and poked a pig with a cane pole while he held the attention of everyone around him with his "yarns." I felt sad, like a piece of me was missing. I had loved Catfish since I was seven, almost sixteen years.

Daddy and the boys watched me as I walked away from them with Marianne and Tootsie.

I knew all of Tootsie's family—her sister, Jesse and Jesse's husband, Bo, and their children; Tootsie's brothers, Tom and Sam, and their wives and children. All of Catfish's other grandchildren were younger than Marianne, and I knew all of their names and ages and what grades they were in. I'd had more interaction with Marianne's sisters and cousins than with my own siblings over the years and I felt more at home in the Quarters than in the big antebellum home on the corner of South Jefferson and Marble Avenue. I wished I could stay in the Quarters and never go back to that empty-feeling house with the blue drapes and carpets and walls that closed in on me.

Tootsie sat at one of the rough-hewn picnic tables. Marianne and I stood behind her, talking, catching up. She looked more mature and even more beautiful than ever, if that was possible. Getting out of Jean Ville and living in Baton Rouge while she was in nursing school for two years had agreed with her. She was self-confident and happy. She even mentioned she was dating someone, although I didn't have a chance to get the particulars.

The chatter of people, mixed with outbursts of laughter and sobs, overrode the crackle of the fire and the whishing sound when fat from the pig dripped into the fire.

My eyes followed Rodney as he milled around with his cousins and I watched him out of the corner of my eye when he walked away from a group of men and strolled to a pecan tree several yards away from the tables. He was alone. He chewed on a long piece of straw and had one knee bent, the sole of his foot against the tree. His suit coat was flung over his shoulder as he leaned into the shade provided by the fullness of greenery that softly filtered a few rays of sunshine that smiled on Catfish this day. Rodney looked pensive. He had been alone at the church—no date, no girlfriend. If he had a fiancée or a wife, wouldn't she have been with him?

I told Marianne I'd be back and strolled towards him, talking to people casually as I made my way to the pecan tree. I knew my dad was watching so I tried to seem natural.

Rodney saw my slow, casual approach long before I reached him and we locked eyes for a second over his aunt's shoulder as I stood listening to a group of women talk. I winked to let him know I wanted him to stay there. He winked back.

By the time I got to him everyone had started moving towards the tables to watch the men spread the roast pig out so they could begin to lift off the crackled skin that Cajuns calle, quoin, and cut the pork into pieces. The focus on the pig created a diversion for me as I made my way to the pecan tree.

We didn't touch. I stood in front of him, my back to the crowd, and tried to make small talk. I asked how things were going, when he'd complete finals and what he planned to do after graduation. He told me he hadn't made a final decision but that his dad had been pressuring him to come home.

"The Toussaint Parish District Attorney offered me a job where I can work my way up to Assistant DA one day," he told me. If he took the job, it began in August. We started to walk towards the cabins, close enough to hear each other but not touching. Both of us watched the ground as we walked to keep from looking at each other.

"Is that what you want to do? Work as a prosecutor?"

"I'm not sure. I always thought I wanted to practice family law, to help people, especially Negroes who can't afford an attorney, but I can't work for free."

"Do you want to live in Jean Ville?"

"I don't know. It's home, and I don't have offers anywhere else."

"How are things here?"

"Better, I think. The federal laws are in place to give us equality, but the South is slow to get on board. There are still active Klan activities and local law enforcement turns a blind eye."

"Oh, how could I ever forget how awful colored people are treated down here? It's so different up north. You'd think that by 1974 people would have learned to live together and accept one another."

"It's better than it was, but it still has a long way to go."

When I remember that conversation that took place forty-plus years ago, I realize that, even now, we still have a ways to go.

"When do you finish law school?"

"I took my last final Wednesday, the day before I came home for the funeral."

"Oh, I still have to take finals and complete my thesis. I'm going back Sunday."

"What then? What will you do after you finish?"

"I have several job offers. I'm also thinking about going to Europe. I've saved some money."

"Oh."

I wanted to ask him about his personal life, attachments, girlfriends but I knew we couldn't talk about personal things, not with so many people, and my daddy, around. We split up and milled around with different people. Rodney went to sit with his uncle and cousins at one of the tables. I stopped to talk to Tootsie and Marianne again then went to stand near Daddy and my brothers. I knew Daddy wouldn't stay to eat with colored people. He talked a good game.

"I'm going to stay a while," I told him.

"No, you're coming home with me and the boys."

"Daddy, please. I feel like I need to be with Tootsie for a little while. I'll walk home."

"I don't like to leave you here with these people."

"I'll be fine. It's the right thing to do." Daddy looked at me with an expression I knew spelled danger if I didn't do what he said, but I'd been away too long and I was no longer a child. I refused to let him control me any longer, or maybe I'd forgotten how his temper could flare and what he could do to me when it did.

Before I left the Quarters that afternoon I told Rodney that my flight to New York was on Sunday, the day after tomorrow. He asked if I was flying out of Baton Rouge and I said, yes.

"Can I take you to the airport?" he asked. He still had his 1966 Mustang Fastback that he said he'd fixed it up, whatever that meant. He wanted me to see it.

"Oh, Rod, that would be too risky."

"How will you get there?"

"I'll take the bus." I looked off in the distance. There were still a few people milling around in the Quarters. I could see Marianne hovering, waiting to have some time with me. "I'm going to leave for Baton Rouge in the morning. I've overstayed my welcome at home."

"Can I see you in Baton Rouge?"

"I'll call you when I get there, okay?" I didn't intend to call him. I think he knew that.

I walked towards Marianne and she and I strolled past the corn fields to the barn. She had lots to tell me.

First she told me about her girlfriend.

"I might be in love," she said. I wanted to be happy for her, but I knew her life would be hard taking that route.

"Why don't you move up north. You can stay with me." I watched her think about my offer, then she shook her head side-to-side.

"I could never leave Mama. That's why I moved back from Baton Rouge after I finished school." I left it at that. We were quiet for a while, sitting with our backs against the outside of the old barn. I took her hand and she smiled at me and squeezed.

"Rodney told me he'd left his summer open," she said softly, almost as if she was considering whether to tell me or not. "He said that in the back of his mind, he planned to go to New York to put things to rest between the two of you so he could move on with his life." I didn't say anything. I let the words find a place inside me.

"He's been dating someone," she whispered. I knew she didn't want to tell me, but she was being honest and I appreciated it, especially after what I considered the deceit I felt three years before when I discovered the truth about my dad and Tootsie. Then she told me about Annette, and my heart sank. Although I felt Rodney had someone else, hearing it made it real and I was crushed. Marianne told me about how Annette faked a pregnancy to get him to marry her and how he didn't date her for almost two years because he said he couldn't trust her. It made me think about my own pregnancy and how I didn't tell him.

"His parents were insistent that he get back with Annette, and Jerry is engaged to her best friend—so somehow they got back together about a year ago," Marianne said. "He told me he's never had sex with her because he still doesn't trust her." I didn't know what to say or whether to believe her, about not having sex.

"Do you think he's in love with her?" I asked, then I realized what I said and I wanted to take it back.

"No, I don't think he loves her, but I think he feels pressured to marry her because of his folks and Jerry and—well, I don't know, because he feels like it's time."

"I don't want to mess up his life."

"Today he told me to tell you he's single. He's going back to Baton Rouge tomorrow to break it off with Annette. He said everything changed when he saw you at the funeral today. He even told his dad he couldn't pretend any longer."

"He told his dad that?"

"Yep. Today at the funeral. He said his dad noticed how the two of you looked at each other. Rodney said he had to be honest with himself and with his dad. He wants to see you, Susie. He asked me to give you his phone number in Baton Rouge in case you don't have it with you."

When I left the Quarters I was torn. I wanted to see Rodney, to be with him. I wanted to finally tell him the truth about everything. But it was still dangerous. And he had a chance at a decent life with someone who was more right for him, who would be accepted by his family and friends, who would support him as an up-and-coming lawyer in Jean Ville, the first colored attorney in Toussaint Parish. I didn't want to take all that from him.

*

"Where is that girl? She should be home by now," I could hear Daddy yelling when I walked in the front door. They were standing in the hall. Mama shrugged her shoulders and walked to the kitchen. He didn't see me come in and he went into the master bedroom across the hall from the kitchen, talking at the top of his voice.

The window air conditioners hummed but the house was stifling.

"I knew I shouldn't have left her with those colored people. There's no telling what Tootsie and her half-breed girl will tell her. Then there's the Thibault boy. I don't like the way he looks at Susie, like he's not colored and she's not white. It's downright disrespectful.

"I have a mind to go find her and drag her home by her hair," he screamed. I couldn't hear what Mama said, but I knew she responded.

"Who does she think she is, anyway? She just waltzes into our house like she belongs here—all high fah-luting because she has all those college degrees. Educated women are dangerous. Does she have any idea how badly she can hurt my political chances? She's too damn selfish to care about me."

"Who are you talking to, Bob?" Mama called out to him.

"Just because I don't give her money doesn't mean she can do anything she wants."

He ranted and raved that I was probably living up there in the North with no morals, screwing every boy I found, making a tramp out of myself, and if that wasn't enough, he had to witness me come to his town and flirt with a colored boy, right in front of him, in front of the town. He'd be a laughingstock once word spread.

"Those Northerners might be open to mixed relations but Susie doesn't need to come to my town and humiliate me this way. Not now when I'm in a tight political race! I'll teach her to stick with her own."

"Are you talking to yourself, Bob?" Mama called from the kitchen.

"Come here, Honey. We need to talk." Mama went into the bedroom with little Al following.

"Fix me another drink, would you Honey?"

I sneaked into the front bedroom and shut the door quietly. I gathered my things and stacked my suitcase, overnight bag and purse near the door in case I needed to make a fast getaway.

Sissy was happy to have me home. She was twelve and didn't mind sharing her space. She and I lay across the bed talking and laughing. Sissy had all the things a twelve-year-old could want in a room, a French Provincial tester bed, a desk and vanity, cork boards where she hung her pictures and ribbons, a trophy case for her awards, a closet full of the latest fashions. I remembered growing up in that room. There were no mementos, no pictures, no ribbons or certificates or trophies when I was there. Oh, I won lots of stuff, but I never showed my awards or displayed them. I kept them in cardboard boxes in the attic. All I had in that big blue bedroom as an adolescent and a teenager was a desk with a stack of books and lots of paper and pens.

Daddy stormed in the room from the short hall that connected it to the master.

"Get out, Sissy. I need to talk to your sister."

"Oh, Daddy, please. Susie's leaving tomorrow. Please let me have some time with her."

"Get out, Honey. Now." Sissy backed out of the room with a scared look on her face. I stood up and faced him.

"Who do you think you are?" He was yelling.

"I'm not sure why you're angry with me. What have I done?"

"You humiliated me in front of a hundred voters, that's what you did!"

"Daddy, you can think what you want, but I didn't do anything of the sort. If you need an excuse to berate me, try something else. I'm innocent here."

"Don't you tell me what to do."

"If you hit me, I'll go to the police this time. I won't take your abuse any longer. I'm an adult. I'm on my own now."

"You are in my house, you impudent little bitch." He slapped me so hard I fell against the footboard of the bed and slid to a seated position on the floor. He was on top of me before I knew what happened. He started to kick and slap me.

Then, on impulse, I caught one of his feet with both my hands and threw his leg in the air with all my might. He staggered backwards, lost his balance and almost fell on his back but managed to remain upright. By the time he got his bearings, I was on my feet with my hand on the doorknob. He got there just in time to slam it shut with his size twelve foot as I tried to pull it open. Then he hit me with his fist. I staggered backwards and my hand automatically covered my cheekbone. I felt a strange darkness come over me and all the fear and anger and hate I'd felt for years bubbled to the top of my brain.

My leg flew up and I sucker-kicked him in the balls, hard.

"You little bitch!" He bent over in agony. I moved in closer and, like a runner taking off from a starting block, I pushed off my back foot and aimed my knee at his face before he lifted it, and hit him, hard. There was a loud crunch when it connected with his forehead and he toppled backwards onto the thick blue carpet. Blood spurted from above his eye.

"It's your turn to bleed on this disgusting carpet," I said. I grabbed my purse and overnight bag and ran out the room, through the front door and down the sidewalk while he yelled after me.

"You have no place to go in this town, you tramp. Everyone will believe me, not you."

The feeling of triumph didn't hit me until I was on the street between our house and Dr. David's. I smiled and felt a glow inside. Those self-defense classes came in handy. Wow! That felt good. I turned to look at the house from the pavement.

Daddy stumbled onto the front porch, bent over, holding his crotch, blood from his forehead dripping into his already swelling right eye.

He called to me as I ran barefoot on the black top road. There were no cars going either way, no one in their yards, no witnesses anywhere.

"I'll get you, you little tramp. You can't hide from me," he yelled. 'Come back here you ungrateful slut. Take your medicine."

Dr. David Switzer opened his front door and walked briskly towards the road. He stopped at the edge of his yard and glared across South Jefferson Street at Daddy, who stood on his porch bleeding, holding himself, and screaming at the top of his lungs. I turned to look at the two men in the face off, then started to run towards the quarters. I heard them yelling.

"What the hell, Bob?"

"It's Susie. That little bitch ran away from me."

"Maybe you should be grateful. At her age, she doesn't have to take it anymore. She should call the sheriff."

"The sheriff won't listen to her. He knows me."

"Does he, Bob? Does anyone really know you? Does anyone know what goes on in that house where people believe a saint and his saintly family live? You'd better get inside and calm down. Susie is all grown up and knows her rights."

"I'm the businessman in this family. She doesn't know anything."

"Suit yourself. I'm going to sit out here and wait."

"Wait for what?" Daddy yelled. I didn't hear any more. By that time I was half-way to Gravier Road.

*

I was out of breath when I reached the Quarters, and the bottoms of my bare feet were blistered from the hot asphalt. I heard someone talking, so I stopped on the side of Catfish's house and peered around the corner. A few women were clearing the long tables and men were packing cars and trailers as the sun set behind the cane fields. I sneaked around to the front of the house, which was almost hidden by several huge oak trees, draped with moss. No one came to the front side of the cabins; all the activity was in the back yard, inside the semi-circle of porches that almost touched each other.

I stepped into the coolness created by the abundant shade and opened the front door. I could see through to the back porch. The doorways that separated the bedroom from the sitting room, and the sitting room from the kitchen, lined up with the front and back doors. "Shotgun house," I remembered Catfish explain.

I slipped into the bedroom and quickly shut the door between it and the next room, in case someone came inside. With the doors closed, the room immediately became unbearably hot. I opened the front window for relief. There was no cross draft, but at least air came into the room from under the shade trees.

I turned my back to the front door and realized I'd only been in Catfish's bedroom once—Tuesday, the day he told me goodbye. I hadn't noticed anything that day, just Catfish, his sunken cheeks, his raspy voice, his weak grip on my hands as he placed the cotton candy side on top of mine and I put my other hand on top of his and stroked the chocolate side with my pink thumb. I remembered the first time I'd touched his two-toned, long fingered hand.

I looked around.

His bed encompassed most of the space in the small room, although it was barely the size of a double bed. I reverently touched the tattered, but clean, pink, blue and white wedding ring quilt that draped the bed almost to the floor. I ran my hand across the one, single pillow, encased in a white pillowslip. A large picture of Jesus was framed above the head of the bed. He had brown skin.

I ran my hand over the only other piece of furniture in the room, a four-drawer chest with a small fan on top and an oval mirror hanging above it between pictures of Martin Luther King and John F. Kennedy. I turned the fan on. Three clean shirts and two pairs of khaki slacks hung on hangers over a pipe extended across one corner of the room. Over the closed door that led to the sitting room was a plain, wooden cross, no Jesus hanging from it.

I fingered one of his shirts and inhaled the smell of Ivory detergent, Faultless starch and dust. I could feel his presence. Tears ran freely down my cheeks as it hit me, like a delayed reaction, that he was gone. I would have to go on living in this world without Catfish in it. He was my source of wisdom, my example of love and acceptance, my image of what a father, grandfather, husband and friend looked like in its purest form. I began to sob uncontrollably.

This was the first time I'd been alone with my grief, a chance to feel the stored up pain inside. I had cried with Marianne and Tootsie Wednesday afternoon, and with the gathering family Thursday, but I had concentrated on helping to ease their grief. I knew they could never understand mine—the emptiness inside, the space left behind that no one could ever fill but Catfish. My Cat.

He didn't get to tell me all his stories. What happened after the two Samuels inherited the property? What was Catfish's mother's school like? I had so many unanswered questions. Without thinking I began to open the drawers in his bureau. In the bottom, right drawer was a yellow legal pad, on its front, in even, almost childlike printed capital letters the word, "STORIES."

I started to flip through the pages, slowly. On each page there was a caption in block print. "Annie," "Mr. Van," "Mr. Henry," "Alabama," "Mama," and some names I recognized but didn't know much about: "Audrey," "Bessie," "Maureen," "Big Bugger," "Lizzie," "George." Each had a one-page explanation of who they were, approximate dates they were born and died, and lists of good and bad traits. Halfway through the tablet, the pages became blank, but I kept flipping faster, driven to find something of Catfish I needed. On the very last page, "Suzanah."

I sat on the edge of the bed and read the words made of painstaking letters that squiggled and curved and dropped below the lines. I knew this was his last attempt at writing and that his aged hands strained to form the sentences.

Suzanah,

I tried to make some more stories for you so when you come back I can remember what to tell you. I know you gonna come back. I hope these help your book.

I missed you.

Love, Cat.

I held the tablet to my chest and wrapped both arms around it and myself, bent forward and cried so hard I began to cough and shake. How could I have stayed away from him for three years? Did he understand, in death, that I was avoiding my own family, not him? Actually I was avoiding myself. I was running from the truth. I left because it was easier than staying—easier than standing up to the *status quo* that said white people could not love colored people. I'd been a coward.

But Catfish was a hero. The stories he told me, and the ones he left me to discover and imagine on my own, were rich with history and truth that he wanted told.

I stood and looked in the mirror hanging between Kennedy and King, two men who declared truths. Kennedy said we should not wait to see what our country would do for us, but what we could do for our country and King said that all men are equal. My eyes were swollen and red and there was a deep gash across my right cheekbone. It was still oozing blood. I found a hanky in the top drawer of the chest and pressed it to my face. I sat on Catfish's bed and thought about how I could make Catfish proud of me.

I would begin immediately to write these stories for Catfish and for my country, and I wouldn't stop until they were printed in national magazines where Catfish's legacy would show people the injustice of slavery and the after effects we carried on through unwritten rules, Jim Crow, the Ku Klux Klan.

But I couldn't do that if I was not an example of how to undo the sins of the past and set a new course for equability and tolerance.

I had to take stance. I would admit I loved a colored boy and show everyone, including my family, that a person's skin color does not determine his worth. I sobbed as I made these revelations to myself.

The larger question was how to live this truth without endangering Rodney and his family, and Tootsie, Marianne and their family. It was quiet as I sat in Catfish's bedroom pondering these dilemmas.

I no longer heard voices outside the cabin, so I crept through the sitting room into the kitchen and peeked out the window. Everyone was gone. I looked around Catfish's kitchen. I'd been in it a couple times, but I'd never been alone in his house, and never with the sadness I felt so heavy in my belly.

His kitchen was so like him, plain and uncomplicated. There was a white enamel sink with a chrome faucet that was extended about eighteen inches up before it hooked downward. I could see him filling tall pots of water. My mind went back to the day I gave him the turtle.

"I'm gonna boil it till I know it's dead, then I'm gonna break the shell, me. It's the meat inside that's good, yeah."

I stepped onto the porch and fell into Catfish's rocker holding the handkerchief over the gash on my face. I needed to be near Catfish so I could think. I couldn't go back to my house. I'd left the suitcase but I had my overnight bag with my personal items and a change of clothes. And I'd had the presence of mind to grab my purse that had my bus and airline tickets, and cash tucked inside.

I felt the cut and swelling on my cheekbone and wondered whether I'd have a black eye in the morning. It was amazing that, after all this time I was still surprised when Daddy hit me. I knew he was angry and I should have been more prepared, I thought. Then I remembered that I struck back, that I left him bleeding and in pain. I grinned.

I was so enveloped in my thoughts that I didn't hear or see Marianne walk up the steps and sit in the straight-back chair I normally occupied when Catfish was alive. Marianne didn't say anything and I don't know how long she sat there before I noticed.

I could tell she was curious, but I wasn't ready to talk just yet. I rocked and thought of Catfish and all the times he sat in this chair and told me stories and the times I caught him sleeping, his mouth opened, a slight drool forming in the corner.

I thought how Catfish was the catalyst for all the good things that had happened in my life—peaceful, loving visits and shared stories, a best girlfriend I came to know and love more than my own siblings, and Rodney, I would never have known, really known him, had we not had the quarters and Catfish's quiet protection. I had learned the real meaning of family and love and acceptance through Catfish. I owed him so much.

I remembered how Catfish opened one eye just a sliver when I got here Tuesday night.

"Missy, you came," he said. His breathy voice was almost non-existent.

"Of course I came. Where else would I be, but with my surrogate grandfather?" He smiled and closed his eyes.

"I'm glad to see you, Missy," he said.

I sat there with his hand in mine and told him stories, for a change. I told him about school and New York City and the job offers and how I was going to write our book. That's what I called it, "Our Book." He grinned when I said it. Tootsie came in and asked if she could sit with him for a while. I kissed him on the cheek, then on the forehead where I rested my lips a little longer and breathed in his mushroomy odor and something that smelled almost like old, wet leaves.

That was the last time I heard his voice, the last time I touched him.

Catfish was the gentle soul who taught me, by example, that not all daddies were mean and angry, not all daddies beat their daughters. Until I knew Catfish, I thought the way my daddy treated me was normal, that every daughter was disciplined that way, that it was how a daddy showed he loved his little girl, how he taught her right from wrong, for her own good.

"Now Mama, she'd make us bring her a switch from the bush and tell us to dance while she switched our legs," Tootsie told me. "But Daddy, no he never raised his voice, much less his hand to us."

I was jealous—jealous of Tootsie and jealous of Marianne. When I confessed my envy to Marianne a few years before, she'd laughed.

"Yeah, you can be jealous of colored folks cause you white," she said. "No Klan gonna come after you because they think you say the wrong thing, forget to say "Sir" or "Ma'am," or use a tone of voice they find offensive. You don't know what you talking about when you say you wish you were in my family, a colored family."

"You're right. I'm sorry, Mari, I don't get it," I whispered, almost like I didn't really want her to hear me. I paused and thought a minute and said, "If being white means waking up in a hospital room and not knowing how you got there, or having your family act like nothing happened to you even when you had a broken arm and black eyes, then I guess you'd want to be white, wouldn't you?" She didn't answer and I didn't continue.

I wondered how she felt now that we were older, more mature.

～Chapter Twenty～

～

Love?
1974

I FINALLY LOOKED AT Marianne sitting next to me on Catfish's porch, waiting to be noticed. She gasped when she saw my face.

"Oh, God, Susie, what happened?" Catfish's handkerchief was soaked in blood and no longer helped to stop the flow. My hand was filled with red fluid and my white silk blouse was streaked scarlet. "That gash on your cheek is huge and your eye is turning black."

"I'm okay. I've been worse."

"You need stitches, Susie," she said. "Let me take you to the emergency room."

I was so ashamed my chin fell to my chest and I heaved deeply. Marianne put her arm around my shoulder. We sat there for a several minutes until I realized I was bleeding all over Marianne's beautiful black suit and sat up straight. I thought about the last time I had been in the Quarters before this trip, the day my daddy showed up at Tootsie's house. I had questions, unfinished business with Tootsie. This was as good a time as any, since I didn't think I'd be back for a long, long time, if ever.

"Where's your Mama?" I asked.

"She's in the house."

"I want to talk to her, privately."

"Okay. I'll go get her. Then will you let me take you to the hospital?" I looked at my friend, my very best friend, perhaps my sister.

"Marianne, does she know I saw him come here?"

"I didn't tell her. We don't talk about him, ever!" Marianne looked at the cornfields, a hollow stare.

"Mari, look at me." Marianne turned to me, tears pooling in her big, hazel eyes.

"Do you think he's your father?"

"I hope not. I don't want him to be my father. I hate him." She walked down the steps.

"Wait, Mari." Marianne stopped but didn't turn around. "Would it really be so bad? I mean, that we might be ... ?" Marianne paused, but she didn't turn around. Finally she continued walking and went into her house next door.

I sat in Catfish's rocker and waited. I missed him deeply. The emptiness was visceral, like a stabbing sensation in my stomach and a burning in my gut. Tears ran down my cheeks and the saltiness burned where it pooled in the gash across the side of my face. I didn't care. If I listened carefully, maybe I could almost hear his voice in the clouds.

Tootsie came up the steps with two glasses of sweet tea and a bag of ice.

"What you doing here?" she asked. She handed me the tea and the ice pack.

"Daddy." That's all I said. She understood.

"Mari said put this ice pack on that cheek." I took the ice and put it over the blood-soaked handkerchief and drank a long sip of tea then put the glass on the floor.

"This was the only place I knew I could come," I said. Tootsie sat in the chair next to me. We both looked out at the cane fields.

"You always welcome here." She said it so softly I almost didn't hear her.

"Except when he's here, right?"

"What you mean?" She sat up straight and looked at me. I stared at the sky. I couldn't look at Tootsie.

"Daddy. When he comes to see you."

"What?"

"Don't act dumb, Tootsie. I saw him here with you." Tootsie looked down and put her face in her hands. She started to cry.

"I'm sorry, Miss Susie," she said. Tootsie never called me "Miss," what was that about? "I don't have no choice. All these years. When it first started I was young, and I didn't know he was married. Then I got pregnant and he tole me he had a wife and a chile and another one on the way. He say he help me financial-like. And he kept coming around and he gave me money from time to time." She put her face in her hands and sobbed. I could feel her pain. I'd felt it too, from him.

"Then when you was born he axed me to work for your mama. He said you need protection. You was just a baby and your mama wanted you dead." She looked at me. "I'm sorry to tell you that about your own mama, but, well, that's why I stayed all those years. I was only fifteen when I went to help her out, and I had a new baby myself. I needed the work and I worried that woman would kill her baby girl."

I listened and saw Tootsie's pain, her shame, her bondage. I'm not sure why her revelation about Mama wanting to kill me wasn't a shock—it didn't even stir me. I guess I was thinking more about Daddy and how it felt to be under his control, like Tootsie. I didn't want to keep questioning Tootsie, I wanted to leave her alone, I'd already pushed her pretty far—but I couldn't stop myself from asking about Marianne. I had nursed my curiosity for three years. It was choking me.

"Is she his? Marianne. Is she my sister?"

"Please don't tell her. She hate him."

"I hate him, too, but she needs to know who her father is, Tootsie. Does he know, does Daddy know about Marianne?"

"I guess he do. We never talk about it."

"Do you mean that son-of-a-bitch knows that Marianne is his child and he doesn't acknowledge her?" Tootsie hung her head and shook it softly, wringing her hands in her lap.

"She's my sister and I'm not allowed to be here? He can come here, sleep with you, make mulatto babies and forbid me to visit?" Tootsie didn't answer, nor did she look at me.

"Tootsie, you need to stop this nonsense."

"I know. I tole him so many times to stop coming around, but he wait a month or so, and start up again. I'm afraid of him. I see what he do to you."

"You should be afraid. He's dangerous. If he hurts you, no one will believe you. He's Bob Burton. Mayor Bob Burton, soon to be Senator." Tootsie didn't look up. I could hear her quiet sobs.

"Tootsie, are you the one?"

"Huh?" She raised her head out of her hands and sat back as if she'd been shocked.

"You know what I'm asking. Did you tell Daddy that I came here? About me and Rodney?" She began to sob and couldn't talk. She tried but she swallowed her words and heaved so hard I thought she'd stop breathing. I wanted to stop badgering her, but, heck, here I was with a gash across my face because she probably told him about my visits to the Quarters and about Rodney. I sat there and listened to her hysteria and felt no compassion. She was as bad as my mother.

We didn't talk for a while. I looked out at the dark, moonless night that made the cornstalks seem like black feathers against the deep blue sky and the trees appeared like tall, ghostly figures with multiple arms. Stillness surrounded me. The only sounds were a hoot owl in the distance, bullfrogs in the ditch near Gravier Road, and Tootsie's quiet sniffles.

I knew the desperation Tootsie felt, held captive by my daddy, not a mistress but a prostitute who could never be free. Like Rodney tried to explain to me, I didn't understand what it was like to be colored, to be oppressed, to feel you have no say in your own life, not even with whom you sleep or have children with—to be afraid of white people, to have to watch the way you talk, your tone of voice, the words you use, eye contact, attitude. It must be exhausting to live that way.

I wanted to cry for Tootsie. I wanted to cry for the entire Negro race. I wanted to cry for myself and for Marianne because of who fathered us.

*

Rodney told me later that he had to keep himself from stepping on the accelerator as he headed down South Jefferson Street towards the Quarters, but he couldn't risk having the sheriff or one of his deputies stop him. They'd throw him in jail just because he was colored, had a college education and the nerve to own a car. He said he tried to act nonchalant with his arm bent on the ledge of his opened window as he drove, unhurried while his heart raced and sweat beaded on his forehead and under his arms.

He said Dr. David waved when Rodney drove past the doctor's house. He waved back. He said he didn't look to his right at my house across the street, but it seemed Dr. David stared at the front door of the antebellum home with a determined look on his face. Rodney said it was strange, and that he couldn't remember ever seeing Dr. David in his front yard swing. Rodney said he had a feeling it might have to do with the phone call from Marianne.

I was sitting at the kitchen table inside Catfish's house when he arrived, holding an ice pack Tootsie insisted I put on my cheek. I heard footsteps on the porch and could feel someone's presence standing at the screen door. I knew it was Rodney because I smelled all the wonderful, manly parts of him that came through the screen and filled the air around me—oil and dust and musk and toothpaste and aftershave and desire.

I looked up when I heard the screen door creak.

"Oh, my God, Susie!! What happened? Your face."

"What are you ... ?"

"Oh, Baby!" He knelt beside my chair and took the ice pack from me and gently applied it to the open cut that had turned purple and swelled like a baseball. "This must hurt. I can see you cheekbone." Poor Rodney, he'd never seen my face after a beating.

"It's not so bad. I've had worse. In fact, it could have been much worse, but I fought back for the first time."

"What'd you do?"

"I kicked him in the crotch and kneed him in the face, or maybe the forehead. I'm not sure where I got him but he was bleeding when I left. He'll feel it for a while."

"That's my girl!" He wrapped his arms around my waist and I put mine over his shoulders and pulled his head to my chest. It fit perfectly between my breasts. One of my hands pressed the back of his head and I ran my fingers through his wavy brown hair, massaging his scalp. We stayed in that position for a long time until I felt my blouse become so wet it stuck to me. I thought it was blood, but when I pulled away from him, my palms on each of his cheeks, my fingernails near his ears, I saw the tears on his face and his swollen, red-rimmed eyes. When he looked at me, his sorrow turned to empathy. I must look horrible, I thought.

"Oh, Baby. I'm so sorry. Let me take you to Dr. David. He is sitting in the swing in his front yard."

"Let's wait until dark. No use making my dad crazier than he already is."

"Do you want to talk about it?"

"Nothing to talk about, Rod. I leave tomorrow and I'm not coming back."

"I don't blame you, Chere. But ... what about ... uh ... what about ... us?

"Is there really an ... us?'"

"Do you want there to be?"

"I don't know if there can be, Rod."

He stood up and lifted me out of the chair, one arm under my knees, the other around my back. I remembered the first time he carried me like that and I put the side of my head on his chest where his T-shirt dipped just enough that I could taste his skin against my lips. I thought he would take me to the bedroom. Instead he walked through the screen door, down the three small steps and put me in the front seat of his car. I didn't ask any questions until he drove into Dr. David's circular drive.

Dr. David got up from the long, green wooden swing that hung from a wood frame under a huge oak tree that must have been over 200-years old. He walked to the parked car, opened the door on my side and picked me up. Rodney followed us through the front door, into the house. Dr. David lay me on a small tan leather sofa in what looked like his home office. It was cozy and cool, with cypress paneling and an oversized oak desk, a medical bag perched on top.

He rang a bell and Josie, the Switzers' help, came into the study.

"Get me some ice, Josie, and some boiling water."

Josie hurried from the room. Dr. David sat on a low stool with rollers and scooted up to me. Rodney sat on the arm of the sofa at my head and gently massaged my shoulders. Dr. David spoke in a low, soft tone and told me what he was about to do. Josie returned with a tray and Dr. David asked her to hold a flashlight steady and aim it towards the gash on my cheek. He gave me a couple of shots in and around the cut and began to stitch it with neat, tiny sutures. He explained in a soothing voice each stick and every prick and dab of the cotton pad he dipped in iodine. He told me the scar would disappear in a few months, just as the last one had. When he was finished he handed Rodney the ice pack and showed him where to hold it while he examined me for other injuries.

"Seems you have a couple of bruised ribs, my dear," he said. "And your ankle is swollen. I don't think it's broken but I'd like to X-ray it to make sure."

"I'm not going to the hospital, Dr. David. I'll just take my chances. I want to leave town as soon as I can."

"I understand. How can I help? I feel like this is my fault."

"Your fault?" I asked and Rodney lifted his eyes and stared at Dr. David.

"I've turned a blind eye to your dad's abuse for years. After what happened three years ago when you were working at the hospital, I thought I'd stopped it. I should have known it was a temporary fix. I wanted to do something when you were seven, when you were twelve, when you were fifteen, nineteen."

"There's nothing you could have done, Dr. David. This is a small town. You have to live and work here. None of this was ever your fault."

"Oh, I could have done a lot."

"Why didn't you Dr. Switzer," Rodney blurted. "You knew that son-of-a-bitch was hurting her. He could have killed her."

"Rodney . . . ," I said.

"It's okay, Susie. I deserve it. That's what I'm trying to say. I don't have an excuse except to say that I'm a coward, and I took the easy way out."

"You could have talked to him, threatened him, turned him in. Something." Rodney was angry. He had never seen my face torn up. The one time he saw me after the beating that put me in the hospital at fifteen, all the swelling and bruising on my face was gone. My arm was in a cast but he couldn't see the internal injuries or the emotional scars.

"Rodney!" I pleaded.

"You're right, Rodney. I took an oath, one I haven't kept. It's my fault. And I'll have to live with my guilt. And you both have every right to hate me for it. But for now, tell me how I can help you. Seems the two of you are in a predicament."

I looked at Dr. David in disbelief. I'd never heard him say so many words at one time. I thought he believed my parents' claims when I was a child. I began to feel as angry as Rodney. Salty tears sprang up in my eyes and burned the swollen one.

"I'm not sure," I whispered, thinking aloud. "We haven't discussed the future, yet. Could we get back to you if we need help?"

"Of course." He walked to the glass doors that overlooked his park-like backyard and swimming pool. Rodney and I exchanged confused looks. Dr. David rubbed his chin with the thumb and forefinger of his right hand while the other three fingers seemed to hold his face up. His left arm crossed his chest, the back of its hand a resting place for his right elbow.

Dr. David and Rodney both helped me into the car. Rodney stood up next to the door and Dr. David knelt on one knee on the paved driveway, holding my upper arm. I felt like we were being watched and I looked across the street. Daddy was standing on the front porch. I gasped.

"Susie, don't worry about your dad. I'll take care of him. He won't get in your way, no matter what the two of you decide to do. Remember: this is your life, not his." Dr. David stood up and faced Rodney. He reached to shake hands and Rodney hesitated. He looked angry.

"I'm sorry Rodney. You should be angry. Susie is a very special girl, uh, young lady. If you love her and if she loves you, don't let Bob Burton keep you apart. Don't let him win. This is your life." Rodney finally shook hands with Dr. David but he didn't speak, didn't thank him, didn't say good bye.

He walked around to his side of the car and noticed my dad starting to walk down the steps of our house, heading towards us in Dr. David's front yard. Rodney slammed his door and walked through Dr. David's front yard and stood at the ditch, glaring at my dad as he approached the street that separated the two houses. I watched from the car as Dr. David walked up and stood beside Rodney, a show of force against the enemy.

"I'm taking her away so you don't kill her. You should thank me," Rodney said.

"You rotten N___r! How dare you," Daddy yelled from the middle of our yard, almost running toward the street.

"Stop right there, Bob," Dr. David said. "If you cross that street I'll have you arrested." Daddy slowed, then stopped when he reached the sidewalk that divided our yard from South Jefferson Street. He had a huge Band-Aid on his forehead and one of his eyes was already turning purple.

"You can't do that. I'm the mayor." He had his hands on his hips and blazing eyes protruded from his face.

"I don't care if you think you're the president. Stay put." Dr. David put his arm on Rodney's shoulder. Rodney's fists were clenched at his sides, his chin was thrust forward. I could tell from the stiffness of his back that he wanted to lunge at my dad.

"I'll have your black ass, Rodney Thibault. And your family, too."

"No you won't, Bob," Dr. David said. "I'll file charges against you and present all the records on Susie's accidents over the years if anything at all happens to the Thibaults. You'll never be a senator. Your political career will be ruined." I looked past Daddy and saw Sissy, Mama and little Albert standing on the porch of our house. Sissy started down the steps but Mama grabbed her by the back of her shirt. A sob caught in my throat as I realized I'd never see my little sister again if I left now.

"Rodney," Dr. David said without taking his eyes off my dad. "Get in your car and take Susie somewhere where you can protect her from any future abuse."

"How dare you!" Daddy yelled, but he didn't move.

"You drove her to me yourself, Mr. Burton," Rodney said. "If you'd have treated her with love and kindness, she wouldn't have needed me."

"You son-of-a- ... ." Rodney turned and walked to the car, got behind the wheel and we drove off. I tried not to look at Sissy and Mama standing on the porch. I was crying so hard I was shaking all over.

Rodney carried me to Catfish's bed, gave me an icepack and left without a word. I sat up heaving and gasping for air. Blood started to trickle down my face and dropped in my lap. I knew I must have burst a stitch or two from crying so hard. I had to get a grip. It was all too much. I'd lost Catfish and Tootsie, maybe Marianne and now... Oh, God, just when I'd decided I couldn't live without him, I'd lost Rodney. Where'd he gone?

An hour went by and I must have fallen asleep. I didn't hear the screen door open, but I felt his presence.

"Don't you think we need to talk, Cherie?" He knelt beside the bed and I turned my head towards him. I was so happy to see him I threw my arms around him and pulled him close.

"Oh, God. You came back. I thought you left me. I thought I'd never ..."

"I went back to apologize to Dr. David. And to make sure my family was okay. And I packed some things." I was out of tears but my chest still heaved as if I was sobbing. He lay his head on my chest a few seconds, then he pulled away and looked at me.

"I love you, Susie." The green specks in his eyes were so bright they cast rainbows on my blood-drenched blouse. I didn't know how to tell him I loved him. I'd never said those words before, not to anyone. They seemed to flow so freely from his mouth, but they stuck in my throat. I felt I would choke if I uttered them.

"You'd like New York," I whispered. It was a deep thought, one I'd buried for so long it surprised me when it came came out of my mouth and hung in the air. I closed my eyes, afraid of his response.

"What are you saying?"

"I'm not sure." I lay on the bed and stared at the ceiling, twisting my hair just over my ear. Rodney opened my overnight bag that was sitting on Catfish's dresser. He found a T-shirt and sat next to me on the bed. He unbuttoned my bloodstained blouse and removed it and my stained, wet bra. He slipped the T-shirt over my head. He made sure to pull the cotton ribbing away from my face so it didn't scratch my wound.

It was all so respectful. He didn't comment on my naked chest or how my nipples hardened when the air hit them. He didn't touch them nor did he stop to stare or show any sort of desire. Once he had my shirt pulled down to my hips, covering my nakedness, he lay me gently back against the pillows he'd fluffed and stacked. I kept waiting for him to say something, but he didn't utter a word. The silence was so loud it echoed in my ears.

He sat on the side of the bed with his butt against my leg and he bent forward, his face in his hands, elbows on his knees. I finally realized he was waiting for me to say something. He'd always been so open and upfront about his feelings for me, but I had never been honest.

"I'm tired of hiding how I feel," I whispered. He turned his torso to look at me, one hand near my arm. "I'm tired of denying it. I'm tired. Period."

"Susie. Do you love me? Do you want to be with me?" I tried to look at him, then averted my eyes to the ceiling again. He put one of his hands on either side of me and his face hovered above mine. He was inches from me and I could taste his fear, smell his anticipation, hear his heart thump, double time—thu-thump ...thu-thump ... thu-thump.

"I wish I'd never met you, Rodney Thibault," I whispered. I knew he could taste my words, every syllable. "My life, your life, would have been so much easier. I wish I'd fallen in love with a white boy. I wish I had been convincing enough when I told you I didn't love you. I wish you would have moved on, found a nice colored girl, married her, had children. Then I would have had to move on, too."

He looked confused. He didn't say anything.

"I'll be honest, Rod. I've tried to move on. I've tried to date other guys and I would think for a while that, maybe, I was over you. Then I'd see your handwriting on an envelope or hear your voice over the phone or, worst of all, see you in person, and I'd have to start trying all over again." What I didn't tell him is that I could never get over him once I had his baby. Other than Josh Ryan and the couple who adopted our daughter, no one knew about that. No one.

I sat up on the other side of the bed, facing away from him. He touched my back and I felt a chill down my spine.

"I've tried, too," he whispered. I was afraid to hear the words. "For a while, I thought I'd succeeded. I even dated someone pretty seriously, went home with her, brought her to meet my family." He stopped talking for a few seconds. I didn't say anything. It hurt to hear about another girl. I couldn't bear to think of Rodney with someone else. He walked around the bed and knelt in front of me.

"Then I saw you step out of your dad's car at the church this morning and I knew I had failed miserably." I finally looked into his eyes as if I could see something in them that might tell me what I needed to know.

"I knew then I could never love anyone but you, Susie. Even my dad saw it. He told me I needed to end it with Annette and go after my dream. He said it wasn't fair for me to settle for half a life just because I'm colored." I stared at his lips while he spoke. So many confusing things. His dad? His dreams? He still loved me? He started to say something else, then he stopped. We didn't touch. He just knelt in front of me as I sat on the edge of the bed.

"I have ... I have ... uh, I have loved you ..." I swallowed hard. Saying that word was so difficult. My dad had used it often, then he'd attack me and call me names. My mother said she loved me, but she wanted me to disappear. Josh Ryan said he loved me until he saw my baby. Gavin said he loved me, but his love did not come with trust. I didn't know how to use the word in a way that said what I meant—that I had wanted and trusted Rodney since I was thirteen years old, that he was the only person in this wide world I believed in, especially with Catfish gone. How does a four-letter word say that?

"I didn't tell myself, not for a long time."

"Are you saying you love me?"

"Is that word so important to you?"

"Of course. It says everything." I guess for Rodney the word love did mean something because all those who had told him they loved him, acted like they loved him. I tried to understand why he needed to hear that word from me.

"Okay, then. I love you, Rod." He smiled and took both my hands where they rested in my lap. His eyes were filled with tears.

"Do you want to marry me?" I stiffened and my mouth sprang open. I swallowed hard.

"Are you asking me to marry you, or are you asking me whether I want to?"

"I'm asking you to go with me to Washington D.C. tomorrow, the next day, whenever you say, and marry me. I'm telling you I will move to New York, or New Mexico or New Hampshire or New Jersey. I'll do anything, go anywhere, if you will marry me."

"I don't want to believe or hope in something that can't really be—and have my dreams shattered."

"I can make it happen, Baby. You have to trust me." I looked at him, trying to believe him, but unable to reconcile my beliefs with his words. He stared at me. Beneath all of my strength and resolve, all of my courage and determination, all of my brave efforts to keep him alive—under that outer layer, I was a vulnerable, sensitive, needy white girl who wanted him ... more than anything.

"Do you trust me?" he whispered. He held the ice pack to my cheek, our noses almost touching. I breathed in his exhale, he sucked in mine.

"Yes."

"Will you marry me?"

*

I sat in Rodney's Mustang the next morning and felt like I was in a time capsule. The front of the car seemed to move forward, to a future, to happiness. The back of the car seemed stuck in the muck and the murk of Jim Crow and the Deep South.

We didn't talk much. Every now and then Rodney would look at me and smile or wink, then look back out the front windshield. I also sneaked a few peeks at him, and tried to read his mind. His expression vacillated between a shit-eating grin that reeked of victory, happiness—and a concerned frown that said he was worried and missing his family already. Then I'd see the almost-smile and deep wrinkles form across his forehead simultaneously. We didn't say what we were both thinking.

Would Rodney's family suffer because of our actions? Would my daddy come after us? Would we live to regret our selfishness after the honeymoon period of our love passed on?

As we neared Baton Rouge and I saw airplanes taking off and landing, I gulped. Would Rodney really get on the plane with me? If he did, if he and I really were to sit next to each other thirty-thousand feet above the ground, would I tell him about our four-year-old daughter? How would I do it? Would we voice our concerns about our future or just delve into it?

I had to walk through the next few hours to see how it played out. Just as my doubts started to get the best of me, Rodney parked the car, turned off the ignition and shifted in his seat until he faced me.

"I love you, Susie." He leaned his body to me and kissed me on the lips. "Tell me you love me. Just say the words. That's all I need."

"I love you, Rodney."

More books by Madelyn Bennett Edwards

The Catfish Stories
Sequel to *Catfish*. Susie writes more of the stories told to her by
Catfish as she and Rodney live out the end of segregation in the
South.

On Good Days
The true story about the killing of six-year-old Jeremy Mardis by two
police officers in Marksville, Louisiana on November 3, 2015, that
captured the nation's attention.

Looking for a Cliff
A memoir about withdrawing from opioids and alcohol and
overcoming childhood traumas.

Go to www.madelynedwardsauthor.com to read excerpts and keep up
with release dates.

On the Cover

The picture that depicts Catfish on the cover of this book is an actual man named, Shadrack White. Mark Reid, who designed the cover, found the picture and checked to see if the photograph could legally be used.

"There are countless images of African American 'slaves' spread across myriad stock libraries," Reid said, "But they never have any soul. Most are staged by modern-day actors and photographers, and there is always something missing." Reid believes that "something" is the look in their eyes that conveys the depth of feeling by those who have experienced hardship.

Reid felt Shadrack White conveyed the feeling we were looking for and sent the picture to me. I fell in love with Shadrack and after Mark removed his beard and walking cane, he became my Catfish.

Shadrack was a real man with a real story. He was the slave of John Randolph, a Virginia plantation owner, who freed his slaves by the terms of his will, executed prior to the Civil War. It took 13 years for lawsuits by next of kin to be resolved and a band of lonely and frightened former slaves to find their way north to the Ohio River.

After crossing the Ohio, the freed men and women traveled by canal boat northward and eventually settled in west central Ohio. A number of them formed the settlement of Rumley, located off state route 29 near McCartyville. A few moved to Sidney. Among them, Shadrack White.

For reasons history does not record, Shadrack obtained the nickname "Buddie Shang." Buddie quickly became a favorite among the residents of Sidney. He was well liked, and was often kidded about his two favorite things: fishing and corn liquor.

Buddie's motto, when referring to his need for the latter, was "I'm dry as a hoss." He lived in Lacyburg, a shanty town that was located along the canal feeder south of Water Street. The settlement was composed mostly of blacks, who were not especially welcome in Sidney.

Buddie ran a shoe shine stand outside one of the local taverns in town in the 1880s but was not permitted inside because he was black. The proprietor would compensate him by providing liquor in a bucket which Buddie would take home with him at night.

October 31, 1889 was a brilliant fall day. At 2 p.m. in the afternoon, as Buddie wandered down the towpath of the canal feeder, he became embroiled in an argument with a young resident by the name of James Edwards. During the dispute, Buddie fired a shotgun he was carrying in the general direction of Edwards, missing him, but striking the cottage of Lewis Nichols, a white man who resided in Lacyburg. Nichols appeared at the door, grabbed a brick laying on the ground nearby, and flung it at Shang. Buddie, then 74 years, ducked and the brick missed his head by inches.

"I was just foolin'" the old former slave shouted, but Nichols renewed his attack by throwing another brick at Buddie. The sound from a blast of his shotgun echoed through Lacyburg, and Nichols fell to the ground. He died several hours later. Sheriff Joseph Raterman arrested Buddie for the murder of "Soapstick," as Nichols was known in the community.

Following his indictment by the Grand Jury, Buddie Shang stood trial for murder. Not many people in town gave Buddie much chance of convincing an all-white jury that he had done nothing wrong in shooting a white man. However, Buddie believed he had acted in self-defense. It was therefore with much trepidation that Buddie Shang faced a jury in the new Shelby County Courthouse on January 27, 1890.

After the evidence was presented, the jury deliberated a total of three minutes - apparently just long enough for each juror to attach his name to a verdict of "not guilty." After the jury had rendered its verdict, Hess slapped the eccentric old slave on the shoulder and said, "You're free again, free for a second time, Buddie. How do you feel?" Buddie is reported to have replied: "Dry as a hoss!"

Buddie Shang lived out the remainder of his years in Lacyburg mostly in the canal feeder and the Great Miami River. He died at the age of 97 in 1912.

"Shadrack was more than a slave," Reid said. "He was more than a man. He was a genuine character, a scoundrel, and during a time when the color of his skin would surely have meant death by hanging in Ohio Penitentiary in Columbus, Shadrack stood his ground, stated his case, and was tried as an equal.

"This is a gentleman that I felt needed to be immortalized, and I feel blessed to have discovered his story," Reid concluded.

It should be noted that Mark Reid is British and lives in Scotland. His penchant for history is only one of the many reasons he is a great book designer.

CPSIA information can be obtained
at www.ICGtesting.com
Printed in the USA
FFOW03n1747010518
46431251-48289FF